Praise f

"Timothy Hallinan's *The F
in a Hallinan novel: indel
moments of hold-your-bre

the *New York Times* bestselling Sookie Stackhouse series

"Ever since Dashiell Hammett introduced us to Sam Spade in *The Maltese Falcon* 83 years ago, hundreds of writers have adopted his formula, flooding the bookshelves with wisecracking private eyes who work both sides of the law, disrespect authority, icily stare down gun barrels and conceal an immutable code of honor beneath a cynical outer shell. This can get awfully tiresome, but every now and then a writer comes along with the imagination and skill to make the whole thing feel fresh and new again. That's what veteran crime novelist Timothy Hallinan has accomplished with his latest series of novels featuring Junior Bender, full-time Los Angeles burglar and part-time private eye-style fixer for the city's criminal element . . . An intricate high-stakes plot, a compelling subplot and heart-pounding suspense." —*Associated Press*

"Timothy Hallinan's affable antihero, an accomplished thief but inept sleuth named Junior Bender, makes a terrific first impression in *Crashed* . . . Bender's quick wit and smart mouth make him a boon companion on this oddball adventure."   —*The New York Times Book Review*

"If Carl Hiaasen and Donald Westlake had a literary love child, he would be Timothy Hallinan. The Edgar nominee's laugh-out-loud new crime series featuring Hollywood burglar-turned-private eye Junior Bender has breakout written all over it . . . A must-read."

—Julia Spencer-Fleming, *New York Times*
bestselling author of *One Was a Soldier*

"Junior Bender is today's Los Angeles as Raymond Chandler might have written it. Tim [Hallinan] is a master at tossing out the kind of hard-boiled lines that I wish I thought of first."   —Bruce DeSilva,
Macavity & Edgar Award-winning author of *Rogue Island*

"This is Hallinan at the top of his game. It's laugh-out-loud funny without ever losing any of its mystery. It's a whole new style and I love it. Junior Bender—a crook with a heart of gold—is one of Hallinan's most appealing heroes, rich with invention, and brimming with classic wit. I can't recommend it highly enough."

—Shadoe Stevens, *The Late Late Show with Craig Ferguson*

"Loved loved loved *Crashed*, Tim Hallinan's first Junior Bender mystery. Great narrative voice, complex plot, 3-D characters. Hallinan's deft comic tone and colorful characters have earned him comparisons to Donald Westlake and Carl Hiaasen. Check it out now." —Nancy Pearl

"A modern-day successor to Raymond Chandler."

—*Los Angeles Daily News*

"Wisecracking Junior is great company . . . There's a satisfying balance between the present-day mystery and the vivid flashbacks."

—*The Seattle Times*

"Hugely,splendidly entertaining . . . Full of delightful characters, and dialogue that provides at least one good laugh on every page, the book is so hard to put down you'll swear it's been glued to your hands."

—*Booklist*, Starred Review (*Little Elvises*)

"A fresh turn on Raymond Chandler . . . In *Crashed*, Hallinan's fabulously convoluted, wise-guy detective potboiler featuring Bender, the California author's voice—intelligent, sarcastic, profane but never coarse, unfailingly honest—is like a fast ride over a potholed road in a vintage Cadillac." —*San Antonio Express-News*

"Junior's levity provides an excellent set-off to the dark underpinnings of the criminal world he inhabits. Along the way to the truth, he strives not only to keep himself alive, but also to bring a sort of justice to those who have been wronged, even so many years later. More please, Mr. Hallinan." —*Deadly Pleasures Magazine*

"This is one of those books you long for, wait for, and find once or twice a year." —Beth Kanell, proprietor of Kingdom Books, Vermont

The Fame Thief

Books by Timothy Hallinan

The Poke Rafferty Series
A Nail Through the Heart
The Fourth Watcher
Breathing Water
The Queen of Patpong
The Fear Artist
For the Dead
The Hot Countries
Fools' River

The Junior Bender Series
Crashed
Little Elvises
The Fame Thief
Herbie's Game
King Maybe
Fields Where They Lay

The Simeon Grist Series
The Four Last Things
Everything but the Squeal
Skin Deep
Incinerator
The Man with No Time
The Bone Polisher
Pulped

The Fame Thief

A Junior Bender Mystery

TIMOTHY HALLINAN

SOHO
CRIME

THE FAME THIEF

Copyright © 2013 by Timothy Hallinan

Published by Soho Press, Inc.
853 Broadway
New York, NY 10003

Library of Congress Cataloging-in-Publication Data

Hallinan, Timothy.
The fame thief : a Junior Bender mystery / Timothy Hallinan.

ISBN 978-1-61695-282-2
eISBN: 978-1-61695-281-5

1. Thieves—Fiction. 2. Private investigators—Fiction.
3. Mystery fiction. I. Title.

PS3558.A3923F36 2012
813'.54—dc23   2012032015

Interior design by Janine Agro, Soho Press, Inc.
Illustration by Katherine Grames

Printed in the United States of America

10 9 8 7 6 5 4 3 2

To Munyin Choy-Hallinan,
first laugher

THE MOST BEAUTIFUL WOMAN IN THE WORLD

Part One

Part
One

1

My Business Plan Calls for Long Periods of Inactivity

Irwin Dressler crossed one eye-agonizing plaid leg over the other, leaned back on a white leather couch half the width of the Queen Mary, and said, "Junior, I'm disappointed in you."

If Dressler had said that to me the first time I'd been hauled up to his Bel Air estate for a command appearance, I'd have dropped to my knees and begged for a painless death. He was, after all, the Dark Lord in the flesh. But now I'd survived him once, so I said, "Well, Mr. Dressler—"

A row of yellow teeth, bared in what was supposed to be a smile but looked like the last thing many small animals see. "Call me Irwin."

"Well, Mr. Dressler, at the risk of being rowed into the center of the Hollywood Reservoir wired to half a dozen cinder blocks and being offered the chance to swim home, what have I done to disappoint you?"

"Nothing. That's the problem." Despite the golf slacks and the polo shirt, Dressler was old without being grandfatherly, old without going all dumpling, old without getting quaint. He'd been a dangerous young man in 1943, when he assumed control of mob activity in Los Angeles, and he'd gone on being dangerous until he was a dangerous old man. Forty minutes ago, I'd been snatched off a Hollywood sidewalk by two walking biceps and thrown into the back seat of a big old Lincoln Town Car, and when I'd said, "Where's your weapon?" the guy in the front said, "Irwin Dressler," and I'd shut up.

Dressler gave me a glance I could have searched for hours without finding any friendliness in it. "You got yourself a *franchise*, Junior, a *monopoly*, and you're not working it."

I said, "My business plan calls for long periods of inactivity."

"That's not how this country was built, Junior." Like many great crooks, even the very few at his stratospheric level, Dressler was a political conservative. "What made America great? I'll tell you: backbone, elbow grease, noses to the grindstone."

"Sounds uncomfortable."

Dressler had lowered his head while he was speaking, perhaps to demonstrate the approved nose-to-the-grindstone position. Only his eyes moved. Beneath heavy white eyebrows, they came up to meet mine, as smooth, dry, and friendly as a couple of river stones. He kept them on me until the back of my neck began to prickle and I shifted in my chair.

"This is amusing?" he said. "I'm amusing you?"

"No, sir." I picked up the platter of bread and brie and said, "Cheese?"

"In my own house he's offering me cheese." Dressler addressed this line to some household spirit hovering invisibly over the table. "It's true, it's true. I've grown old."

"No, sir," I said again. "It's, uh, it's. . . ."

"The loss of American verbal skills," he said, nodding, "is a terrible thing. Even in someone like you. I remember a time, this will be hard for you to believe, when almost everyone could speak in complete sentences. In English, no less. What have I done, Junior, that you should laugh at me? Get so old that I don't frighten you any more?"

"I wasn't—"

"I bring you here, I give you cheese, good cheese—is the cheese good, Junior?"

"Fabulous," I said, seriously rattled. This had the earmarks of one of Irwin's legendary rants, rants that frequently ended with one less person alive in the room.

"Fabulous, he says, it's fabulous. What are you, a hat maker? Of course, it's fabulous. The Jews, you know, we're a desert people. The two gods everybody's killing each other over now, Jehovah and the other one, Allah, they're both desert gods, did you know that, Junior?"

"Um, yes, sir."

"Desert gods are short on forgiveness, you know? And we Jews, we're the chosen people of a desert god and hospitality is part of our tradition, and now I'm going to get badmouthed for my cheese by some *pisher*, some *vonce*—you know what a *vonce* is, Junior?"

"No, sir."

"It's a bedbug, in Yiddish, great language for invective. I'll tell you, Junior, I could flay the skin off you using Yiddish alone, I wouldn't even need Babe and Tuffy in the next room there, listening to everything we're saying so they can come in and kill you if I get too excited. My heart, you know? A man my age, I can't be too careful. Someone gets me upset, better for Babe and Tuffy just to kill them first, before my heart attacks me."

"I'm sorry, Mr. Dressler. I wasn't thinking."

"But *thinking*, Junior, that's what you're supposed to be good at." He reached out and took some bread off the platter, which I was apparently still holding, and said, "Down, put it down. Did I offer you wine?"

"Yes, sir." He hadn't, but I wasn't about to bring it up. I put the tray in front of him on the table. Inched it toward him so he wouldn't have to lean forward.

"I still got arms," he said, tearing some bread. "What were we talking about before you got so upset?"

"My franchise."

"Right, right. You may not know this, Junior, but you're the only one there is. You're like Lew Winterman when he—did you know Lew?"

"Not personally." Lew Winterman had been the head of Universe Pictures and long considered the most powerful man in Hollywood, at least by those who didn't know that the first thing he did every morning and the last thing he did every night was to phone Irwin Dressler.

"When he and I thought of packaging, we had to get horses to carry it to the bank, that's how much the money weighed," Dressler said. "You know packaging? *You can have Jimmy Stewart for your movie, but you also gotta take some whozis, I don't know, John Gavin. And every other actor in your picture and also the cameraman and the writers,* and he represented them all, Lew did. For about a year after we figured it out, he was the only guy in Hollywood who knew how to do it, and he did it ten hours a day, seven days a week. You know how much he made?"

"No, sir. How much?"

"Don't ask. You can't think that high. So you're like that now, like Lew, but on your own level, and what are you doing? Sitting around on your *tuchis*, that's what you're doing. That whole thing you got going? Solving crimes for crooks? And living through it? You got Vinnie DiGaudio out of the picture for me with every cop in LA trying to pin him. You helped Trey Annunziato with her dirty movie, although she didn't like it much, the way you did it. When four hundred and eighty flatscreens got bagged out of Arnie Muffins' garage in Panorama City, you brought them back, and without a crowd of people getting killed, which is something, the way Arnie is.

You're it, Junior, you're the only one. And you're not working it."

"Every time I do it," I said, "I almost get killed."

"Ehhh," Dressler said. "You're a young man, in the prime of life. What're you, thirty-eight?"

"Thirty-seven."

"Prime of life. Got your reflexes, got all your IQ, at least as much as you were born with. You're piddling along with a franchise that, I'm telling you, could be worth millions. Where's the wine?"

I said, "I'll get it."

"*You'll* get it? You think I'm going to let you in my cellar?" He picked up a silver bell and rang it. A moment later, one of the bruisers who'd abducted me and dragged me up here came into the room. He was roughly nine feet tall and his belt had to be five feet long, and none of it was fat.

"Yes, Mr. Dressler?"

"Tuffy," Dressler said. "You I don't want. Where's Juana?"

"She's got a headache." Despite being the size of a genie in *The Thousand and One Nights*, Tuffy had the high, hoarse voice of someone who gargled thumbtacks.

"So mix her my special cocktail, half a glass of water, half a teaspoon each of bicarbonate of soda and cream of Tartar. Stir it up real good, till it foams, and take it to her with two aspirins. And get us a bottle of—what do you think, Junior? Burgundy or Bordeaux?"

"Ummm—"

"You're right, it's not a Bordeaux day. Too drizzly. We need something with some sunshine in it. Tuffy. Get us a nice Hermitage, the 1990. Wide-mouthed goblets so it can breathe fast. Got it?"

Tuffy said, "Yes, Mr. Dressler."

I said, "And put on an apron."

Tuffy took an involuntary step toward me, but Dressler raised one parchment-yellow hand and said, "He just needs to pick on somebody. Don't take it personal."

Tuffy gave me a little bonus eye-action for a moment but then ducked his head in Dressler's direction and exited stage left. Dressler said, "So. People try to kill you."

"Occupational hazard. I'm working for crooks, but I'm also catching crooks. If I solve the crime, the perp wants to kill me. If I don't solve it, my client wants to kill me."

"Nobody's really tough any more," Dressler said, shaking his head at the Decline of the West. "You know how we took care of the Italians?"

I did. "Not really."

"Kind of a long way to say *no*, isn't it? Three syllables instead of one. So, okay, the Italians came out to California first, and when we got here from Chicago it was like Naples, just Guidos everywhere, running all the obvious stuff: girls, betting, alcohol, unions, pawnshops, dope. Well, we were nice Jewish boys who didn't want to make widows and orphans everywhere so you know what we used? Never mind answering, we used baseball bats. Didn't kill anybody except a few who were extra-stubborn, but we wrapped things up pretty quick. See, *that's* tough, walking into a room full of guns with a baseball bat. Ask a guy to do that these days, he'd have to be wearing Depends."

I said, "Huh."

Dressler nodded a couple of times, in total agreement with himself. "But let's say the people who want to kill you, give them the benefit of the doubt, let's say they could manage it. And all that nonsense with a different motel every month isn't really going to cut it, is it? What's the motel this month? Valentine something?"

"Valentine Shmalentine," I said, feeling like I was drowning. "In Canoga Park."

"Valentine Shmalentine? Kind of name is that?"

"Supposed to be the world's only kosher love motel."

"What's kosher mean for a love motel? No missionary position?"

"Heh heh heh," I said. He wasn't supposed to know about the motel of the month. *Nobody* was, beyond my immediate circle: my girlfriend, Ronnie; my daughter, Rina; and a couple of close friends and accomplices, such as Louie the Lost. But, I comforted myself, even if word about the motels had leaked, I still had the ultra-secret apartment in Koreatown. Nobody in the world knew about that except for Winnie Park, the Korean con woman who had sublet it to me, and Winnie was in jail in Singapore and had been for seven years.

"So the motels don't work," Dressler said, "not even taking the room next door like you do, with the connecting door and all, to give you a backup exit. It's a cute trick though, I'll give you that. So I'll tell you what you need. Since you can't hide, I mean. You need a patron, so people know you're under his protection. Somebody who's got the kind of weight that people wouldn't kill you even if they caught you playing kneesie with their teenage daughter, and you know how crooks are about their daughters."

"What I need," I said, "is to quit. Just do the occasional burglary, like a regular crook."

"Not an option," Dressler said. "You agree that everyone, even a schmuck like Bernie Madoff, has the right to a good defense attorney?"

I examined the question and saw the booby trap, but what could I do? "I suppose."

"Then why don't they deserve a detective when some *ganef* steals something from them? Or tries to frame them, like Vinnie De Gaudio? You remember helping Vinnie Di Gaudio?"

"Sure. That was how I met you."

"See? You lived through it. You got told to keep Vinnie out of the cops' eyes for a murder even though it looked like he did it, and you kept me out of the picture so my little line to Vinnie shouldn't attract attention. This was a job that required tact and finesse, and you showed me both of those things, didn't you? And now you're eating this nice cheese and you're about to drink a wine, a wine that'll put a choir in your ear. So quitting is not an option."

"What *is* an option?" I held up the platter, feeling like I was making an Old-Testament sacrifice. "Cheese? It's terrific cheese."

"You can lighten up on the cheese. I know it's good. You thought this dodge up all by yourself, Junior, and I respect that. Something new. Gives me hope for your generation. Like I said, a patron, *patronage*, that's what you need. And an A-list client, somebody nobody's going to mess with."

"A client and a patron," I said. "Two different people?"

"That's funny," Dressler said gravely. "You gotta work with me here, Junior. I've got your best interests in mind."

"And don't think I don't appreciate it. But I—"

"I *do* think you don't appreciate it," Dressler said, "and I don't give a shit."

I said, "Right."'

"And also, I gotta tell you, this is a job I wouldn't give to just anybody. The client, for example—"

"I thought you were the client."

"Literal, you're too literal. I'm the client in the sense that I'm the one who chose you for the job and the one who'll foot the bill. But think about it, Junior. Am I somebody some crook's going to hit?"

"No."

"How stupid would anybody have to be to hit me?"

"Someone would have to be insane to take your newspaper off your lawn."

"Not bad. Sometimes I get glimpses of something that makes me think maybe you're smart after all. No, the client, in the sense that she's the one who got ripped off, the client is—are you ready, Junior?" He sat back as though to measure my reaction better.

I put both hands on the arms of my chair to demonstrate readiness. "Ready."

"Your client is . . . Dolores La Marr."

There was a little *ta-daaa* in his voice and something expectant in his expression, something that tipped me off that this was a test I didn't want to fail. So I said, "You're kidding."

"Dolores," he said, nodding three times, "La Marr."

I said, "Wow. Dolores La Marr."

"The most beautiful woman in the world," Dressler said, and there was a hush of reverence in his voice. "*Life* magazine said so. On the cover, no less."

Life ceased publication on a regular basis in 1972, which I know because I once stole a framed display of the first issue, from 1883, paired with the last, both in mint condition. I got $6,500 for it from the Valley's top fence, Stinky Tetweiler, and Stinky turned it around to a dealer for $14 K. A year later it fetched $22,700 at auction while I gnashed my teeth in frustration. So it seemed safe to ask Dressler, "What year was that?"

"Nineteen-fifty. April 10, 1950. She was twenty-one then. Most beautiful thing I ever saw in my life."

The penny dropped. Dolores *La Marr*. Always referred to as "Hollywood starlet Dolores La Marr" in the sensational coverage of the Senate subcommittee hearings into organized crime at which she testified, reluctantly, during the early 1950s.

I said, "She'd be what now, eighty?"

"She's eighty-three," Dressler said. "But she admits to sixty-six."

"Sixty-six?" I said. "That would mean *Life* named her the most beautiful woman in the world when she was four. I know journalism was better back then, but—"

"A lady has her privileges," Dressler said, a bit stiffly. "She's as old as she wants to be."

"Well, sure."

"I gotta admit," Dressler said, "I didn't expect you to know who she was. What're you, thirty-eight?"

"Thirty-seven," I said again.

"Oh, yeah, I already asked that. Don't think it's 'cause I'm getting old. It's 'cause I don't care. But you know, you're practically a larva, but you remember Dolly."

"Dolly? Oh, sorry, Dolores. I remember her because I'm a criminal. I read a lot about crime. I pay special attention to that, just like some baseball players can tell you the batting averages of every MVP for fifty years. I read the old coverage of the Congressional hearings into organized crime like it was a best-seller."

Tuffy came in with an open bottle of wine and a couple of glasses on a tray. To me, he said, "Say one cute thing, and you'll be drinking this through the cork."

I asked Dressler, "You let the help talk to your guests like that?"

"Tuffy, be nice. If Mr. Bender and I don't reach a satisfactory conclusion to our chat, you have my permission to put him in a full-body cast." Dressler looked at me. "A little joke."

I waited while Tuffy yanked the cork and poured. Then I waited until he'd left the room. Then I waited until Dressler picked up his glass and said, "Cheers." Only then did I pick up my own glass and drink. An entire world opened before me: fine dust on grape leaves in the hot French sun, echoing stone pas-sageways in fifteenth-century chateaus, the rippling laughter of Emile Zola's courtesans.

"Jesus," I said. "Where do you get this stuff?"

"Doesn't matter," Dressler said. "They wouldn't deal with you. Tell you what. You take care of Dolores and I'll see you get a case of this."

"And a case of the one we had last time," I said. "I've thought about it every day since I drank it."

"You drive a hard bargain. Done. If you can fix things for Dolores. If not, I'll let Tuffy pay you."

"I don't need threats," I said, feeling obscurely hurt. "If I say I'll do something, I'll do it. And I'll do it the best I can."

"That's fine," Dressler said. "But I might need better than that."

2

And Makes Me Poor Indeed

"So," I said, halfway into the second glass, "what did somebody do to Dolores La Marr?"

"What's the most valuable thing we've got, Junior?"

"We?" I asked. "Or me?"

"Let's start with you." Dressler rang the bell again.

"My daughter," I said. "Rina."

"Okay, that's you. That's good, family should always come first, but think bigger. Look, there's one thing you've got that someone can steal, you listening? Of course, you're listening. And once they steal it, they're no richer, but you're a lot poorer. You know what it is?" Tuffy came into the room. "Be a nice guy," Dressler said to him, "and get us some green olives. The big ones with that weird red thing in it."

"Pimento," I said.

Dressler said, "Did I ask you?"

"Sorry."

"In the refrigerator. In the door, second shelf down, on the right. Jar with a green label. Don't bring us the jar, just put three olives each on six of the big toothpicks, in the second drawer to the left of the sink, put them on the good china with some napkins, and bring them in. That's eighteen olives on six tooth-picks. And don't touch them with your fingers."

Tuffy's forehead wrinkled in perplexity, and I thought he probably did that a lot. "How do I get them on the toothpick without touching them?"

Dressler said, "You want I should come in and do it myself?"

Tuffy took a step backward. "No, no, Mr. Dressler."

"Good. You figure it out. Every time I have to do something myself, I figure that's one less person I need."

As Tuffy scurried from the room, and I said, "I admire your management style."

"We'll see how much you admire it when it's aimed at you. Answer my question. What do you have that somebody can steal and it hurts you but doesn't give them *bupkes*?"

"Oh," I said. Rephrased, there was something familiar about it. "I've got a kind of tingle."

"So tell your neurologist. Do you read Shakespeare?"

"Yes."

He looked at me, one eye a lot smaller than the other. "And? What is it?"

"My good name," I said. The window to my memory opened noiselessly, and in my imagination I dropped gratefully to my knees in front of it. I closed my eyes, and said,

> "*Good name in man and woman, dear my lord,*
> *Is the immediate jewel of their souls.*
> *Who steals my purse steals trash; 'tis something, nothing;*
> *'Twas mine, 'tis his, and da-*da, *da-*da,*-da-*da—"

"Has been slave to thousands," Dressler prompted, and I fin-ished it up:

"But he that filches from me my good name
Robs me of that which not enriches him,
And makes me poor indeed.

"Iago," I said. "Not someone who deserves a good rep."

"If he hadn't had one," Dressler said, "he'd have been hung before the end of Act One. Play should have been called *Iago*, not *Othello*. Why name a play after the mark?" He drank the wine as if it were Kool-Aid. "Who needs a good reputation better than a crook?"

"Good point."

"That was a question."

Context is everything, and we'd been talking about Dolores La Marr. "An actress."

"I could learn to like you," Dressler said, "maybe. First the Shakespeare, then the common sense. They shouldn't call it common sense, you know? Nobody's got it any more."

I didn't think there had ever been a period in human history when common sense had been thick on the ground, but it didn't seem like an observation that would interest Dressler. So I said something he'd undoubtedly heard a lot of. I said, "You're right."

"Everything, the girl lost everything. She was getting good parts in bad movies, working up to bad parts in good movies, and then Lew was going to give her a good part in a good movie. Her whole life, she wanted one thing, just one thing, and she worked like a bugger to get it. And then somebody took it all away from her. *He that filches from me my good name,*" Dressler declaimed, "*Robs me of that which not enriches him—*"

"*And makes me poor indeed,*" I said in unison with him. We both gave it a little extra, since the wine had kicked in, and Tuffy, coming in with a plate in his hands, stopped as though he'd found the two of us sitting shoulder to shoulder at the piano, playing "Chopsticks."

"I couldn't do it," he said, looking worried. "I brought the olives and the toothpicks, but the olives are just rolling around on the dish 'cause I couldn't get them on the toothpicks. I ate the ones I touched. I figure the genius here can figure it out."

"In my sleep," I said.

"Just put it down," Dressler said. "Where's Babe?"

"He's, uh, he's taking a nap."

"What *is* this? Juana's got a headache, Babe's asleep, and you can't put olives on a toothpick. I've gotten old, I've gotten old. Nobody's afraid of me any more."

"I am," I said.

"You don't count. Wake Babe up. He can sleep tonight."

"Yes, Mr. Dressler." Tuffy was backing up.

"Aahhh, let him sleep," Dressler said. "They got a baby at home. Probably up all night."

"Yes, sir." Tuffy licked his lips and fidgeted.

"Just fucking say it," Dressler said.

"Kid's teething," Tuffy said.

Dressler lifted a hand and let it drop. "Achh, I remember. My sister, two of my nieces and nephews. Misery, it's misery. Okay, let him sleep."

Tuffy left the room rather quickly, and Dressler said to me, "Give me an olive."

"I don't know how to do it, either," I said. "How to get them on the toothpicks without touching them."

He pulled his head back, a snake preparing to strike. "Yeah? And suppose you'd been Tuffy just now, and I gave you an order you didn't know how to carry out. What would you have done?"

"I'd have been all over the olives with my fingers."

"And then lied about it?"

"Absolutely. That's why God gave us lies. So we could get out of things."

"The hell with the toothpicks," Dressler said. "Just give me a goddamn olive."

Forty minutes later, there was a second bottle of wine on the table and Dressler and I were discussing techniques for soothing a teething baby, and Tuffy was in the kitchen, singing Barry Manilow's "Copacabana" and heating some chicken noodle soup. Outside, a long summer afternoon had done its slow fade, and the windows had gone a glassy black. Dressler's house was completely surrounded by hedges and fences, with gates front and back, so there were no lights to blemish the darkness. Tuffy had gotten to the verse about feathers and long hair, and he was giving it quite a bit. He had a lot of vibrato.

"Is Tuffy married?" I asked.

"No, and it's not in the cards," Dressler said. "Not until they change the law." He harpooned an olive. "But that doesn't mean he couldn't whip you thin enough to spread on matzoh."

He'd said it cheerfully enough, so I thought I'd give it another try. "You really think I should do this Dolores La Marr thing."

"I not only *think* you're going to do it," he said. "I know you will. I like you, Junior, although it's probably mostly the wine, but you're going to do this for me. If you don't, you're going to have to find a new place to hide, and wait there until I'm dead."

Dressler, as near as I could figure, was ninety-two. That wouldn't be so long to wait, and I already had the perfect hiding place, in the Wedgwood Apartments in Koreatown. It was the most successful secret of my life. So I listened a bit smugly.

"And you should do it even if I didn't want you to do it," he said. "She's your neighbor, Dolly is. Thou shalt love thy neighbor as thyself," he said. "Jesus said that, right?"

"I guess so." I thought about the block in Tarzana where Rina lived with my ex-wife, Kathy, and then I ticked off the names of the people who lived in the nearby houses. "Dolores La Marr lives in Tarzana?"

"No, stupid," Dressler said, quite a bit less cheerfully. "In the Wedgwood, same as you. In Koreatown."

3

Figurative Smoked Glass

The "China" apartment houses—so-called not because they're Hollywood-Chinesey in design but because their names (The Wedgwood, The Royal Doulton, and The Lenox) all denote makers of fine china—were built in the late 1920s on what was then the western edge of the city of Los Angeles, near the appropriately named (at the time) Western Boulevard. They're masterpieces of twenties California architecture, art deco in three dimensions, and were designed to allow members of the upper middle classes to live in close proximity to each other, well above the peons on the sidewalks, and under conditions of comfort and even grandeur.

Twelve-foot ceilings, mahogany paneling, oak floors, wrought-iron fixtures, hand-built deco windows, no two alike. Only four apartments to a floor, their front doors opening into a cathedral-ceilinged, vaulted hallway high and wide enough for four men on horseback, side by side. The cowboy actor Hoot Gibson famously did ride his movie horse, Goldie, down the fourth-floor hallway one gin-fueled evening in 1929.

The China apartment houses were close enough to the film industry—then budding in dusty Hollywood—to house an historic assemblage of actors, actresses, writers, the occasional director, and a great many mistresses. The studio moguls lived at first atop the hills of Los Feliz, near the newly expanded Griffith Park. As the city spread west, toward the sea, the moguls and the stars migrated to Beverly Hills and Bel Air, and the neighborhood the Chinese apartments graced had slid imperceptibly downhill. The second-tier actors and actresses and directors moved away, the mistresses were relocated farther west for ease of access, and the writers stayed, as writers usually do, to the party's bitter end.

By the 1960s, the party was no longer even a memory. The blocks north of Pico and Olympic, and east of Western, had become working-class, many of the grand duchesses among the apartment houses broken up into smaller units and offered at low rents. In the 1970s and '80s, the Koreans moved in, recognizing good value when they saw it and building—over the course of decades—a Koreatown that has the highest population density in LA and more Koreans, during business hours, than any other city outside of Korea. The men, and the occasional woman, who govern Los Angeles looked on with mixed emotions. On the one hand, here was an inspiring local immigration success story that had the additional benefit of displacing some of the city's more lethal gangs and bringing down the crime rate sharply. On the other hand, as all-Korean shopping malls the size of small cities began to spring up, accompanied by literally hundreds of all-Korean strip malls, restaurants, and night clubs, the city rulers' palms began to itch.

Where were the rake-offs? Where were the taxes on all that investment money? Where were the corporate profits? There they were, the leaders of Los Angeles, good twentieth-century political hacks, looking greedily through a smoked-glass window at a thriving private economy of cash, favors, handshakes, and barter.

That figurative smoked glass made the extremely peculiar

renovation of the China apartment houses possible, and with almost no profit to the city. Operating on the ancient Asian principle that ostentatious living should be confined to interiors, surrounded by drab exteriors designed not to arouse envy, the Koreans who renovated the China apartment houses left the grass long and the sidewalks cracked and the paint peeling, left the window shutters hanging crooked, left the neon signs missing the letters that turned The Lenox into the toxic-sounding *The nox* and the The Royal Doulton into *The Royal Doult*. They even left the elevators and the hallways threadbare and shabby. In some cases, they distressed them further, installing non-conducting electrical wires and letting them dangle from the ceiling and doing the occasional Mexican-restaurant trick of punching holes in the plaster to expose the bricks behind it.

But the apartments, behind their triple-locked doors, were brought back to the sheen and grace of the 1920s, fitted out with the finest appliances, invisibly heated and cooled by the best systems money could buy. And then, bribing a great many building inspectors to allow them to do so, the Korean owners' syndicate created a single enormous garage that stretched beneath all three buildings, separated only by thin but deceptively solid walls, each with a locked door, the numbered keys to which were distributed among the tenants. As a result, a tenant could take the driveway beneath the Nox when he or she was actually going to the Wedgwood, or walk into the Wedgwood and walk out of the Royal Doult. The landlords knew who their customers would be: people with something to hide. And they'd attracted a fine group of the rich and shifty, people who needed to conceal their incomes, their identities, and themselves. At a million to three million a pop, depending on the size of the apartment and which floor it was on. Most of the tenants, though not all, were Korean.

Traffic on the major boulevards surrounding Bel Air was brutal by the time Tuffy and Babe drove me back to the street in Hollywood where they'd snatched me. They were in a lighter mood, since Dressler and I had apparently gotten along so well. The death threat hadn't carried into the kitchen, where Babe had been sleeping in a breakfast nook with his head back and his mouth open and Tuffy had been working on his dance moves.

So they were fairly pleasant on the drive, including me in a conversation about who would buy the Dodgers now that that prick Frank McCourt was on the way out, and was Matt Kemp really worth $160 million bucks. On the latter topic, Tuffy and I disagreed, he saying you could get a whole team for that much and I saying that in the last half of the last season, Kemp had pretty much *been* the whole team, and we'd have made it to the World Series if he'd been allowed to bat nine times in a row instead of bringing the other guys to the plate.

"Designated runners," I said, wise on Dressler's wine. "That's what you need. Three pitchers, three designated runners so you've got one for each base, and Matt Kemp. World Series guaranteed."

"Yeah?" Tuffy said. "Then who's on first?"

I said, "Yes."

"No, I mean, who's playing first?"

"Who."

"You had too much wine, huh?"

"Nobody remembers Abbott and Costello," I said. "It's a poorer world."

Babe said slowly—Babe said everything slowly—"I always liked Martin and Rossi. Every time that little fat guy said *Hello Dere*, I cracked up."

"*Hello Dere*," Tuffy said, and laughed.

"*Hello Dere*," Babe said, and laughed.

Given the option, I would choose a really ripe case of cholera over fifteen minutes of Martin and Rossi. I said, "You can drop me up here."

"*Hello Dere*," Tuffy said, and laughed, and then he wiped the tears of mirth from his eyes and said, "Got a couple of blocks to go."

"No problem," I said, all but clawing at the door handle. "I could use the walk."

"*Goodbye Dere*," Babe said, pulling to the curb, and the two of them laughed so hard they fell over sideways and banged shoulders. I got out while the car was still moving. In fact, it kept moving until it banged into the bumper of the parked car in front of it. That set Babe and Tuffy off again, and I could still hear their laughter, spiced with the occasional *Hello Dere*, when I was half a block away.

My anonymous white Toyota Corolla had, as always, been ignored by car thieves and cops alike, and I climbed in and pointed myself South and East, toward Koreatown and the most beautiful woman in the world.

4

The Patron Saint of Lost Causes

The Wedgwood, the Nox, and the Royal Doult occupy a corner just north of Olympic, at the intersection of two narrow streets which, for the purpose of getting to the end of this sentence, we'll call Courtney Lane and Baltic Way. They're not on a map, so don't bother looking for them.

Normally, when I visit the Wedgwood, I do an intricate little dance of dead-end streets, double-backs, park-and-waits, and other routines for spotting a tail. Ever since the lease was signed over to me by the now-incarcerated Winnie Park—who owes me every breath she's taken since around 4 P.M., March 9, 2001, when I persuaded someone to put a gun away—I'd kept the existence of Apartment 302 in the Wedgwood from the entire world, even my ex-wife and child. It was my ultimate hiding place, the one real secret of my life, the safe spot I could run to if I ever got one of the behemoths of the local scene mad at me.

Well, Irwin Dressler was the bull behemoth and had been for more than seventy years, ever since the Chicago mob sent him out to domesticate Los Angeles and make it theirs in the early 1940s. He'd exceeded their expectations, not only making the city theirs but also making it better. He created banks. He guided the studios and helped them with their labor problems.

He prevented a strike on the day the Dodgers first played ball at Chavez Ravine. He kept the money flowing back to the Windy City and guided its reinvestment in the Big Orange. He was instrumental in the creation and growth of Palm Springs and Las Vegas. And over the years he pursued a long-range, private program to turn all of it, every little scam, every hundred-million dollar business, legal. He'd never been arrested, never been indicted. He'd testified before Congress so often half the House of Representatives called him by his first name, and he never—not once—was challenged on his testimony, although he arguably never—not once—told the whole truth.

And he knew where my refuge was. The question was, how many other people knew?

I turned into the driveway for the Royal Doult, on Baltic, parked my car beneath the building, and went through two locked doors marked *¡Peligroso!* with an electric-looking, bright red lightning zigzag beneath the word, until I was in the garage beneath the Wedgwood, two buildings away and fronting on Courtney Lane. My escape car—different color, different make—was parked here, and in the apartment upstairs were excellent papers for two new identities, complete with active credit cards and bank accounts, and about $120,000 in cash. I could literally drive in on Baltic Way as me and drive out, half an hour later, in a different car onto a different street, Courtney Lane, as a different person. It had all seemed perfect until about three hours ago.

The Most Beautiful Woman in the World lived on the ninth floor, the next-to-the-highest in the building. I got into the elevator, waved at the hidden camera that was beaming my image to some extremely bulked-up Koreans in the lobby area, and looked for the button for nine.

It required a key.

"*Anyong haseo*, guys," I said to the microphone in the left

front top corner. I heard a buzz and the elevator started to climb—
someone above me had rung for it. "I'm supposed to go see Miss
La Marr on nine, and I haven't got a key. What do I do?"

There was no reply, but the elevator passed the first floor,
slowed and then stopped, and then started back down, as whoever it was up there above me leaned impatiently on the buzzer.
The doors opened, and I found myself in the amazingly dilapi-
dated lobby, facing the Korean guard I privately thought of as
Pyongyang because of his unfailingly threatening expression.

The guy above me buzzed again, and Pyongyang looked up
and muttered, "*Pabo*," which means stupid. Then he said, "She
knows you come?"

"She does."

"You live here," he said. "So if she yell at me, you—" He made
a motion with his hands like someone wringing out a washcloth.

"Got it," I said.

"You bettah." He leaned in and slipped a key into the little
lock where the button for the ninth floor should have been. And
I began my ascent to meet Dolores La Marr.

The reason for the key became apparent when the elevator opened
directly into a private entrance hall, which got my attention.
Apparently, the entire ninth floor was a single apartment. That
meant it was about 12,000 square feet.

The dominant object in the room was the hollowed-out
lower leg, complete with foot, of an elephant, obviously pro-
cured in the days before PETA. At the top, about four feet
above floor level, it erupted in an enormous bouquet of dusty
peacock feathers. Behind it, the entire leg-and-feathers assemblage was duplicated, dust and all, in a single gigantic gold-
veined mirror that extended from corner to corner and from
floor to ceiling.

The place smelled dry and papery, like old books that have been boxed up for decades.

The floor was wood, black enough to be ebony. Brazilian ebony, the last time I looked, was going for about thirty bucks a square foot. If this whole place was floored in ebony, that had been about a $360,000 decorative touch. Dolores La Marr was obviously not in danger of winding up on food stamps.

I called out, "Hello? Miss La Marr?"

"Come through the archway in front of you and down the hall," said a voice from above me. I looked around and saw a small speaker, a cube about five inches to a side, tucked into a high corner to the right of the elevator door. It was a nice voice, not conspicuously old or young, although it was shot through with a barely noticeable tremor, just the hint of a vibrato.

"Coming along," I said. I took another look at the elephant's leg and went through the archway.

The hallway was high-ceilinged and painted a pale greenish-gray, like faded pewter, if there were such a thing. Every two or three feet on either side, illuminated by a pinspot, hung a large photo of a woman's face in satiny black and white, shot from every imaginable angle and lighted by the same masters who made the Hollywood black-and-white films of the thirties some of the world's most beautiful dream-images.

It was quite a face. The eyes, with long, heavy upper lids that continuously threatened to close, were wide-set and obviously a very light blue that photographed a dreamy translucent gray and gave me the illusion I could look through them into the mind of the woman who owned them; the nose was straight and delicate, a faint seashell-whorl defining the nostrils; and the mouth had enough lower lip for two lesser and more forgettable mouths. And all of it was framed by a luxurious waterfall of dark, wavy hair that brushed her neck and shoulders with an

easy familiarity that gave me a pang of envy, and set off the flaw-
less skin so the face seemed to leap out of the photo. I had the
sense that if I were to close my eyes and slide my hand over the
surface of the image, I would feel the contours of the woman's
features. The last picture was the *Life* cover. The most striking
thing about it—the thing that made it a plausible representation
of the most beautiful woman in the world—was the fact that the
subject of the portrait seemed to be laughing at the whole situation: the camera, the lights, the photographer, herself.

"Don't dawdle," the amplified voice said again. "Bring him
in, Anna."

I didn't see Anna, but it was only a few feet more before the
hallway emptied into a living room the size of an Olympic pool,
ringed with spiky, asymmetrical Art Deco windows, windows
so good my palms itched with the urge to steal them right out
of the walls. The ones that looked east framed the vertical glit-
ter of downtown. The furniture was all white, glaring against
the ebony floor like unmelted pockets of snow floating on dark
water. Five groupings of chairs and tables barely filled the place.
They rose above the liquid darkness of the floor like extremely
comfortable islands, each group gathered in a circle of yellowish light cast by a standing lamp with stained-glass shades that
could have been Tiffany. I'd have to get closer to the lamps to
look for the confetti glass or the silvery lead or the turn-paddle
on-off switch, or any of the other genuine Tiffany giveaways.

"Ah, the patron saint of lost causes," said the woman at the
far end of the room. Three pinspots set into the ceiling con-
verged on her, making the place where she sat the brightest spot
in the room.

She was enormous, nearly wide enough to fill the three-
cushion sofa on which she sat. The hair was still dark—or dark
again—and the face, perhaps because it was so plump, seemed

almost unwrinkled. She wore a shapeless black gown or dress or muu-muu or something very loose, just a parachute of dark cloth with an opening for her neck and long, draping sleeves. As I got closer, it sparkled at me, and I saw it had jet beads sewn to it.

"Is the cause lost?" I pulled the nearest armchair back a foot or two, just to give her some space, and sat. Up close, she could still be recognized as the woman in the photographs, but much bigger and decades older.

"It's been sixty years," she said. A little earpiece-and-microphone thing stretched from her ear to her mouth, and I could hear her voice twice, once up close and then echoing from the hall. "Most of the people who had anything to do with it are dead."

"Dressler doesn't seem to regard death as an obstacle."

She shook her head, but not in disagreement. Jet earrings swung back and forth with a little chittering noise. From this distance I could see a fine line of snow-white hair at her scalp and the impasto of makeup, artfully applied but definitely not for daylight. Her eyebrows looked tattooed on. Even on Hollywood Boulevard, where dogs sometimes ride bicycles, she'd have drawn stares. Still, the bone structure was perfect and clearly visible, even beneath the extra weight. "That's Winnie. His entire life he's been looking at the world, seeing a problem, and fixing it. I doubt it's ever occurred to him there's anything he can't fix."

I stopped staring at her and said, "Winnie."

"Irwin," she said. "Winnie. I can't call him Irwin. It makes him sound like an accountant."

"Winnie's got its problems, too."

"I've known Winnie since 1948," she said, and disagreement intensified the quiver in her voice. "I've known you two minutes.

If you don't mind, I'll let things drift along as they are. What's your name?"

"Junior Bender. And no, Junior's not a nickname, it's my given name. My father was named Merle and he wanted to name me after him, but after a lifetime of being called Merle, he thought it over and just named me Junior."

"Well, you're not really in a position to criticize anyone's name, are you?"

"Who's Anna?" I asked.

"Oh," she said. Her mouth tightened for an instant in what might have been irritation. "Anna."

I waited. When it was evident I'd be allowed to wait quite a while, I said, "I ask because you seemed to suggest she was escorting me down the hallway, but I didn't see anyone."

"No," she said. "You wouldn't. Maybe you'll see her later."

"She's very small?"

"She's . . . shy." Dolores La Marr cleared her throat as a punctuation mark.

"All right," I said. "Let's talk about your problem."

"I don't have a problem."

"Well, I'm glad to hear it. Would you mind calling Dressler and telling him? I'd kind of like to go home and forget all this, if you really don't care."

Something sparked in her eyes, and I caught a glimpse of the humor I'd seen in the *Life* cover. "It's not that easy. Nothing is ever that easy, certainly you've learned that by now. What are you, thirty-eight?"

"Thirty-seven." Maybe, I thought, I should be using my girl-friend, Ronnie's, moisturizers.

"Sorry. You have an air of maturity, if you'll accept that as an excuse for thinking you're older than you actually are."

"No problem. Why isn't it that easy?"

She leaned across to extend a very white hand and tapped my knee with the tip of her index finger. I looked for the Norma Desmond talon but was surprised by the bitten nails; also by the swollen knuckles and curling fingers of advanced arthritis, the most telling sign of her age. Two rings bit into one of her fingers, almost disappearing in the flesh. "Because it's *Winnie*," she said. "Winnie has *decided something*, and when Winnie decides something, it's like gravity. You can try to ignore it, you can try to deny it, but if you trip you'll still fall down." She looked around the room as though searching for someone, and I had an impulse to turn and look for myself. "So here's the situation as I see it. You don't want to do this and I don't particularly want you to do it, but Winnie does. So the best thing for me to do is to give you whatever I can to make it easier for you, and then say goodbye. If you find anything out, you can tell Winnie, not me. I stopped caring fifty years ago."

"Is there something you want?"

"Many, many things, my dear. But why do you ask?"

"You keep looking around as though you hope the butler has come into the room. Do you want me to get you something?"

"Aren't you perceptive?" She clapped the crooked hands once. "In the kitchen, which is through that door, you'll find an old-fashioned cold pantry, and in the pantry are some very nice bottles of Pouilly-Fuisse. Why don't you get one and a corkscrew and a couple of glasses, and bring them all back in here. At least we can lubricate the next hour or so, even if we can't skip it."

The door led through a substantial formal dining room with an oak table that seated twelve, uncovered. It had a dull oakish gleam, but the corner nearest the kitchen door was quite dusty; I could see the little border left by the edge of the dust rag. The room's size was emphasized by a cathedral ceiling with long, thick, rough-hewn beams running beneath it. Since there was one more floor of apartments above this one, the cathedral ceiling was lower than most. I figured I could almost touch the beams if I went on tiptoe and jumped just a little. I trailed a finger through the dust on the table's corner as I passed, leaving a conspicuous jet trail.

In the kitchen, it took me about two minutes to find the wine and the glasses, but the corkscrew stumped me. I stood there, looking at approximately twenty closed drawers, and then something feathery and steamlike kind of blew against the side of my face and straight through my skull, planting a thought: that the second drawer from the left in the top row to the right of the sink just might be the one. I opened it, and there was the corkscrew.

I looked around the kitchen, much as Dolores La Marr had looked around the living room, said "*WEEoooo WEEooo WEEooo*" quietly and asked myself where the tray was. This time I just closed my eyes and stood there for a moment, waiting for the next bit of guidance, and when I opened my eyes again, I was looking at one out of a large number of closed cabinets. In that cabinet, I found the tray.

I might have hurried a bit getting back to the living room.

"You may pour," Dolores La Marr said, a bit grandly, when I was seated.

When I had the cork worked out, I poured her a good full glass, waiting for her to say, "Stop," but she didn't. I was still feeling the wine from Dressler's house, so I was in *do-I-don't-I* mode, but the wine smelled like a green hillside with a hint of cut grass, so I poured myself some, hoisted my glass, and said, "Cheers."

"And cheers to you, dear. Are you married?"

"Divorced. One daughter, thirteen."

"Pretty?"

"So pretty it's too bad *Life* isn't still publishing."

"That was a mixed blessing at best," she said. "I think that was what tipped everything over."

"How so?"

"People," she said vaguely. "Do you get to see your daughter?"

"Yes. My ex-wife and I are polite to each other, through our teeth sometimes, but we both love her too much to make her the rope in a tug of war."

"Good for you. So many parents these days—"

"Miss La Marr," I said.

"Dolly."

"Well, Dolly, I'm not trying to be rude, but you're not giving me your time to talk about me. We're here to start trying to understand what happened to you."

"Actually," she said, and the quaver was back in her voice, "actually, I'm giving you my time *precisely* to talk about you, at least at the beginning. I need to know who's going to be bulldozing my past. I need, for example, to be relatively certain that whoever it is has the wit to figure it out and the discretion not to sell it to the tabloids. Is that you, dear?"

I said, "I've been a professional burglar since I was fifteen. That's twenty-two years now, and I've never been caught. I have no criminal record. I've been working as a kind of detective for crooks, some of them extremely *muscular* crooks, for fifteen years, and none of them has decided to kill me in the aftermath. And except for one richly deserved incident in which I used what I'd learned for blackmail, I've never violated a confidence."

"How does someone deserve to be blackmailed?"

"When the crime he committed involved a young girl who was terrified about the story coming out. At the same time, though, the man who messed with her was on the verge of messing with someone else. Someone thirteen years old. My client had forbidden me to kill him, so I used what I knew about Girl Number One to force him to abandon his plans for Girl Number Two. He was famous, so being exposed as a child molester was pretty firmly in the *No* column."

"And would you have killed him?"

"If it had seemed to be the only way to stop him without publicly involving the first girl. If he'd called my bluff, I didn't have a fallback position because I'd told the first girl I wouldn't expose her."

"So you *would* have killed him."

"My daughter is thirteen."

"Well, that covers discretion. What about wit?"

"Up to you," I said. "What am I going to do, tell you I'm smart? Want to see me do calculus on my fingers?"

She pushed her lower lip out and looked down into her wine. Then she looked up at me and then past me, letting her eyes float around the room until they came to rest on something, and once again I had the urge to turn around. She nodded. "I see," she said. "Do I see?" She waited a moment and then nodded again, and her eyes came back to me. "Yes, I see."

I said, "Can I have a vote next time?"

"Why not?" she said. "It's not really like I have a choice. There's Winnie, up there in the clouds pulling the strings, and he's probably checking his watch right now, wondering how far we've gotten. A million years ago, Al Hirschfeld—do you know Hirschfeld?"

"A caricaturist, right?

"You might say that. He was a genius, but he was a caricaturist, too. Anyway, he did a poster for *My Fair Lady*, the Broadway version, of George Bernard Shaw peering over the tops of clouds and manipulating two puppets representing Rex

Harrison and Julie Andrews. That's the way I think of Winnie sometimes, although Shaw was more benign than Winnie is." She held out her glass, which was empty. "Top me up, please."

I picked up the bottle and poured. "I once knew a con man," I said, "a gay guy, probably the biggest *My Fair Lady* fan on earth, who told me that poster was the first modern representation of God he'd ever seen, and he always visualized Shaw when he thought of God."

"There are probably worse gods than Shaw, if you don't mind relentless rationality. Me, I'd prefer some mysticism, even some quirkiness." She drank and put the glass down, hard. "We really *are* all over the place, aren't we? Here's what you came to find out. Do you want a pen and some paper?"

"I'll remember it."

"Fine." She reached up to the microphone-ear-piece rig and pushed a button. "No reason to tell those adorable Korean boys downstairs all my secrets."

"Is that what that thing is for?"

"Partly. My cleaning people come in once a week, not that they do much, and I use it to talk to them, too. I don't get up very easily these days. Mostly, though, it's to let the boys downstairs know I'm still breathing."

"I interrupted you. You were about to tell—"

"The tale of me. I was born in a trunk—not really—in a year that was not numbered, in Scranton, Pennsylvania. One of America's rust capitals. I was a pretty child, and my mother, who had always wanted to be an actress, et cetera, et cetera. You can fill it in. She finally made it out here with me in her suitcase when I was sixteen and she hauled me to every agent in town until one of them looked at me and saw in me precisely the kind of young woman after whom one of the moguls of the day, Max Zeffire of Zephyr Pictures, perpetually lusted. And I mean insatiably.

If he'd been offered nine of me before breakfast he'd have done all of us and still made it to the table before his eggs got cold. So I entered womanhood, so to speak, on Max Zeffire's casting couch while my mother remained demurely in the outer office, talking race horses with Max's receptionist."

"How did you feel about it?"

"I was sixteen, dear, what did I know? It hurt, but it would have hurt exactly as much if I'd given it up to some pimply Scranton boy destined to die in a coal mine at the age of twenty and abandon me to a cold little house full of black dust." She tipped back the glass, and once again her eyes searched the room behind me. "Instead, I got into the movies, a much better deal. Through Max and some other—oh, let's call them flirtations—I actually made it up onto the screen." She wagged a hand back and forth, minimizing the accomplishment. "Along with a thousand other girls who'd *flirted*, in quotation marks, with the right men. But there were *ten thousand* others—this is one of the things that kept us going, dear—there were ten thousand *other* girls who'd given it up to every rake in Hollywood, some of them multiple times, and never even got through the studio gates. So we were a meritocracy of sorts, even if it was a whorish meritocracy. Am I boring you?"

"Not even a little bit."

"Good. You didn't want to get involved in this in the first place, dear, so it would be awful if you had to be bored, too. Where was I?"

"A meritocracy. You were in the movies."

"I was, I was. Have you ever been in a movie?"

"I've been on sets."

"Then you know. People who haven't made movies think it's glamorous, but it's mainly getting up while it's still dark, having makeup pasted on you and getting pinned into a costume that someone else has sweated into, and then standing around for hours and hours without wrinkling your clothes until it's time to step into the light and say your line or raise your eyebrow or whatever you've been hired to do. Not tremendously interesting work, but not exhausting, either. For a girl my age, it was wonderful. There were handsome men everywhere, some of them famous, and everyone looked at me, and for the first time in my life, I had enough money. And if I had to sleep with people—men and, once in a while, women—well, so what? Some of them were beautiful and some of them were rich, and some of them were both." She smiled at me. "But none of them was neither."

"And Los Angeles was nice back then."

"It was very, very not Scranton. We had an orange tree in the yard of our apartment house. It took me a year to get over having an orange tree in the yard. I ate the damn things green, I didn't care. And then we moved to Beverly Hills, the flats, not the fancy part, and we had *several* orange trees, plus rattlesnakes. Beverly Hills used to be infested with rattlesnakes."

"It still is."

"Yes, but back then, they warned you before they struck. So I was moving up in the world of movies, going from *Girl in Background* to *Second Chorine* to *Ellie's Friend* and then all the way up to where I got my first character with a name. Judy, she was called, Judy, and Judy had a really good moment in a Boston Blackie movie—do you remember Boston Blackie?"

"Not really."

"Budget detective series, but they had their audience. So Judy—who, you'll recall, was me—had a good moment when her necklace got caught on Chester Morris's bow tie and her pearls bounced all over the place but she couldn't bend to pick them up because the necklace was still tangled in his bow tie—he was wearing a tuxedo—so they leaned down together and bumped heads and wound up in a kiss. Fade out, except that was the moment that brought letters in from the hinterlands and got me into Universe, and into movies that didn't have Chester Morris in them. With a contract. *Regular money*. My mother was in heaven."

"Universe Pictures was the studio Dressler helped to run."

"He helped to run all of them, dear. And the banks and the racetracks and both the movie unions and the studios that hired them, although lesser people might have seen that as a conflict of interest. Nobody did anything important in Los Angeles in those days without Winnie. He was the man behind the screen, like in *The Wizard of Oz*. You know, *Do not look at the man behind the curtain*. So I met Winnie, and he took an interest in my career—all very up-and-up, because of Blanche. Winnie never fooled around on Blanche, even though he had all sorts of romantic yearnings for pretty girls—and he got Mr. Winterman to notice me, and I began to get better parts."

"Blanche," I said.

"Winnie's wife. Winnie was the Husband of the Century."

"Is she dead?"

"I have no idea, dear. It would be a misery if she weren't. She had advanced senile dementia, got it very young and had it forever. Practically the only thing she remembered, poor thing, was that her older sister had died of scarlet fever when Blanche was twelve. She did nothing but cry for years."

I'd seen no sign that Dressler was married, nor had I read about it, although very few aspects of his private life ever made it into print. "Did you meet her?"

"I'd never have met her, not in my circle, but practically nobody did. She was from an old family, listed in the Los Angeles Blue Book. Gentile, of course, in those days, and her parents were frantic not to have it get out that she'd married a Jew, and a *gangster* Jew at that. She and Winnie eloped, got married by a justice of the peace in Santa Barbara, and lived very quietly. But, in the interest of time, let me get back to my story. The funny thing was that it wasn't Winnie who got me involved with organized crime. It was George Raft."

"I remember George—"

"Georgie was dumb," she said. She was looking down into her empty glass as though she could see tiny figures from the past in it. "A sweet man and great in the sack, but dumb as a bag of nuts. I was never sure he could actually read or write. I know he had his movie scripts read to him, because I'm the one who read some of them. Here's how dumb Georgie was. He wanted to get out of his contract at Warner Brothers, and that prick Jack Warner was sick and tired of him, so he asked Georgie what it would take to terminate the contract. Warner was thinking he'd have to pay Georgie a hundred thousand, a hundred and a half, to get out of the arrangement, but Georgie said, ten thousand. Warner practically leapt at it, but before he could write Georgie a check, Georgie wrote *him* one." She shook her head. "Dumb, dumb, dumb. Ten thousand was a lot of money in those days. My big contract at Universe, I made three hundred fifty dollars a week."

She looked up at me and gave me a smile that almost melted me, the smile that had sold a hundred thousand copies of *Life*. "Poor Georgie. He made Bogart a star, you know. Turned down *High Sierra* and *The Maltese Falcon* and *Casablanca*, turned down half the scripts that transformed Bogart into Bogey. Everybody thought Bogey was the tough guy, but Bogey was a tennis-playing socialite and Georgie grew up in Hell's Kitchen, with real gangsters, not the movie kind. It wasn't his fault he was dumb. One of his friends when he was a boy was Owney Madden. Don't tell me you haven't heard of Owney Madden."

"I remember. The Killer, right?"

"Right, that was his nickname. The Killer. Little cocky English guy, but he grew up in New York near Georgie, got famous as the kid who was shot eleven times one night on 52nd Street and lived. After he got out of the hospital, the boys who shot him began to turn up in the East River. Showed his talent early. He grew up to be a big man in the mobs, much to Georgie's envy. Owned the Cotton Club in Harlem, owned part of The Stork Club—where I had some of the best nights of my life. Probably Owney's most famous murder was when he killed Vincent 'Mad Dog' McColl, whom I'm sorry to say I never met. Nickname like that, I'd have liked to have a drink with him. Most of the guys with the horrific nicknames were pussycats. Anyway, Owney Madden was Georgie's friend, and I was also Georgie's friend. And you know what they say about the friends of my friends."

"They're your friends."

"Good, you're listening." She shifted her weight forward and put both hands on the coffee table. "Here's something you're too young to know, dear. Getting old shrinks your bladder to the size of a tear duct. I'm going to go to the little girl's room, and that'll give you an opportunity to snoop around. Oh, and after you've snooped, open another bottle, would you? Now look away for a minute. Stare at the nice view."

I got up and went to the east-facing window with its bright downtown spangle and watched Dolores La Marr's reflection in the glass as she leaned far forward over the table, put both hands down, and pushed herself up with an audible grunt.

"A gentleman wouldn't have heard that."

I said, "Heard what?"

"You're a nice boy," she said, on her feet. She swayed a moment and then edged left, between the couch and the table. Once free of the furniture, she reached behind the couch and rolled out a walker I hadn't noticed, and launched herself down the length of the room, aiming for a door that undoubtedly led to the bedrooms and bathrooms.

The wheels of the walker squeaked. It was one of the saddest sounds I'd ever heard. I waited at the window until she'd vanished down the hallway, so as not to let her see me watching her. And then, with the squeaks from her wheels echoing over the hard, bare floors, I started to snoop.

5

The Whore of Babylon

Burglars are expert snoops. We have to be. It's a hard-and-fast rule that the longer we spend in a place, the more likely it is that we'll get caught. For me, twenty-five minutes is the maximum. I've gone through some pretty roomy houses in twenty-five minutes, and I like to think I found and removed everything worth finding and removing. And done it without leaving a mess behind, because the other hard-and-fast rule is that the longer it takes the pigeon to discover the burglary, the safer the burglar is. I've learned to ransack a six-room house in less than half an hour, selecting things as I go, and leave without even disturbing the nap on the carpet. In that regard, successful burglary is like surgery. If you want to remove the appendix, you don't start at the lungs and work down. You try to get in and out without leaving a scar.

I was almost sorry she'd given me permission.

People like to hide things on bookshelves, mostly because there are so many objects there that they think a crook in a hurry will give them a pass. So smart crooks head straight for the bookshelf.

La Marr's was a bonanza. In addition to some nice books— from a reader's perspective, not a burglar's—she had a row of very fine ivory figurines, Japanese *netsuke*, maybe eighteenth century, the ivory rubbed so smooth it almost felt soft. *Netsuke* were originally small carvings designed to dangle from the sash of a man's kimono as a counterweight to a hanging box that served as a pocket. A cord looped through the sash connected them, and man could tug on the *netsuke* and tuck into the sash to bring the box within reach. As time passed kimonos grew pockets, and *netsuke* became purely ornamental. The ones Dolores La Marr had collected were exquisite: a sleeping fox; a duck; a very naughty one featuring a man and a woman in the ever-popular rear entry position; and two beautiful *anabori netsuke*, hollowed out to display beautiful ivory filigree, and derived from the form of a clam's shell, partly open. Next to the *netsuke*, on a ravishing Meissen platter so thin it was translucent, were half a dozen drop-dead gorgeous, hand-painted blown-glass Christmas-tree ornaments, almost certainly Victorian, the kind of stuff that brings beads of sweat to the forehead of the San Fernando Valley's premier fine-swag fence, Stinky Tetweiler. In the middle of the fiction section I found a thick book that was actually a little safe, jammed almost uncomfortably full of cash, all in banded bundles of hundreds. Maybe $60,000 in all.

I resolved to speak to her about that. She needed to do better with that kind of money, Korean guards or no Korean guards.

On the top shelf, lying on its side, was a photo album that hadn't been dusted in years. I opened it and entered the glittering demimonde of the 1940s.

Dolores La Marr, stunning in every photo, at a great number of tables in a great many night clubs, the linens white enough to make me squint and the silverware shining, a thicket of glasses and bottles gleaming in the camera's flash. I'm not much of a drinker, but I have a sneaking admiration for the days when people just damned their lungs and livers and sailed full speed ahead, smoking and drinking with both hands as though the morning hangover and cough were a century in the future and they didn't expect to live long enough to suffer.

And they had a point, or at least the men in these pictures did. They came from a different planet, and had a shorter expected lifespan, than the women with them. The men, sitting between the delicate females in their white satins and silks and looking like the bad teeth in a row of good ones, were dark, porcine, dangerous. Their eyes looked through the camera, half-expecting a gun to materialize out of the flashbulb's glare. Their hair was slicked back, their chins shadowed with evening stubble. There were a lot of cleft chins, a lot of petulant mouths and budding jowls. A lot of really well-tailored tuxes and double-breasted suits. Here and there, a slumming star: Raft, George Jessel, a couple of Catskills comics. In one picture, captured mid-laugh with his eyes still dangerous, Sinatra.

The mobsters included some box-office names: Tony "The Ant" Mostelli; Georgie's buddy, Owney Madden; the puppet-master himself, Antonino "Big Tuna" Accardo; Accardo's show-off front-man, Sam Giancana; Roberto "Bobby Pig" Pigozzi; John "Handsome Johnny" Roselli; and a dozen others, a shifting cast of wise guys, on top for the moment and feeling good about it. They had the eyes of people who could see through walls, although a lot of them would fail to see the last gun aimed at them.

The women, beautiful as they were, had something interchangeable about them, a faint air of desperation, like flowers blooming in the dark. They glittered a little too much. They laughed a little too hard. In no photo were any of the men looking at them. The men looked at each other, they looked at the camera, they looked through the walls, not at the women—with one exception.

The exception was Dolores La Marr. In quite a few pictures, one or several of the men had their eyes on Dolores La Marr. As beautiful as most of the other women were, Dolores La Marr made them look like hat-check girls or the women who sold cigarettes from table to table. She was also the only woman at any of the tables who paid no attention to the camera. She had the sleek, quietly pleased appearance of someone who knew she brought a lot to the party. She seemed to be in her natural element.

No Irwin Dressler. These were not the kinds of parties at which Dressler would have been photographed.

I closed the album and re-shelved it, and someone blew warm air in my ear.

I whirled so fast that one foot slid out from under me on the polished floor, and I tottered there, off-balance, my right hand hanging onto the bookshelf, and looked around the big, empty room. My heart was doing its best to escape my chest via my throat, and the hair on the back of my neck was standing at attention.

Purely instinctive, I told myself. A person thinks he's alone in a room, and someone breathes into his ear. It's too intimate, it's a violation of our expectations, our animal assurance that we'll sense something before it gets that close to us. That our senses will warn us in time to let us protect ourselves from whatever it is.

What it was, it appeared, was nothing. This did not actually reassure me.

But there was *something*, maybe: a kind of light spot on the floor, moving away from me, an odd little patch that was like a shadow in reverse, a shadow that was paler than the light in which it fell. It seemed to be going toward the dining room, and halfway there it disappeared.

Ooooookaaayyyyy.

I don't believe in anything. I'm not religious, I don't buy into the warnings and promises of politics. I don't believe the Mayans or Nostradamus knew squat about the end of the world, I don't think there's a national cause worth dying for unless the politicians are willing to die first, and I have no faith that there's such a thing as luck. I *certainly* don't believe in apparitions. But something had led me to the corkscrew and the platter. Something had blown into my ear. Something was causing that odd gleam on the floor.

Something was giving me goose bumps.

So I took refuge in reason. First, there wasn't anything there. Second, all whatever-it-wasn't had done was show me where things were. Third, whatever it wasn't, it was moving away from me, which seemed like the right direction, toward the dining room and perhaps through it to the kitchen.

Oh, I thought. Maybe whatever-it-wasn't was reminding me that Dolores La Marr had asked for another bottle of wine.

See? Another bottle of wine? How scary was that? I'd just had a *thought*, that's all. I'd just remembered to go get some more wine. Nothing more than that. The thought had blown into my ear somehow, but I could worry about that later. Right at that moment, it seemed like an excellent idea to do what the thought was reminding me to do. Especially since it could blow into my ear.

So I followed the path the little, ummm, patch had taken, into the rather dim dining room. Nothing in there seemed to beckon to me, so I made another line on the dusty table with my fingertip and went into the kitchen. Completely free of ectoplasmic entities as far as I could see, and much, much brighter than the dining room. Bright was good.

I went into the cold pantry, quite a bit dimmer and a hell of a lot colder than the kitchen. Cold pantries are an engineering feat now lost to the all-thumbs jugheads who build modern houses, a room that draws drafts of cool air from underground, courtesy of a wide, vented pipe. The people who built the Wedgwood— and, I assumed, the other China apartment houses—had run the pipes right up the center of the building, creating a cold pantry in two of the four apartments on each floor. Presumably, since she owned the entire ninth floor, Dolores La Marr could have had a second one somewhere. Maybe she kept her furs in it.

The pantry had shelves on the three walls that didn't contain the door. The wine was right where I'd found it before, on the bottom shelf, which was the coldest. As I reached down to pick it up, the temperature seemed to drop a few degrees, and the room got just a touch dimmer. Thinking the door might be clos-ing behind me and not at *all* happy at the thought, I turned, still bent forward, and my elbow swept a jumbo-size box of cereal off a knee-high shelf.

I stood there for a moment, holding the wine bottle by the neck like a club, and put out a few cautious feelers. Things were fine. I was in a cold, dim room, with a bottle of very good *Pouilly-Fuisse* in my hand, and I was not being shut in. This was not, I reminded myself, Dracula's castle. It was a building I lived in from time to time, a building I loved and admired. I was being an idiot.

So I bent down to pick up the box of cereal, which provi-dentially had not spilled its contents, and went to put it back. And right there, behind where the box had stood, were seven little brown plastic bottles, about two inches tall, with big white screw tops. I put the cereal box down on the floor and picked up the nearest of the little bottles and read the label. *Lunesta*, it said. Three milligrams, thirty tablets. I poured the little blue pills into my hand and counted them. Thirty.

The next bottle I opened seemed to have about the same number of pills in it, and so did the next. So: seven bottles, let's say 210 tablets at three milligrams each. Six hundred and thirty milligrams. I was aware, because I'd known the woman who took them, that it was possible to recover from three hundred milligrams of Lunesta, although it had been a tight squeak. Six hundred and thirty milligrams had a very final ring to it.

I was looking at one of two things: a medicine hoarder's stash or a suicide's hope chest.

In either event, it seemed deeply, terrifically wrong.

So I poured a dozen or fifteen pills out of two of the bottles and into another, then poured all but three of the pills out of a third and evened them up so there were ten or eleven pills in each bottle. I put the three partially emptied bottles back on the shelf, pocketed the four full ones, and then put the cereal box back in front of them, doing math in my head: roughly thirty-three tablets at three milligrams, a little less than one hundred milligrams. I thought, *nope*, and moved the cereal box again, but at that moment I heard the squealing wheels on Dolores La Marr's walker, and I remembered that the effect of medications varied with body weight. The woman who had lived through three hundred milligrams had weighed about 95 pounds, and my guess was that Dolores La Marr was pushing three hundred and twenty. She'd probably sleep for eighteen hours.

"Where are you?" she asked. It was a normal tone of voice, and it was coming from a speaker just outside the pantry. I called out, "Getting the wine," and closed the pantry door behind me.

"They were *fun*," she said. Her first glass from the new bottle was half-empty, and the additional wine seemed to be energizing her, or maybe it was the memory of those long-dead gangsters. "When a girl had gotten used to going out with men who wore more makeup than she did, it was exciting to be with someone who could barely be bothered to shave and whose suits were tailored to hide a shoulder holster." She held the glass out for more, and I purposely misunderstood and clinked it with my mostly-empty one. It was getting on toward 10 P.M., and I had to drive back to the Valley, back to where Ronnie would be waiting in the Valentine Shmalentine Motel.

"They were real, do you know what I mean?" Dolores La Marr said. She gave her glass a disappointed glance. "If they got shot, they really bled. Sometimes, they really died. They lived with the knowledge they could die tomorrow, so they made everything they could out of today. Or tonight, if it was dress-up time. The men in Hollywood, most of them, half-believe that after they die they'll be brought back for the sequel."

"How were they with women?"

"Awful, mostly. But not with me. They treated me fine. Even the crazy ones, because there were some crazy ones. Like Nitti, who was a complete bedbug. But they knew that the not-so-crazy ones would punch holes in them if they got wrong with me, so everybody was a gentleman. As much of a gentleman as they could be, I mean."

"So there you were, making movies in the daytime and going out at night with gangsters."

"Going back and forth to New York, too, once or twice. Owney Madden owned part of The Stork Club—oh, I already told you that, sorry—and we were treated like royalty. And Georgie was still a star, then. Even my own wretched little career was taking off. I'd made *Hell's Sisters* with the Queen Bitch of Hollywood, Olivia Dupont, and even though it was a quickie, it packed them in, at least, in the middle of the country and the South. Variety's headline was SISTER HISSER HITS IN STICKS. The *Life* cover came out. This was all in the first half of 1950. Mr. Winterman was talking to my agent, Dickie Will-eford, about giving me a good small part in a bigger movie." She held out the glass once more. "Toast me again, and I'll pour the rest of it into your lap."

"Olivia Dupont," I said, tilting the bottle. "I remember her. Come to think of it, I remember *Hell's Sisters*. I saw it on Turner a few years back. I'd never seen women go at each other like that in a film that—that—"

"That old," she said. "Like I said, it was 1950, which is sixty-two years ago. Jesus, where did the time go? Livvy and I were good at going after each other because we just purely, chemically loathed each other. She was a rotten little bitch who'd been sleeping her way sideways for years and years, and she felt she was *far* too good for the movie, and, by extension, me. She wasn't pretty, but she had one of those faces the camera assembled. It loved her eyes, and the eyes kind of dragged the rest of her face along with them."

"Your eyes aren't exactly forgettable."

"*I've* forgotten them."

"Well, I haven't. When I saw the movie, I remember thinking it was a film about women's eyes."

"That's very kind of you, considering it was actually a pot-boiler about two sisters in an old house, with one trying to drive the other one crazy so she could stick her in an asylum and inherit everything. What *I* remember was restraining myself from breaking Livvy's neck. We actually knocked each other around a bit in one of the fight scenes. I put a nice mouse under her left eye and they had to shoot what she called *her bad side*, as though she had a good one, for days and days. The only time I was happy on the whole miserable shoot. And the clothes were awful."

"But it was a pretty good movie."

"There's no relationship between how happy a set is and how good the movie is. As much as I hate to say it, Livvy was better than I was. She had the good part, by which I mean the bad sister. It was my fate to be the good one, the one who suffered silently off to the right while Livvy exuded malice, screen center. My luck. If I'd been playing the bad one, I probably could have survived the scandal and the committee hearings."

The bottles of pills were digging into my leg, and I was having trouble reconciling Dolores La Marr's vitality, as she looked back on her life, with the enormous, elderly woman on the couch, a woman who had probably gained all that weight as a protective layer for the beauty she had once been. A woman who'd stockpiled a lethal cache of sleeping pills. I said, "But you weren't the bad girl. You were playing the innocent."

"And there I was in real life," she said, "up to my neck in the mob." She leaned back on the couch, lifted her head, and closed her eyes. Her eyelids were almost translucent, and with her chin lifted, I could see that she'd had work done on her neck and, possibly, at her hairline: a neck lift, a face tug. Her mouth, I realized, was less full than the lipstick made it. For a moment, she almost looked her age.

"It was June 23, 1950. Friday. I was going to a weekend party in Las Vegas. Georgie had invited me. Sam Giancana was there, and a couple of other *capos*. Also a six-pack of the big-knuckle guys who were always around as human shields. It was in a hotel, Bugsy Siegel's Flamingo, in a huge suite Johnny Roselli had taken for the weekend. Poor Johnny. Got caught up in that crazy CIA plot to kill Castro, wound up floating in an oil drum off of Miami with his legs sawed off. Handsome Johnny, they called him.

"Anyway, usually the Vegas cops were clued in and the guys were left alone, but this night, some local cops and a couple of Feds kicked the door in, and with them were two freelance photographers, paparazzi, you'd call them today. We were all photographed to death in the suite, which the photographers messed up first to make it look like the leftovers of a massive orgy, and then we were booked, but everyone was bailed out within an hour or two. Everyone but me. The cops forgot to haul me into the night court to set bail. The photographers came back the next morning and shot me through the bars. No sleep, no shower, no hairbrush, my makeup all over my face from crying. A nightmare picture. It was *everywhere*.

"In the next few days, a dozen other stories came out, leaked from who-knows-where. Where I'd been, who I'd been with. Vegas, New York, Scandia Restaurant, Ciro's, and the Moulin Rouge, here on Sunset. Pictures taken with a long lens. Known criminals and me. Bathing suits next to swimming pools, one with my top off, although my back was turned, and a man—Johnny Stampanato, it was, the one Lana Turner's daughter killed—oiling my back. Johnny had just gotten out of the Marines, and he—oh, never mind. One day, I was the wide-eyed innocent from Scranton who was hitting it big in the sticks, and a week later I was the Whore of Babylon, I was a gun moll, I was a paid companion. I was a prostitute." She put the empty glass down and sat slumped, looking at it. "I was over."

I said, "It was a setup."

She looked at me as though I were a personal disappointment. "Of course, it was. And that's the actual reason you're here, isn't it? To find out who set me up."

6

Valentine Shmalentine

I pointed the car west on Olympic, then took LaBrea north and grabbed the ramp in the Cahuenga Pass that leads to the Hollywood Freeway. It was drizzling, as it often does in February, and drizzle turns LA roads into skating rinks, so I kept a lot of space between me and the car in front of me.

I had a list of names of people who had known about Dolores La Marr's choice of nocturnal companionship back at the end of the 1940s. It was quite a long list. Then I had a list of those of them who were still alive, or might be. This was a much shorter list.

I was going to spend the next week or so with senior citizens.

Interesting senior citizens, to be sure. A former director, Doug Trent. The dragonlike Olivia Dupont, apparently too mean to die. A writer, Oriole Finlayson. A one-time gossip columnist and the reputed squeeze of a couple of studio heads, Melly Crain. The longtime editor of the Las Vegas paper, a guy reputed to have been mobbed up to his teeth, Abe Frank. A woman who had worked in publicity under Bugsy Siegel, back before he got his left eye blown out in his girlfriend's living room, Delilah Polland.

Both Abe Frank and Delilah Polland were still living in Vegas, so I guessed I was going to Vegas.

And I still couldn't see who was going to benefit from all this effort. Dolores La Marr, if suddenly absolved of all sins, would remain a hugely overweight woman in her eighties. Her career was not simply on hold, the waiting film sets silent with hushed anticipation, and she knew it. The sense I'd gotten from talking to her was that she saw the whole thing as a lot of useless fuss, but since it was *Irwin Dressler's* useless fuss, she was willing to cooperate.

We'd barely touched on it, she and I, but there was also the chance that my activities could backfire somehow and put the spotlight back on her, in a way she wouldn't want. There's no story modern journalism loves more than the wreckage of beauty, the destruction of high hopes, the fall of a star, all the way from the top of the highest marquee to the most sodden trash heap. It had been more than sixty years since Dolores La Marr was a star, and she hadn't been much of a star even then, but the laziest editor in the world would see the value of that *Life* cover side-by-side with a 300-pound woman with hair darker than Elvis's and tattooed eyebrows. On a slow day, it would lead every ten o'clock news show in the country.

Mine was not to reason why, not where Irwin Dressler was concerned.

Almost eleven, and traffic to the Valley was still slow. As I approached Van Nuys Boulevard, I took a chance and dialed the cell phone that belongs to my daughter, Rina. I knew she kept it beside her—if not actually surgically attached to her ear—at all times, so the ringing probably wouldn't wake up my ex-wife, Kathy.

But it did wake up Rina.

"H'lo?" Although she's only thirteen, my daughter sings bass when she's awakened, and the voice was something that might have come from a very large, very deepwater fish.

"Were you asleep?"

"No," she said. Then she mumbled something to herself and said, "Of course, I was asleep. But for some reason, everybody always says no. Why is that?"

"You're not actually expecting me to give you an answer, are you?"

"You woke me up," she said. "You've got to do something."

"Okay. At a guess, it's so the person who called won't feel like a schmuck for interrupting your sleep."

"And do you?"

"Do I what?"

"Feel like a schmuck."

"No. Would you like me to?"

She stretched, and I could hear it in her breathing. "You're no fun."

"Estes Kefauver," I said.

She said, "Listen to me not say *gesundheit*. Who is Estes Kefauver, and why do I care?"

"You want to earn money, right? For the Mac Air? Well, here's how."

"Spell *Kefauver*."

"Figure it out yourself, and bill me. Twelve-fifty an hour. Senator Estes Kefauver presided over hearings into American organized crime back in the early fifties, and I want either transcripts or video of the testimony of one witness."

"Any old witness?"

"An actress called Dolores La Marr."

"L-a-m-a-r-r-?"

"No. The fancy way, in two parts *La* and *Marr*."

"Dolores La Marr," Rina said. "Why do I have a feeling that's not her real name?"

"Good point. Her real name is Wanda Altshuler."

"Are you looking for anything special? Or just a data dump?"

"I don't know. Or maybe I do. I want to know what the panel asked her. Somebody set her up, practically framed her, and she was hauled to Washington to testify."

There was a pause, which was good because I was changing lanes to avoid someone who wanted to drive up my tailpipe. "I don't get it," Rina said. "What are you supposed to be doing? Somebody framed her, you said. It would seem to me you'd be looking for the person who framed her, even if it *was*, like, sixty years ago."

"And you'd be right."

"Then why do you care what she was asked?"

Why *did* I care what she was asked? "Someone went to a lot of trouble to bring her down, probably paid off cops and even got the Feds into it. It was dangerous and complicated. In fact, maybe it was too dangerous and too complicated just to wreck the career of a B-movie actress. So maybe they wanted to destroy Dolores La Marr, and maybe they didn't actually care about that. Maybe they wanted to put her somewhere where she'd have to answer a specific question."

"You mean about someone else?"

"Presumably."

"What you're saying," Rina said, "is that Dolores La Marr might not have been the victim. She might have been the weapon."

"You are *so* my daughter," I said.

I'd been living in motels since I left the house in Tarzana in which Rina and Kathy still lived. My routine is simple: a new motel every month. It's one of the ways I try to be available only to those who are relatively unlikely to kill me. This month, as Dressler had somehow discovered, Ronnie and I were at Valentine Shmalentine, the pinkest building in greater Los Angeles, a city in no danger of running out of pink buildings. In its gray semi-industrial area of Canoga Park it stood out like a boil, but just in case both of the lovers in urgent need of a room were color-blind, a giant neon heart, the sizzling purple of a power-mad fuchsia, burned in front of it twenty-four hours a day.

The architect, or animator, or whoever designed the place, had put on the roof a revolving statue of Cupid, looking like a baby who was going to grow up into someone with a weight problem, and had tricked out the building's corners with little hearts, stucco versions of those chalky valentine candies nobody ever gave me in elementary school. In a final desperate stab at inspiration, he or she had surrounded it with a sort of ditch full of water—or moat—that, according to a sign, was The River of Love.

It had probably seemed like a good idea at the time, but now The River of Love was half-full of an alarmingly green, viscous-looking liquid with a lot of fast-food packaging floating in it. Heavy chains connected the bridge to the front of the building, suggesting that the whole thing could be drawn up in the event of an attack by the unromantic, or a mob of militant interior decorators. Wasn't anyone going to wade through the gunk in that moat.

One drove graciously over the bridge and made a dramatic entrance into a small parking lot, unadorned except that the lines marking out the parking spaces were hot pink, and then one proceeded right through a tunnel in the middle of the building and into the much larger parking lot behind the building, where no one driving past might spot and recognize a car. The guy who built the place must have gotten a deal on the skip-loader, because the moat ran all the way around the back of the parking lot. In the eleven days Ronnie and I had been there, we'd already had one paralytic drunk sink his brand-new car in the water. Places like Valentine Shmalentine, if there *are* any places like Valentine Shmalentine, attract a lot of people who have nothing to do all day but sip and *shtup*, and there must have been twenty of us gathered out there, blinking in the cold winter sunlight and avoiding each other's eyes, when they finally pulled the car out, definitively ridded of that new-car smell.

Ronnie's little something, a mystery car made in Albania or some other country that's been closed for a while, was in its usual spot. I pulled in beside it, got out, and, from force of habit, put a palm on the hood. I felt vaguely ashamed of myself, but also reassured that it was cool to the touch, so she'd been home, or at any rate, *here*, for a while. Okay, I'm a skeptic, but Ronnie isn't exactly addicted to the truth.

One of the things I liked best about the recently widowed but defiantly unmournful Ronnie Bigelow was that she didn't care where she lived. She had a bright, if somewhat twee, little apartment in the Boys' Town section of West Hollywood, but she'd been with me at Valentine Shmalentine since the day I moved in. We'd never even discussed it. When my endless month at Marge 'n Ed's North Pole was finally up, she helped me pack and had me follow her to her place, where I sat around uselessly as she banged some stuff into a small suitcase, pulled four books off the shelves, and trotted helpfully behind me as I toted it to the car. Since then, she'd only gone home for a couple of new books.

Appalling as it was, Valentine Shmalentine was sort of appropriate because Ronnie and I were still in the *oh-brave-new-world-that-has-such-creatures-in-it* stage, the enchanted interlude during which we both found charming the traits we'd probably hate in each other a couple of years down the road. Even Rina, the person I loved most in the world, liked Ronnie. My ex-wife, Kathy, hadn't been polled on the question yet and hadn't volunteered an opinion beyond a certain tightness around the mouth when the conversation drifted in Ronnie's direction. The duet with Ronnie was my first attempt at the boy/girl thing since my divorce, and it was going well enough to make me stop thinking about Dolores La Marr, Irwin Dressler, and a case that made no sense to me whatsoever.

So there was a spring in my step as I bounded up the stairs of Valentine Shmalentine, beginning at the ground floor—or, as the management called it, "Infatuation," containing the smallest, darkest, cheapest, mustiest, most overtly threatening rooms—and continuing up through the higher-rent districts, "First Love" and "Love in Bloom," to the fourth floor, "Obsession," which was all suites, if dividing a small room into two smaller rooms creates a suite. Ronnie and I ruled our kingdom of passion from Obsession IV (Roman numerals only on the fourth floor), which had an expansive view of a large reddish hole that, according to a rusting sign, had been dug, in a more optimistic year, to hold a bank. The drizzle through which I was hurrying had arrived on the heels of two days of rain, and the hole held about eight inches of muddy water, reflecting a featureless sheet of black sky.

As I pulled the hot-pink card key, the one marked HIS, from my shirt pocket, I heard voices inside, both female. It slowed me down. This was a first. Ronnie reserved most of her dazzle for the opposite sex, and if she had any close female friends she'd kept them away from me. We'd made friends with Marge, the woman who ran Marge 'n Ed's North Pole, but Marge tended not to stray more than a couple of blocks away from her vodka bottle.

So, then, who?

Just in case I was the topic of discussion, I knocked lightly, counted a discreet three, and then slipped the card in and turned the handle.

Ronnie smiled at me from the dangling contraption hanging

from the ceiling, a sort of basket chair with a strategically placed hole in the seat that could be raised and lowered via a complicated setup of ropes and pulleys, and which had almost killed me the one time we tried it out. She gave the chair a bounce and said, "Look, Junior, your friend Debbie is here." I glanced over at the woman sitting on the love seat, registered the face, checked it against my internal database, and felt my heart stop.

I said, "Huuuuh," as though I'd been kicked in the stomach.

"Junior," Debbie said. "No kiss for an old friend?"

I said, wondering where the closest weapon was, "A kiss?"

Ronnie said, "I can turn my back if you'd like. But not for long."

"Not necessary," Debbie said, getting up to her full five feet two, as unthreatening as a sea monkey. Her face fell naturally into a smile, eyes permanently crinkled, dimples in play, the *gamine* features surrounded by a soft fluff of reddish-blond hair. She was holding a sort of carpet bag that looked heavy. "There's nothing I want to do to Junior that I can't do in front of you."

That didn't necessarily make me feel better. "Then let her leave," I said.

"In a few minutes," Debbie said. "Maybe."

Ronnie said, "*Let* me leave? Have I lost free will somewhere along the way?"

"Stay where you are, Ronnie," I said.

Debbie put her hand into the bag. "Junior," she said. "What you want to do is sit on the bed and not say anything else, especially anything that would tell Ronnie, whom I like quite a bit, anything she doesn't need to know."

Ronnie said, "Such as what?"

"You really, really *don't* want to know," Debbie said. "It has nothing to do with Junior. He and I don't have any history, one way or the other. In fact, we barely know each other." She looked over at me. "Why aren't you sitting?"

"Sitting," I said. I lifted my hands, fingers spread wide, and tugged my sleeves up in the traditional magician's gesture to demonstrate that I wasn't holding anything that might surprise her. Then I sat on the bed.

I got a cute smile of appreciation. With her Reddi-Wip hair, button nose, and child's frame, Debbie Halstead was cuter than Hello Kitty. *Cute* was the professional stock in trade that had allowed her about a dozen times, if what I'd heard was accurate, to get close enough to someone to slip a tiny gun into the other person's ear, an effective point of entry although it probably muffled any parting words she'd been asked to deliver. Still, who was going to complain? In the world of crime, where originality is rare, a distinctive signature is a good way to raise your profile among potential customers. Among other things, the small-gun-in-the-ear approach, which said, DEBBIE HALSTEAD WAS HERE, was a good way to keep people, initially, at least, from wondering who ordered the hit. By the standards of the criminal world, Debbie was having a great career.

"I'm here on personal business," she said. "Not on the job, so to speak."

"Then take your hand out of your purse."

"What job?" Ronnie asked, and I was seeing something in her eyes that indicated a very bad next thirty or forty seconds.

I got up and said, "Debbie does a job you don't need to know about." When her eyes came to mine, I actually went on tiptoe to reinforce my words. "It would be better for all of us if you didn't know about it. It would be best of all if you poured water on your temper and sat the fuck down."

Ronnie opened her mouth, closed it, and sat.

"You let him talk to you like that?" Debbie asked.

Sitting again, I said, "She'll get me later."

Debbie tilted her head to one side, evaluating it. "And you know that, but you talked to her that way anyhow. It's enough to make a girl envious." She took her hand out of the purse, empty, and waved it at me. "Now, why don't we all take three or four deep breaths and start over? Ronnie, honey, can you do that? Really, none of this has anything to do with you."

"I have a question," I said before Ronnie could reply. "Why don't we let Ronnie leave? That way, you and I can talk without worrying about what she does or doesn't know."

"I'll make a counterproposal." Debbie smiled a smile cute enough to be on a Japanese T-shirt. "Since I have some sensitivity about people leaving my sight this early in a relationship, to do who-knows-what, why don't I tell you why I'm here, being a weensy bit careful, and if it seems to me that we're getting into territory that it wouldn't be safe for Ronnie to explore, I'll raise a hand and she can step out of the room for a minute or two."

I said, "Ronnie?"

"This is stupid," Ronnie said. "I mean, what could be that awful?"

There was a silence long enough to learn a new language in. Then Ronnie said, "Oh."

Debbie lifted both hands, palms out. "I'm harmless," she said. "You're safe as milk. It's a profession, not a hobby." She looked back to me. "Are you strapped?"

"No." I patted my shirt and pants to demonstrate the absence of a gun-bulge. I hit the little bottles of Lunesta but kept going. "And there's nothing in the apartment."

"Where *is* the gun?" Debbie asked Ronnie. She leaned over. "Whisper it to me."

Ronnie gave me a look that should have peeled the skin off my face, and whispered something into Debbie's ear.

Debbie leaned back and said, "Junior? Where did she tell me you've put your gun?"

"In storage compartments. She doesn't know where."

"Compartments, plural? You have more than one gun?"

"I lead a rich and varied life."

"That's why I'm here." She put the carpetbag on the floor beside her feet, and I relaxed a little bit. "I have a problem, and I'm told you can solve problems."

"Who told you? In fact, who told you where I was?"

"Do I have to say?"

"Not unless you want help."

She chewed at the left corner of her mouth for a moment, and said, "Louie the Lost."

I said, "That fucker."

"I thought you were friends," Debbie said.

"We are. That's why I'm pissed. Nothing personal, but most people wouldn't be grateful to someone who handed you their address."

"I guess not."

"It's like giving directions to the Grim Reaper."

She nodded. "I get a lot of that."

"And he didn't even call to warn me."

"Well," Debbie said, "I'm afraid that was my fault. I told him I'd—you know—"

"Kill him," Ronnie said. "Let's just say it out loud, so we can finish in time for Craig Ferguson."

"Exactly," Debbie said, looking grateful. "I told him I'd kill him."

"Okay," I said. "So now we're all friends. What can I do for you?"

"Someone is looking for me," Debbie said. "She says she's my daughter."

"That's sweet," Ronnie said. "How long since you've seen her?"

I said, to Debbie, "And what?"

Debbie grabbed a breath, puffed her cheeks out, and then blew. "And two things. One, I need to know whether she really is my daughter. And, two, if she is, I need to know whether she wants to kill me."

7
Killers Need Friends, Too

I said, "Twenty-five hundred up front, before you even tell me about it."

Ronnie said, "You don't look old enough to have a daughter."

Debbie said, "I like her better than I like you."

"I'm not looking for your vote," I said. "I have rules, and that's one of them."

"So Louie said." Debbie was alone on the love seat, and it dwarfed her, making her look like a ten-year-old. A ten-year old who had a great many notches on her water pistol. "I'm going to pick up the bag now," she said. "Don't get your intestines in a knot." She bent down and hoisted the carpetbag, just barely muffling a grunt.

"Jesus," I said. "What's in there, your bowling equipment?"

"It's mostly makeup," she said, up to her elbow in the bag. "Don't you carry a lot of makeup?"

"I think that one was for you," I said to Ronnie, who was watching Debbie as though she were something coiled in a circle on the other side of a plate of four-inch-thick glass.

"No," Ronnie said, keeping her eyes on what she could see of Debbie's hands. "I kind of do it in the morning and forget about it."

"You've got that kind of skin," Debbie said. "Wish I did. Hold this." She extended a hand that had a 22 automatic in it. "I keep bending my nails on it."

Ronnie took the gun and gave me a helpless look.

"That should relax everyone," Debbie said rooting around in the bag.

"You've got others," I said.

"Well, sure I do. And that one's empty, anyway. It was just a gesture. What kind of moisturizer?"

"Clinique," Ronnie said. "The yellow stuff."

"Pricey."

"You're only young for free once. After that, they charge you."

"Ah, here we are." Debbie pulled out a thick envelope. "You can thank your little friend Louie for one thing. He inflated your fee for saying yes."

"He'll hit me for the difference," I said. I got up and took the envelope, giving it an experimental heft. "How much?"

"Thirty-five hundred."

"The piker," I said. "He could've said five."

"With all due respect to you and your friendship, he was walking a balance beam. He figured you wouldn't want me to be too highly invested in the outcome. As a disappointed customer, I'm a nightmare."

"I don't have any disappointed customers."

"Not what I hear. Trey Annunziato isn't crazy about you."

"Trey's the only one."

"Or Jake Whelan."

I said, "Oops."

"Just messing with you. He thinks you're terrific."

"That's a relief." Jake Whelan, once Hollywood's hottest producer, had paid me some of the money he had left over after buying all the cocaine in the western hemisphere, and had received in return a picture he thought was a genuine Paul Klee. I'd been waiting for that shoe to drop for more than a year. "You've been busy."

"Attention to detail is essential to success." She said it almost automatically, as though it were a mantra. "Don't you find that?"

"Sometimes," I said.

I got the pursed mouth of disapproval. "If you don't, you won't be in business long."

"I also believe in unprepared improvisation. You can't always have a plan. Sometimes you have to make your leap and grow your wings on the way down."

"Did you make that up?"

"No," I said, "but I believe it. So, your daughter."

She waggled her hand, *mas o menos*. "My daughter *maybe*."

"Okay. Take it in order. How do you know anyone is looking for you, why do you think it might be your daughter, and why—if it is your daughter—would she want to kill you?"

"That's what I like about men," Debbie said. "No emotions at all."

"I didn't see you break out a hankie."

"How do I know someone is looking for me, right? That was the first question. Someone, a young woman of about eighteen, has been knocking on doors in my hometown—"

"Which is?"

"Las Vegas."

Ronnie said, "I didn't think anyone came from Las Vegas."

"Yeah?" Debbie said. "Where are you from?"

"Trenton," Ronnie said.

I said, "Or Albany." Debbie's smile slipped, and I said, "She and I are still discussing it."

"I don't always tell the truth," Ronnie said.

"And you think she might be your daughter why?" I said.

"She says she is. And she's about the right age."

"And part three of the question. Why would she want to kill you?"

Debbie shook her head, and her hair bounced adorably. "I didn't say she did. I said I wanted to *find out* if she did."

"Why would you think—"

"Not important," Debbie said. "Drop it."

"Nothing about the reason might help me?"

"I don't know. For now, let's just save it for later. If I actually need to tell you."

I decided to let it pass. "How many people do you want me to talk to in Las Vegas?"

She sat back. This was more comfortable territory. "Four. All women."

"I'll need names and addresses, numbers, all that stuff."

"I have to talk to them first. They're not in the business, but they're not exactly not in the business, either. Or at least two of them aren't."

"I don't care if they make socks out of kittens," I said. "I just need to talk to them."

"They don't need to know much about me," Debbie said. "Two know better than to ask certain kinds of questions, but the ones who do ask, well, stiff them as much as you can. So you'll go? To Vegas?"

"Sure," I said. "I have to go anyway."

Ronnie said, lighting up like a spotlight, "We're going to Vegas?"

"No, I am."

"You don't have to take that kind of talk," Debbie said to Ronnie. She reached down into the bag and pulled out the little gun again. "I'm just going to load this so I'll be comfortable on my way out. Don't let it bother you."

"Before you put in the bullets," Ronnie said, "don't tell me what kind of talk to take or not take, okay? This relationship may not look perfect to you, but I'm a long way from finished."

I said, "Finished?"

"With changing you."

"Good luck with that," Debbie said, sliding the magazine in with a decisive *click*. "I've tried, but it never took." She glanced up and caught Ronnie's stare. "Not with Junior honey, relax."

"Put the gun away, now," I said. I waited until she had. "Let's get the details straight. I'm going to find out whether someone is looking for you and who she might be, and I'll give you the information you need to decide whether it's your daughter or not, if I can. As to what her motives are, I don't read minds. I'll ask you for more money when and as I need it, but the minimum you're going to pay me, if I find her, is twelve thousand five. The maximum could be double that."

Debbie said, "Jiminy."

"If I don't get enough information for a positive identification, you don't pay me beyond ten thousand."

Debbie thought about it for a moment, her eyes wandering the room, lingering on some of its odder features, of which there were many. "Okay," she said.

"Good. How do I get in touch with you?"

"I'll leave you a card. It's got phone, email, Facebook."

Ronnie said, "Facebook?"

"Sure," Debbie said. "Killers need friends, too."

Five minutes later, Ronnie said, "God. I thought she'd never leave. At least, not with both of us still alive."

"Changing me, huh?"

"Well, I am," she said. "One stubborn little atom at a time."

"What's wrong with me?"

"Puh*leeeeze*. Planning to go to Vegas without me? Hit-women dropping in at all hours? Living in this pop-up porno book of a motel? Where should I start?"

I wiggled my eyebrows at the enormous pink bed. "How about there?"

She pushed her foot against the carpet, setting the contraption in which she was sitting on a long slow swing back and forth. "How about the Death Chair?"

"How about a narrowly missed pelvic fracture?"

She pushed again, and the ceiling creaked. "I'm not worth a narrowly-missed pelvic fracture?"

"Of course you are. Tell you what. This time *you* lie on the floor."

"With you on the seat? Never work. Physiology, remember? Not even worth a try."

"Oh, ye of little faith," I said, getting up. "Put on your red hat."

8

Outliving People Is a Pale Victory

Demographically speaking, I was all over the place. A crowd of people in their eighties on one hand, and Debbie's 18-year-old, or thereabouts, on the other.

The age gap suggested an approach to organizing my time, which was that I speak first to those who were more likely to die of old age. That decision also reinforced my instinctive sense that, scary as Debbie Halstead was, Irwin Dressler was scarier by several magnitudes, golf slacks or no golf slacks.

So by 10:30 A.M. the next day, I was in a small living room with a pumpkin-orange leather couch and a coffee table of blue-green Coca-Cola glass, regarding the magically smooth face of Doug Trent.

Trent—the director of *Hell's Sisters* and about thirty other movies, according to Wikipedia—had been a very good-looking young man, and he was doing everything money, medical science, and a high pain threshold could accomplish to make him a very good-looking old man. His skin had the fraudulent flawlessness of a wall that's just had graffiti sandblasted off it. And if that wasn't enough to put me off him, his naturally silver hair was as blue as a delphinium and curled into long commas that fell over his Teflon forehead. To make it a trifecta, he was also wearing an ascot, tucked into the open neck of a loose white shirt.

"Yeah, yeah, Dolly," he said. He touched the tips of his fingers to the corner of his right eye, as though checking to make sure the masonry was holding. "Terrible, terrible thing, what happened to her. Beautiful girl, just beautiful. Couldn't act for shit, of course, but it didn't matter, as long as she hit her key light. Light went right into those pale eyes, and the audience just filled them in with whatever emotion the background music had to offer. Do you know how Mauritz Stiller got those long, heart-wrenching close-ups of Garbo?"

"No."

"He got the light exactly right, put the camera a foot from her nose, and told her to count to ten."

I said, "In Swedish?"

Trent, who had moved on to patting the skin beneath his eye, stopped and gave me a first-rate cold look. "How would I know? The *point* is that a lot of what an actress gets credit for is actually due to the director."

"I'm sure," I said. "I mean, makes perfect sense."

"Trust me," Trent said. "I know actresses. I married six of them."

"What was it like, being married to six actresses?"

"Like being married to one of them. They're all pretty much alike."

"Why'd you keep doing it, then?"

"'Hope is the thing with feathers,'" Trent said, "that tickles your scrotum at the moments when you most need a clear head."

"How'd you get along with La Marr on *Hell's Sisters*?"

"She was fine," he said. He looked around the room, and sighed with apparent regret. Doug Trent was living out his sunset years in an over-furnished one-bedroom apartment in Encino, only eight or ten miles from Valentine Shmalentine, and everything about him telegraphed that he regarded it as a comedown. "Everybody liked her. Of course, it helped that the other one was . . . was. . . ." He put the tip of his index finger between his eyebrows and closed his eyes.

"Olivia Dupont," I said.

Trent said, "Don't *do* that. I have to fight this thing, or it'll get me. When I go adrift, you just sit there. If you must do something, cross your fingers for me."

"Sorry." I liked him for the first time.

"Olivia. What a flaming, seven-day-a-week bitch she was." He lifted his head, angled his face away from me by about twenty degrees, and regarded me out of the corners of his eyes. It was pretty stagy. "Am I right? *Was?*"

"Is, actually."

"I should have known it. She'll live forever, sucking the blood of the unborn. I directed pictures for more than thirty years and never worked with a bigger shit than Olivia Dupont. Oh, I mean, there were some big stars who were almost in her league, but not many even of those. But Livvy was never a big star."

"Dolores La Marr said she slept her way sideways."

"For years. Before I knew about that, it amazed me that she kept working. I was in a pre-production meeting at Warner once, and when someone read her name on the cast list, everyone groaned." He circled a thumb and index finger and pushed his other index finger in and out of the opening. "The front office," he said. "She was boinking every executive producer at every studio in town." He looked down at his hands and put them in his lap. "Directors, too, if they were on the A-list."

"How many times did you work with her?"

"Twice. The first time, I asked for her, and the second she was forced on me, and I caved in."

"*Hell's Sisters*? Was that the first or the second time?"

"The second. The first time, I was an almost-big name and she did the sweet-young-thing act. As you've probably deduced, I have a weakness for actresses. The second time, I was, let's say, somewhat faded, and I couldn't say no."

"Why faded?"

He pursed his mouth, as though to spit out a seed. "Bad judgment. I associated with the wrong people, politically. I was big enough for the anti-communists to go after, but not big enough to be one of the Hollywood Ten." He gave me a very small smile, something the corners of his mouth might have been doing on their own, without permission. "Even in times of disaster I wasn't big enough for top billing. If there had been a Hollywood Fifty-three, I would have made the cut."

"But you got *Hell's Sisters*."

"It was the last one, under my own name, and it wasn't much of a picture. Nobody was more surprised than I was when it did business. But by then, even a hit couldn't help me. From that point on, I worked in television as a *consultant*, under the name Albert Paris, showing neophyte TV directors where to put the camera and how to figure out which takes to print."

"What do you think about what happened to Dolores La Marr?"

The ascot had popped partway out of his shirt. He maneuvered it back into place and sighed, and I realized he was tiring. "Well, on one level, of course, she was asking for it. It wasn't like she went on the occasional *date* with a hoodlum. She was *surrounded* by them. It was odd, because she was such a sweet girl. I knew a couple of other—well, molls, I suppose. I directed Virginia Hill, for example, the one who told the Kefauver

Committee that her male friends gave her money because she was 'the best cocksucker in town.' They were all like that—hard girls, the kind of girl who'd get punched occasionally and come back for more, if there was some money or a nice little diamond in it for her. But Dolly was genuinely sweet. Those clowns must have gone crazy for her. I blame that idiot, Raft, for getting her into it. This was a guy who couldn't remember from one day to the next how many fingers he had, but she liked him. And he took her down to his level."

"Who hated her enough to dime her out?"

"Well, of course, Livvy," he said. "But Livvy hated everyone. I'm not sure she'd have exerted the energy to bring Dolly, or anyone else, down. I think she would have blown up the entire town if she could have, but damage just *one* of them? Hardly worth it."

"Anyone else then? Or just Livvy?"

He raised his fingers to the corner of the eye again and massaged the skin in a tiny circle. "No one," he said. "Everybody else liked her. Just Livvy."

"Let's turn it around, then. Who was closest to her? I mean, you say she was open about the people she spent her time with, but some people must have known more than others. More specifics, maybe—dates, specific restaurants or hotels, things that she wouldn't share with just anyone."

Trent frowned, bringing the tendons in his neck into play. Not much a plastic surgeon can do about those. "Her friends," he said.

"Sure. Who better to dime you out than a friend?"

"Hollywood is different than most places," Trent said. "In this business, people make friends—or enemies—during the filming of a picture, and then they all move on. If you were on the set of *Hell's Sisters*, you'd have seen Dolly hanging off the neck of Alec Roxfield, who was the not-very-good male lead. You'd have thought they were inseparable. But after the picture was finished, they never spoke again, except to say hi and good-bye. Livvy was different; Livvy preserved her hates in formalde-hyde to keep them fresh, but for most of us, a picture was like a lifeboat. We were shoved together night and day for as long as it took, relationships blossomed, people loved each other or loathed each other, and then the director called 'that's a wrap,' and everybody went home and picked up where they'd left off."

"But still," I said.

"Okay. She had a young PR person, Pinky Pinkerton, who had been with her for a year or two, and they seemed to get along great. He's alive, Pinky is, still in business, if you can believe that. Has a little office somewhere, probably low-rent Holly-wood. The girl who dressed her, I can't remember her name—" He closed his eyes again, and this time I waited. "Nope," he said, looking around the room as though he hoped it had gotten a little better while his eyes were closed. "Can't remember. But that's not—you know—the age thing, it's just that it wasn't my job to remember the names of dressers. Dolly wanted her, asked for her. It was the only thing she asked for, as far as I remember. You might find her name on IMDB, or get a copy of the movie. It'll be one of two or three names under 'Costumes,' if it's there at all. Call me and read them to me, and I'll tell you which one it was."

"But we don't know whether she's alive."

"Nope. Oh, Alec Roxfield, the male lead Dolly was so close to? He died six, seven years back." He sat back on the couch and crossed his arms. "I have to tell you, when you get to be my age, outliving people is a pale victory."

"But preferable," I said.

"Not as much as you'd think."

"Listen, before I go, tell me what you know about these people." I read him the names Dolores La Marr had given me: the screenwriter, Oriole Finlayson; the gossip columnist, Melly Crain; the Vegas editor and P.R. woman, Abe Frank and Delilah Polland.

"Oriole wrote *Hell's Sisters* and a half-dozen other pretty good movies. I liked her. She knew how to keep a story tight without all the machinery showing. She alive?"

"As of last night."

"Well, good. Melly was a psychotic with a byline, in bed with everyone who could give her a tip, and pathological about her importance, which was negligible. Tell you the truth? If I had one bullet in my little gun and a promise of no prosecution, and both Olivia Dupont and Melly Crain were within range, it'd take me a long time to make up my mind. The other two, the ones in Las Vegas, I don't know."

"Did Melly have it in for Dolly?"

"No more than she did for anyone else."

"Did she run the story? About Las Vegas and the arrest and all that?"

He shrugged. "Everybody ran it. For a few months there, and then again after she talked to the Senate subcommittee, you'd have thought Dolly was a real star, not just one more girl who'd accidentally made a good movie."

"Was that what she was? Just one more girl?"

"Honey," Doug Trent said, rubbing his eyes. "There are thousands of them." He looked around the room again and cleared his throat. "They're the fuel that Hollywood burns."

9

In Real Life, He Smiles When Somebody Gets Hit by a Car

I go months without setting foot in Hollywood, and I can't say I miss it much. Whatever enchantment it may have had vanished into the black hole of time long ago, and all the hundreds of millions of dollars pumped into glitzy redevelopment just make the rest of the place look even more decayed. I think of Hollywood's lost glamour as a kind of urban phantom limb syndrome; it's been gone for decades, but every now and then the city of Los Angeles feels an itch and reaches out to scratch it, and up goes another ugly building.

But Pinky Pinkerton had set up shop in a *genuine* artifact of Hollywood glamour, the still-beautiful—if rundown—art deco tower at the corner of Hollywood and Vine now prosaically called The First National Bank Building. Built in 1927, it was the tallest structure in Los Angeles until City Hall went up, way downtown, seven or eight years later. The building seems especially fine now that it's across the street from the multi-purpose melanoma of the Hollywood and Highland Center, which contains the Kodak Theater, where the Oscars are given, and at least one outlet for every Eurotrash label on the planet.

As a general rule of business, if you don't call ahead, you run the risk that the person you want to see might not be in. On the other hand, if you don't call ahead, there's no chance of being told that he or she won't see you. So when I climbed into the vintage elevator for the ride to the floor that housed Pinky's P.R. agency, creatively named Pinkerton Ink, I hadn't called ahead. And sure enough, when I got to the end of the dim, dingy 12th-floor hallway, there was a sign taped to Pinky's door. It said, BACK LATER.

The lettering was done in a dark brown my mother would probably have called sable, and it was shiny. On a whim, I ran the tip of my finger over the word LATER, and it smeared. Some of it came off on my finger. I looked at it and thought, *eyebrow pencil.*

So I'd had a little hole punched in my day. I could either get all upset about it or go find something to eat. And right down the block, facing out onto the sad, if occasionally diverting, decline of Hollywood Boulevard, was one of my favorite restaurants, Musso and Frank. The place has been right there, watching the town bloom and wither, since 1919, making it one of the oldest restaurants in Los Angeles, and the waiters have been using every moment of that time to perfect their indifference. Any time I want to have a good meal and feel like the Invisible Man at the same time, I go to Musso and Frank.

It seemed a little odd that Pinky's office would be closed in the middle of a working day, without even a secretary to answer phones and tell the unlucky caller when they'd be back. As I waited for my salad, I called. I got a recording, a chipper enthusiast with a somewhat quavery voice, who informed me that they were out of the office at the moment, probably assisting a client, but to leave a message at the beep and they'd surely get back to me soon.

I hung up and used the time between the salad and the steak to indulge in mild regrets. I'd never been particularly interested in movies, and had virtually no interest in older films—say, films of Dolores La Marr's vintage. My ex-wife, Kathy, had loved them, had talked about the different standards of glamour between that age and our own, about the way the movies of the Depression raised the country's spirits and how films had brought the country together during World War II. She'd tried to share it with me, but aside from infecting me with her enthusiasm for Hollywood black-and-white photography, she'd failed. In the end, we had almost nothing in common except our love for Rina. I think the divorce, when it came, was a relief to her. For one thing, she could stop worrying about the cops knocking down the door some night and hauling me away as Rina looked on.

So here I was, up to my eyebrows in old movies, eating lunch alone, just one more father who saw his kid once a week, if he was lucky. Ultimately, Kathy and I split because I wouldn't change into who she wanted me to be. At moments like that one, I wondered what in the world I'd been defending from her attempts to improve it.

At about two o'clock I called again, and this time I got a live one, a somewhat snappish woman who popped the plentiful Ps in "Pinky Pinkerton" as though she had a grudge against them. I waved at the waiters until one of them deigned to notice me, paid the bill, and trudged the Walk of Fame, stepping on as many stars as possible back to Highland and Pinky's building, trying not to speculate about the person who went with that p-popping, somewhat querulous voice.

Which was probably just as well, because what awaited me was a woman who would have been called a tootsie back in the 1940s, and probably had been. She sat behind a scratched wooden desk in a small reception area the precise brown of chewing-tobacco spit. In addition to the desk and its singular occupant, it housed two leather armchairs liberally repaired with duct tape. The walls were enlivened, sort of, by head-shots of actors whose faces I hadn't seen in years, but the face that commanded attention belonged to the woman at the desk. She was defiantly styling her way through her eighth or ninth decade in a bright print dress with Joan Crawford shoulder pads and kelly-green silk Chinese frogs for buttons, and her silver hair hung down around her shoulders in those long, tight '40s curls that look like Slinkies. The general effect was an extremely lively mummy with excellent retro taste in clothes. The look she gave me said, essentially, that she'd seen me and a thousand more of me, and there'd been no indication over the years that we were getting any more interesting. I couldn't help noting that her mouth was painted scarlet and that she'd left her blood-red signature on the pile of crimped cigarette butts in the crystal ashtray located just behind the sign that told the world that her name was, I swear to God, EDNA.

I said, "I can't believe they let you smoke in here."

She said, "I can't help what you can't believe, sweetie. Whad-dya want?"

"Pinky."

"Yeah?" Edna picked up the live one from the mountain of butts and decreased its life expectancy by half. "And who's lookin' for him?"

"Junior Bender. Seriously, how can you smoke in here? Last I looked, this was a non-smoking city."

She batted her big flat-screen computer monitor cockeyed so I couldn't see it, and showed me some lipstick-red teeth. "Who's gonna tell me no?"

"Good point."

"We're the oldest leaseholders in the joint," she said. "We got privileges. And I never heard of Junior Bender."

"Well, then this is your lucky day."

She said, hitting the keys so fast I couldn't see her fingers move, "Listen to the man."

I couldn't help myself. She'd exerted all that energy to keep me from seeing what she was doing, so I asked. "What are you doing?"

"This?" She clicked a long red nail against the edge of the big monitor. "Ahh, why not? I'm putting a pop-up flag, says *Pinkerton Ink*, on the pictures of this dump on Google Earth."

"My, my."

"I may be old," she said, "but I live in the same world as you."

"So. Is Pinky in?"

She looked up at me, giving me a reflection of the fluorescent overheads in her glasses. "What's it about?"

"Doug Trent suggested I talk to him."

"*That* old fart."

A spasm of coughing came through an open door at the end of the room.

"He speaks well of you," I said.

"A kidder," Edna said to the ceiling. Her eyes were lined in kohl-black, definitely not the sable in which the sign had been printed. "What the world needs, another kidder."

"He thinks, Doug does, that Pinky might be able to help me with something."

"Why would he?"

"The milk of human kindness. An opportunity to extend a hand to a fellow journeyer across the barren plain of life."

More coughing, followed by a long, painful-sounding throat-clearing and a very clearly pronounced *ptui*.

"He's not in," Edna said.

"Yeah?" I said. "He forgot his lungs?"

She looked me straight in the eyes and said, "He coughs so much it echoes around in there when he's gone."

I held her gaze until I started to laugh. She didn't laugh with me, but when she picked up her butt and stuck it into her mouth, she sort of grinned around it.

"Jesus, Edna," said a breathless voice from the other room, "Whyn'cha just let the kid come back? Whaddya think I'm doing back here?"

"I know better than to ask," Edna said.

"Come in, kid. And don't feed the dragon."

I waved at Edna, who took the butt out of her mouth and picked a shred of tobacco off the tip of her tongue. I looked again at the ashtray, and there wasn't a filter in sight. "Live dangerously," I said.

"Yeah," she said. "I'm worried sick."

I heard her nails on the keyboard as I went into Pinky Pinkerton's office.

"You gotta 'scuse Edna," he said, going through some gyrations that looked like part of his body wanted to get up to greet me but the rest of him wouldn't go along with it. I waved him down, and he relaxed, sinking gratefully into the big leather chair that made him look even smaller.

At first glance, Pinky Pinkerton was the size of a ventriloquist's dummy. He wore his clothes as though they'd been buttoned on him thirty years ago, when he was normal-size; he seemed to be sinking into them to the point where it was easy to envision his clothes sitting here empty in another five or ten years, long after Pinky slid out, probably down a pants leg. His chin hardly cleared the shiny surface of his desk, bare except for a name plaque that read PRESIDENT. He was being worn by a dark jacket and a blue shirt with a bright yellow tie, and even though the shirt was buttoned all the way up, it was loose enough to get a clenched fist inside it. His face had shrunk away from a truly remarkable nose that dominated not only his face but his entire upper body, or at least the part of it that was visible above his desk.

Since my command performance at Dressler's, I'd spent a lot of hours talking to people in their eighties, although most of them seemed to have dodged some of the erosion long stretches of time usually bring. But every year that had somehow missed Dressler and Dolly La Marr, every year that had been scraped from the face of Doug Trent, had landed directly on top of Pinky Pinkerton. He was as wrinkled as a tree root and as spotted as a foxed book.

"Sit, kiddo, sit," he said in a voice like the scrape of a match, and then he doubled over and coughed, and I found myself staring at the part in a toupee ancient enough to have jewel-like little beads of rubber cement at the part. He coughed so hard one of his feet came up and kicked the underside of his desk, and that seemed to calm the spasm. He wiped his eyes with the palms of his hands and said, "That'll hold her for a minute or two."

"You take your medicine?" Edna called.

"Nah. Couldn't find it in all this fucking smoke." He winked at me, then coughed again.

"Right top drawer," Edna said. "You need water?"

"I've never in my life needed water." His eyes, bright with tears, wreathed in wrinkles and separated forever by the mountain range of his nose, came to me. "So, kiddo. Doug Trent, huh?"

"Doug Trent."

"Who's he married to these days?" The noise was half laugh, half cough, sort of a *caugh*. "Christ, I think the only one he missed was Garbo."

"He's single."

"He musta run out. Or he's just counting the days, huh? Like the rest of us. So, what about Doug?"

I said, "Actually, it's about Dolores La Marr."

All the merriment vanished from his eyes. He said, "Dolores . . . ."

"La Marr."

"Edna," Pinky called. "*Where's* the medicine?"

"Right top drawer."

"Hang on, hang on," he said to me. He rolled the big chair back and opened a drawer, then pulled out a brown bottle with a white pharmacist's label on it. He took his time unscrewing the top, put a thumb over the open neck so he could shake the bottle, read the label as though he'd never seen it before, took a slug, winced, waited, took another slug, and then extended the bottle over the desk, eyebrows raised in invitation. The whole show had taken almost a minute.

I shook my head, and he put the top back on the bottle. I said, "Dolores La Marr."

His tongue licked quickly at a corner of his mouth. "What is this? You writing a book or something?"

"Doug said you were a friend of hers."

"Some kinda documentary? *Girls Gone Wrong* or something?"

"Was Dolores La Marr a girl gone wrong?"

"Who sent you to Doug?"

I sat back and looked at him. I have a face I've developed for conversations with the police, and it's about as drained of expression as a face can be. It would be sleepy if it weren't for an under-layer of hostility. I've learned it makes people nervous, so I used Garbo's trick to prolong it and counted silently from one to ten. When Pinky had scooted back and forth in his chair a few times and cleared his throat, I said, "You really don't need to know that."

"Kiddo—"

"No, listen. There were some very powerful people in Los Angeles back when you and Dolores La Marr were pals, and some of them are *still* very powerful."

The wrinkles around Pinky's eyes deepened and his eyes got even smaller. He said carefully, as though one of the words in the sentence might explode if he pronounced it wrong, "Someone who was powerful back then."

"And who is not patient with obstructions."

Pinky's chair squeaked as he sat back. He said, "Fuck me. You're kidding."

"I'm not kidding. I haven't told you anything."

He was shaking his head before I finished. "We weren't friends, Dolly and me."

"Not what Doug says."

He lifted his hands, palms up, the picture of reason. "P.R., you gotta understand, we're like *everybody's* friend, you know? It goes with the job. The client's gotta trust you, so you make like friends, but it's over the minute they fire you. Not even a hello in the street."

"They've got to trust you why?"

"Okay," he said, nodding. "This is my P.R. speech. I gave it to everybody I ever hired. P.R. is the crossroads between who somebody really is and who they want people to think they are. You get that?"

"When I fall behind, I'll wave at you."

Pinky folded his hands on the desk, a miniature professorial. "So on the one hand, you're like a painter doing a portrait, you know? Making the, um, nose smaller, filling in some hair, maybe putting a friendly smile on someone who, in real life, he smiles when somebody gets hit by a car. Putting a picture out there that's the way your client wants to look. That's half the job. On the other hand, you're not just a painter, you're a makeup artist. You gotta know where the warts are, which teeth are rotten. Not just so's you can cover it up, but so's you're prepared when the warts suddenly show."

"In a column like Melly Crain's."

"Sure, in the stone age. These days it's the fucking Internet. *Unlisted, F-Bomb, Hollywood Scoop, Celebrity Dogpile*, all the other ones. Make Melly Crain and *Confidential* magazine look like Saint Clare. But the point, see, the *point* is, the P.R. person has to *know* about this little wart and that fondness for Girl Scout uniforms and that, I don't know, Olympic-size dope habit. So for the client to be comfortable with that, they have to believe that the P.R. person is a friend."

"So your relationship with Dolores La Marr—"

"Was professional. Nice girl, but really, I hardly knew her."

"But you were one of a small number of people who knew where the warts were."

"Now, wait, wait, don't jump to—"

"You can't have it both ways. Maybe you weren't friends, but you knew her secrets."

"Well, look at it that way—"

"Maybe easier for someone who knows the secrets but *isn't* a friend to sell the other person out."

He sat up straight, or at least that was what he seemed to be trying to do. "I never sold out anyone in my life."

"No matter how much was offered?"

"Wouldn't have made any—"

"Or who was offering it?"

He started to cough again, but abandoned it halfway through the first one, so the medicine might have been helping. "That's more like it, if I ever did. Who, not how much. But I didn't. Terrible for business. It gets out one day—and sooner or later

everything gets out in this town, even if it's only to certain people—and you're marked dirty for life. Never get another client,
not if you walked down Hollywood Boulevard with a sandwich
board, said, PUBLIC RELATIONS, CHEAP."

"But you knew about her—her dates."

"Well, sure, sure. Everybody did, but listen, listen to me, you
gotta understand. I was second-rate, okay? I was the first guy
people hired, on their way up, and then they either dropped out
of sight or got billed above the title, and either way, I lost them.
But Dolly, Dolly was different." His face lit up when he said her
name, and he looked thirty years younger. "I was really *doing* it
for her. I got her the *Life* cover, I made a huge noise about her
reviews in *Hell's Sisters*. I *arranged* some of those reviews. I had
every photographer on the West Coast lined up to shoot her. I
was hounding Max Zeffire to offer her a picture, and he would
have. You gotta believe this, Dolly was going to be a star, and
she knew that I was the one who was making it happen. She
woulda stayed with me. She woulda been my first real star client. My whole life would have changed." He blinked, and his
eyes softened. "I'd have been big." He coughed once, not even
bothering to cover his mouth. "And she was a nice girl."

I didn't say anything. Pinky glanced toward the outer office
and then came back to me, and I realized I hadn't heard a peep
out of Edna for a while.

He lifted a hand and let it fall on the desk. "So."

"So," I said. I got up. "Did you maintain a clip file on Dolores La Marr?"

"Sure. I maintained a clip file on everyone."

"I want to see it."

"That's sixty years ago."

"I know, but I doubt you threw it away. That was your best
shot, as you've just finished telling me."

"It's not here," he said, sulking. "In storage."

"Can you or Edna get it?"

"You mean, today?"

"Why not? It's not even two o'clock."

Edna cleared her throat sharply in the other room.

"Yeah," Pinky said. He licked his lips and blinked. Then he patted his palm on his forehead, which was damp with sweat. "Tell you what. Give me your phone number and I'll call you when we got it."

"Today."

"Sure, yeah, today. Jesus."

"Great," I said. I got up. On the way out, I said, "Thanks, Edna."

While the door was still closing behind me, I heard the buzzer on Edna's desk. I let the door close and put my ear to it.

"Okay, okay," Edna said. "I'll get him for you. Hang onto your horses for a minute."

I double-timed it down the hall and then slowed, almost to the elevators, as I heard the door open. It stayed open for a moment and then closed, and I knew that Pinky was making his call. Maybe later in the day, I'd find out to whom.

Part
Two

DOLLY (1950)

There were no orange trees here, but Dolly was in love with the way the leaves on the California sycamores that rustled just outside her windows, held the light. Three months ago, when she moved into the upper floor of the big Hancock Park duplex, what had caught her attention was the space—seven big, graceful rooms, all hers. But after a few days, she began to see the leaves through the tall, inward-opening windows in the living room, and she got into the habit, on the days she didn't have to go to the studio, of taking her morning coffee to the couch in front of the windows, where she curled up and lost herself in an orchestra of greens. The green she loved best was the brilliant emerald of the newer leaves when they were lighted from behind by the still-rising sun. When they brought back that high, singing note.

At the age of five, Dolly had discovered that certain sounds streamed colors through the air. The new-leaf green of the sycamores was the color that had curled around the room when her mother listened to classical orchestral concerts on the radio back in Scranton. The strings, in their upper register, produced a vital, living green that she'd never seen in nature until she looked out the window at the sycamores.

Not that she wanted to think about her mother. Mom had finally gone, moved in with the second assistant director who'd picked her up on the Boston Blackie picture, when Dolly was still a minor and the law said that her mother was supposed to be on the set. So Mom was living in Studio City now, and Dolly had her new place—and herself—*to* herself, for the first time in her life. Just her, the gleaming oak floors, the deep, glazed indigo of the tiles surrounding the big fireplace in the living room, and the green music of the trees.

She learned when she was seven or eight not to talk about the colors. They frightened her mother, not so much—Dolly thought—because her mother was afraid her daughter was crazy, but because it might interfere with her becoming a moviestar. Dolly was thirteen before she learned that *moviestar* was actually two words. Her mother had always run it together into three shining syllables with their own color, a kind of light piney brown. *Moviestar* was what Dolly—Wanda back then, of course, Wanda Altshuler—was going to be if she was very good and always did what Mother told her and never asked questions and let Mother choose her clothes and stayed away from Scranton boys and brushed her hair two hundred times a day and didn't eat enough to get full. If she did all those things, and some others she learned about later, after they came to California, then the future was *moviestar.*

When she first tried to figure out how *moviestars* were different from ordinary people, Wanda pictured them like the men and women she saw in the church windows and the paintings of Bible times, people with a little gold plate shining around their heads. The gold plate announced immediately that these people were different, the same kind of different, she thought, as *moviestars*, shining somehow, less coarse and earthly than those around them.

When she was ten, Wanda learned the gold plates were called halos. When she was sixteen and called Dolly, she learned that *moviestars* not only didn't have halos but also that they were, by and large, unlikely candidates to earn them.

The only problem with the duplex, she thought, as she allowed the front door to close behind her and entered the cool of the living room, was that there was no gate at the bottom of the stairs. Anyone who knocked on Dolly's front door was already upstairs, just an inch of wood and a couple of locks away from her. The door to the lower unit was at the foot of the stairs, and the older couple who lived there had declined her offer to put in a gate with a buzzer. They rarely had visitors, they said, and they didn't want to be running back and forth when people pushed the wrong button. *People*, the old man had said, in words Dolly saw in an unpleasant brown, coming to visit a pretty little thing like you.

She went through the living room with a glance at the trees outside—the sun too high to bring out her favorite colors—and put her bags on the dining room table. Just a few things for the trip: some expensive shampoo, a new hairbrush, makeup, a sweet pair of heels that had been cheap enough to buy on impulse.

She was cutting it close. Less than forty minutes before the car arrived.

She had to shower and dress and pack. Obviously no time to use her new shampoo and dry her hair, which put her slightly out of humor. She hated to go a day without shampooing, even though her mother had told her a thousand times that her hair would go dry and frizzy and then fall out if she didn't stop *soaping* it so often.

"I'll wash it twice tomorrow," she said out loud to the mother who wasn't there.

The weekend shimmered in front of her, night clubs and

music and big air-cooled rooms and casinos and those . . . those *interesting* men. Men who had killed people, men other men were afraid of, but who made her feel safer than she'd ever felt in her life. Men who treated her as though a coarse word would chip her. Men who tiptoed around her and took the edges off their voices when they spoke to her, no matter how they treated the other girls.

And she'd get to spend some time with Georgie.

All right. What first? Well, of course, pull the suitcase out of the closet and open it on the bed.

Two people had recognized her in the department store, a new record. She'd signed autographs for them, and then out of nowhere there were a dozen people, all holding out something for her to write on although most of them probably didn't know who she was. She was going to have to do something about her autograph, she thought, folding clothes and wrapping them in tissue to keep them from wrinkling. The signature she'd been working on for the past year or so was too fancy. Looking at it now, it was almost embarrassing, florid and—and insecure. *Junior-high* insecure. And when, a year or so from now, there were thirty or forty people waiting—or a hundred, she'd seen a hundred or more gathered around for Joan Crawford—it would take far too long.

She'd work on simplifying it while she was on the plane.

She stood there with two pairs of slacks in her hand, trying to decide between them.

Georgie signed his name like lightning. He could carry on a conversation and sign autograph after autograph, as fast as people could hand him the paper. It might be the only thing he knew how to write, but he had it dead to rights. You could even read it. He always carried a pen, too. She'd need to buy a nice pen, silver, like Georgie's, and keep it with her. It was easier to do a good autograph with a nice pen. And nice for the fans. It showed that you've been thinking about them.

Both pairs of slacks, she decided, and the phone rang.

She folded the slacks carefully and put them on the bed. Just because she had more nice clothes now, that was no reason not to take care of them. The phone was in the dining room, and by the time she got to it, it was on its fourth ring.

"Miss La Marr? This is Patricia at the answering service. Isn't it a beautiful day? You've had five calls."

"In an hour? My, my. Let me go get a pad, and I'll—"

The doorbell rang, and then rang again.

"Patricia, I'm sorry, I've got someone at the door. I'll have to call you back."

She hung up, glanced at her watch—getting pretty late—and went to the door.

"Who is it?"

"It's me, Dolly," said a queasy-yellow voice, a voice the color of smokers' teeth. "Livvy."

"I'm in a hurry, Livvy. Can't this wait?"

"Oh, for Christ's sake." The door was kicked from outside, down low, not lightly. "Open the door. I'm no more eager than you are to play a long scene."

"All right, but just for a minute." She undid the bolts, wishing she had the courage to be ruder.

"I was in the neighborhood," Olivia Dupont said, as though daring Dolly to contradict her, "and thought we might have a chat. Are you going to invite me in?"

"I suppose." She stepped aside and Livvy brushed by, shorter, as always, than Dolly remembered her, and dressed for the California summer in a bright floral print sundress and seamed stockings. The seams were perfectly straight, as usual; Dolly figured Livvy's stockings were too intimidated to go crooked.

"This is cute," Livvy said, giving the room an uninterested once-over. "A girl alone and so on."

"Thanks. What do you want?"

"I want to know who's—" She stopped as the phone began to ring.

"Hold on." Dolly took the two steps up to the dining room, picked up the receiver, turned so she could keep an eye on Livvy, and said, "Not just yet, Patricia—"

"Not Patricia, Dolly," a man said. "Tell me, how does Randolph Scott sound?"

"Kind of nasal," Dolly said. "Like a farmer. Who is this?"

"I meant, how does he sound as a co-star? This is Max, darling."

"Max." She squeezed her eyes shut for a moment, trying to find the voice. "Oh, *Max*." She hadn't spoken to him in more than a year. "So nice to hear from you. *What* about Randolph Scott?"

At the name *Max*, Livvy put down the little piece of ivory she was inspecting and wheeled around to face Dolly, and her eyebrows rose when Dolly said Randolph Scott.

Max hadn't spoken. "You mean for *me*," Dolly said, feeling a little slow. Studio heads didn't call girls at her level and offer them leading men. "For a picture?"

"Well, of course, darling. For a picture."

Livvy said, making no attempt to lower her voice, "Is that Max Zeffire?"

Max said, "Who's there?"

"Nobody," Dolly said.

Livvy said, "*Nobody*?"

"It's Olivia Dupont," Dolly said.

"That bitch," Max said. "Tell her I said fuck her *and* her overbite."

"I'll let you tell her yourself. Listen, Max, about the picture—"

"It's the female lead," Max said.

Dolly's heart dropped a few inches, and she put a hand on the table to steady herself. She said, "The lead," and watched Livvy's mouth tighten into a straight line. Then she said, "Gosh, Max, I'm flattered, but you've got to talk to Lew—"

Livvy said, "You gotta be kidding."

"Of course, I'll talk to Lew," Max said. "I just want to know if you're interested."

Dolly took a moment, just enjoying the anticipation, and said, "What's the story?"

"What's the—Dolly, it's the *lead* in a *Randy Scott picture.*"

"If it were the lead," Dolly said, "you wouldn't call it a Randy Scott picture."

Zeffire had been using his mellow, persuasive radio announcer's voice, but now it tightened a little. "Randy's top-billed, but it's the girl's picture."

"A western, right? If it's Randolph Scott? How can a western be the girl's picture?"

Dolly watched out of the corner of her eyes as Livvy sank to a sitting position on the arm of the sofa. She interlaced her fingers, put them between her legs, and closed her knees. It was an unusually vulnerable position for Livvy.

"It's a new story," Max said. "Never heard one like it before, and that's saying something. Dolly, it *needs* you. It needs somebody who's dynamite but not a real star yet, because you don't want to give the end away. Randy's an old gunfighter, right? Wants to hang them up and farm, and he's living in a little town, just a dirt road, a general store, and a saloon. Are you with me?"

"Memorizing every word."

"Funny girl. But you will be. Okay, so a new girl comes to work in the saloon, and she seems to like Randy, all right?

They're getting acquainted when Randy learns there's a kid after him—a young gun who wants to take him down. And then, sure enough, a kid rides into town, packing double, and sits around staring at Randy. But Randy won't put his gun on, and one day he's in the saloon, talking with the girl, when she pulls a shotgun out from under the bar and blows away the kid, who's just come through the door behind Randy."

"So far, not so new."

"Be patient. Not so new, except for this. The *girl* is the kid who's after Randy. She gunned the other kid down to get Randy's trust, but she's the one who was hired to kill him. Are you following me?"

"You have no idea," Dolly said. She'd forgotten all about Livvy.

"So she goes home with him to the farm, thinking she's going to kill him, but they fall in love, and she finally tells him the truth. By then, though, the black hat who hired her has sent someone else to do the job, and in the final shoot-out, she's on Randy's side. He wins, but she gets killed, and Randy buries her and puts his guns on and rides off into the sunset."

Dolly said, "I want it."

"Everybody's going to want it, darling. But talk to Lew, and you can have it. I mean, you'll have to meet Randy, but he's a sweetheart. Hey, listen, do me a favor. Ask Livvy if she's read the *Variety* review."

"You mean, there's a review in—"

"Just ask her."

Dolly looked across the room to see Livvy staring at her with an expression of undiluted hatred. "Max wants to know whether you've read the *Variety* review."

"That asshole," Livvy said.

"I think she has, Max. What's it say?"

"You'll love it. It calls the picture a tidy low-budget thriller, says a couple of nice things about Dougie Trent, and Oriole's script. But then it goes on to say, 'As the good sister, Dolores La Marr manages to be sympathetic and intelligent at the same time, and she's on the way to being one of the screen's great beauties. As the hisser-sister, Olivia Dupont is so convincingly awful that those of us who don't have the pleasure of knowing her personally will probably think she's playing herself.'"

"Ooohhhh."

"Talk to Lew, sweetie."

"I'm going away for the weekend, to Vegas. I'll call him first thing Monday."

"Tell him not to hold me up. This'll make you a star, and he could use another star."

"Thanks, Max."

"You were good in the picture, Dolly. I knew it the first time I saw you. *Kid's got something*, I said to myself."

Yeah, and you took it when I was sixteen, Dolly thought, but what she said was, "Talk to you Monday." She hung up, her head whirling, looking down at her hand on the receiver.

"Well, well," Livvy said. "Little Miss Marvelous. Max Zeffire calls you at home."

"I'm in a hurry." Dolly felt a rush of embarrassment at the pleasure she was taking in the moment. "You must have wanted something, or you wouldn't be here."

"I want to know who's doing your P.R."

"I'll bet you do."

"These reviews. They're reviewing the movie they were told about, not the movie they saw."

"Olivia, I have a car coming in ten minutes. Don't you have an acting class or something?"

Livvy turned back to the shelves beside Dolly's favorite

window. She picked up one of the ivory miniatures. "Who gives these to you?"

"Someone you'll never meet."

"Expensive?"

"I can't imagine," Dolly said, "why you think you have the right to barge in here and ask me questions. Just trot your extra-wide bottom through that door and let me get back to business."

"Business," Livvy said. She put the ivory figurine back and threw up her hands in mock-surprise, as though just remembering something. "Oh, right. Las *Vegas*, all those hoodlums. Picking up some spare change, are we?"

"Hard to believe that would even occur to you, considering how *widely* you do it for free."

"Melly Crain," Livvy said dreamily. "Louella. Hedda. Doris Lilly. *Hollywood Secrets*. Don't you think they'd be *fascinated* to know that one of the screen's great new beauties spends her weekends on her knees under nightclub tables, servicing gangsters?"

"Coming from you? Any of them, even Melly, would consider the source."

"It's too good a story to turn down. Hollywood's sweet new innocent, tugging on Johnny Roselli's dick. You'd be working as a car hop. Who got you the *Life* cover? Who got you these reviews?"

The phone began to ring.

"Just leave that," Livvy snapped. "And give me the name."

Dolly was on her way to get the phone, but she stopped. She tilted her head down a little and gazed at Livvy, thinking. She was right, it was a good story. And, unfortunately, partially true, so there wouldn't even be a retraction.

"I know why you do that, that thing with your head," Livvy said. "Lowering it like that. I saw you do it every time the camera was at eye level. You do it because it shortens your upper lip, don't you?"

"I tried a mustache," Dolly said, "but it didn't come in."

"The name. You know I can cause you trouble. This is not a point in a girl's career when she wants trouble."

"If I tell you, will you leave?"

"I'll be a streak."

"Pinky Pinkerton."

"That little hack? He couldn't have gotten that cover—"

"You asked. I told you." She went to the door and pulled it open. "Go away."

"You swear? Pinky Pinkerton? If I find out otherwise—"

"It's a nice day out," Dolly said. She made a little shooing motion toward the door. "Go ruin it for someone else."

11

June 23, 1950

"Oh, Georgie," Dolly said, leaning against his shoulder. She breathed in the soothing fragrance of the baby powder he always wore on his neck to keep the stiffly starched shirts from chafing him. "I hate myself when I'm with her. She turns me into her."

"She does it to everybody, Button," Raft said. "Don't think about it."

"She's such a—"

Raft put a hand on her wrist. He had the warmest hands of any man she'd ever known. "Look around, okay? You see her? She on the plane?"

"No, of course, not."

"So why are you inviting her along? She's with us as long as you're stewing about her. You want to toss her off? Stop thinking about her."

"All right. But she almost made me late."

He laughed, showing his beautiful, even teeth. "We ain't taking off without you, so relax."

They were the only people in the passenger compartment, which seated eight. Georgie traveled first-class, even when he couldn't afford it, perhaps especially when he couldn't afford it.

Through the open door to the cockpit, Dolly watched the pilot reach up to snap a bunch of switches and then press his earpiece against his head so he could hear the instructions from the tower. Cloverfield Airport, out in Santa Monica, was smaller than the new Los Angeles International, but it got busy on Fridays.

The plane shuddered and began to roll forward, and Dolly grabbed the sleeve of Raft's beautiful suit, wadding it up in her hand. "These little planes scare me."

"Nothin' scares you," Raft said. "That's one of the things I like about you." Gently, he pried her hand off the sleeve. "Take it easy on the fabric, Button. These things ain't free."

"Okay, I'm not scared," Dolly said, sitting back. "I just like the cloth."

Raft reached over and put an arm around her shoulder. "Then go back to leaning on it." He waved his free hand at the little window to his left. "Take a look at that, willya?"

Dolly leaned across him to look out. The light was mostly gone, and through the eucalyptus and palm trees the sky was the pure, deep blue Dolly associated with sadness, the blue she saw when cellos played slow melodies. A curved, cream-yellow melon-slice of moon dangled just above the treeline, and the first stars were beginning to make their tinny appearances, getting ready to brighten as the sky went to black.

"Beats the pants off Hell's Kitchen," Raft said.

"Not to mention Scranton. The night sky in Scranton was like coal. Actually, everything in Scranton was like coal."

The moon slid sideways across the window and disappeared as the plane pivoted to take its place on the runway. Takeoffs always made Dolly nervous and chattery, and she said, without thinking, "Max Zeffire called me today," and then wished she could kick herself.

"Really," Raft said. He pursed his lips and looked down at

the shine on his shoes. "Just called you out of nowhere? He don't even return mine."

"Oh, Georgie. He probably figures you're too big a star for—"

"Yeah, right. What did the little twerp want?"

"He offered me a movie," she said, glad the cabin lights were dim so he couldn't see her blush. "With Randolph Scott."

"Yeah? You'll like Randy."

"I probably won't get it."

"You'll get it. If Max wants you, you'll get it, Button. He owns the place." The airplane shook and rattled as the engines rose in volume, taxied forward, and then slowed. "I didn't know he had Randy."

"He said he did."

"Coming up in the world, old Max." Raft turned and stared out the window, and Dolly looked at his hair, seeing for the first time that it was thinning in back. Still facing the window, he said, "Good part?"

It felt like bragging, given what was happening with Georgie's career, but he'd asked. "I think so. I think it could be great for me."

"Tell Georgie the story."

She told him the plot as the plane taxied and slowed again, and when she got to the part where her character was revealed as the hired gun, he whistled.

"Choice. Sounds like Max wants his own *Duel in the Sun.* Who's directing?"

"I forgot to ask. Livvy was there, and I was mad enough to spit."

"Save your spit for someone who's worth it. And forget what I said, that stuff I said, about Max. They're all the same, the studio big shots. He's no worse than any of them. Little men in big suits, trying to act like they deserve what they got, like they don't wake up every morning and pinch themselves. No, I take that back, Meyer is worse. Making those family movies so he can slide his hand up Judy's dress."

"Judy?"

"Garland."

"Oh," she said, feeling a now-familiar rush of excitement. This was the world she lived in now, a world where she knew people who called Judy Garland "Judy," as though she were Judy Karnow, who lived just down the hill from them in Scranton. "Is that true?"

"People say. They say he did it with Temple, too. That's *Shirley* Temple." He gave her the smile she liked best, the one that seemed to come out of nowhere.

"I know, I know. But to hear you just say 'Judy' like that, I practically get goose bumps. Georgie, can I tell you something and you promise you won't get mad?"

"Mad at you? Not a chance."

"All the stars, when I first started to see them up close up, to meet them, I mean?" She put her hand, fingers spread, in the middle of her chest. "They just took my breath away. It felt like they were so bright I should have squinted at them, and I couldn't have thought of anything to say if my whole life had depended on it. But *you*, my mom never let me see the kind of movies you make, so I wasn't afraid of you. I liked you right away and I didn't even find out you were a star until later."

Raft dropped his heavy lids and looked her in the eyes. "Really?"

"Is that okay?"

He leaned across and kissed her cheek, and the talcum fragrance bloomed around her. "Better than okay. It's great. You'll find out when you're a star. You never know whether someone means what they say or whether it's just because—you know."

"That must be awful," she said, trying to imagine it. It didn't sound all that awful.

"Well," Raft said, "I won't have to worry about it much longer, not the way things are going."

"Come on, Georgie, that's not—"

He held up a hand to stop her, and then he took her chin and turned her face to his. "Nah, nah. Let's tell each other the truth," he said. "We always have."

"But maybe it's just a slump, right?" She suddenly felt the icy lake of fear at her center, stirred by the notion that anything could happen to throw her—to throw *anyone*—out of this wonderland. "Everybody goes up and down. Don't they?"

Raft seemed to be studying the wall between them and the pilots' cabin as though it were a screen and rushes were flickering across it. He reached into his shirt pocket, pulled out a cigarette, and lit it. She waved the package away when he extended it to her, and he turned his head to blow the smoke against the window. "Tell you something, Button, but it's a secret." He dragged on the cigarette again, its bright orange coal reflecting in the dark windowpane. "You gotta promise me it's a secret. Nobody except you and me."

"Cross my heart."

He leaned back and closed his eyes, and she watched the climbing filigree of smoke. "Meyer—you know, Meyer Lansky."

"I know who he is. I haven't met him."

"Meyer's made me an offer. I'm getting charity from a gangster. Down in Cuba. He's going to open a casino and give me a little piece of it, and I'm going to work for him."

"You mean—quit acting? Leave Hollywood?"

"Acting's quit me, Button." He lifted the cigarette to his lips again and inhaled. "And, yeah, I gotta be in Havana to work in Havana."

Banished from Eden, she thought, the chill fear lapping at the bottom of her heart. "But . . . doing what?"

"Being Meyer's pet movie star. Meet the gorillas, the high rollers, have a drink or two with them, sit at a table once in a while with a crooked deck, winning for everyone to see. Press the flesh, wear nice clothes. Gleam a little."

"But Georgie—"

"I'll make more money down there in a month, off my piece of the skim, than I made here in a year. I'll do it for a couple years, three, retire rich. The hell with Jack Warner and Max Zeffire and the whole bunch of them, all the big shots and all the Olivia Duponts, too. I'll be rich, I'll buy a penthouse in Manhattan and just turn into a rich old man, great clothes and shiny women."

She looked into his eyes but didn't see the regret she expected. *If it can happen to Georgie. . . .* "But people will miss you."

"They'll have Bogey."

"He's not you."

He turned to look into her eyes. "No, he's a *real* star. You know what *I* was, Button? I was the only guy in town who could do what I did, back when pictures were a small business. If they wanted someone like me, they got me. Now pictures are a big business, and there are half a dozen of me."

Raft returned his attention to the wall in front of them, chewing on the corner of his mouth, and Dolly could sit back and look at him. Georgie was one of only three people she'd ever known who put out colors of their own, not just in their voices, but in the air around them. His was a kind of silvery fog, as though mercury were smoke, and from the moment she'd seen it, it had relaxed her, made her feel safe. But now it seemed roiled, even stormy. She said, "There's only one of you for me."

"Won't happen for a couple of years. Meyer's got to build the place first."

"Still too soon for me."

"Maybe not, by the time it happens. You're gonna be a big star. Stars look at other people different, you'll see. I'll just be somebody to smile at."

The engines roared into real life, no rehearsal this time, and the plane rushed toward the end of the runway.

"I'm still me," Dolly said, grabbing his hand to steady her nerves. "I'm just Wanda Altshuler from Scranton." And she thought, *Am I?*

"Not for long," Raft said. "Two years from now you'll barely remember me." The front end of the plane tilted upward vertiginously and they were climbing, getting side-punched by winds in off the Pacific. He extended a hand, fingers straight, and mimed a smooth ascent. "Like this plane," he said. "You're going up. It's like—like—you know the word, Button. Sounds like a dangerous reptile."

The rear end of the plane skewed right and then fought its way back again, and the sound of the engines increased. The cold lake sloshed inside her chest. "A dangerous—"

"Yeah, you know." Raft squinted at the black rectangle of the window. "Says one thing but means something else. Not alligator, but—"

"Allegory."

"Yeah, one of those." He reached into the breast pocket of his jacket, pulled out a thin silver flask and unscrewed the top before handing it to her. "Dolores La Marr," he said, and there was something dangerous in his grin. "Going up."

She drank half of it in one long pull.

○ ○ ○

G.R., hard to read in a floral scroll of fine lines, was engraved into the side of the flask, which dangled loosely from his hand. Dolly eased it away from him and screwed the top back on. She put it on the divider between their seats, sighed, unfastened her belt, got up, and crossed the aisle to the opposite window seat to watch the world go by below. She felt the gaze of the pilot, craning around to watch her. Probably trying to figure out who she was, this woman with George Raft.

Georgie's head was tilted back, his eyes closed, and his mouth open. In the overhead light his face looked slack and much older than it seemed when he was awake. While he was awake, being "George Raft," he had the muscles of his face under total control, but now his age showed. Before she stepped in front of a camera, Dolly thought, she wouldn't have known about that muscle mask, but now—now she'd felt it shoulder aside her normal face every time the lights went on and the cameras started to roll. Not rigid, not stiff, just sort of electrically responsive, slightly tauter than life. A complete awareness of every square inch of skin, bone, and muscle she bared to the camera's eye.

Acting, she had discovered, was both harder and easier than she'd expected. She didn't really know anything about it, and she wasn't sure she wouldn't rather keep it that way. Now that she was used to the cameras, the lights, and the army of silent people, frozen in the darkness just beyond the lights with their microphones and makeup and clipboards, acting was like a water faucet. When she turned the spigot, either it flowed easily or nothing at all came out. When it flowed, she could forget even that her face felt twelve times bigger than usual the moment the sound man called "Rolling" and the director said "Action." The flow—when it came—filled her up and told her what to do with her arms and hands, and where in a speech the emphasis belonged.

When the faucet went dry, she'd learned to pretend it hadn't. As stiff and uncomfortable and *orphaned* as it felt, as unconvincing as she thought she must be at those times, she'd learned the hard way that it usually didn't matter. Later, watching herself on film, in the daily rushes she used to dread, she couldn't tell whether the faucet had been flowing or not.

The lights of Los Angeles were far behind. Now the land slipping by below was mostly dark, save for the little yellow constellations of small groups of houses or the glistening starfish of a town, its streets radiating outward and dimming as they moved away from the center. A ribbon of highway, Route 66, unrolled itself through the darkness, a fragile tendril of moving lights leading from one place to another. Maybe from one life to another. Taking people from someplace to someplace else, where they probably hoped things would be better.

That had been her mother and her down there only four years ago, headlights slicing open the endless darkness as her mother grimly pushed the old Plymouth west, one anxious mile at a time, one eye glued to the rearview mirror. After the two-day drop south and east from Scranton to pick up Route 66 in Springfield, Illinois, before it made its downward dip through the panhandle of Texas, her mother had stopped the car beside the sign that marked the final right, the one that would put them on the road to dreams and oranges. She had passed her forearm over he face, wiping her eyes.

"Honey," she said, "from now on, you're an adult."

And it had turned out to be true, in ways her mother had probably not intended.

Dolly pressed her face against the cool windowpane and looked down at her life.

12

Route 66 (1946)

Wanda hadn't thought she'd be able to sleep when she climbed into bed, fully dressed beneath her nightgown, and forced her eyes closed. But it seemed to be only a moment before her mother shook her awake, standing over her in the tiny, dark bedroom with her index finger pressed to her lips, commanding silence. The streetlight outside provided just enough yellowish light for Wanda to see the things she'd slipped beneath the bed, the brown paper supermarket bags jammed full of her favorite clothes, her diary, and the small yellow stuffed horse she'd had since she was two.

No makeup. Even after she turned sixteen, her father had forbidden makeup, and her three tubes of pale, barely noticeable lipstick were hidden a block away, along with her face powder and a dried-out, cracking cake of mascara, in the bedroom of her friend Betty, whose mother didn't notice anything that wasn't directly between her easy chair and the cupboard where she stored her bottle.

But, Wanda thought, there would be plenty of makeup in Hollywood.

Her father was a snorer, especially now that he was working extra shifts to mine coal. He was in top form that night, the racket following them through the house as they tiptoed from room to room. In the pantry, her mother reached up for a canister that turned out to be full of fives, tens, and twenties, the booty—she said later—from more than a year of skimping on the groceries and pocketing the difference. The house seemed smaller to Wanda than usual, her father's bed just feet away wherever she was, every noise they made amplified, but still he snored on, and she realized she had the tail of her mother's blouse wadded up in her hand. Her fingers seemed cramped as she let it go. Her palm was wet and cold.

Room after room, stop after stop: a basket of food pulled from the oven, the one place her father would never find anything, two small cardboard suitcases, smelling new in the darkness, from the cramped, spidery space beneath the stairs, coats and hats—it was April, but still cold—from the closet just inside the front door. Wanda held her breath when her mother opened the closet because the hinges creaked like a joke on a radio show, but it swung wide without a whisper, and Wanda smelled the oil her mother had used to silence the hardware. The front door also opened without a murmur, and the cold slapped Wanda on the face as they hurried across the dead, stiff little lawn toward the old, high-roofed Plymouth. The car was a black silhouette against the ghost-light of the city, reflecting off the low clouds—snow clouds, her father had said the previous evening. Remembering that, Wanda felt a sudden clutching in her heart: her *father*.

The car had been backed into the driveway. It was a two-door, and the trunk always groaned when it was popped open, so her mother eased the passenger door outward and crawled in, leaning over the seat to put the food basket on the backseat, and then taking the suitcases Wanda handed to her and sliding them over the top of the seats and easing them to the floor. Last were the bulging supermarket bags, stowed on the floor beneath the dashboard; when the car was a safe distance away, their contents were to be transferred to the suitcases. Suitcases, her mother had explained, would be less conspicuous.

And, standing there, looking at her breath drift by in the air and listening to the crumpled complaints of the bags being pushed into place, Wanda wondered why they needed to avoid being conspicuous.

A little chill rippled over the skin on her back and arms as her mother scooted over to position herself behind the wheel and waved Wanda in. "Don't close the door," her mother said. "Just hold it shut until I tell you." Then she closed her eyes and bowed her head until her forehead rested on the steering wheel and said, "Dear Lord, please bless this journey and carry me and my little moviestar to the fields of glory. Amen."

Wanda echoed the "Amen," although her eyes remained open. With her back curved like that, her mother looked smaller than usual, and her voice had been higher and less steady than usual, smearing the air with a dirty topaz color. But then her mother straightened and said, in her normal tone, "Hold onto that door." She released the parking brake and pushed the clutch to the floor, and they began to roll down the driveway.

"We're off," her mother said, grabbing Wanda's arm and squeezing it so hard that Wanda almost cried out. At the bottom of the drive, she wrapped both hands around the wheel and steered right, down the hill, the car gathering speed until she reached down and turned on the ignition and popped the clutch. The engine dragged at them and then caught with a cough, and her mother pressed down on the gas and said, "Slam it, moviestar. We're free."

Half an hour later, with the sky beginning to pale in the west, her mother pulled the car to the curb in front of a house with only one lighted window, and the two of them pulled out the bags and packed the suitcases. To Wanda, it felt like a shared moment, she and her mother doing the same things at the same time, but then she folded a blouse too quickly, and her mother reached over and slapped her hand and said, "Lazy." Wanda snatched her hand back and re-folded the blouse, blinking against the little sizzle of pain. When she'd placed the blouse in the suitcase, precisely folded and all its wrinkles smoothed out, her mother said, without looking up from her own suitcase, "We have to do everything carefully. This is your adventure, Wanda, and the thing you never read in stories about adventures is that people who are having one have to be very, very careful. Do you understand?"

Wanda said, "Sure," putting a little sullen edge into the word.

"Don't give me that, sweetie. This is a small car, and we're going to be in it for a long time. If we're not going to get along, tell me now, and we'll turn around and go home."

Wanda recognized the dare and almost called it, but the word *moviestar*, echoing in her mind, made her clamp her teeth together against the impulse. "Sorry, Mom."

"That's my baby." The color of her mother's voice lightened toward yellow, closer to her normal color. "Tell me, sweetie, what do you like most in the world? What's the smell you like most in the world?"

"Shalimar." It was her mother's perfume. At the age of eight, Wanda had been spanked and sent to bed without dinner for sneaking into her mother's and father's room and pouring half a bottle of the scent over herself.

"Well, sweetie, we're floating to Hollywood on a cloud of Shalimar." She picked up her purse, put it in the center of the open suitcase in her lap, and pulled out a small, circular bottle with a tapering glass stopper. "Close your eyes."

With her eyelids pressed together so tightly she saw little red fireworks, Wanda heard the whispery sound of the stopper sliding out, and then the fragrance bloomed around her with its own delicious color, a clear cool aquamarine, and she felt her mother's fingertips behind her right ear and then her left, leaving cool spots where the alcohol was evaporating, and the smell thickened and gathered strength, and the color lightened and deepened and rippled, the clearest, cleanest water in the history of the world, and Wanda surprised herself by laughing.

"Me, too," her mother said, and Wanda opened her eyes to see one of her mother's rare smiles. She was almost pretty when she smiled. "It used to make me laugh, too." She dabbed a finger behind each of her own ears and said, "The hell with it," and poured a few precious drops on the dashboard. She slid the bottle back into her purse, inhaled deeply, and said, "Flowers all the way." As the smile faded she leaned forward and studied the sky. "Getting light. We've got to get some miles behind us."

It went wrong almost immediately.

At 9:30 the first night, the two of them yawned in unison and her mother hooked a left off the highway and bumped east through the dark on a narrow, pot-holed, tree-lined road for half an hour, chasing the moon above a ragged treeline until they came to a small, paint-peeled town with a crumbling stucco motel in it. Wanda was ordered to stay in the car, the heat on full, while her mother talked to the clerk, visible through the window of the office, and then came back clutching a big key with a plastic tag that said 12. With a glance at the clerk, whose nose was already buried in a big copy of *Life*, Wanda's mother steered the car to the far edge of the parking lot, squinting at the room numbers until she cranked the wheel left, toward the doors, hanging a wide U-turn that ended when the right front wheel bumped up onto the walkway in front of number 12, so close that Wanda could almost have hit the building with her opening door.

"Stay put," her mother said. She climbed out of the car and toted the suitcases and the food basket into the room while Wanda, who had never been in a motel, tried to get a look at the room. After the third trip, her mother came out to the car and opened Wanda's door.

"Get in there," she said, almost a whisper, but with a lot of whip in it. "And stay in there."

Wanda climbed out and darted four feet across the sidewalk into the room, feeling foolish. She wasn't a moviestar yet. Her mother shot an index finger at her and said, "Don't you dare set foot out that door." Then she hurried around the car, climbed in, and started it. Without turning on the lights, she backed it out of Wanda's line of vision and then drove to Wanda's left, away from the road. When the sound of the engine had dwindled, Wanda disobeyed just enough to put her head out for a look and she saw the car disappearing behind the last unit in the motel. She ducked back in and sat on the double bed, listening to her mother's shoes scuffing on the walkway until she reappeared in the door, zipping her purse shut. She pulled the door closed and leaned her back against it, her eyes pressed shut.

Wanda said, "I'm hungry."

"Too late. Everything's closed. That's what the basket's for."

"There was a restaurant back there—"

Her mother pushed herself away from the door and dropped her purse onto the bed. "Are you listening to me? Get something out of the basket." She turned her back to Wanda and threw the chain latch and then felt around the doorknob, looking for another lock.

Wanda said, "I want something hot."

"Children are starving in China."

"I'm not in China. I'm in wherever we are."

"No restaurant."

"Why not?"

"And no questions."

"Why'd you move the car?"

At the low, four-drawer dresser, her mother leaned forward and looked at herself in the mirror. She turned her head left and then right, then lifted her chin, her eyes never leaving her reflection. The overhead light in the room was so yellow it looked like it was coming through layers of old wax. She unclipped one of her round, orange earrings and looked down at it, bright in her hand. "Getting old," she said.

"You look fine. Why'd you move—"

"Wanda." Her mother tightened the hand with the earring into a fist and turned to face her, resting her bottom against the top edge of the dresser. "I have driven several hundred miles today. I didn't nap, like you did, and I got up an hour earlier than you. Now stop bothering me. Just leave me alone."

Wanda said, "You *hid* the car."

Crossed arms were always a bad sign, high and tight over the chest like a wall around the heart. "And if I did?"

"Why can't I go to the restaurant? Why would you hide the car?"

"That's enough." Her mother's mouth was as straight as a knife-cut. "I am not going to put up with all these questions, young lady. All of this, everything I'm doing, is for you. I've interrupted my entire life for you. I'm driving thousands of miles, to a place I've never been before, for you. All for you. What am I going to get out of this?"

"How would I know?"

Her mother uncrossed her arms and took a quick step, halv-ing the distance between them. "Young lady," she said, "you are one minute away from getting your face slapped."

Wanda flopped onto her back and rolled across the bed to the far side, coming to rest facing the wall, her back to her mother. "This is going to be fun."

"You'll have *fun*," her mother said, spitting the word across the room, "in *Hollywood*. If you're hungry, eat now. I want to turn off this light and get to sleep."

"Both of us?" Wanda asked. "In one bed?"

"Unless you'd prefer the floor. Do you need the bathroom?"

"I don't need anything."

Her mother said, "Oh, for crying out loud," and slammed the bathroom door behind her.

Things didn't get better as they headed south toward the Golden Road. The car shrank around them and the Shalimar scraped at the back of Wanda's throat as it aged, the high, aquamarine floral notes fading and revealing a bark-brown base that smelled like Scranton on a bad day, when there were no breezes and the place stank of deep, damp earth and coal smoke. Wanda took to sitting in the backseat, knowing that it irritated her mother. Every few moments, her mother's eyes would find hers in the rearview mirror.

Wanda had always seen her mother as a confidential partner, the person who knew her secrets—who had *invented* her secrets. Her mother had always been there, an inescapable presence in the house and in Wanda's life, a steady breeze no more change-able than the shape of the house itself. But now as the distance between the car and home lengthened, her mother began to emit irregular, unpredictable spurts of energy, flaring up and dying down at random intervals like a defective Halloween sparkler.

When the energy was at its highest, her mother's eyes always came to Wanda's in the mirror.

Late on the third day, Wanda had moved from one side of the seat to the other, only to see her mother reach up and re-angle the mirror. "Why do you keep staring at me?"

"I'll look at you all I like."

"But why? What are you thinking about?"

"You don't want to know."

"What I *do* want to know," Wanda said, her fingers digging into the tops of her thighs, "is why you make me stay in the car all the time. We get gas, I stay in the car. If I have to go to the bathroom, you make me wait until you can pull the car around so nobody can see me. If we stop at a restaurant, you go in alone and I sit here in this stupid car, going crazy, while you get to go inside and order."

"Those are my rules."

"It's not fair."

"All right," her mother said, and the flatness of her tone made Wanda pull her head back as though something had been thrown at her. "You want to know what I'm thinking, here it is. Are you ready?"

Wanda pushed back against the seat and brought her knees up. "I'm not sure."

"Too bad. Listen, my dear, and listen hard, because nobody's ever told you this before. You're a very ordinary child. You're not especially smart—"

"I'm not?" The words struck Wanda like bullets of ice.

"Let me finish. You're not especially smart, you're not especially charming. You're not witty. People who meet you don't remember you very long. You don't make an impression."

Wanda said, "But—"

"Hush. Left to your own resources, this is what your life will

be. A few months from now, when you're seventeen, some idiot
who can barely remember his middle name will get you preg-
nant. You'll marry him, thinking you've got everything, an adorable baby and a husband who believes he's married Snow White.
But what you'll really *have* is a husband who will have to quit
school and work at some three-dollar-an-hour job that gets his
hands filthy and has no future, and as that sinks in, he'll begin
to hate you. And your adorable baby will be a screaming bundle
of snot and piss who will wake both of you up thirty times every
night, in your awful little apartment with the neighbors banging
on the wall every time the baby starts up." Her eyes flicked to
the mirror. "Close your mouth."

"It's not—"

"It is, and it makes you look stupid. You need to be aware of
that. You need to be aware of everything, because you're going to
another country now, a place where the competition makes the
people you know back in Assholeville look like monkeys." She
jerked a thumb back over her shoulder, in the general direction
of Scranton. "I haven't finished with your future, dear. About a
year after you have the baby, Prince Charming will start coming home later and later, and he'll smell of whiskey and sometimes perfume. And sooner or later, when you're in the middle of
reminding him how grateful he should be for his life, he'll paste
you. If you're lucky, he won't knock out a tooth, because you
won't be able to afford a dentist, and he won't break your nose
and spoil the one and only valuable thing you possess. Do you
know what that is?"

Wanda didn't answer, just turned to her left and watched the
cold, bare woods whip by, trees lifting bare branches toward
something they'd never be able to reach.

"I asked you a question."

"My face."

"That's right. And your face is no good to you in Scranton, it's just bait for the stupid, do you understand me? People who want it without even knowing why. When it's gone—and it will be after your husband belts you a few times and you give up on the idea that life will ever be better—when it's gone, you'll be just another beat-down, hopeless woman sweeping the coal dust out of a house her husband doesn't even want to come home to. Am I being clear?"

"What you're being is awful."

"Well, someone had to say this to you."

"But you—I mean, you and Daddy. . . ."

Her mother accelerated but didn't respond.

"I mean, you. . . ." Wanda looked at the back of her mother's head, so familiar, and avoided the eyes in the mirror, not familiar at all. "Did he—did he ever. . . ?"

"On the other hand," her mother said, as though Wanda weren't speaking, "you could take this one thing you've been given, this precious gift, this *accident*, someplace where it can give you a life you can barely imagine. A place where people will look at you and see—stars."

The world wavered, and Wanda blinked the ripples away.

Her mother's shoulders were so hunched they were practically touching her ears. "*That's* what I'm doing for you, Wannie. And what I need in exchange for this favor is for you to shut up and follow my rules, let me take this face where it will matter, without your rubbing it against the world everywhere, wearing it out like a piece of chalk. You will *keep it to yourself* until I say it's time to show it, do you understand me?"

Wanda said, "Daddy *hit* you?"

That afternoon, with Route 66 less than ten miles away, they pulled off the road and into a motel. The sun was still up, and Wanda's mother once again drove straight to the door of the room and unloaded the car by herself before opening Wanda's door and watching her scoot into the room. Once Wanda was inside, her mother came in and popped the latches on her suitcase and took out a roll of papery masking tape.

"I'm going to get us something to eat at the Sit 'n Sip that we passed on the way in. You will not open this door. I'm putting a piece of tape across the outside of the door when I leave, and if you open the door, the tape will tear. If this isn't in one piece when I get back, I swear I'll leave you here."

"You don't need to tape the door."

"Prove it. Don't open it while I'm gone."

"Why did we stop so early?"

"Because we're getting up at one. From now on, we're driving mostly at night." She held up the roll of tape, her index finger through the opening, and wiggled her hand left and right. The tape rolled back and forth, and Wanda's mother said, "Don't tear it. Start to earn my trust."

The door closed behind her, and a moment later, Wanda heard the car start, only a few feet away on the far side of the door. She sat on the bed, feeling like the world around her was very large. The room had a small television, but Wanda didn't turn it on, just sat looking at the black screen and thinking about the baby she wouldn't have.

When the sun was fully up on the first day on Route 66, at about 9 A.M., her mother pulled off the highway and began to take the little, local roads, reading street signs aloud and keeping up a running commentary of uncertainty about which way to turn, almost hopping the curb at one moment because her eyes were on the rearview mirror, in spite of the fact that she'd insisted that Wanda sit in front. They'd been on the road since 1:30 in the morning.

They were on a flat, wide street, little soda-cracker houses with dead lawns on either side. People had parked cars on some of the lawns. When they almost hit the curb, Wanda said, "What are you looking for?"

"Shush," her mother said, looking again at the mirror. "I've got enough on my mind without a lot of questions."

"The sun rises in the east," Wanda said. "If you keep driving away from it, you'll be going in the right direction."

"That's fine, Miss Smartypants. What about noon? What about the middle of the day?"

"Get back on the highway."

"And what if I know where I'm going?"

"Then, like I said, what are you looking for?"

"*As* I said."

"As, as, as." Wanda slapped her open hands down on her thighs and was rewarded by seeing her mother jump. "Who cares?"

Her mother hit the top of the wheel with the side of her right fist. "You *will not use bad grammar*. You will take your voice down out of your throat and into your chest, the way I showed you, so you don't sound like a squeaking door. You will be polite. You'll sit the way I told you, your back straight, with your ankles together and your knees to one side. And you will think before you talk. Nobody will hire a stupid actress."

"I'm not stupid."

"That's still an open question."

"Mom," Wanda said, "you're acting like you hate me."

"Please, please," her mother said, looking up at the roof of the car. She checked the rearview mirror again, tapping the brakes when something back there engaged her attention, and Wanda fought the urge to turn around and look, too. With a sigh, her mother made a right onto a narrow street that curved sharply left. Once they were out of sight of the road they'd left, she pulled the car to the curb, behind an old Dodge with half its paint sanded off. A kid of ten or twelve lazily rode a bike past them on the sidewalk, wiping his nose on the back of his hand and followed by a yawning dog. The boy glanced into the car, looked away, and then snapped his head back to Wanda's face so fast his bike wobbled.

"Sit tight," her mother said, craning back to watch the boy and the dog. After a long moment, she opened her door and said, "Come on."

The world had looked warmer through the windshield than it actually was. A wind, taking courage from the fact that there was nothing much to interfere with it, whipped across the brown lawns and pierced Wanda's double-breasted swing coat, which had looked so warm in the store. She shoved her hands into the pockets of her plaid wool skirt, glad for the first time that it hung below her knees, and hunched her shoulders to make herself smaller. "Why are we out here?"

"So I can move around a little. I'm sick of the car, and if we're going to have a fight, I don't want to have it in there."

"We don't have to fight. I just want to know why you're acting like we're bank robbers or something, keeping me away from everybody, driving at night, always looking at the mirrors. This morning when that police car was behind us, I thought you were going to start to cry. Why can't we just stay on the highway? Why can't I go into restaurants and, and gas stations? Maybe I'd like a Coke, did you think of that? Maybe I'd like to walk to the bathroom instead of being driven to it. I feel like I've done something wrong."

"Honey," her mother said, and Wanda snagged her toe on an uneven pavement square. When her mother called her *honey*, it didn't mean anything good. The last time she'd been called that it was because her mother had gone through her closet and found the pair of slacks she'd bought and hidden on the hanger holding her longest skirt. She had loved those slacks, even if she didn't have anywhere to wear them.

"I didn't want to talk about this until later, until we were *there* and the trip was behind us." Her mother's hands were folded in front of her as she walked, a deceptively meek pose that, Wanda knew, didn't usually last long. "It's your father," she continued, and Wanda had to get a step closer to hear her. "He's going to be looking for us."

"He's in Scranton."

"He'll have the police after us."

"Why? How could he? What did we do wrong?"

Her mother stopped walking. Wanda stopped, too, but moved away a little in case this was the first sign of an explosion, but then she heard an engine, and a big car backed out of a driveway right in front of them. The woman at the wheel took off in the same direction they were walking in, without a glance at either of them.

"He could say I abducted you."

"But I wanted to come. How could you abduct me if I wanted to come?"

"He doesn't know that you—"

"Sure, he does. I left a note."

"You left him—"

"All it said was that I love him and that he shouldn't worry about me. And that I'd call him sometime soon."

Her mother lifted her eyes to the sky and blew out a ragged puff of air. "And you think *that* helped?"

"Well, sure, I mean, at least he'll know I wanted to go, and . . . ."

"He doesn't care about that. He knows you wanted to come."

"Then why would he tell the police that you—"

"Because *he* didn't want you to come."

Wanda turned up the collar of her coat, threaded her finger through some hair that had blown into the left corner of her mouth, and pulled it free. "But then what's the *crime*? Betty's mother left her husband and took Betty with her, and the cops never—"

"He'll claim something else," her mother said. "This is the last way I wanted you to learn about this."

"I know he didn't want me to come. Why else would we have snuck out in the middle of the night? But still, what's the crime?"

"All right, all right." Wanda's mother stared down the street as the woman in the car turned a corner, and then all Wanda could hear was the wind over the dry, dead grass. Without turning to face her daughter, Wanda's mother said, "Have you ever heard of the Mann Act?"

"No." Looking down, she rubbed the sole of her loafer over the rough sidewalk. She was trembling, but it wasn't entirely the cold.

"It punishes people who take someone across state lines for—for immoral purposes."

The tremble centered itself in Wanda's abdominal muscles. "But you're not—"

"It's what he *thinks* that matters." They had still not looked at each other: Wanda's eyes on her shoes and her mother's looking down the empty street.

"And what," Wanda said, her voice grating oddly in her ears, "what does he think?"

"Let's walk," her mother said, turning to take Wanda's arm. "This way." They went on in the direction they'd already been taking.

"Who could live here?" Wanda asked.

"What's the difference? Scranton is better? Most people

spend their lives in shitholes, sorry for the French, honey, and even though they *know* they're living in a shithole they stay there because it's familiar. Because they're afraid of anything new. But you and I—"

"What does Daddy think?"

"He thinks he knows how Hollywood works. He thinks no actress gets into a movie unless she's nice to the men in charge."

"Nice," Wanda said, although she knew what her mother meant.

"Do—favors for them. Be nice to them."

"Sleep with them," Wanda said. "Is that what you're saying, sleep with them?"

"It's not me, it's your father. That's what he'll tell the police, that I took you to Hollywood so I could make money by—you know."

Wanda took her arm back and walked beside her mother. She began to count the cracks in the sidewalk. If her mother didn't say something by the tenth crack, she decided, she would turn and run in the other direction.

Seven. Eight. She raised her head.

"Yes," her mother said. "Sleep with them." Both of them kept their eyes forward, looking at where they were going.

Three steps later, Wanda said, "But."

"Of course not," her mother said, and once again her voice had that peculiar tobacco-yellow color. "It's just your father. He doesn't know how things work out there."

"But you do."

"I've been thinking about this for years, since the first time I realized what a beautiful baby I had."

"So I'm not going to have to sleep with them."

"Oh, sweetie," her mother said, her voice the color of fouled beeswax. "How could you even ask?"

There was a rattle from behind them, and the boy cruised by on his bike again, staring openly at Wanda, taking the bike up a driveway in front of them and then across the lawn and back to the street so he could circle them once and then twice. The dog lagged behind, its tongue hanging out of one side of its mouth too, its eyes—also on Wanda—the same corrupted yellow-brown as her mother's voice.

"Then," Wanda said, "what am I going to have to do for them?"

"Wait until we're there," her mother said, taking her by the arm and turning her back to the car and never, not then, not at any time during the journey, saying what she meant, even though Wanda knew what it was. What her mother didn't say was, *Whatever they want.*

Five days later, there was the dazzle of sunlight, the sprawl of Los Angeles, the big Chinese- and Egyptian-looking theaters, the iron gates of the studios, closed as they drove by; and then the eye-ringing gleam of oranges peeking out from dark leaves.

Then there were new clothes for Wanda from big, gleaming stores and men with suits and ties and offices, men with eyes that swallowed her whole, indifferent most of the time and sometimes a little too interested. And sixteen months after they arrived, Wanda had given Max Zeffire what he wanted on the couch in his big white office. When she thought back, later, on that confused, embarrassing, and sometimes painful transaction, what she remembered most clearly was the dirty-yellow sound, through the closed office door, of her mother laughing at something Zeffire's secretary had said.

Her father, Dolly thought. She hadn't spoken to her father in years. Even after the *Life* cover, he'd hung up on her whenever she called.

Motion reflected in the airplane window snatched at her attention, and she turned to see Georgie yawning and rubbing the back of his neck. And the plane banked to the left, and below them the lights of Las Vegas spilled out across the desert.

"Landing," Georgie called across the aisle. He glanced down at the flask as though surprised to see it there, picked it up, and shook it. What he heard prompted a satisfied nod. He unscrewed the top and said, "Come on back over here, Button."

As she sat, he tilted the flask vertical and swallowed whatever was left, then lowered it and put the top back on. He took a perfectly folded display handkerchief from the breast pocket of his jacket, ran the lowest fold precisely around the bottom of the flask's cap, and dropped the flask back into his inside pocket. Then he scissored his long index and middle fingers over the still-folded handkerchief and slipped it back into place, and Dolly saw that it had the same ornate GR monogram as the flask

"We need to talk," he said. "I know I got you into this, but you gotta quit with these guys, these gunsels."

"Listen to you," Dolly said. She took the perfect Windsor knot in his tie between her fingertips and centered it. "You sound like Livvy."

Georgie automatically fingered the knot to confirm that it was in the right place, and she slapped the back of his hand. "Whaddya mean?"

"Livvy says one day I'll wake up and the whole world will think I'm a moll."

"Button, if *Livvy* knows, too many people know. Much as I hate to say she's right, she's right." He tapped the flask through his jacket as though hoping to find it refilled. "But that's only half of it."

The plane shuddered as it descended into an updraft, hot air from the desert floor. "What's the other half?"

He touched his index finger to the tip of her nose and leaned in, close enough to kiss her. "The other half is sooner or later you're gonna hit the sack with one of these guys, and everything will change."

Dolly pulled her head back and looked down at her lap, feeling the heat in her face. Georgie didn't know, she thought, there was no way he could know. And anyway, he wouldn't toy with her, he'd just slap her one and say *knock it off*. She said, "Why? What would change? I mean, I'm not going to do that"—her voice sounded thin, badly recorded, in her ears—"but if I did, what would change?"

"Think about it," Raft said. "Right now, there's you and then there's all the other girls. The minute you fuck a guy, you'll become one of *all the other girls*, just another punchboard. And then there'll be jealousies and all that, guys trying to use you to score on other guys, and you'll become a way for people to get to whoever it is that you're *shtupping*." He made a rolling motion with his hand, looking for the word. "Not a lever but the other thing, the thing you put the lever on—"

"The fulcrum?" The plane slowed suddenly and dropped quickly enough that if felt as if Dolly's stomach was floating in the air.

"Yeah, like that," Raft said. He took a quick look out the window. "You'll be a weak spot, you'll be a weapon. You gotta remember, just because they're all sitting around a table together tonight, drinking and telling jokes, that doesn't mean they won't try to kill each other tomorrow. These are nervous guys, dangerous guys. They're going to look at you, they're gonna see an opening in your boyfriend's armor."

"I'm not going to go to bed with any of them," she lied.

"See that you don't." He put a hand on her arm as though to strengthen the connection between them. "Do yourself a favor, Dolly. Finish up with them, once and for all. It wouldn't be good for you if it got out. There's too many pictures of you with them already."

"All right." She wanted to tell him her secret, but she couldn't. It wouldn't be safe for him. "I don't even have to do this thing tonight," she said. "I can take the plane back without even getting off."

"You promised," Raft said. "No point in pissing the guys off. Just go, have a good time, and go home. Then have your publicity guy put it out that you're getting serious with some pretty little movie boy, and you can use that as an excuse not to come back."

The pressure inside the plane increased, and Dolly opened her mouth wide to try to get her ears to pop. Outside the window, the lights rose up to meet them and the wings tilted left and then right again as the plane homed in on the end of the runway.

"Takeoffs and landings," she said, taking his hand. "Flying would be swell if it wasn't for takeoffs and landings."

"Much smoother," Raft agreed. "Course, you'd never get anywhere." The plane bumped down with a squeal of rubber, bounced, and then bounced again. "There," Raft said. "You landed three times, and you're still alive."

The unease at her center had intensified. "Maybe I *should* go home. This doesn't feel right."

"Gonna be tough," Raft said, looking out the window. "We got a welcoming committee." He cupped a hand to the window to get rid of the reflected cabin lights. "Got a photog and everything. Looks like Pigozzi and a couple of his guys. They got flowers and champagne, Button. Ain't for me."

Dolly pulled out a mirror and gave her hair a few strategic tugs. Her makeup seemed okay. "I don't know Pigozzi."

"He's a tough guy," Raft said. "Roberto Pigozzi. Bobby Pig. Supposed to be on the rise."

"I don't know."

"Listen to me. You're here, and you can't turn around without making a scene. Anyway, the plane's probably got somewhere else to go. I don't own it, you know." He got up as the plane slowed its taxiing and smoothed the wrinkles out of his suit, put his fingers on the perfect knot in his tie. "This thing really straight?"

"Perfect," she said, and the plane stopped. George eased past her and went to the rear of the cabin, where the crew had stored the bags. When he came back he had a suitcase in each hand and a beautiful, pale brown cashmere coat draped over his shoulders. The silvery smoke around him had settled, just gleaming softly in the air.

"Isn't it a little hot for the coat?" The pilot popped the door open, and she heard the stairs being wheeled into place.

"It's not a coat," Georgie said. "It's money. Never go into a negotiation looking like you need anything. Meyer's a friend, but the first thing he's gonna do tonight is guess how much this coat cost."

She started down the aisle. "That's smart, Georgie."

"Nobody ever calls me smart," Raft said, and as Dolly approached the open door, a man pushed his way through it, a wide, dark man with the heaviest eyebrows she'd ever seen. Two other men crowded in behind him, but they were just there to carry an enormous all-white bouquet and a bottle of Champagne four times the usual size.

The wide man had jet-black hair slicked back, tight against his head, from a sharp widow's peak. From beneath the caterpillar eyebrows, his eyes were hard enough to be bulletproof. He spread his arms and said, "Here she is." He cupped his hands over his heart and said, almost singing it, "The face that launched a thousand ships."

His voice was the oily green she sometimes saw on spoiled beef in the supermarket, and her lungs were suddenly tiny. She was sure he could hear her wheeze as she fought for breath.

Bobby Pig drove an elbow into the man to his left, and there was a tremendous *bang*. Dolly's knees gave way, and she grabbed onto the top of the nearest seat as the Champagne cork slapped into the cabin wall and bounced off.

"Dolores La Marr," Bobby Pig said, baring tiny, uneven teeth. "Have we got plans for *you*."

UNREDEEMABLE

Part Three

Part
three

13

Valley Tartlet

"He's *here*," Tyrone called, turning his head in the direction of Rina's room in the house that used to be mine, back before Kathy and I split up. Tyrone was almost improbably black, so dark his skin had bluish highlights, but his eyes were the dry, pale brown of a pile of fallen leaves. I glanced at his midsection, hoping he had packed on some unsightly weight, but his form-fitting T-shirt showed off the form it made to fit, and his waist was still narrower than Rush Limbaugh's worldview. He was also, apparently, still an important part of my *daughter's* worldview.

"Hey, Tyrone." I looked at my watch: 4:50 P.M. "Kathy around?"

He wiggled his head, side to side. "Not so's you'd notice. But don't worry, we're being so good my own mama wouldn't—"

"I trust both of you completely." I put a lot of honesty into it, but the word *completely* was oversell, and Tyrone's eyes gleamed with amusement.

"Even if I tried to be bad," he said, "which I wouldn't, your daughter knows what's what."

"Thank you, Tyrone," I said. "As a parent, that's very reassuring."

"Daddy," Rina said, materializing in the hallway door. "You owe me money."

"What have you got?"

"This and that." She whirled around, giving me a quick shot of a long tear in the rump of her jeans. "Come on down."

Tyrone bowed slightly from the waist and dipped a long arm through the air to usher me in. His fingers looked as long as my legs. "After you."

"What's the thing with her pants?" I said.

"Her pants?" Tyrone's Teflon-smooth brow wrinkled and then cleared, and I got the smile that would probably make the kid rich someday. "Ah, the *pants*. Fashion. Valley tartlet style. You know, a little bit bad but not too bad."

"You like it?"

"Daddy," Rina called from her room. "Come in here."

"I could lie," Tyrone said, "but—" He lowered his voice a surprising octave. "*But that would be wrong.* Quick, what president said that?"

"Nixon. And he's not a role model I'd suggest to any kid who wants to keep seeing his, uhh, his, uhh—"

"Girlfriend. Naw, I can see that. No daddy gonna want a guy who sweated like that, guy who got five o'clock shadow at one o'clock. Guy who got little bubbles of spit at the corners of his mouth. Uh-*uh*. But, you know, the pants? You probably ought to talk to *her* about them."

"I was kind of hoping to avoid that."

"I'll bet," Tyrone said.

"Well." I took off down the hall, Tyrone following me noiselessly. As we passed my old bedroom, now shared by my former wife and God knows who, I said, as nonchalantly as possible, "Is what's-his-name still around?"

"Naw. She got a new one now. Probably shouldn't be telling you that."

"What's he like?"

"Old. Even older than you. Got different-color eyes."

"What, like brown and blue?"

"Red and green," Tyrone said. "You don't know whether you're coming or going. Yeah, sure, brown and blue. What you think?"

"I think no one with different-colored eyes should be trusted. What's his name?"

"You asked," Tyrone said.

"Yes," I said. "It was such a short time ago that I still remember it."

"Just reminding you. Name of Dick."

I stopped. "This is way too trite."

"Dick Stivik. S-T-I-V-I-K."

"Tyrone," Rina called from her room, "you're a gossip."

"Man asked," Tyrone said, following me in. "What am I supposed to do?"

"Dick's okay," Rina said to me. "Not anyone you'd lend ten dollars to, but nice enough. I guess." She was sitting at her computer, which was where she seemed to spend most of her time when she wasn't in school, and when she was there she probably spent most of her time in front of a school computer. She'd swiveled the office chair I'd bought her part of the way around, giving me a glance of a piquant profile, heartbreakingly young, that was, thanks to whoever is in charge of such things, inherited largely from her mother.

"Where's your mom?"

She didn't even dodge the question, just rolled right through it. "To be precise, you owe me sixty-six dollars and sixty-two, no, round it up to sixty-three cents."

"Ho," Tyrone said. "*Round it up,* she says. Try that with someone you're not related to."

"Tyrone—"

"That's not what the world *does*," Tyrone said. "Get out of school, the world's gonna round you down. Every chance it gets."

"Five hours and twenty-six minutes," Rina said. "Twelve-fifty times five-point-three-three and a little more. Sixty-six dollars and sixty-three cents."

"Roundin' up," Tyrone said.

"Here." I took out a fifty and a twenty and held them out. "Seventy bucks. You owe me three dollars and thirty-eight cents' worth of work. Where's your mom?"

"With Dick." She got up to take the money, but I pulled it back.

"That's swell," I said. "Doing what, at this hour of the day?"

She stopped, her hand still out. "I don't want to tell you."

"Why not? What in the world could she be doing that I shouldn't know about?"

Tyrone said, "*Listen* to the man."

"Well, sure, there's *that*," I said. "But we're not married any more, right? So that's stopped bothering me." I looked at Tyrone, who had made a sound that was too close to a snicker to be mistaken for anything else. "Any more," I said. "After that duck hunter."

"Give me my money," Rina said, snatching it from my hand, "and listen to what I've got."

Something glittered on her face. I squinted at her and took a step forward, and she instantly backed up, sat down, and gave me the right profile again. I said, "What the hell is that?"

Rina said, "It's my nose."

"I'm well aware it's your nose. What have you done to it?"

"I meant *it's my nose* in the sense that it's not anyone else's nose. Yours, for example."

"That doesn't give you a license to poke holes in it. Did your mother say—"

"This?" she turned the chair to face me again and pointed at the golden ring in her left nostril. "Is *this* what you're talking about?" She sounded quite a lot like her mother.

"Yes, that, that and . . . and . . . *look* at you, your butt is hanging out of your pants, you've practically installed plumbing in your nose. Where's your mother in all this? Too busy hanging with Dick, or—"

I stopped because they were both laughing. Tyrone sat down on the bed heavily enough to bounce, and Rina had both hands over her face. I stood there, feeling my heart rate triple. The childish piping treble of youthful laughter, no matter what the poets say, is one of the most profoundly irritating sounds in all of human experience.

"What?" I demanded. "What?"

"You got to be an honest man," Tyrone said, wiping tears from his eyes. "'Cause you'll believe *anything*."

Rina drummed the heels of her shoes against the floor. "Your face," she said. "If you could have seen your—" She dissolved again, bent so far forward her chin practically touched her knees.

"I've already seen it. What the hell is so—"

"Look," Rina said. She reached up and yanked the ring out of her nose and then bounced it on her palm. "One of mom's clip-on earrings." She started laughing again.

"The pants," Tyrone said, way too happily. "Tell him about the—"

"You know the bench out by the pool? The one mom was always asking you to drive the nails into?" She put her palms to her eyes and rubbed them dry. "I sat on it today and when I scooted down to make room for Tyrone—"

"Valley *tartlet*," Tyrone said. He fell over sideways, emitting a falsetto laugh that sounded like someone ironing a puppy. "Little bit bad but not *too*—"

"Dick Stivik?" I said. "Different-colored eyes?"

They both stopped laughing, so abruptly it sounded like the power had been cut. "Well, no," Rina said. "He's as real as acne."

"And where are they? What are they—"

"I'll tell you after I show you this stuff, okay? Otherwise we'll never get to it."

"That's not very reassuring."

"You're a grownup, Daddy. It's not my job to reassure you."

"You'll be a grownup someday yourself," I said, "and believe me, you're going to want some reassuring."

"Dolores La Marr," she said, over me. "God she was beautiful." She spun to the computer and hit a few keys with the assurance of Vladimir Horowitz, and Dolores La Marr popped onto the screen in high-def black-and-white. A moment later, the picture faded, to be replaced by another. "Slide show," Rina said. "There are five websites just about her and four others she's featured on, and she's all over some of the gangster-groupie sites, guys who think of gangsters as action figures."

"She really was something," I said, watching the pictures succeed each other.

"Wanda Altshuler from Scranton," Rina said. She cocked her head to the left, as though she saw better, or at least differently, that way. "Jewish on her father's side, but her mother wouldn't go for it, so she was raised a generic blue-stripe gentile. Her mother was apparently a total dragon. Wait a minute, here she is."

La Marr's face was replaced by an angular woman as thin as the Duchess of Windsor but not as warm-looking. Her face was a collage of acute angles culminating in a mouth with a pronounced trumpeter's lip and a chin sharp enough to puncture balloons. I could see a hint of her daughter in the cheekbones and the shape of the forehead, but otherwise there was no resemblance. "A dragon how?"

"Fought with everybody. Wanda—I mean, Dolores—was a minor when she did her first movie, like sixteen, although they tried to pretend she was seventeen. Anyway, young enough that she needed her mother on the set with her, but mom kept getting tossed off. Which meant there had to be like a social worker or something, which meant extra money, which meant Wanda got fired off a couple of pictures, poor kid."

"What happened to her mom?"

"After Wanda turned eighteen, mom married some guy she met on a set, a guy who later turned into a big deal in the union. There was some kind of power struggle, and he was out front, like a vice president, but then they split up or something. Look here. Isn't she phenomenal?"

Filling the screen was a picture from the *Life* session. I recognized the lighting and the gown. Dolly was laughing and looking past the camera, probably at the person who'd cracked the joke. It was enough to make me jealous.

"She's so young," I said.

"Not really," Rina said with the mercilessness of youth. "Twenty-one."

"That is *fine*," Tyrone said behind me, and I stepped aside to let him get closer to the screen. His arm was touching mine. I put my hand on my daughter's shoulder, and for a moment, we had a circuit: there were three of us, and it felt all right.

"You've got a good eye, Tyrone," I said.

"Have to be blind," Tyrone said, "not to see *that*. She'd be beautiful through a wall."

"Here's a poster from the good movie." Rina hit a key and I was staring at Dolores, looking apprehensive in close-up. She was strongly lighted from the left, the pale eyes drinking in the light and giving nothing back, while a sharp-featured Olivia Dupont, her hair drawn back in a bun so tight it looked painful, glared at the back of Dolly's head, one hand raised with the fingers curled into claws. Behind them was your basic spooky house, all dark shadows and curving stairs. Lurid, flame-edged type stretched across the image to inform us it was from HELL'S SISTERS, and below that was the cutline: *They were sisters IN MURDER!* Way down toward the bottom, in the kind of print mortgage lenders use for foreclosure conditions, it said, *Directed by Douglas Trent.*

"They weren't sisters in murder, you know," Rina said. "The awful one pushed the good one down the stairs once and tried to scare her to death about a hundred times. Not a bad movie, but they saved a fortune on light bulbs."

"Big film *noir* trick," Tyrone volunteered. "Keep the light low, you can fill the set with junk."

I looked around the room and said, "Who said that?"

"Gonna be a film student." Tyrone said. "Document racial injustice."

"You'll need a lot of film."

"Film," Tyrone said, although "scoffed" would be a more precise word. "Pixels. Drive space. Processing power."

I said, "Talent."

"You guys interested in this?" Rina said. "What *is* it about men?"

"I'm interested."

"Good. Because look." She hit a key hard enough to make it snap, and the screen was flooded with the words FALLING STAR, a headline from somewhere or other, the paper creased diagonally through the type. She hit the key again, and there was Dolly. She was a nightmare: her hair in knots, stalactites of mascara streaking her cheeks, her hands wrapped around the bars, her mouth wide, screaming at the photographers.

Rina said, "The end. Everywhere, this was everywhere. I mean, every paper in the country, seems like. And these, too." Dolores La Marr in an off-the-shoulder gown in some dark color, sitting looking baffled and dazed on a bed with its blankets and sheets rumpled suggestively and pulled back to the foot of the mattress and behind her, glaring at the camera, three unusually swarthy Guidos, one of whom I recognized as Johnny Stamponato.

"The photographers did that," I said. "Messed with the bed like that."

"Talent," Tyrone said. "Somebody had an eye."

"In the printer," Rina said, "there's a list of the people who were arrested. Two other women, four men. The men were all gangsters, according to what I found. One of the women was referred to as a showgirl, and the other one, it said 'Occupation unknown.' Although one paper in New York called her a 'party girl.'"

I said, "Ouch."

"What's funny is that someone bailed everyone else out. Like instantly. Even the girls. I mean, I can see somebody paying to get the guys out, but the girls? But they left her in overnight for the photographers."

"Setup," Tyrone said.

"That's it." I looked over the list of those arrested. Other than Stamponato's there were no familiar names. "Do you have stuff on these people?"

"In this," Rina tapped a beat-up three-ring notebook, with a picture on it of some kids who were apparently called The Jonas Brothers. They had been extensively restyled with facial hair, glasses, warts, and ugly hats in practically every color a marker comes in. She looked at me, looked back down at the notebook, and said, "From fourth grade. Disney dorks."

I picked it up and was rewarded by its heft. "Good work."

"Mostly junk," she said. "The guys have all got the same story, and most of them ended up floating in oil drums."

"First thing on the job questionnaire," Tyrone said. "*Do you float?*"

Flipping through the notebook, I backed up until the bed hit the backs of my knees. I sat. "What about the Kefauver Committee? The testimony?"

"There's a *ton* of it," Rina said. "But it's not cross-referenced, and it's not searchable, and it's not all in one place. Most of it's indexed by gangsters. They made her come in, Dolores La Marr, I mean, to testify, and it got almost as much publicity as the jail thing. Place was full of cameras. I found some video and stills of it, and she looks nervous, poor thing. Some of the real wonk sites say she went back again, but I haven't found anything about that. Go to the third tab in the notebook, there's a transcript."

I leafed through it. After the swearing in and all the formalities, they got right down to business.

Senator Durkee: Is it fair to say that you know John Roselli?

Miss La Marr: I don't know whether it's fair, but sure, I know Mr. Roselli.

Senator Durkee: How well would you say you know him?

Miss La Marr: Better than I know you, better than I know my milkman. How well compared to what? You got some kind of scale in mind?

Senator Kefauver: Miss La Marr, you will be civil while you're in this hearing room.

Miss La Marr: Well, how about him asking a straight question?

Senator Durkee: This might be a way to approach it, Miss La Marr. Do you call him Mr. Roselli or do you call him Johnny?

Miss La Marr: Johnny.

Senator Durkee: And Owney Madden?

Miss La Marr: What about him? You mean, do I call him Johnny, too?

Senator Durkee: Do you call him Owney?

Miss La Marr: Actually, I call him Killer. It's a nickname.

Senator Durkee: And a colorful one, too. Just to move things along, I'm going to read some names of people we believe to be your acquaintances. You just answer "first" or "last," depending on whether you call him by his first name or—

Miss La Marr: Yeah, yeah.

Senator Durkee: —or his last. Sam Giancana.

Miss La Marr: First.

Senator Durkee: Anthony Mostelli.

Miss La Marr: First. Tony, not Anthony.

Senator Durkee: Thank you for the clarification. Benjamin Siegel.

Miss La Marr: He's dead.

Senator Durkee: But when he was alive, you called him—

Miss La Marr: Benny.

Senator Durkee: Not Bugsy?

Miss La Marr: I didn't have enough life insurance to call him Bugsy.

Senator Durkee: Roberto Pigozzi.

Miss La Marr: Bobby Pig. That's what other people call him. I don't call him anything. I only met him that—that day.

Senator Durkee: You are referring to the day of your arrest?

Miss La Marr: Actually, it was the day before, when we landed in Vegas. I was arrested in the A.M. on the next day.

Senator Durkee: Noted. Thank you. You say "we" arrived in Vegas? Who else was with you?

Miss La Marr: You know who was with me.

Senator Durkee: For the record, Miss La Marr.

Miss La Marr: For the record, you know who was with me.

Senator Durkee: I must insist that—

Miss La Marr: I was with George.

Senator Durkee: George. That would be the film actor George Raft.

Miss La Marr: Good heavens, it would.

Senator Durkee: Mr. Raft is married, is he not?

Miss La Marr: For ages.

Senator Durkee: But you travel with him.

Miss La Marr: It was a plane, not a railroad car.

Senator Durkee: How many other passengers were aboard?

Miss La Marr: None.

Senator Durkee: Sounds intimate. You are, in a sense, intimate with all these men?

Miss La Marr: Not in any sense I recognize.

Senator Durkee: Intimate enough to fly to Las Vegas alone with one of them and to go to a party where the others were guests.

Miss La Marr: (Consults with counsel) George is a friend. The party was a party. Like a million parties.

Senator Durkee: And how many female guests were there?

Miss La Marr: You already know.

Senator Durkee: The booking records at the Las Vegas jail indicate three females.

Miss La Marr: Well, cops can usually tell the difference.

Senator Durkee: So there were only three women present. And four men.

Miss La Marr: Is that a question?

Senator Durkee: Not a very large party, was it?

Miss La Marr: What's that supposed to mean?

Senator Durkee: An intimate gathering. One and one-third men per girl.

Miss La Marr: It was a (expletive) party.

Senator Kefauver: Order. There will be order in this committee room. Young woman, you will watch your language.

Miss La Marr: Dirty minds deserve dirty language.

Senator Durkee: Do you know what Anthony Mostelli does?

Miss La Marr: He's in business.

Senator Durkee: What Sam Giancana does?

Miss La Marr: He's in business, too.

Senator Durkee: What Benjamin Siegel did?

Miss La Marr: He owned things. He owned the hotel we were all in.

Senator Durkee: So you're telling us that you're unaware that these men are, or were, all suspected of being engaged in organized crime?

Miss La Marr: Not now, I'm not.

Senator Kefauver: You're saying you're not aware?

Miss La Marr: I'm not unaware.

Senator Kefauver: Please make an attempt to be clear in your answers.

Miss La Marr: Tell him. Tell him not to ask his questions backward.

Senator Kefauver: Miss La Marr—

Miss La Marr: "So you're unaware"? How am I supposed to answer that? Jeez, get a new writer.

Senator Durkee: You are an actress, I believe.

Miss La Marr: You believe correctly.

Senator Durkee: The other two women at the party with you, the party of June 23, 1950 in the Flamingo Hotel in Las Vegas, are they actresses, too?

Miss La Marr: I don't remember. We didn't talk.

Senator Durkee: Would it jog your memory if I were to tell you their names? They are Miss Kelly Brannigan and Miss Ella Cowan.

Miss La Marr: Kelly's an actress, or supposed to be. I think Ella's a showgirl. In Vegas. They have a lot of showgirls in—

Senator Durkee: So. With only three women present, all either actresses or "supposed to be actresses" or "showgirls," and all the men accused criminals, how would you describe the tone of the party?

Miss La Marr: Refined. Regular Amy Vanderbilt get-together. I'd call it a *soiree*.

Senator Durkee: Please share with the committee the names of the men who were present.

Miss La Marr: You mean, before or after?

Senator Durkee: Before or after what?

Miss La Marr: The cops came. Before the cops came, or after they were there?

Senator Durkee: After the police—

Miss La Marr: Gee, there's a surprise. All the big guys left just before the—

Senator Durkee: With all due respect, everything you say here goes into the permanent record and must be verified. The men who were there when the police arrived were booked by the Las Vegas police. That means I have a source I can use to verify your answer.

Miss La Marr: Yeah, right. Probably nobody's paying you at all not to bring up the names of—

Senator Kefauver: Miss La Marr. You will confine your answers to the questions that are asked you.

"Boy," I said, closing the notebook. "She gave as good as she got. I'll finish reading this at home."

"She didn't stand a chance," Rina said.

"Bunch of old white men," Tyrone said. "Nothing's changed much."

"Okay." I got up. "You've earned your money. Try to find the rest of her testimony. Now where's Kathy, and what's she doing?"

"Out with Dick," Rina said. She hooked her hair with her fingers and combed it back behind her ears, something she did when she was nervous, although she wasn't aware of it. "Looking at houses."

"Excuse me?"

"She's looking at houses. He's got like five of them lined up for her."

"Has she inherited money? Is there oil in the back yard?"

"Dick's a realtor." Rina blinked rapidly and licked her lips and shot a glance at Tyrone. "He says she can make a lot of money if she sells this place and buys a cheaper one."

"In a fucking cow's hat," I said. "She is not selling—"

"It's hers, Daddy," Rina said.

"And let me guess. Good old Dick, he represents the sellers of the houses he's showing her. And he'll represent her if she sells this one. Double-dipping."

"Double-what?"

"He gets both commissions. Not even legal in eight states. How do you feel about it?"

"I hate it," Rina said. "This is my house. It's where I *live*."

"Different color eyes," Tyrone said. "Sees everything two ways at the same time. Smile at you, cut your throat, both of them look just fine."

I said, "Huh?"

"My mama. My mama doesn't like people with different color eyes."

"I'm with your mama. Tell Kathy to call me," I said to Rina.

She fanned herself with her hand, looking even younger than usual. "I'll *ask* her, not tell her. She's been waiting for you to get all crazy about this."

"Well," I said, "tell her she hasn't even *seen* crazy yet."

"Dick says he's the man who *owns* Tarzana," Rina had said as she walked me out. And in some respect, he did: As I zigzagged the streets, feeling my blood pressure mount into the Yosemite Sam zone, I saw sign after sign: FOR SALE BY RICHARD "DICK" STIVIK. A significant number of the signs also said, like a melancholy footnote, REDUCED. I had a feeling these weren't the houses old Dick was showing to Kathy.

Our house wasn't just walls and a ceiling on a piece of dirt. It *meant* something. I rebuilt half of it by hand. I dug part of the swimming pool before coming to my senses and hiring some nice guys who, in retrospect, were probably in the country without official blessing. Employing my special expertise, I replaced every door and window in the place, most of which would have yielded to a weak argument, with stuff even I'd have trouble opening, including a metal front door you could hit with a Humvee and still not break down.

It was the house Rina grew up in. Kathy and I had been happy there, as happy as we got, anyway, and that was pretty happy in the year or so after Rina was born.

I scribbled down addresses as I went, and then I pulled over and called Louie the Lost.

"I forgot this number," Louie said when he came on the line. "Been so long since I seen it, feels like I been reincarnated or something. You know, all wavy, like something you see underwater."

"And how are you?"

"Alice—you remember Alice?"

Until he made a memorable wrong turn one night, Louie the Lost had been one of LA's top getaway drivers, and the thing about getaway drivers is that there's no hurrying them. "Yes, Louie, I remember Alice."

"I'll tell her that. Hard to get a smile out of her lately, what with you not around. Anyway, she's gotten into pots."

I looked at my watch again. After six. "Pots."

"You know, *pots*. The things you put stuff in and they break when you drop them. Pots."

"Got it. Pots."

"There's more to pots than dried mud," Louie said. "Who'da thought?"

"I certainly wouldn't. *Pots*, you say, and I think *mud*."

"They throw them, did you know that? *Throwing pots*, you heard anyone say that?"

"I may have."

"Well, forget it, it's not what you'd think. You know, Alice tells me her women's group—she has a women's group—is gonna start throwing pots, I'm picturing these middle-aged—if most people live into their hundreds—these middle-aged ladies going to Builders Emporium or someplace, buying a bunch of pots and tossing them at each other. Like stress reduction or something: Tense? *Break some pots*. But nope, that's not—"

"Louie."

"—not it at all. Not even close. You wanna know what it really means?"

"Not particularly."

"Too bad. It's a dilly. You still at Valentine Shmalentine? You and Ronnie, I mean. Boy, if love can survive Valentine Shmalentine, it's built solid. Got *foundations*, you know?"

"And who else knows we're at Valentine Shmalentine?"

"This is a question with an accusation behind it. I can hear it."

"I ask because Irwin Dressler knows about it, too."

"Don't look at me," Louie said. "I ain't on Irwin Dressler's level. He wouldn't ask me for a minute if I owned time. He giving you problems?"

"Not really. He just knows things I'd rather he didn't."

"Like what?" Louie asked promptly.

"Oh, well," I said.

"Trust is the foundation of every relationship."

"Glad you brought that up," I said. "Seen Debbie Halstead lately?"

"She told you."

"She did."

"You gotta understand. . . ." His voice faded away, and then he swallowed.

"If you're waiting for me to complete that sentence, you're going to be on the phone a long time."

"Listen to you," he said. "Voice sounds good, you're breathing regular, you're okay. I knew she didn't want to do nothing to you."

"And I know you'll be safe, too."

"Say what?"

"When you start checking her out for me."

"Wait a minute."

"Think of it as a karmic debt. At least I'm not sending her to your door. Without so much as a tip-off call."

"I can explain all that." I waited for the explanation. Instead, he said, "What do you want to know about her?"

"Whatever you can get. Especially anything you can find about her early life—up to the time she popped up here, killing people. What did she do before, where's she from, was she ever married, that kind of stuff."

"Okay. I don't like it, but okay. Is that why you called me? To bust my balls?"

"Actually, I have a paying job for you. I need some plausibles. About six of them. With good IDs."

"We got plausibles coming out of our ears," Louie said. "The Internet has really put a crimp in con games, at least the ones you play in the flesh. Million-dollar accounts in Nigeria, phony AARP dues, they're doing great."

"Louie."

"Here's how bad it is. I know a few plausibles—you know one of them, too, Handkerchief Harrison—they're working as extras in the movies."

"Handkerchief is?" Handkerchief was a widely admired con man, among those who admire con men.

"On a cop show, if you can believe that. Irony is so cheap."

"Handkerchief would be great. He and about five others. Some of them in pairs, looking married."

"Who are they supposed to be?"

"House-hunters. Their paper has to look plausible enough to be taken seriously."

"Papers are rough these days."

"I'll get some credit histories from Stinky."

"If you can afford credit histories, you're not paying me enough."

"Nobody's going to spend anything. They'll be on loan. I just need them to stand up to a surface check."

"Stinky's not easy. Call me after you talk to him. No point in my wasting your money till you know you're covered."

A beep in my ear announced that someone else was on the line. "Call you back," I said. "After I talk to Stinky. But go to work on Debbie Halstead, okay?"

I disconnected and picked up the incoming call.

"Mr. Bender?" It was a thin, old voice, a little wavery.

"Yes. Who's this?"

"It's Pinky, Pinky Pinkerton." He coughed once, then said, "I've got your stuff."

I looked out the windshield and was surprised to see that it was dark. I'd been so fixated on the FOR SALE signs I didn't even remember turning on my headlights. "I'm in the Valley," I said. "It's, what? Six thirty? Traffic will be terrible."

Something brushed the mouthpiece of the phone and then there was a long pause. Finally, Pinkerton said, "Don't worry. I'll wait for you." He really did sound weak, years older than he had a few hours earlier.

"You seem tired," I said. "Why don't you go home, and I'll come tomorrow? In the morning sometime."

"No," he said. Then he said, "Wait a minute. I need some water."

Again the sound of something brushing the mouthpiece. When he came back, he said, "Now or never. I'm leaving on vacation tomorrow for—for two weeks. I don't want to leave this material here all that time."

"Edna can show it to—"

"No, she can't," he said, and his voice scaled up a few tones. "She's not going to be here, either. Nobody will, not for weeks. If you want to see it, come here now. I'll wait one hour, no more." He disconnected.

I sat there, listening to my car tick as the engine cooled, and took stock. Here I was, in the neighborhood I once thought I'd spend the rest of my life in, safely south of Ventura Boulevard in the gently expensive hills of Tarzana, once part of the giant Edgar Rice Burroughs estate. It suddenly felt to me like I had fallen a great distance from the certainties of that time and that place, and the prospect of driving all the way to Hollywood, at rush hour, on what was essentially a crook's errand for the über-crook himself, Irwin Dressler, suddenly became a journey of absolutely symbolic proportions. Every mile I traveled in the direction of Pinky Pinkerton and the evidence of Dolly La Marr's fall from grace represented flight in the wrong direction. What I wanted was here.

But, of course, what I wanted was five years ago, back before Kathy decided, probably correctly, that I was never going to change into a weekly-paycheck guy with a 401(k). What I wanted was this neighborhood with my family in it, intact and optimistic. What I wanted was this neighborhood with the streets as they were when I carried Rina along the sidewalks, riding on my shoulders. What I wanted was this neighborhood without all these fucking FOR SALE BY RICHARD "DICK" STIVIC signs in it. And that neighborhood didn't exist any more.

And if it had, I wouldn't have been welcome in it.

I started the car, bumped my forehead against the steering wheel several times, and headed south, toward Hollywood.

But here was the thing. I didn't like any of it.

I didn't like the errand, sure, but I *really* didn't like the way Pinkerton had sounded, like someone who'd just stopped crying. I didn't like the quaver in his voice. I didn't like the sudden vacations.

I didn't like the sound of something covering the mouthpiece.

And I liked it all a little less with every mile I drove.

It was rush hour, but most of the traffic was coming at me, heading north out of LA toward the Valley's bedrooms, not going into town. I was making pretty good time, as I always do when I'm heading someplace I don't want to go, so I took the Woodman offramp and went down to Ventura, choosing the more leisurely route. Looking for a long line of red lights.

But, of course, red lights are like cops: when you need them, they're not around. I felt like the president, one light after another obediently going green and bowing down in front of me as I proceeded, at a stately thirty-five miles per hour, toward the declining ZIP codes of Hollywood. I couldn't even find a traffic jam in the Cahuenga Pass, which is usually denser than the molecular structure of lead. Nope, whistled right up the hill and back down again, for the first time in memory not getting stuck long enough to have a birthday or two at the stoplight that marks the Hollywood Bowl.

So I was well within the allotted sixty minutes when I turned left on Hollywood Boulevard, my dimming hopes pinned to the very good chance that there wouldn't be a parking space within miles. And there probably wasn't until the very moment that I hoped I wouldn't find one, but precisely then, not thirty feet from the entrance to the Tower, someone at the curb started the turn indicator ticking and pulled out in front of me, leaving a yawning space. I checked the nearest sign: legal at this hour. I had almost no change, but the meter had more than an hour left on it.

Fate can really be pushy at times.

At 7:23, I shoved open the door to the half-lit lobby. One of the elevators had been taken out of service, dark and open behind a sign announcing it would be available again at seven the next morning. I looked at the other elevator, thought for a second, and went to the far end of the lobby and took the stairs.

A lot of stairs. My legs were leaden by the time I reached the twelfth floor, where I stopped on the landing and let myself breathe heavily before I opened the door. The dim hallway tapered away in front of me, in accordance with the laws of perspective. It took me a moment to assemble the floor plan in my mind: the offices radiated off both sides of a U-shaped hallway, with the stairs at one terminal of the U and the elevator at the other. There were offices in the center of the U, so the elevator wasn't visible to me and—I thought, with an odd sort of easing in my chest—I wasn't visible from the elevator. Or to anyone who might be watching the elevator.

Pinky's office had been the last door in the hallway leading away from the elevator, the numbers rising as the elevator receded. So if a visitor wanted an office with a number higher than Pinky's he or she would have passed the door that opened into Edna's lair and turned left along the bottom of the U to keep going. That meant that I had to take the hallway in front of me and follow the turn to the right. When I got to the end of the short hall at the bottom of the U, I'd be looking at Pinky's door.

So I did exactly that, moving on the balls of my feet and making about as much noise as the average fog. As far as I could tell, the offices I passed were all empty. Every other ceiling light in the hallway was off, and no strips of light gleamed beneath the office doors. Just for the hell of it, I tapped on one, about halfway along the corridor, which listed itself on a laser-printed sign as FANFARE MAIL SERVICE, probably a one- or two-person outfit that responded to fan mail. It was that kind of building, catering to the disposable fringes of show business. No one answered, and the door was locked. So was the next, and the next.

When Pinky's door came into sight I stopped, for two reasons. First, because my body declined to carry me any further, and second, because the door was ajar.

In detective novels, doors that are ajar *always* precede the discovery of a body. If fictional detectives took the time to read detective fiction, the moment a door swung open at their touch, they'd be in full retreat all the way to the street, not even pausing to straighten their fedoras.

Of course, I wasn't fictional, so the rule didn't apply. Still, I'd be lying if I said that the door, gaping open a couple of inches like that, didn't give me pause. In fact, it gave me about five minutes' worth of pause, which is quite a long pause for someone who's standing in a boring, empty hallway and listing to his heart thump irregularly in his ears.

At first, it looked to me like the office was dark, open door or not, but by using the old trick of looking past it, to the right, I could see that it actually wasn't. If I'd been forced to explain the skim-milk-pale light that peeked around the straight, hard edge of the door, I'd have theorized that the lights in Edna's room were off, but at least one light was burning in Pinky's inner sanctum. Which made sense, of course: He would have sent Edna home to whatever stone tower she curled up in after hours, and he'd be sitting there, glancing impatiently at his watch.

Speaking of which.

About six minutes remained of the hour he'd given me. It seemed like a very good idea, if he was going to come out at the end of that hour, to wait for him. As opposed, I mean, to going through that door. So I leaned against the wall to my right and waited.

The building creaked and settled around me, thousands of tons of iron and cement tucking itself away for the night. At the end of Pinky's corridor, the one functioning elevator groaned upward, sending me into full scurry mode backward toward the stairs, but it kept on going, and about a minute later, it went down again, with less protest. Somewhere behind me a phone rang for a very long time. Just as it stopped, the building's air circulation system filled its giant tin lungs and blew at me, making a *whoosh* that sent me twelve or fourteen inches into the air. The moment my feet hit the tile, the phone began to ring once more.

Outside, down on the street, neon was burning, cars were honking, people were moving along the sidewalks, staring at the freaks or being stared at by the straights. Some of them were probably chemically deranged, others certifiably schizophrenic, and an improbable percentage of them, in this richest country in the world, were undoubtedly hungry. I would have traded places with any of them.

At ten minutes past the hour, with no sign of Pinky, I took the prudent, if not the boldest, course. I removed my left shoe, stepped away from the wall to get a better angle, lifted my left leg for the windup, and let fly, at a respectable sixty-five miles an hour or so, at Pinky's door.

The shoe hit with a loud bang, and the door opened about four inches, snagged on something that slowed it for an instant, and then kept opening, having broken through whatever had been—

Bright light, the kind of hot white light that tells people in nuclear-war movies that they haven't got the time they need to get close enough to their asses to kiss them goodbye, and then a whole NFL line of sound, six 300-pound linemen wide, muscled itself at me, turning my ears inside out and shoving me back as the door snapped shut again, so hard that it broke in half lengthways and the side without hinges on it arced slowly through the air at me. Or maybe it wasn't all that slow, because a corner of it caught me in the ribcage and put me on my butt on the cold, hard linoleum.

A wall of smoke charged and then surrounded me, and I sat there, hacking and coughing in a cloud of dust and asbestos and God knew what else, until I rolled away and crawled, as fast as I could, around the far corner, the one that led back down to the stairs. Then I rested my back against the wall and sat there, choking and sneezing and retching as my ears continued to vibrate like the world's biggest tympani. A few minutes passed, during which two things did not happen: there was not another explosion, and no alarm began to shrill.

Nor did I hear the elevator coming back up or footfalls on the stairs. Those two things, I realized later, probably meant only that I was deaf, but I was sufficiently rattled at the time that they reassured me enough to get to my feet, grab a breath of relatively nonpoisonous air, and head at a dead run for Pinky's office.

Edna's desk was resting on end, leaning against the wall at a seventy-degree angle with its center drawer lolling open like a dog's tongue. The desk was partially covered in a snowy drift I guessed had erupted from the cushions of the two old leather chairs, now mostly scraps. The hundreds of little white cards on the floor had been sprung from Edna's Rolodex.

Belatedly, the fire sprinklers awoke to the situation and it began to rain.

Edna was not under the desk, nor was she recognizable in any of the fragments of various substances pasted around the office by the explosion. Wiping water from my face, I opened the door to Pinky's office, which was closed tight. It opened out, into the reception area, and it had undoubtedly been blown closed in the explosion.

Pinky was in his chair, leaning forward, resting his head on his desk. The door had spared the office most of the force of the blast, but that couldn't have mattered much to Pinky. The thick, dark pool of blood covering the desk, now being diluted by the water pouring from the sprinklers, made it pretty clear that his throat had been cut.

I'm normally an easy queasy, but the explosion had probably desensitized me, because I knelt beside his chair so I could make sure that I'd guessed correctly. I had, and whoever did it had been very strong or very angry, or both, because the slash was uselessly, horribly deep. He had been such a weak little man.

There were no boxes of files in the room.

On the way out, barely knowing I was doing it, I grabbed some of the papers from the floor and stuffed them into my pants, then headed for the stairs. I was all the way down to street level, filthy and dripping, and out through the doors and on the way to my car and drawing no more than the usual quota of interested glances, before I heard any sirens. And suddenly there were red lights bouncing off everything, so they'd been closer than I thought. Opening the door of my car, I found myself in the center of a peculiar bell of silence for such a busy boulevard and realized I was virtually deaf.

For the moment, it felt like a blessing.

15

Stunned and Numb

As luck would have it, when my hearing came back, the radio was playing "Stairway to Heaven."

I read somewhere that "Stairway to Heaven" has been played more than three million times on the radio, with every million plays representing about 50,000 broadcast hours, or more than 5.8 years of continuous Led Zep. Multiply that by three, and you've got a total of 17.4 years of nonstop "Stairway to Heaven." It just *seems* longer.

I know it's a minor detail, but I'd be more likely to believe in a God who participates in our daily life if one of His infinite self-assigned tasks was to keep count on the number of times a song has been played, and when that number exceeds reason, to incinerate instantly the disk jockey who's just put it on. Not only would we be spared another hearing of "The Wind Beneath My Wings," but there would be a much higher turnover among disk jockeys, and wouldn't that be nice?

Time to turn the radio off. Time to pull over. Time to stop taking refuge in the world's irritants and focus on what had just happened.

The person who told me about Pinky Pinkerton had been Doug Trent. Hard to see a reason why Trent would send me to

Pinky and then kill him so he couldn't talk to me. The only other person who knew I'd even heard the name was Irwin Dressler, for whom I had outlined my day over the phone that morning.

Hmm. Irwin Dressler.

Nope. Same objection: why hire me to answer a question and then kill someone who might give me part of the answer?

Of course, Pinky wasn't the only intended victim. *I'd* been on someone's mind, too. Someone had wanted me to come through that door. If I hadn't thrown that—

Shoe.

Not until that moment, sitting in my car on a residential street in North Hollywood, did I realize I was wearing only one shoe. I'd been so stunned and numb that I hadn't even noticed it. I'd limped down Hollywood Boulevard, dripping wet and covered in carcinogens, wearing a single shoe. A hundred people must have seen me.

On the other hand, it *was* Hollywood Boulevard.

But that was nit-picking, just a delaying mechanism to postpone the real issue. The issue was not whether anyone had noticed me on Hollywood Boulevard. The issue was almost infinitely more serious than that.

The crook's first reaction, our most ingrained reflex, is to ask ourselves: *Does this implicate me?* And I'm ashamed to say that I stopped thinking about Pinky Pinkerton and his undoubtedly terrifying and painful death in order to devote full attention to my missing shoe.

It was a cheap shoe, probably made in China, since everything else is. I'd bought it at a shoe outlet in Marina del Rey, a gigantic barn filled with off-brand, anonymous footwear. Unlike some *mode du jour* denizens of Hollywood, I wore socks, although I wasn't dumb enough to believe that DNA couldn't push its treacherous little fingerprints through a pair of socks.

One shoe at a murder scene was going to attract a certain amount of attention. Even Deputy Dawg would count the shoes on Pinky's feet and wonder where the third one came from and whom it belonged to, and most LA Homicide detectives aren't Deputy Dawg.

My DNA isn't on file anywhere that I know of, although that can be rectified in ten seconds by a cop with a search warrant and a Q-Tip.

Also, speaking of fingerprints, a shoe undoubtedly will take and hold one.

And, of course, Doug Trent had sent me to Pinky. When this story broke tomorrow, he'd open the paper and reach for the phone.

I was a very good crook. It's a point of pride with me. In a career that had begun twenty-two years earlier, when at fifteen I broke into the house of the man next door and superglued every single thing he owned in place (I had good reason), I had never been as exposed as I was right now. And this wasn't some crap burglary. This was *el supremo*, the pinnacle, the pimento in the Big Olive of crime. This was premeditated murder.

Little me.

Breathing whenever I remembered to, I took Lankershim north until I came to a booming shopping center, one of the ones the recession had somehow missed. The lights in the stores were winking out right on time, at 8:30. There were enough cars rolling through the parking lot that I didn't feel conspicuous as I eased around the front of the complex and cruised behind it to a Dumpster the size of an ocean liner. As an efficient criminal, I keep track of the trash pickup dates for about a dozen commercial locations, and I knew that this whopper would be emptied tomorrow in the blue light of dawn. I drove aimlessly past the container, looking for a surveillance camera without seeing one. I pulled around the corner anyway and put on a billed cap, yanking it low over my eyes. Keeping my face down and my shoulders hunched to give myself an oldster walk, I went to the Dumpster, tossed the shoe in, and drove off. My stomach muscles were on *vibrate*, and I could see my fingers on the steering wheel trembling.

As I traveled the ugly, too-familiar streets, an inevitable sequence of events kept running through my head in high definition. Cops find shoe. Story appears in paper. Doug Trent calls cops to say he sent me to Pinky. Edna remembers me. I'm so all over that shoe I might have been licking it for a month.

I'm up to my eyes in trouble.

Rina. Kathy. Ronnie. Rina again. One cheap shoe could end everything. I mean, they'd all recover eventually, but Rina—how could I do that to Rina? Kathy was finished with me, dallying with duck hunters and—Jesus!—realtors, and Ronnie and I were burning bright, but the roots, to mix a metaphor, were still shallow. But *Rina*. Rina's father fingered as a murderer. The betrayal of trust. The kids in her school.

This could *not* happen.

I drove toward Canoga Park, toward Valentine Shmalentine and Ronnie, trying to figure out what, if anything, I could do to prevent it.

I pulled into one of the few open parking spaces—the full lot a testimonial to the enduring appeal of adultery—and worked out of my pocket the wet wad of papers I'd snatched off the floor in Edna's waiting room. The first thing I saw as I separated them was a business card for EDNA FRAYNE, EXECUTIVE ASSOCIATE, whatever that meant. There was a cluster of phone numbers at the bottom. I was worrying the other sheets apart when my cell phone rang, instantly tying my innards into a large, uneven knot. I didn't recognize the number, but I took a deep breath and answered anyway.

"I haven't heard from you," a woman said.

"Who is—oh, Debbie. No. No, you haven't." This was just exactly what I needed.

"Is there a reason you'd like to share with me?"

"Well, I doubt you've got time."

"Come on, Junior. I work when I work, I make a lot of money, and in between I have nothing but time. Tell Debbie about it. So she doesn't think you're just blowing her off."

"Fine, fine." I tried to think of something persuasive and failed to find anything more persuasive than the truth. "Okay, here goes. Through no fault of mine, which is to say I haven't done anything wrong—"

"Please."

"Well, I haven't done anything *new*. Anyway, I think I'm just a few hours away from a first-degree murder charge."

She whistled, which is something few women do. "I can see where that might get your attention."

"I'm coming to realize that I lack the skills to survive being suspected of murder."

Headlights in my rear-view mirror drew my attention. The car, a distinctively clunky silhouette, glided past me and pulled into a spot four or five away.

"If it's any comfort," she said, "most of the people who develop those skills don't get to practice them very long. You really didn't do it?"

I said, "Of course not," hearing the hurt feelings in my tone. I'd shot and killed one person some time ago, but that was letting him off easy, all things considered, and it had never cost me a moment's sleep.

"Well, listen," Debbie said. "Don't take this wrong. I wouldn't make this offer for just anybody, but is there someone I can take out for you? As a freebie? Someone the cops need to make the case?"

The door to my car opened, and Ronnie leaned in and smiled at me, widened her eyes at my disheveled state, and then got in, sitting as far away as the seat would let her.

"That's really sweet of you," I said, genuinely touched. "No one has ever offered to do that for me."

Ronnie raised her eyebrows and leaned toward me just enough to hear the other end of the conversation.

"Like I said, don't take it wrong," Debbie said. "It's not a pass or anything. I really liked Ronnie, although I think she's too pretty for you."

"She is," Ronnie said.

"She's there?" The temperature on the other end of the line dropped about twenty degrees. "She heard my offer?"

"No." I raised my index finger to my lips and gave Ronnie the big scary eye. She did not look terrified, although she did pinch her nose closed and wave air at me. "I'm in my car, and she just got in a second ago."

"Well, if you want to discuss this, call me back when you're alone."

"No, I mean, listen, this is a very generous offer, but I couldn't possibly take you up on it. I mean, how in the world would I repay it?"

"Don't worry. Just think about it. How about this? Would you feel safer if I sort of hung around for a little bit? Invisibly?"

"Actually—and don't take offense at this—until the moment you said that, I couldn't think of anything that might make me more nervous than I already am, but you've managed to do it."

"Up to you. Well, the offer stands. And don't tell Ronnie about it."

"Of course not," I said, ringing off. I checked to make sure the phone was dead and said, "Debbie just offered to kill somebody for me. For free."

Ronnie's eyebrows went up. "Anybody at all?"

"Why? You got someone in mind?"

"Lot of people. But she didn't make the offer to me, did she? And that brings me to the obvious question. Why did she make it to you? And who dragged you through a pile of burning tires?"

So I told her.

One of the things I'm coming to love—yes, I suppose that's the word—about Veronica Bigelow is that her first reaction to practically every problem is, "What can we do about it?" And her second reaction is to start proposing solutions. Add those traits and her unshakeable nerves to a not-unprepossessing physical appearance, culminating in a sort of genetic dessert topping—the finest, brightest, goldest hair I've ever seen—and you've got someone it's easy to look at for long periods of time without the need to rest your eyes. Add the steel under the skin, and she's precisely the kind of woman I thought would never put up with me.

So, since I was still emotionally and intellectually stuck in neutral and she was Ronnie, it was her plan we acted upon. At ten forty that night, after I'd showered and changed, she putt-putted out of Valentine Shmalentine in her little Hupmobile or whatever it was. I gave it about a minute to let some traffic glide past and then pulled out behind her with my ears still popping from time to time, trying to keep one eye on her and the other on my rearview mirror, looking like Jean-Paul Sartre and searching for a tail on either or both of us.

There was only a slight chance that anyone would be there, but I had to play find-the-watcher anyway, just in case whoever had tried to kill me back at Pinky's office knew about Valentine Shmalentine. It seemed improbable. A bomb is an indiscreet way to kill someone, and most murderers, given the choice, will go for something a bit lower-profile. These guys hadn't, and to me that argued that they didn't know where to find me.

Still, I couldn't expect that state of affairs to last forever, so Valentine Shmalentine was now a memory, and not a very fond memory at that, and Ronnie was returning to the safe, sunny little apartment she'd vacated in West Hollywood to join me in the motel-of-the-month lifestyle I'd thought would keep me safe.

Two miles later I'd decided there was no one behind her, no one behind me. We had the cell phones on and connected, and I directed her up to Ventura and then across it, sending her south of the boulevard to make a turn that would take her parallel to it while I stayed on Ventura. I cruised along until I pulled over a few parking spaces before the street I'd just told her to take back down. No car pulled to a stop behind me, and when she came through the light and made her right, toward LA, she wasn't towing anyone.

"You're okay," I said. "I'll take a different route and drive by your apartment in about an hour. If everything's all right, turn on the light above your door."

"I don't know," Ronnie said. "I don't know why I have such rotten taste in men. Car thieves, drug dealers, British journalists, and now whatever you are."

"I am sort of indefinable," I said.

"You certainly are. Are you sure you wouldn't like to park about half a mile away and come in and stay with me? Danger makes me feel sexy."

"That probably explains the taste in men you were just—"

"You think? Huh. Probably does. Maybe I should see a therapist."

"If you do, make up some different names."

"Doctors can't tell."

"Fine. Then just change *my* name. For all I care, you can show him pictures of the others."

"Think about it. Coming by, I mean."

"Nope. The point right now is to keep me away from you."

"You expect me to waste the way I'm feeling?"

I said, "I'm sure you'll find something."

"I will. And I won't have to listen to it snore, either."

She hung up, and I made the call I'd been thinking about for more than an hour. I called Dolores La Marr.

And got no answer.

16
Black Lake

In the dream, the leaves she loved so much—leaves of that pale, tender shade of spring green thrown off by the sound of strings in their high register—were brushing her cheek, soft as cobwebs. In the dream, she turned her face to them, her young, beautiful face, and let the leaves caress her, let their green light wash over her. In her dream, she laughed.

The leaves scratched her.

She opened her eyes. The only light came through the big window across the room from the bed, just junk light, a stew of colors from the city. She'd forgotten to close the blackout curtains. The wine slammed in her head. Her mouth tasted sour.

The touch, soft as moving air.

She said, "Anna?"

There was no response except a sudden vision—almost projected on the darkness—of herself, on a narrow beach ringing a black lake, the lake full not of water but a thick, sticky, liquid terror, a deep hole filled with fear. From where she stood on the beach, the lake was to her left, the direction, in the room, where the touch had come from. Where, she thought, Anna was.

"What is it?" She realized she was whispering. She looked

around the room, identifying the vague shapes she knew: the dresser, the darker rectangle of the open closet door, the table with the big flatscreen television on it. The glimmer Anna sometimes gave off was nowhere to be seen, but if Anna wasn't here, where was the fear coming from? She reached for the clock on the table, touched its top, and got a cold blue glare: 9:24.

She'd been asleep a little more than an hour, and she hadn't undressed or gotten under the covers. *Got to watch the drinking,* she thought, *one bottle is more than—*

A sound, not from the left, but from the right, the direction of the living room, at the other end of the hallway that led to her bedroom. Dolly felt her mouth go dry.

It wasn't much of a sound, but she knew what it was: one of the floorboards in the living room. The building was around ninety years old, and wooden floors will develop creaks after all that time. She supposed, Dolly did, that she had a mental map of every creaking board in the entire—

Another noise, the masticating sound of something crunching, as though someone was stepping on a wad of paper or popcorn or something harder, but still brittle enough to be crushed underfoot. One, and then two.

Working against her weight, this weight she'd carried for years and *still* hadn't grown accustomed to, she pulled herself to a sitting position and invested every bit of her energy in listening. From the left, at the very threshold of hearing, there was a sort of frantic papery/whispery sound, one of the things she associated with Anna.

But, maybe, just maybe, Anna wasn't real. The sounds in the living room—here came another one, another *crunch,* a sound like old dried bones being pulverized beneath a boot— were real.

Someone
was
out
there.

She turned herself slowly, muffling a grunt of effort as she swung the big, half-useless legs over the side of the bed. How slender, how strong those legs had been, how they'd carried her across the brightly lighted space in front of the cameras, across the dance floors in those envy-filled nightclubs as she whirled. How they'd lifted her, effortlessly, as she flew up the steps to her Hancock Park apartment, the one place she'd been happy, before everything went away.

How they'd shone in silk stockings.

Well, they were no good to her now. Another papery whisper from Anna, if Anna existed, and Dolly saw, in her mind's eye, that burglar whom Winnie had sent, whatever his name had been, standing in her pantry, holding a wine bottle like a club. She reached out and found the bottle she'd emptied and pulled it across the table toward her so she could grab it by the neck once she was up. You could do a lot of damage with a wine bottle, she thought, or someone else thought and sent it to her. Satisfied that she could locate the bottle one-handed, she swung her hand through the air, searching for the aluminum edge of the walker.

She went an inch too far.

The sound it made hitting the wooden floor almost split her head open. And even so, over it, she could hear that frantic dry-grass whisper from Anna, cutting through the noise as though the whisper was being made far inside her ear. Folding herself forward, flailing frantically above the floor for the fallen walker, she heard a deep growl from the living room and then slow, heavy footsteps, the sound rolling down the hallway and through the door in a dark, choking cloud of a red she'd never seen before, a thick, arterial, almost fragrant red, and it enveloped her and cushioned her as the sounds came closer and the shape appeared in the doorway, and it seemed to her for just a moment (almost the last moment) that the cloud even, *somehow*, lessened the force of the first, massive blow.

17

The Aftermath of Tiny Explosions

I was stinking with sweat by the time the elevator doors opened.
For once, I'd skipped all the evasive maneuvers, driving as fast
as I could without getting pulled over, ignoring the usual switch-
backs, and—for the first time ever—dropping directly down
the driveway of the Wedgwood instead of using the entryway
around the corner. When the elevator doors opened, I called
up to the microphone in the ceiling to say I'd need the key to
Miss La Marr's place on the ninth floor, but halfway through the
sentence, I saw it. It was hanging there, right where the button
would have been if a key weren't required.

I backed out of the elevator as though the key had been a six-
pound black widow and went back to the car and popped the
trunk. I'm an optimist in spite of a lifetime of evidence to prove
that living optimistically is likely to be as disappointing as taking
astrological advice, so I never carry a gun until I realize too late
that the moment calls for one. This moment was no exception,
but under the trunk lining, fastened to the underside in a Velcro
sheath, was a very slender and very sharp knife, its handle flat
and not much thicker than a couple of silver dollars. I palmed it,
point up my sleeve so it wouldn't be visible to anyone watching
the closed-circuit feed, and went back into the elevator. I said,

"Hi, again, going straight up," and twisted the key, expecting to hear something authoritative in an Korean accent.

But I didn't get it. What I got was an elastically prolonged elevator ride, its length stretched out by my anxiety, past floor after floor until the car shuddered to a stop, did the terrifying little three-inch downward plunge it always offers up when it reaches its destination, and then hung there motionless until the doors reached an agreement to slide apart, revealing Dolores La Marr's Hollywood-Gothic entry hall.

The precise moment I stepped out of the elevator, it hit me: a cold wet sheet of something weightless and invisible and without any texture at all, just chilled, distilled, heart-clutching *anguish*. Just a shriek of the nerves, a sense of tragedy on a par with the final, rending moments of a Greek play, when the malice of the Fates is finally revealed and every illusion that makes life worthwhile is stripped away.

Anguish that constricted my chest, almost made it hard to breathe.

Without willing it, I flailed at the air with my arms, trying to repel whatever it was and hoping to create an empty space around me, the way I had tried to wave away the smoke in that office hallway earlier in the evening. I had a sense of the presence, whatever it was, receding, retreating a bit: letting go of me, but not going far. The terror and sadness remained.

I stepped back into the elevator, and instantly it all stopped, as sudden and complete as a film cut. I'd been *there*, now I was *here*. I stood there, my heart doing tympani triplets from the experience, but it was memory now, not present-tense. I was—the only word I could find—*alone*. Whatever that was, it couldn't follow me out of the apartment.

The entry hall yawned in front of me, still dusty, still dominated by the elephant's foot and the peacock feathers, something left over from a William Powell or Carole Lombard movie. Sort of silly, sort of saddening, sort of—

Something made a wet sound, a bit like a cough underwater. Just once.

I got goosebumps in places I didn't know I could get goosebumps. I backed up so fast I hit the rear wall of the elevator, and the doors chose that precise moment to begin to slide closed. Without a moment's thought, I jumped forward and pushed them open again.

They opened, bounced a little, and then stayed open. It felt *patient* to me. It seemed to be saying, *Up to you, buddy. We tried.*

I said, "Fuck this," and stepped back into the apartment.

Immediately the cold sheet was back, but this time I had the feeling it was maintaining a distance of a few inches, as though it knew it would chase me off if it wrapped itself around me again. I had the notion of the scream you don't hear, someone's last shrill of pain and terror, wasted on the far side of a thick wall, not reaching another human ear.

I said, very quietly, "*Anna?*"

And the space around me seemed to clear, as though some vibration on a barely perceptible wavelength had ceased, or rather, been damped down. I felt free to move, so I stepped farther into the apartment, and the elevator doors snicked closed behind me, and I figured, *Okay, like it or not, I'm in,* and headed down the hall, calling out "Miss La Marr?"

Halfway down, I saw little spots of white on the gleaming black floor in the living room—not very big, irregularly shaped, like the aftermath of tiny explosions, fuzzy little galaxies seen from millions of light-years away. I slowed and stopped calling out. For the second time that night, I took off a shoe, but this time I took off both of them.

From where I stood, not yet out of the hallway, I was looking across the living room at Dolores La Marr's bookshelves. To my right, but not visible to me, the living room stretched off to the window facing downtown, with the couch, table and chair in front of it. That end of the room opened onto the dining room with its big, empty, dusty table and then the kitchen and the cold pantry. In the part of the living room to the left of where I stood, the other hallway led to the bedrooms and bathrooms and closets.

I'd never been in the part of the apartment to the left of the entry hall, but I've burgled enough floor plans to make it easy to visualize the area: the biggest bedroom, the one La Marr used, at the far end of the hall with its own bathroom, and two other bedrooms and a second bathroom opening onto the hall from both left and right.

Doors, I thought, I'd just as soon not pass in front of.

Operating on habit, I had slowed my breathing, making it as noiseless as breathing can be. I put the shoes down very quietly, wrapped my right hand around the hilt of the thin, razor-sharp knife, and slid my stocking feet over the smooth floor toward the living room. I was dreading a sound that would tell me I wasn't alone, but most of all I was dreading a repeat of that terrible wet noise.

At the end of the hallway I chose the right wall, put my shoulder against it, and looked quickly into the end of the room where the couch and window were. Nothing except Los Angeles, gaily glittering away as though nothing bad had just happened.

I *knew* something bad had just happened. I think I would have known it even without the anguish-saturated fog that had clung to me the moment I stepped off the elevator. I pushed all of that away, plus all the emotion that went with it, busying myself by looking toward the bookshelf. Everything seemed to be there, even the fake book with all the money in it.

I stepped into the room and turned, looking down the hall-way toward the bedrooms. The lights in the hall were out, although light from the living room bled partway down it, mak-ing the floor gleam and setting off the black rectangle of the open door at the far end of the hall. I felt another sharp-winged flutter of anguish, but then it left me alone.

The little splashes of powder on the floor weren't completely white. I leaned forward and saw tiny bits of blue, irregular little gray-blue tatters, like flakes of lizard skin. And then I knew what they were, and all the hope I'd been trying to muster drained away. I stood absolutely still, listening as I've learned to listen in a house I'm not certain is empty, and knowing that there was something terrible in one direction and something almost as bad in the other. I chose the less-bad first. I kept my right arm loose with the elbow crooked slightly, the hand with the knife tilted upward, at the right angle—about seventy degrees—to slip beneath the rib cage, and I headed for the kitchen.

But it wasn't necessary to go all the way, because the dining room floor was littered with empty prescription bottles, two or three of them smashed into the hardwood and dragged over it, hard enough to leave a pattern of gouges. Just to make sure, I went on through, into the kitchen, stepping around the shards of a broken glass glistening in a pool of water in the center of the floor, and continued to the open door of the cold pantry. The floor in there was inches deep in loose cereal from the carton, now torn to scraps, that had hidden the bottles of Lunesta. All of which were gone.

I was seeing fury. A plan interrupted. The cereal box shred-ded, the glass shattered. The bottles tossed and stamped on, the remaining pills crushed to dust.

Which left me with nothing to do except the thing I dreaded. I was reasonably sure I was alone in the apartment now, and I moved quickly and quietly back out through the dining room and down the length of the living room to the other hallway, threading my way through the splotches of white powder. Out of the habit of caution, I stood at the entry to the hallway, barely breathing, for a count of one hundred, and then I went straight down the hall to the door at the end and slid my hand over the wall until I hit the light switch. At the same time, I kicked the door against the wall as hard as I could, just in case.

The sound seemed to drive the dark away, seemed to bring into existence and solidify the dreadful display in front of me.

I had to close my eyes.

It must have been twenty or thirty seconds before I could force them open again. The bed, high, wide, canopied, was an abattoir. I couldn't look at Dolores La Marr for more than a second or two, but when I did, my heart stopped. On the pillow, only a few inches from the ravaged face, was the headset she'd been wearing. The wet sound I'd heard when I came in—

I forced myself across the room and gently took the wrist dangling off the end of the bed, silently asking permission. Still warm, still supple. No pulse. Closing my eyes again, I leaned down, close enough to her to put my ear a few inches from her mouth.

She wasn't breathing.

Straightening up, I felt a surge of the purest, whitest, coldest rage. It almost crumpled me. Whatever had happened in 1950, bad as it had been, hadn't closed the books. The books had been closed tonight. Whatever it was that had destroyed Wanda Altshuler/Dolores La Marr so ruthlessly, way back then, had been patiently waiting until it felt that it was necessary to finish the job.

It was still out there. And by accepting Irwin Dressler's assignment, I had brought it back to life.

Which meant that, as far as I was concerned, the books weren't closed. They wouldn't be closed until I closed them, and I would do that, no matter who I had to cross.

I pulled my shirttail loose and backtracked through the place, using the shirt to wipe everything I could remember having touched. Then I went into the hall and peeled my socks off, putting my bare feet directly into my shoes without letting them touch the floor. I slipped my hands into the socks and went back into the living room, where I pulled the book full of money off the shelf and popped it open. There was just enough room for four of the *netsuke*, and I wedged the others into my pockets.

On the way down, I remembered the headset. There *must* have been time for her to scream. I stopped the elevator at the lobby level. One look at the floor was all it took: footprints in the distinctive brownish red of drying blood, leading away from the room where the guards were stationed. Avoiding the bloody spots, I used my shirttail to pull the door open and found myself looking down at the man I'd thought of as Pyongyang. His throat had been cut. He was on his side, one hand stretched straight up, as though he'd hoped something might reach down and take his hand and snatch him to safety.

Two throat-cuttings in one night. People who use knives are different than you and me.

Down in the garage, moving with slow deliberation and keeping my mind as still as possible, I returned the knife to its hiding place and put the book full of money into the trunk. Then I powered up the driveway, made a right and then another. The street with the Nox on it led me down to Olympic, and I sat there for all of three or four seconds before turning right, west, toward Bel Air.

WHO WE WEREN'T

Part
Four

Part
Four

18

A Knife to the Ivory

Irwin Dressler looked one hundred and fifty years old. All the frailty, all the vagueness, all the fretfulness, all the tremors—all the palsies and neural misfires and cosmetic damage he'd been holding at bay all these years—had joined forces and knocked him sideways. He sat on the enormous couch, folded forward over another bright pair of golf slacks, hugging himself tightly and rocking back and forth like someone who is keening.

He said, "But." It was the fourth or fifth time he'd said it.

Tuffy stared at him from the doorway to the dining room, his forehead so furrowed he looked like a Basset Hound. He had his hands jammed in his pockets with his fists balled up, the picture of helpless concern. Babe was rattling things around in the kitchen, whipping up something or other that, from the sound of it, involved pans and glasses.

"It happened between seven-forty-five and ten," I said. "Probably closer to ten, because she was alive when I went in, just alive enough to make one sound that I heard over the speakers. You know about the speakers?" He didn't respond, and I said, "Do you know about—"

Dressler waved me away and said, "Junior—" It was a warning.

"No," I said. "With all due respect, Mr. Dressler—Irwin— we're at a new stage in our relationship. Tonight I've almost been killed, I've put myself in the frame for a murder charge, and I've seen something I'll never forget, even if I—if I live longer than you have. I'm not just on a case any more."

"No," Dressler said, sounding like he was being strangled. "What are you on?"

"A fucking crusade. I am personally going to deal somebody the big one, and I hope I get to do it in a really unpleasant fashion."

"Here, Mr. Dressler," Babe said, coming into the room at a half-trot, balancing a small tray on his upraised hand. In the center of the tray was a clear glass coffee-cup, almost full of something steaming hot, a kind of muddy, nondescript brown. Babe put it on the table, and Dressler reached for it.

All three of us watched his hand shake.

Babe reached over and pushed it closer.

"What is it?" I asked.

"Whiskey, Worcester Sauce, V-8, Vitamin B-12, and four dissolved capsules of Tryptophan."

"I'll take one, too," I said, "but leave out everything but the whiskey."

Babe automatically glanced at Dressler, who was trying to lift the cup without spilling all over his terrible slacks. He dipped his head about a quarter of an inch.

"Fine," Babe said, a bit disapprovingly.

"A big one," I said. "And not hot."

Tuffy jammed his hands even more deeply into his pockets.

I said to Dressler, "Do you want a hand?"

"You give me a hand," he said, more gasp than voice, "and I'll have Tuffy kill you right here." He sipped the drink, swallowed, and sipped again. "On my good carpet."

"That's better," I said. Tuffy relaxed his arms, bending his elbows slightly. This was a good move, since he'd been on the verge of shoving his pants down over his thighs.

"What do you mean," Dressler asked, a little more voice in it, "*you're* on a crusade? What about me?"

"What *about* you?" I pulled the chair closer to the table, putting a big ripple in his good carpet. "When I took this on, I didn't ask you any of the questions I would have asked anyone else in the world, because—well, because of who you are. But that doesn't count now. I was alone in that room with her, and nothing counts any more."

Dressler waved the back of one spotted hand at me as he drank. The awful putty-gray color was leaving his face. When he lowered the cup, he said, "How do you know you didn't *cause* what happened? How do you know—how do I know— you didn't make some incredibly stupid mistake that told them where she was?"

"*Where she was* is a different topic, and we'll get to it. I did make a mistake. I didn't ask you, when you gave me this job, whether you thought all that malice was still out there. Whether that particular play was finished, or just in a long intermission."

Dressler's eyes tried to look straight through my head, an eagle's glare, and then faltered. He blinked, started to drink again, and stopped, the cup still close to his lips. "No, you didn't," he said, "and that was my fault. I made it sound. . . . I—I *guess* I made it sound . . . like history."

"And because of that, I made another mistake, a second mistake," I said. "Talking to Pinky Pinkerton, when he got a little difficult, I tried a scare tactic. I told him that there were people who were dangerous, way back then, and that one of them was still dangerous today. It terrified him."

Dressler put down the cup. His hand wasn't shaking. He was looking at me, but I could see calculation behind his eyes, like someone pretending to pay attention while doing math in his head. "What was the mistake?"

"I thought the person he was frightened of was you. But it wasn't."

"How do you know?"

"He didn't call you today, did he?"

"How would Pinky—what is it, Pinkerton?—how would *Pinky Pinkerton* call me?"

"He didn't," I said. "He didn't call you, but he had his secretary call *someone*. She was dialing the call as I left, but she came out and made sure I was out of earshot before she went back in and finished."

"Mmm-hmm." He put his hand on the cup again, and just then Babe came in with a tall glass in his hand. "One for me, Babe," Dressler said.

"Worked, didn't it?" Babe said proudly, putting the drink down in front of me.

"Like a charm." He aimed a knuckle at my glass. "Is that the good stuff?"

Babe said, "Ummm."

"Take it back, take it back. Bring the—"

"Hold it," I said, snatching the glass just before Babe wrapped a hand the size of a leg of lamb around it. "Bring him the good stuff, but leave this with me. Give me a chance to compare."

Babe looked at Dressler, got a *what can you do?* lift of the eyebrows, and trotted out of the room.

"So," Dressler said to me, settling into the notion. "Someone else."

"Someone else with weight," I said. "And I'm going to figure out who it is, with you or without you."

"Don't get carried away. Just because you've seen me get knocked flat for a minute, don't think that—"

"Why now?" I asked.

"You've interrupted me several times tonight. Don't make a habit of it."

I said, "Finished?"

"Finished."

"Why now? It's been sixty-two, sixty-three years since someone pulled the rug out from under Dolores La Marr. Why open it up now?"

Dressler cleared his throat and swiped an index finger under his nose. "It's personal."

"I know it is." I pointed at the shelves of jade figurines on the opposite wall. "Remember how we met? The judge and his stolen collection of jade? That jade over there?"

"There are very few things in this long life, Junior," Dressler said measuring the words, "that I've forgotten."

"Well, good." I lifted the glass, knocked back a couple of fingers' worth, stifled the gasp, blinked away the tears, and picked up Dolores La Marr's hollow book. Dressler's eyes followed it all the way up to the top of the coffee table, and when I flipped the little latch, he said, "Tuffy," and Tuffy, his hands suddenly out of his pockets, covered most of the distance between us in the time it takes me to blink.

"It's not a weapon," I said. "Or I don't know, maybe it is. I should have known the minute I saw them." I took out two of the *netsuke* and put them on the table.

Dressler's right hand knocked the cup sideways, and a long crack appeared instantly, like a bolt of lightning, across the glass tabletop. He sat there, peering at the little figurines, his mouth hanging half open, and then he twisted himself around so that his shoulder was pointing toward me and his face was averted, and he made a noise like someone trying to swallow and speak at the same time.

Irwin Dressler was crying.

There was no way I could look at this; he deserved that much. I got up, feeling Tuffy's stricken eyes on me, and said to him, "Let's go into the kitchen and see if we can't help Babe."

In the end, it was Babe who got him through it. He sat with Dressler—a good, safe two or three feet away—and the sobs and the coughs rolled toward us, toward Tuffy and me as we sat in the breakfast nook, avoiding each other's eyes. After one particularly racking seizure, I got up and went into the kitchen and saw the bottle of whiskey on the counter and filled my cup to the brim. I drank half of it straight down, filled it again, and rummaged in the cabinets until I found another matching cup, poured some whiskey into it, and took it in to Tuffy.

I tried to put it down, but Tuffy swiped it from me six inches above the table. He tilted his head back and drained it, then started to get up. I waved him back down, took his cup, and handed him mine. When he'd emptied that one, too, I took them back into the kitchen, where I poured the rest of the bottle into them.

We'd drunk most of what was in our cups when he said, in that acid-washed voice, "Never thought I'd see this." He looked into the glass, into the remains of the pale amber liquid. To it, he said, "I seen him have his heart attack, and then I seen him have his other heart attack."

For want of anything else, I said, "That must have been rough."

"Nothin'," he said. "Compared to this, nothin'." The pale blue eyes came up to mine again. Like a disproportionate percentage of men who make their living hurting other men, Tuffy had beautiful eyes, a clear, transparent blue, set into the battered face like sapphires in a pudding. "What'd you do to him, anyways?"

"Reminded him of someone."

"Yeah? Who?"

"Himself, I think."

Tuffy said doubtfully, "He's crying for himself?"

"In the end," I said, "I think that's what we all cry about. Who we weren't."

"Yeah?" He shrugged. "You say so."

"Did he ever talk about her? About Dolores La Marr?"

He didn't even think about it. "Nah. He talked about the Missus, he talked about Carole Burnett, but those were the only women I ever heard—"

"Carole Burnett?"

"He loves her. Got all the old shows on disk. You should see him when he watches, you know that *Gone with the Wind* thing when she comes down the stairs—"

"With the dress and the curtain rod across her shoulders?"

"He just falls on the floor," Tuffy said. "He seen it a thousand times, and he still laughs."

I said, "Me, too."

Tuffy said, "Me too," and started to smile. Then we both laughed until a sort of Old-Testament wail came from the living room, followed by a series of clucks that had to be Babe.

"But the Missus," I said.

"Batty as a hen," Tuffy said. He shook his head. "Years and years. I mean, I been with him twenty-seven years, and she got locked up long before I came aboard."

"He loved her."

"Oh, Jeez." Tuffy reached up and laid the back of his hand against the dark glass of the window, as though he needed to feel something cool. "How does anybody know what he feels about anything?" Another howl from the living room. "'Cept this," he said. "This, you can tell pretty good. But I heard him say once, about someone—talking real mild, like the guy went through a door first when he should of waited—he said, *He's a nice boy but he should know better*, and two days later a dog found the guy's foot in Griffith Park. The missus, he always talked like he loved her. I mean, he said stuff like *Poor Blanche, lost in that nightmare*, and he went to see her every week even though for all she knew he'd come to sell her a set of encyclopedias. But yeah, I suppose he loved her. He respected the hell out of her, that's for sure, and he loved her memory. You know, who she was before."

"When she was herself," I said.

"I guess." He pushed his lower lip out, far enough to look down at it, and just left it out there to dry. "What I mean," he said at last, "is that you don't never know what he's thinking, but that doesn't mean I don't love him, Babe doesn't love him. 'Cause we do. There's something in the middle of him that's all clear, you know? All salted away proper, all in the right place, and once he knows down in there that you're okay, you'd really have to fuck up like a world war for him to turn on you. And he'd kill somebody for you without even thinking about it. Makes it hard to see him like this."

"I know what you mean."

Movement at the corner of my eye caught my attention, and I looked up to see Babe coming in with the platter, which held a pyramid of wadded tissues. He glanced at me without much friendliness and said, "He wants you. Give him two minutes."

Dressler used the minutes to change his shirt and to paste his sparse hair back over his scalp so it didn't hang in gray, deranged-looking spikes over his eyes, and he'd found some calm somewhere, as though something basic had shifted inside him. The look he gave me as I came across the room toward him was nowhere near as stonily remote as before. His eyes looked almost human.

"Sit, sit." He had a glass of whiskey in front of him and when he lifted it, his hand was steady as a gyroscope. "You're right, we've reached a new stage in our relationship."

"If we haven't," I said, "we don't have a relationship."

"At ease, Junior. This is hard enough for me without some junior executive, excuse the expression, going all branch manager on me. Sit."

I sat, and Dressler raised a hand for Tuffy's attention. "Bring us a bottle," he said, "and then you and Babe get out of here. Go to a movie. Tell Babe to go home to the baby. Drive to Omaha. Do whatever you want, but get out of here."

"Are you sure?" Tuffy asked.

"Since when do you ask me if I'm sure? Go, go. Junior and I have things to talk about. You and Babe will be happier not knowing them. Bring the bottle, go get him, and go out the back door. We're not saying a word in here until that gate closes behind your car."

"Yes, sir." Tuffy turned and double-timed it into the kitchen, although there was a certain amount of miffed flounce in it. Dressler held out a hand, palm up, and I looked at it, and then he nodded at the *netsuke* closer to him. It was my favorite, the sleeping fox, its spine a perfect curve, the carving so artful, making such expert use of a reddish color variation in the ivory, that I half-expected soft fur when my fingers closed around it.

"Eighteenth century," he said in a voice I hadn't heard before, the kind of voice he might have used with a child. He put the carving to his cheek and closed his eyes for a moment. "Some anonymous master, guy with no name." He was looking at me again. "One of the things I like about the Japanese is their willingness to do perfect work in private, not for credit, not for money, just to make something right. The thing, when it's finished, it is what it is. It doesn't need a signature. After all, no real fox is signed."

"Like the artists who carved stone and colored glass for the cathedrals," I said.

"Not such a happy comparison for a Jew," he said. "Those things, those spires, towered over us like threats, like raised fists. They cast a lot of shade, reminding us that we were allowed to be there just as long as we were useful."

"Fine," I said. "Then like all the things you've done in this city. All the businesses that are here because of you, all the pieces you made and then fit together, making the city work, and never signing anything."

He tilted his head a bit, accepting it, but he said, "Brute force," and he held up the fox as though to show it to me. "Compared with this, it was—"

"He took a knife to the ivory," I said, and blinked away a vision of the cuts on Dolores La Marr's face and shoulders. "The ivory was cut from a living tusk."

"But this is," he said, and then he inhaled deeply. "This is beautiful." He started to go on, but instead he closed his mouth and ran the tip of his index finger over the fox's back. "Beauty always counts, doesn't it? You can enjoy things that are useful, you can admire things that help people, things that stand the test of time, things that are so well built they won't let themselves be . . . eroded. They're all good. But something beautiful. Something beautiful blesses the space it occupies."

I said, "I'm not going to argue with that."

"Any room she was in," he said, and stopped. He was blinking fast.

"I'm sure. She still had some of that when I met her."

He reached out again, and I gave him the other piece, the pillow-book piece, the man and woman making love. He put the carvings side by side, then tapped the head of the pleasantly occupied man. "Nothing dirty about it. *This is what people do,* is what it says. *Here's something you might want to try. Look, they're smiling, you might like it.* This was probably part of a set given to a newlywed couple. It's sweet, when you think about it. Two young people, they barely know each other, they've hardly talked, one of them is a virgin, guaranteed. And these things are right there, next to the mat on the floor, glistening at them. They're beautiful, they're sexy, they're even funny. How sane is that? Helping those babies over the first steps like that."

"I didn't know any of that."

"Do you know how valuable they are?"

"Probably. Within ten, fifteen percent."

"This one." He tapped the couple.

"Sixty-five."

Dressler's eyebrows went up, an inquiry.

"Thousand," I said.

"Not bad. Pretty close. You're a little under, maybe. So look at you, Junior, you know where they came from, you know when they were made, more or less, you know what they're made out of, and you know what they're worth. But you don't know about that blushing girl, so frightened, that boy hoping he doesn't blow it." He put his open hands up, a couple of feet apart, and slowly brought them closer together, as though compressing something. "The *concentration* of that moment, two lives coming together, maybe for good, maybe for bad, and so much riding on what happened *right then,* as those kids tried to become one person. And someone loved them enough to put this there. Look how *little* it is, Junior. Look how light-hearted it is. It couldn't be threatening if it tried."

I said, "Why now?"

His chin came up, and he looked more like the old Irwin Dressler. "I'm getting to it, I'm getting to it. How come only old people, who have so little time left, know how to be patient?"

"I'll look into that when I'm older. So you were lovers, you and Dolores La Marr."

"Listen, you. I sent Babe and Tuffy out of here because I didn't want to have to live with them after tonight, after I talk about what happened, after what I'm about to tell you. You want to stay on my good side right now, Junior, you don't want me stewing about this, about what I've told you, for the next month or so."

"Please," I said. "Take things at your own pace."

"You know I was married."

"I'd heard something about it."

"Blanche Millyard." He was blinking again "Blanche."

There didn't seem to be anything to say.

"She was—not, not . . . one of us." He ran his tongue over his upper lip a couple of times, fast. "Upper crust, rich, went to good schools. Pasadena rich, *old* rich for LA. Thought the world was polite. What was I? A *schmendrick* off the streets, had holes in his shoes when he was a kid. I mean, yeah, I was smart, but I was street-smart. Didn't have grammar, didn't have polish. Didn't know how to dress, what to say once I got past 'Hello.'" He squeezed his eyes shut and let them pop open again. "That's enough of me, right? But I was *faster* than anybody she ever knew, I thought faster, I moved faster. People like the Millyards, they looked at a situation and they saw two, maybe three ways to handle it. I looked at the same thing and saw ten. Of course, some of them involved fucking people up."

"I married one, too," I said. "Not *that* kind of upper crust, but too upper for me."

"We're mutts, you and me. I know, I know, mutts, that's garbage, that idea. I mean, whadda *they* got? Money they didn't make. Houses they didn't build. But they got a *shine*, you know what I mean? They've read things, they've been places. Okay, their world is only about an inch thick, like frosting on a cake, and they think it goes all the way down. But we know, you and I, that down underneath the frosting there's yeast working to keep things up and weevils working to bring it down. But these people, they haven't heard the news, and the way they live, it's like the weevils aren't there, it's like everybody reads books and has clean fingernails and everybody's grandparents knew each other. They say *Bring the car around*, and somebody brings the car around. And they bring it around the right way and it's the right car, the right color, and polished like a star. And it takes them to the right places, the brightest places, and they think that's the world, and they think it was built just for them."

I said, "Makes them prime marks."

"Doesn't matter," Dressler said. "Not for this story, it doesn't. The way it worked, I was me and she was her, and she looked at me and wanted me, and there was no way I could say no. So I said yes, and guess what? Disaster, that's what. We ran away, we closed the door on her parents and her friends, and it was awful. For one thing, we didn't have these guys." He poked the copulating couple with his index finger. "Disaster. I'd been with girls, dozens of girls, and you know what kind of girls they were. Roll them over, jump on, kiss them on the cheek when you're done, and leave a couple hundred on the dresser. You want to do something they don't want to do, that's just the first move in a negotiation. But *Blanche*, nobody had told Blanche about any of it, and Blanche really hated it. Hated all of it. Thought it was undignified, thought it was ugly. Thought *I* was ugly. Thought it hurt, hell, it probably did hurt, the way she felt about it. In six months, that part of our life was over, not that it ever really got started. And there wasn't much left after that. She tried to go home, they closed the door on her. And she started to go—" He looked up at me as though he were startled to see me there, as though he'd thought he was alone. "She started to go crazy."

I needed to say something matter-of-fact. "When was this?"

"Nineteen forty-five. We got married on August 7, 1945. It was over, everything that mattered, by May of '46. She was alone in the world. The people she'd left, family and friends, they wouldn't even look at her. She hated me, she hated everyone I knew, and she had nowhere to go. So she went . . . away. I thought then that she went into the past because she couldn't stand the present, but later I found out it ran in the family, there was one every generation or two. By 1949, she was in the home, talking to her dead sister."

"And that's when you met—"

"Through—well, no matter who it was through. He's dead for years. It was her face first, I couldn't believe Dolly's face. But, come on, a face is just a face. It was who she was, Junior."

"Who was she?"

"A little half-Jewish girl with a crazy *shiksa* mother, that's who. A mother who hauled her across the country to whore her out to the studio bosses. So she—*Mom*, I mean—could feel like a star. And Wanda, sorry, Dolly, was just as cut off from everything as Blanche was. Her father wouldn't speak to her, tried to get her mother arrested on the Mann Act, treated his daughter like a street whore. People in Scranton thought she was a freak; she'd been in the *movies*. But she had the steel. So many people, they look tough, they talk tough, but they haven't got the steel. Dolly, she looked like an angel who took a tumble and wound up here by accident, but she had it. She played the game, she caught the eyes she needed to catch, she made it work, fair and square. I got her into Lew's studio although any of them would have taken her at that point, because he was a gentleman, he'd leave her alone and make everyone else lay off, too. And she was going to be a star. All on her own, she was going to be a star."

"What about the gangsters? What about George Raft?"

"Raft was a good guy, dumb but a good guy. He had honor. The gangsters, they were like a thrill ride. They didn't mean anything, not until that last night, when they meant everything. She wasn't doing anything with any of them, except George once in a while."

"And that was okay with you?"

For five very long seconds, I didn't know whether he'd answer me or shoot me. "We weren't—we weren't like that. Tell you the truth, and I hope I don't regret saying this, we tried. But I couldn't. I couldn't get past Blanche. I'd given Blanche my promise, and she was paying for it with her life. If I didn't keep my word, the world I live in, I'd have been dead years ago. So I kept my promise. To Blanche."

I sat back in the chair. It creaked loudly, and Dressler said, "Careful, that's an antique," and then he said, "Ahhh, break the fucking thing. Give it a kick for me, too." He picked up the two ivory carvings and his drink, and then he sat all the way back on the couch, brought up both legs, and slammed them down on the cracked coffee table, which split in two and caved in toward the center as I grabbed the bottle of whiskey and jumped out of my chair.

"That's better," he said, and without even grabbing a breath, he was shouting. "*No*, it wasn't okay with me. What are you, crazy? I loved her, but to her I was a friend. Special, yeah, a special friend, but a friend as far as she was concerned and me, she was the only person in the world I ever loved. No, it wasn't okay with me, none of it was okay with me." He got up, a carved piece of ivory in each of his dangling hands. "*Why now?* you ask. Because Blanche died eight days ago, because I felt like I could finally do something for Dolly, because it wouldn't matter if the whole fucking world found out, that's why. And now that you know all that," he said, leaning toward me as though he was going to take a bite out of the center of my chest, "how are you going to catch this cocksucker?"

19

The New Garbo

"Where'd you get this stuff?"

We were in the breakfast nook, sitting at a more solid table, and Dressler was paging through the loose-leaf notebook Rina had put together. He'd stopped flipping and started reading when he hit the transcript of La Marr's testimony.

"My daughter," I said. "She found it on the Internet. She's tracking the rest of it down now."

"Internet," he said. "One more thing I haven't kept up with. Am I in there?"

"In the Internet?"

"Yeah, yeah. Am I?"

"In highly edited form."

He flicked the open page with his forefinger. "These people the committee schmucks asked her about, Roselli and them, they're dead."

"Well, somebody isn't. The way Pinky acted proves that."

"The secretary, his secretary. She'll know who he called."

"I'm going to try to find her tomorrow." The thought of Edna reminded me of my shoe, and all my *let's get going* energy took a nose dive.

"Still," Dressler said, "I'm pretty sure everybody's dead, the guys in the outfit. Forget about me, most gangsters don't live so long. It's not like we're orchestra conductors."

"The girls," I said, tapping the transcript pages. "Do you recognize any of the names?"

He shook his head. "Girls," he said, "I didn't really know many girls. Not my vice." He bent closer to the page. "But this one, this Ella Cowan, she was a showgirl. If she stayed in Vegas and she's still around, I can probably find her. I've still got weight in Vegas, and old showgirls, they're like a club."

"Can you help me with Abe Frank?"

"Jesus, he still alive? That was one of the nice things about Vegas, owning the editor of the town paper. Sure, I can fix that up. But why?"

"He's one of the people Dolly named. Doug Trent, whom I talked to; Pinky; the screenwriter, Oriole something; Olivia DuPont—"

"Oy," Dressler said. "Olivia DuPont. A name I'm glad not to have heard lately."

"Seems to be the consensus. And Melly Crain, the gossip columnist."

"Forget Melly. She's gaga. Been at the Motion Picture Home, trying to learn the alphabet all over again, for years. Anyway, what's she going to know?"

"Who gave her the story."

"Maybe, maybe. But she ran it late, if I remember right. Picked it up from the Vegas paper, like everybody else. So good idea, talking to Abe Frank. But the secretary, she sounds best to me."

"Me, too. I just have to find her." I went for the last of my whiskey. "I want Babe or Tuffy or someone like that. Three or four of them."

"For what?"

"I need someone to watch the people I talk to. Before, during, after. I'm not interested in being responsible for any more deaths."

"You weren't responsible for anything. That little PR guy, he did something dirty, he knew who brought Dolly down because he was in on it. And he called whoever that was to rat you out, and he got himself killed."

"Humor me."

"Okay, you're humored."

"You know," I said. "The cops are going to be all over this. A case that gets the kind of publicity this will get, especially when they connect Dolores La Marr, the murdered security guard, and Pinky—well, they're going to work it hard."

"And?"

"And they'll find the person who did it."

He nodded. "And?"

"Just seems worth mentioning."

"The person who did it," he said, sounding patient. "When they find the person who killed her, he'll already be dead. And they won't find the person who *really* did it, the person who killed Dolly twice."

I put my face in my hands and closed my eyes. I was slowing down. Of course, he'd be dead.

"So," Dressler said. "More questions?"

"One. Who knew where La Marr lived?"

"No idea," he said. "When she moved, she kept it quiet. A couple friends, her awful mother. But she's been living there a long time. No telling when they found out she was there."

"It was a while ago," I said. "Before you hired me. Whoever killed her hid a stockpile of sleeping pills in the apartment, behind a box of cereal too low on the shelf for her to bother with it."

"You mean, they went in and out? To put pills there? Kind of sense does that make?"

"She was drinking pretty heavily, so getting in and out wouldn't be so tough, especially if they were getting up by paying the guard they killed. I think they've been planning to kill her for a little while, but they were going to make it look like suicide."

Dressler was shaking his head as though I were speaking a foreign language that he was translating as I went along, and the translation had gone wrong. "Wait, wait, how would you know about the pills?"

"I found them, by accident, when I was getting her a bottle of wine."

"How do you know they weren't hers? Why would the killer put them there?"

"I know they weren't hers because whoever killed her saw that most of them were missing from the pantry and threw a fit, stamping all over the ones that were left."

"Missing?"

"I took most of them. I was afraid she was stockpiling them for—well, you know why."

He was looking at me oddly. "You took some."

"Most of them, actually."

"Stole them."

"So she couldn't—"

"Well, sure." His gaze was a little embarrassing. "You're a mensch," he said. He put a wrinkled hand on top of mine and gave me a pat. "But why go through that *mishegas*? Why not just bring them when he needed them?"

"She had people who came in and cleaned once in a while," I said. "I think the idea was that the cleaners would see them, and after—after she was dead—they'd testify to that, and it would look more like. . . . "

"Yeah, yeah, but it still doesn't make sense. How do you make somebody take a few hundred—"

"There was a broken glass on the kitchen floor, in the middle of a pool of water. I think he ran water into the glass and then went to get the pills so he could dissolve them, maybe grind them up first. My guess is he was going to inject it into her."

The words hung there. Looking down at the center of the table, Dressler said, "Somebody who knew where she lived. Something else to think about. I come up with anything, I'll let you know."

The day's events suddenly clobbered me. It was all I could do to sit upright. "So," I said.

"A suicide," Dressler said. "Would have made news all over the place. Would have been the second suicide in that apartment. That's how she got it so cheap."

"The second? Who was the first?"

"An actress, Swedish girl, back around 1940. Supposed to be the new Garbo, but it didn't happen."

"What was her name?"

He thought about it for a second. "Anna," he said. "Anna Akers."

In room 104 of the Continental Tiki Hut in Reseda, I discovered I was too tired to sleep.

I'd snapped off the light, mercifully hiding the glowering plastic Polynesian tiki statues and the Eiffel-Tower wallpaper, and flopped onto the bed fully clothed, kicking my shoes off just before slipping my feet under the covers. I closed my eyes, lay still for about fifteen minutes while I watched little retinal fireworks, and then got up again.

Thanks to the Continental Tiki Hut's Wi-Fi, Google sure-footedly took me to a site dedicated to the memory of Anna

Akers, with an absolutely breathless piece about her last day on earth by a screenwriter named King Folden, who was with her when the final aces and eights were dealt.

Anna's achingly beautiful face, all fine bones and long, hooded eyes in the Garbo tradition, gazed out at me in glorious Hollywood black-and-white. She looked like someone who could be sliced open with a sharp word, and as King Folden made clear, she'd suffered more than her share of them.

Her dreams of stardom were not to be, King wrote, possibly in violet ink. *The English language defeated her. Despite months and months of drill on the studio lot, Anna's accent refused to yield. What were supposed to be starring roles became supporting roles and then bits. Instead of replacing Garbo, who was a year or two away from retiring, Anna entered the floating battalion of Hollywood rejects, accepting "gifts" from prominent "gentlemen"—as if there were any gentlemen running the Hollywood studios—and eventually becoming a pass-around for the powerful.*

August 14, 1940 was a Wednesday. The day of the week is important because Wednesday was, by strict agreement among the all-male membership, "Mistress Day" at the Elgin Club, an "exclusive" watering-spot for studio power players at the Sunset Tower Hotel on the fabulous Strip. As far as the wives knew, the Elgin was closed on Wednesdays, but for the sunglasses-and-jodhpurs-set it was the day to parade the latest conquests. At ten past five on that day, just as I was getting ready to go home, Max—

I looked up to the top of the piece and found that "Max" was Max Zeffire, the head of Zephyr Pictures, a grade-C outfit ranked somewhere between Warner Brothers and Republic that had fought its way out of Poverty Row on the strength of some unusually good B pictures. I remembered Dolly saying Zeffire had taken her virginity, and I flipped open Rina's notebook and found that Dolly had made her first two films for Zephyr and had been given her name there. Just for the hell of it I looked up Max Zeffire and discovered he'd died in the crash of a private plane in 1956. So I went back to King Folden:

. . . Max came by my office and said to come with him so we could talk about the story problems on Queen of the Moon, *which was all story problems. I got into the car, and there was a beautiful girl whom Max introduced as Anna Akers. I said hello, and she nodded, and Max said, "She doesn't speak English so good," and then he ignored her and we talked about the script. Anna looked out the window. After we'd failed to solve any of the problems and we were a couple of blocks from the Elgin, Max said, "Get this picture right, King, and we'll give it to Anna."*

She turned from the window and smiled for the first time. "You won't," she said, but she kissed his cheek. There was something—and I don't think this is just hindsight—broken-hearted about her. Despite the beauty, she knew she wasn't going anywhere. She probably knew that Max went through women so fast he got their names mixed up, but she still smiled again when Max said, "We've got to do something for Anna."

Anna made a reproving tsk-tsk sound and said, "We are here." Her English was heavily accented, but she had a beautiful voice, low and sweet as a cello. The car pulled to the curb, and the driver hopped out to open it. We went through the lobby and down the stairs to the Elgin, with Max scanning the crowd as he always did, although this time he was probably making sure he didn't see anyone who knew his wife. Anna turned a lot of heads, and once Max was satisfied he was safe, he grabbed her hand like a boast, just making it clear to everyone who she was with. At the door to the Elgin, Gottfried, the maitre d', looked flustered. He was waving his hands and getting in our way, trying to say something, but Gottfied had the most imitated stammer in Hollywood, and he couldn't get it out. Max shouldered him aside, saying, "Later, Gottfried, when I've got a week or two," and opened the door from the anteroom into the bar and dining area.

The first thing I noticed was how quiet it was. Normally, people were laughing and talking, but if I'd gone in with a blindfold on, I'd have thought the place was empty. Second thing was that most people were on the edges of the room, as though someone in the middle was holding something that might explode. The third thing was Max's back, because I walked straight into it. He'd frozen, about a quarter of the way into the room.

And there they were, the explosives, right where they shouldn't be on Mistress Day: four wives, and one of them was Lenore Zeffire.

They were all dressed to the nines. It looked like Oscar night. The clothes were top of the line, the jewelry glittered, and their hair was perfect. All around the room, mistresses peeked around the men they were hiding behind. Max started to say something, but he sounded like Gottfried. It was the only time I ever saw him tongue-tied.

Lenore Zeffire was taller than Max was, which wasn't unusual, but I'd never seen her look taller than she did at that moment. "We can go now, girls," she said, stepping forward. "You were right. There's nothing here but whores." And she pushed past us toward the door, slowing just enough to spit in Anna's face. Then she and the other women filed out.

I've never been in a more silent room. Nobody looked at us. We might as well not have been there.

When he came to his senses, Max turned to Anna and said, "Let's get you cleaned up, darling," but Anna backed away from him, all the way to the door. When she felt it behind her, she said, "I will go home now" in that accent, and left. Max said to me, "Go after her," and I did, but I have to admit I didn't try very hard to catch up with her. I had no idea what I could say that would have comforted her.

At about nine that night, Max sent some of the boys from the studio over to the Wedgwood to check up on her, but by then she'd climbed up onto the dining room table, thrown a long sash over one of the ceiling beams, tied both ends around her neck, and jumped off the table. The police doctor said the sash was long enough, and Anna was tall enough, that she could have stood on the floor on tiptoe with the sash around her neck without choking. He theorized that she'd hugged her knees to her chest, like someone doing a cannonball into a swimming pool, when she made her leap. "It's almost impossible," he said in his report, "not to straighten the legs and try to stand. The urge to survive is the most powerful instinct of all. She wanted very badly to die."

I yanked my eyes from the screen and turned all the lights on. The plastic tiki gods and the Eiffel Tower wallpaper looked pretty good. For the first time in years I felt like crying—for Dolly, for Anna, for all the beautiful and not-so-beautiful girls everywhere who lose their way in the world without stumbling over anyone kind. But I was too tired to sleep, too tired to cry.

Somehow, though, I did sleep. In the morning I woke up with my head on the desk beside the laptop. I brought the machine out of standby mode and went to the *LA Times* site, and there was a photo of Dolores La Marr from about 1948, with Chester Morris in the famous scene from the "Boston Blackie" movie,

and the headline FORMER STAR MURDERED IN "CURSED" APART-
MENT. Below that, relegated to smaller type by the death of
someone who had been billed just below the title, was a story
on Pinky's murder, complete with a photo of the devastation in
Edna's room. Much farther down, almost at the bottom of the
page, was yet another headline, this one reading, VETERAN HOL-
LYWOOD DIRECTOR KILLED.

During the night, someone had cut Doug Trent's throat.

The chain. Dressler had sent me to Dolores La Marr. Dolores La Marr had sent me to Doug Trent. Doug Trent had sent me to Pinky Pinkerton. Other than Dressler, I hadn't mentioned Trent to anyone.

Except for Pinky Pinkerton; I'd told him that Trent sent me. He'd sounded terrified when he called me. The man with the knife had plenty of time to learn how I'd found my way to Pinky's office.

On one hand, I thought, not liking myself very much for considering it from this perspective, the news meant that Trent wouldn't be calling the cops to point them in my direction. That left the shoe, which would only be useful once the cops already had me, since my DNA and fingerprints weren't, so far as I knew, on file, or at least not on any legally available file.

On the other hand, what did the news mean for Edna? Edna, who hadn't been in the office, alive or dead, when the bomb went off.

It used to be that only cops and the phone company had access to reverse phone directories, but with the advent of the Internet, anyone can use one. Problem is that many of the free sites are just honey traps—plug in a number, and a demand for paid membership pops up. Others have special relationships with law-enforcement agencies, carefully preserving the IP addresses and names of the curious and relaying them to the cops. Someone attracts the wrong amount of attention; some nerd cop hits a keyboard, and there it is: whoever that person requested info on, or whoever requested info on that person.

No, thanks.

A year or so back, a plausible—a con man—who specialized in defrauding the estates of the recently-deceased rich had made the mistake of trying to dip into the postmortem arrangements of the late father of a friend of mine. I'd put a pin in him, and as part of his settlement—in addition to returning everything he'd swiped, plus 20 percent interest—he'd shared with me a short list of Web resources that could be accessed with confidence by those of us who live outside the narrow focus of the law. One of them was a reverse-directory service. A membership cost $1,200 per year, a bargain for an active burglar.

I brought up the site and entered the "after-hours" phone number on Edna Frayne's business card, and there we were.

Edna lived about ten minutes from Pinky's office, in the hills near Beechwood Canyon, up above Hollywood Boulevard. The houses in the area had been built mainly in the twenties and thirties, probably priced originally at five or ten thousand bucks, now running in the low seven figures. If Edna changed houses as often as she changed her hairstyle, she'd probably paid less than fifty thousand, back in the early fifties.

I drove past it, waited fifteen minutes, and then drove past it again, in the opposite direction. There were no patrol cars or likely plainclothes cars sitting out front. Still. The cops had to have been here.

And they had to be coming back.

It was a vaguely European-style cottage, probably designed in the thirties by someone moonlighting from the studios, gray stucco with cheesy bits of exposed timber and brick and mullioned windows, topped by a sharply-pitched roof that curved up at the edges and seemed to cry out to be thatched. A ficus hedge obligingly hid most of the place from the street, and Edna's driveway ran obediently right past it, allowing me to park the car and get out without disturbing the view from her neighbors' windows.

The morning was slate-gray and cold by LA standards, but the drizzle of a day or so earlier was still evaporating from the ground, raising the humidity and dulling the edge of the chill. I turned my collar up anyway. I was too tired to resist the cold, and it seemed to blow straight through me. As I looked at the side of the house and saw the yellow crime scene tape, something in me relaxed a tiny bit. Even if bad things had happened here, the worst of it would have been cleared away. And I could *sense* that nothing was wrong inside. I've learned to trust my senses.

I made a note, as I walked around to the front door, to review my belief systems and see how I might be able to account for Anna.

Behind its crime-scene tape, the door was locked. I knocked earnestly several times, the knock of someone confident in the unimpeachable innocence of his errand. The doorbell worked, giving out the classic *ding*-dong tune. Nobody answered, which is what one would expect from a clearly identified crime scene. Still, I earnestly rang again, counted to twenty, and walked around to the back of the house.

A tiny pool, in bad need of some chlorine, reflected the gray sky behind a chainlink fence. The back door was locked, too, but it might as well have been standing open for all the resistance the lock put up. Given that there actually are good locks in the world, it never ceases to amaze me that so many people use hardware no more secure than the lock on a teenage girl's diary. I could have picked it with a fingernail, and there wasn't even a chain on the inside.

The door opened into a little utility area, industrial-gray linoleum beneath the washer, the dryer, and the hot-water heater. All were spotless. The whole room smelled of ammonia. Edna apparently used a lot of Windex.

Normally, the smell would have made me pause, wondering whether someone had been thinking about fingerprints. But it just didn't feel that way. I opened the door to what I supposed was the kitchen, since builders tend to keep the plumbing close together, and it was indeed the kitchen. A few drawers were open, but the search, if there had been one, had been polite. I stood just inside the room, looking at the autographed photos from the Big Band era on one wall, mostly white female vocalists who'd sung their way out of Idaho and Tennessee and South Dakota in the days of radio, the days when it didn't really matter what the singers looked like. And many of them didn't look like much, which I found sort of reassuring. From the perspective of a time when most stars have been buffed and sanded and capped and snipped and Photoshopped, it was a kind of relief to look at these real faces with their too-big chins and crooked noses and unfixed teeth and tight, beauty-shop hairdos.

I knew there was nobody in the house. This is a topic on which I am an expert. Nevertheless, I stood there studying the Bettys and LaVernes and Margarets for a couple of minutes, and then I went through the place.

I had to wonder about Edna. I'd assumed that she and Pinky were longtime partners, probably everything all proper and above-board, but neither of them keeping any big secrets from the other. And yet here I was, just a few miles from the office where

Pinky had been killed, looking at a house that had been abandoned in a very orderly, and—from what I could see—unhurried manner. The contents of the bedroom closet had been reduced by about half, judging from the gaps in the hanging clothes; many of the drawers were open and empty; and the neatly made bed still showed rectangular indentations where two suitcases had gradually gained weight. To cinch the notion of an unforced departure, the medicine cabinet in the bathroom was mostly empty, the toothbrush was gone, and there was a plastic laundry basket placed neatly beneath the mail slot in the front door. No unsightly spill of mail for our Edna.

So while Pinky was being tormented, while he was phoning me, while he was trying desperately to believe that the knife was just a threat, that it wasn't *really* going to be drawn across his throat, Edna had been at home, packing. The only way I could see it was that she'd made the call, waited until the errand boys, and maybe whoever sent the errand boys, arrived, and then drove calmly home and got ready for her trip. And then . . . ? *Edna fugit.*

And don't forget: before she'd finished dialing, she'd gone to the door to make sure I wasn't listening.

It all seemed pretty cold to me. But consistent. Whatever was behind all this, whoever had been behind it for decades, had a rich, inexhaustible vein of coldness.

I went back into the utility room. At about light-switch level beside the door was a rectangular button, clear plastic with a little orange light in it to make it easy to find in the dark. I pushed it and watched through the window in the upper half of the door as the garage door rose. Sitting there, neatly centered, was a dark Infiniti sedan, a couple of years old. So someone had picked Edna up. Without much hope of finding anything, I went out the door, popping the latch so it couldn't swing closed behind me, and skirted the chainlink fence and the stagnating pool to the garage.

The car and the garage were as clean as the house. Storage boxes, all labeled in an even, slanting handwriting, rose in careful vertical stacks on either side. I took one labeled *Linens* and opened it to find linens. Rattled one labeled *China* and heard what sounded like china.

I took the one that said *Photos* and put it in my trunk. Then I went back inside, moved the laundry basket to the rear of the hall so Edna's mail would be scattered all over the place, and went back out through the utility room, closing the garage door as I went.

I'd just finished booking a plane to Vegas under one of the aliases I kept stored at the Wedgwood when the phone rang. It was still in my hand.

"Dick's found a house Mom likes," Rina announced. "She's taking me there this afternoon, and she says she might make an offer."

I had pulled over, most of the way down to Hollywood Boulevard, to make the reservation, and I was still idling there. "Hang on a minute while I get a pencil," I said as two black-and-whites went past me, heading uphill, probably to Edna's. A long moment later, they were followed by a black unmarked car that had probably missed the light.

I grabbed a pen off the sunshade and flipped over one of the papers from Pinky's office, now dry and stiff. "Did you get the address, like I told you?"

"Of course, I did," Rina said. "I got the address like, or rather, as, you told me. Are you ready?"

When I was finished writing, I said, "Go with her. Don't be too negative, there's no point in getting her upset with you. Just nod and be polite."

"What if I love it?"

"Keep it to yourself."

"I'm just pulling your chain," she said. "I'm not going to love it. I want to stay here." She hung up.

I called Louis the Lost as yet another unmarked car went by. Gonna be a cop party at Edna's.

"I got you Handkerchief Harrison," he said. "And he's paired up with a girl, looks like, who was that girl singer from the fifties, made all those movies with what's-his-name?"

I took a wild stab. "Doris Day."

"Yeah, her. Looks just like her. Handkerchief's gonna want some money."

"And I'm going to give him some. Where can we meet up?"

"Time is it?"

I had no idea what time it was, which meant I was even more tired than I felt. I can usually guess the time within three or four minutes. It was almost too much work to look at my watch. "Nine forty. Where's Handkerchief coming from?"

"You think he'd tell me?"

"Right, sorry. Okay, noon at Stanley's on Ventura, near Woodman. I'll buy you lunch, you and Handkerchief, but not the girl. I don't want the girl to see me. And I'm going to need a few more couples, so you might keep looking."

"No need. I got enough couples to cast *A Midsummer Night's Dream*." Louie was one of the few crooks who made good use of the free time crooks have so much of. For the past two years he'd been taking adult classes on Shakespeare.

"Keep them in reserve."

"Believe me, they got nowhere to go. Times are hard. You know a country's in trouble when the crooks are unemployed."

o o o

Stinky Tetweiler was the San Fernando Valley's premier fence and had been for more than a decade. He could tell fake from real across an impressively broad spectrum—paintings, jewelry, furniture, fine silver, antiques of practically any kind. But all that taste and even refinement didn't mean he wouldn't back a truck over you, literally or metaphorically, if he felt like you needed tire treads on your chest.

I rang the bell of his Cubist fantasy of a house, high above the Boulevard, and was ushered in, to my surprise, by the same Filipino boy who'd opened the door for me several months earlier. Stinky was known on both sides of the Pacific for funding tours by Philippine dance troupes, almost all of which went home one dancer short. I'd just seen ads for a troupe performing down at the Shrine, which was Stinky's venue of choice, so I figured he was doing another trade-in.

But nope. I got the same smile and the same assurance that Stinky would be delighted to see me, which was almost certainly not the case in any emotional sense. Stinky and I regarded each other warily across the great capitalist divide, each secretly believing he was somehow being cheated by the other. But as is always the case with those on opposite side of the great capitalist divide, we needed each other.

"Junior," Stinky said, whittling a bit off the warmth of the welcome by not getting up. He was sitting at a new/old piece of furniture, a high, two-sided partner's desk that I automatically classified as mahogany, Hong Kong or Southeast Asia, roughly 1880.

"Ting Ting's got staying power," I said after my guide had shimmered noiselessly out of the room. "I figured you'd have him all set up in a flower shop by now."

"Ting Ting is different," Stinky said, and for a heart-clutching moment I was afraid he was going to bare his soul to me, but

I should have known better. "Marvelous conversationalist, just ripping." He was continuing to cling to an English accent he'd picked up on a decades-old visit to old Blighty followed by years of eating more than his share of scones. "What have we here?" He was looking at the thing under my arm.

"We have money," I said. I pulled up a chair, uninvited, to the other side of the partner's desk, sat, and opened Dolores La Marr's big hollow book. "I'm here as a buyer, not a seller."

"Pity," Stinky said. And he meant it. As much as Stinky loved money, what he loved most was the first sight of something he really, really wanted. Born into the family fortune generated by the invention of the perfume strip, he'd taken up a life of crime because it eased his access to beautiful things. He regarded the money I revealed when I opened the book with the air of someone who already had lots of it, probably newer and more neatly folded than what I had to offer.

"Be nice to me," I said, "and I'll show you something so sweet the memory of it will warm your feet all winter."

Stinky Tetweiler had been given at birth the small features you sometimes see in drawings of aliens, and he'd had various doctors sawing away at them pretty much ever since, until the front of his head was as smooth as someone wearing a stocking mask. He touched his microscopic nose whenever something interested him strongly, a tic of which he was blissfully unaware. He touched it now, just brushed at the side of it as though he suspected there might be a grain of soot there, sniffed, and said, "We'll see, we'll see."

"Four IDs," I said. "With financial weight behind them."

"Astronomical," Stinky said promptly. "Much more than you have in your cunning little box."

"Not so fast. First, the financials don't have to stand up to forensics. They just need to look solid to the basic credit check."

Stinky didn't look impressed. "And second?"

"Second, not a penny will be transferred out of the marks' accounts. These are for show only, and I'll return them to you in short order, still all shiny and ready to sell."

"Even if I believed that—and, since we're old friends, let's pretend I do—time is quite literally money in this case. Every single hour from the moment an identity is lifted there's a greater chance that it'll be detected and reported and everything will be closed down."

"Yes, Stinky, and thank you for reminding me of that. If you'd also like to remind me that ice melts, or that tomorrow is another day, I'd be glad to sit here, looking interested, until you're finished."

"Touchy, touchy."

"The loan, not the purchase, of four IDs, each to be used only for two days, returned as promptly as possible, without a nickel nicked."

"This is for a game," Stinky said with an exaggerated air of discovery.

"It is."

He looked at me the way he might have looked at an automobile mechanic who had just revealed a passion to perform Chopin. "Stick to stealing," he said. "You're good at that. Games require strategic thinking."

"Gee," I said. I reached into my pocket and pulled out one of the two *anabori netsuke*, this one in the form of a partially-open clam shell. Painstakingly carved inside the shell were a miniature Japanese hut and the juniper tree that shaded it, with a stocky little peasant sitting on the ground in front of it, carving a tiny *netsuke* that was shaped like a partially-open clam shell. I spread my hand flat with the piece dead-center on it.

Stinky went after his nose as though it were trying to escape.

"Modestly interesting," he said, sounding like someone swallowing a sock. He reached across the desk. "May I?"

"You may not." I closed my hand over it. "You may not see the really good one, either."

One aggrieved blink. "You brought them here for a reason. You didn't just pull on those awful jeans this morning without being aware you had a hundred thousand dollars' worth of old ivory—"

"You think so?" I opened my hand and looked at it again. "Wowzer, I figured—"

Stinky was blushing for the first time in my memory. He'd made a duffer's mistake. "You said you had another," he said, just barely not stammering. "I meant both of them, of course, assuming the other one is much, *much* better than that old thing."

"I do believe it is. Four IDs, just for a few days, no actual money spent. Thirty thousand."

"Ho," Stinky said. "Ho, ho. Sixty, and the ivory."

"Three IDs for thirty-five and one piece of ivory. I hold the other one in reserve. If any money is spent out of the marks' accounts, you'll get it. Otherwise, it's part of my trousseau."

"Open your hand."

I did, and Stinky looked at the *netsuke* so hard my palm heated up.

"The other one," he said.

"I'll show you the signature," I said.

Stinky rubbed his nose. Dressler had been right; most Japanese carvers released their work into the world unsigned. But that made a signed piece by a master craftsmen even more valuable. While Stinky was busy with his nose, I pulled out the other carving, holding it below the edge of the desk, and turned it in my hand until only the signature showed. I held it up.

He swallowed. "Is it damaged?"

I was shaking my head before he finished his question. "It is not."

"Three for forty," he said.

"Thirty-five plus the one I showed you. Another five plus this piece if any money is removed from the accounts."

Stinky looked longingly at the signature again, clearly resisting an impulse to lean across the desk and lick it. "Done." He rubbed his nose. "But only because I like you."

21
Handkerchief

Four murders, I thought, four murders in one night. Three of them throat-cuttings. All of them because Irwin Dressler had decided to look into the destruction of the career of an as-yet-minor actress sixty years earlier.

Someone—I forget who—once said that, if the universe was created in order to produce humanity, one would hope for a better equivalence between the size of the machine and the amount of the product. Four murders and an attempted fifth, against me, seemed out of proportion to something that probably wasn't even a crime, spiteful though it might have been, when it was done back in 1950.

So that was a possible key to the locked box. The sheer violence of the present-day reaction. Something to consider.

I tried to consider it at my apartment in the Wedgwood after I toted up the box labeled PHOTOS from Edna's garage, popped it open, and spent a few minutes looking at a lot of people I'd never seen before, unable even to recognize Edna. I tried to consider it as I grabbed the papers bearing the name I'd used for the airplane and the hotel in Vegas, tried to consider it as I drove up and out the driveway of the Nox and worked my way back toward the Valley, conscious that I might be late for lunch and, more importantly, my flight. Tried to consider it as I took one of my Glocks out of a storage facility and hid it in the trunk. Tried to consider it and got nowhere.

Except for one thought: This all could be sheer, simple terror. The malice might have been exhausted half a century earlier—in fact, it was difficult to imagine anyone fanning away at it, keeping it burning that long—but the terror could be new. Just kick-started, in fact, by the news that I was turning over rocks.

Four murders, almost five. That's a lot of fear.

Stanley's Restaurant was an anomaly: a nice little place serving good, basic American food that wasn't owned by Worldwide Quick Eats or some other globe-gobbling corporate monolith. I spotted Louie the moment I went in, facing me over the shoulder of a man I presumed was Handkerchief Harrison, although I didn't remember the yarmulke-size bald spot gleaming up through the yellowish hair on the back of his head. Even crooks get older. As Louie's eyes found me, I raised my hands palms up, and shrugged, meaning *Handkerchief?* and Louie gave me a tiny nod, but not too tiny to escape Handkerchief's notice. He twisted around like Wild Bill Hickock hearing someone come into the saloon, and I twiddled my fingers at him, Oliver Hardy-style, as I wove between the booths toward them.

Handkerchief had the kind of faded, attenuated, over-refined handsomeness that just missed being silly: a long, narrow Collie's nose above an upper lip so long it always looked as though a mustache had just been stolen from it, downward-sloping eyes, a touch too close together, and eyebrows that rose in the center like a roof. He always looked a little like he smelled something unpleasant and was very politely not suggesting it was you.

Still, that family-portrait face and the Hitler Youth coloring and a wardrobe Tom Ford would have envied—reinforced by an attitude that announced clearly that he was accustomed to someplace much better than wherever he was—had pried millions of dollars out of the rich and credulous, men and women alike. And Handkerchief had blithely spent it, always secure in the assumption there was plenty more where that came from.

And here he sat, flat broke and wanting in on a petty scam in Van Nuys.

"Handkerchief," I said, shaking the softest hand this side of the Duke of Wales and registering the hankie of the day, a meticulously folded flag of oyster-white silk with tiny red dots, protruding exactly correctly from the breast pocket of his navy blue blazer.

"*So* good to see you, Junior." Handkerchief ran his thumb over his palm, wiping away the contagion of the common. "Been dog's years, hasn't it?"

Louie said, "Handkerchief's English this week."

"Really. He should have a chat with Stinky."

"I been telling him, this is a snap, just him and Doris—"

"*Amanda*," Handkerchief said, so firmly that I could have told from across the room that her name, whatever it might have been, was certainly not Amanda. "Yes, yes, Amanda," he said, subsiding a bit. "Delightful girl."

"Don't take this wrong," I said, "but maybe you could move the accent three or four thousand miles West. Say, Ohio or something like that. Unless Amanda is from Knightsbridge or Kensington."

"Fine," Handkerchief said. "No problem. The flat inflections of the great American heartland, the tone-deaf vowels of Carl Sandburg." He sounded like a Cleveland weather man.

Louie rolled his eyes and gave his leather jacket, in which his cigars awaited death by fire, a longing pat.

"You've explained it all?" I asked him.

"It's almost a disappointment," Handkerchief said. "Like hiring a great heart surgeon to fix a deviated septum."

"Well, yes," I said. "But it's *my* deviated septum."

"Today, you said."

I felt a sharp edge emerge, tried to hide it, and figured what the hell. "Unless you have something better going."

"No, no, no, *no*." Handkerchief tossed a quick look at Louie. "Just, you know, the old calendar."

"Well, assuming we have a suitable blank in your datebook, here's your paper. Credit cards, Social Security, a California driver's license. Louie will take you to a guy not half a mile from here who'll put your face on it." I fanned it out over the table, and Handkerchief gave it a glance half a second long, which was all he needed.

"And twelve hundred," I said, putting a number-ten envelope on top of the identification. "Nothing bigger than a fifty, nothing brand-new. You can count it after I leave."

"You ain't eating with us?" Louie said.

"Got a plane to catch." I got up. "Nice to see you, Handkerchief. Oh, just for clarity. You use those papers once, exactly the way Louie told you, and an hour later, Louie's got them again. Not one dollar will be spent out of this particular borrowed pocket, got it? Not a necktie, not a pair of nice silk socks. *Nada*."

"Of course," Handkerchief said, a little stiffly. "Honor among thieves and all that."

"And all that." I scooped up the documents, just in case, but left the envelope with the cash. "Louie will bring these back to you. Walk me to the car, Louie?"

"I thought you'd never ask." Louie the Lost got up just as a waitress arrived with their food. I didn't waste any time wondering which of them had ordered the burger and which the prime rib.

The moment we hit the sidewalk, Louie lit up, trailing smoke behind us like some car that had chugged all the way from the Dust Bowl. "Guy gives me the creeps," he said. "Tell you the truth, they all do."

"We rob and steal for a living," I said. "Good, honest work. They tell lies for a living. Rubs away at the soul."

"You look like shit," Louie said.

"Always nice to have a suspicion confirmed." I blinked hard, trying to clear what felt like a pound of sand out from beneath my eyelids. "I need you to be no more than half a block from Handkerchief until you've got all those papers back. And I need you to count them three times."

"No problem."

We got to my car, and as I started around to the driver's side, Louie put a hand on my arm. "About Debbie Halstead," he said. "Near as anybody knows, she never had a kid."

The temperature in Las Vegas was a balmy seventy-two degrees, the sun was dyeing the western sky tangerine, and the humidity was nosebleed-low. On the way out of the McCarren Airport parking lot in my rented Flahoolie or whatever the hell it was, I wondered what McCarren had looked like back in 1950, when the little plane with Dolly and George Raft in it had touched down. Probably a coat-hanger scratch in the desert, barely long enough for a two-engine prop plane.

Abe Frank, the one-time Vegas newspaper editor, lived out in North Vegas, in a relatively new development that was mostly unsold. Brand-new houses sat behind dead lawns. Tumbleweeds had blown up onto their porches and plywood masked more than a few windows. Chain link, the world's most melancholy fencing material, surrounded some lots, and here and there the chain link was topped with razor wire for that welcoming hello to hopeful house-hunters. The streets had been laid out in long gentle curves to compensate for the resolute flatness of the terrain, so the empty shells revealed themselves gradually as I followed the turns. Here and there on a neutron-bombed block a house light gleamed.

Frank's house, sitting on a quarter-acre of barren sand, looked as unoccupied as the ones on either side except for the lamp in a front window and a yellowish porch light that was hosting a convention of large moths. I slowed when I saw the car parked across the street, tinted windows rolled up against the heat, but then the driver's-side window slid down and Tuffy gave me an ironic salute. I pulled up next to him and lowered my own window.

"How long have you been here?"

"Longer than you can imagine," he said. "Feels like a week, but it's actually—" He looked at his watch. "Four hours."

"Any movement?"

"One fabulously thrilling episode when he went to a liquor store and I followed him. He was alone. He went in alone. He came out alone. I went in, too, and he didn't talk to anyone while he was in there except to buy a gallon of gin. He said, 'How much?' He came home."

"Does he know you're here?"

"He hasn't come to the window and waved. He hasn't brought me an iced tea. He looks pretty frail. He might not have noticed me."

"Okay. You want to run out and get something to eat while I'm in there?"

"Babe made me a turkey sandwich on bread he baked this morning. I'm okay."

"Great. Well, then."

"Ending a conversation is a bitch, ain't it?" Tuffy said, raising the window.

I pulled the car around to the other side of the street and parked directly in front of Abe Frank's house, which was Spanish-influenced in the same way a kosher burrito is, which is to say around the edges: just a pale stucco box with reddish tiles on the roof and the porch cowering from the sun beneath an archway. Long, one story. No stairs for a man who, according to Wikipedia, had been born in 1923.

A dog barked at me from inside as I went up the walk, and turned it up when I rang the bell. It didn't sound big, but it sounded like it had a lot of teeth. I put my foot against the bottom of the screen door, which opened out.

I was about to ring again when the inner door opened. The woman who was standing there was almost certainly American Indian, her high-boned, coppery face perfectly framed by a long shawl of straight black hair, and a pair of eyes that looked at me twice and seemed not to be horrified by what they saw, which was a definite sop to my vanity. I put her age in the early forties, a period when some women finally become comfortable with their beauty. This woman had a lot to become comfortable with.

At her feet, a small white dust-mop yapped at me.

"Yes?" Her voice was a pleasant contralto, with quite a lot held in reserve, despite the eyes.

"I'm Junior Bender," I said, wishing, as I often do, that my name was *Anthony Dash* or something with a little more swash and a few buckles. "I think Mr. Frank is expecting me."

She gave the dust-mop a deft bit of sideways action with her bare foot that produced a soprano squeak, but it stopped barking. "Are you going to upset him?"

"I don't know. Does he upset easily?"

"He was upset when he spoke to your friend in Los Angeles today."

"Irwin is a more upsetting person than I am."

She looked at all of me again, head to feet and back again. "You're cute," she said. "But that doesn't mean I won't take the bat to you if you get him upset."

I said, "The bat?" but she was already using one foot to shove the dust-mop back across the tile floor like a hockey puck and unlocking the screen door. She pushed it open and stood aside. "He's in there," she said, indicating a room to the left of the entry hall.

"Don't I get to follow you?"

"Not in this lifetime. Beer?"

"Sure. Thanks."

She turned and headed off in the other direction, managing it very skillfully. The dust mop growled at me twice and then trotted over, wagging its tail, and I scooped it up and went into the living room with it licking my face.

From the couch, where he was lying full-length, propped up on a mountain of pillows, Abe Frank said, "Sic him, Waldo."

He was olive-skinned and bald except for a four-inch frizz of gray hair that stood almost straight up from the center of his head, as though he had balded from the sides rather than the center, like everyone else. He had deep, almost black circles—badly discolored skin—hanging beneath a pair of spaniel's eyes. Everything in his face had yielded to gravity: The skin beneath his chin trembled like a turkey's wattle, and his cheeks sagged heavily enough to tug down the edges of his mouth. His nose drooped. Even his earlobes seemed unnaturally elongated. His face was a monument to mournfulness, a Mount Rushmore for depressives, set atop a hollow chest and a protruding belly. His feet were up, and the bottoms of his slippers were so unscuffed that I wondered whether he got around by crawling before remembering that Tuffy had followed him to the liquor store. A wheeled oxygen tank, complete with a little Dennis Hopper breathing mask, stood on the floor beside him.

"This is Waldo?" I hoisted the little dog and used one of its paws to wave at Abe Frank.

"He hates that," Frank said. "Anything cute, he hates it." The voice was mainly breath, pushing a smoker's rasp in front of it. Still had a little twist of New York, after God knew how many years.

"Keep him away from mirrors," I said. "He'll kill himself."

"Don't make me laugh. Orinda will hit you with the bat."

"Orinda is a little startling."

He gave me an even line of false teeth. "Isn't she? I can still pull 'em."

The room was largely empty, just the sofa, an overstuffed armchair, a small, banged-up wooden coffee table, and the oxygen tank. One picture, an idealized print of a soft-looking pastel desert, hung very crookedly above the couch. No rug on the reddish Saltillo tiles. And the place was *cold*.

"Good air-conditioning," I said, taking the armchair and putting Waldo on the floor. He jumped into my lap.

"Best made," he said. "I've lived here seventy years and hated the heat every fucking day. I'm gonna die cool. So what's Irwin got on his mind?"

"What happened back in 1950 to Dolores La Marr."

"That poor girl." Frank shook his head, and various droops wobbled. "Prettiest thing I ever saw in my life. Sweet, too. Most of the girls who gravitated to the wiseguys, well, they looked a lot better than they were. Like wax fruit. But that one, that one was good all the way down." He looked at me and then past me. "Does Irwin think what happened back then was related to—to what happened last night?"

I didn't say anything.

"Jesus," he said. "I hope not. I got enough to regret in my life without that."

I let the pause settle in the room before I broke it. "You met her how many times?"

"Who knows? Four, five, maybe more. Whenever I could, right? I interviewed her for the paper once, mostly because I wanted to see if I could put a move on her. She turned me down so nice I couldn't even get upset." He had been looking at the dark window, but his eyes flicked to mine. "I looked different back then."

"You wrote a nice piece?"

"So nice Georgie thanked me, the poor lug, winding up the way he did, a trained monkey for Lansky." He reached over and snapped a fingernail against the oxygen canister, which produced a surprising bell-tone. "I met a lot of them," he said. "The stars, I mean. When Bugsy, the schlub, started flying them in to the Flamingo, when the other places opened. When playing Vegas was the thing to do, when an act could make more money here in a week than in a year anywhere else. I met 'em all. Some were assholes, some were drunks, some had heads so big you couldn't figure how they got through a door. Some of 'em were okay. Georgie, he was a good guy. Jane Russell, really nice girl. Clayton Moore, the guy who played the Lone Ranger? I know, I know, you don't think he was a real star, you probably don't even remember him, but you shoulda seen my kid when I told him I met the Lone Ranger. And how good it felt for me to say, Yeah, Buddy, he's a great guy." He wiggled his shoulders and the sunken chest, trying to squeeze another degree of comfort out of the pillows. "Where was I?"

"Dolores La—"

"Yeah, yeah, Dolores La Marr. Poor baby. Not the biggest star I ever met, that was probably Elvis, but the most beautiful. Maybe the most beautiful woman I ever saw in person. And one of the nicest. I don't know, nobody knows, how she would have wound up. After they'd been at her for a while, after she realized she wasn't gonna be beautiful forever. They hadn't used her up yet. Some of those gals, they got so used up you could see right through their face, see bones and nerves and, and . . . mostly nerves, I guess."

"But Dolores La Marr didn't get to that point, did she?"

He looked stricken, but before he could answer, Orinda came in pushing a little tin trolley that made a clanking noise. "Beer for you," she said, bringing the trolley to a stop. She picked up a bottle of Samuel Adams and said to Abe Frank, "He treating you okay?"

Abe Frank said, "Hunky dory."

"Then you get your beer." She handed me the bottle and an old-fashioned beer glass that widened toward the top. Then she came up with a bold blue ceramic cup and saucer, probably Mexican, and handed it to Frank. "Chamomile," she said. "With a shot."

"A big shot?"

"A shot. And as nice as this man is, you're going to have to eat in about twenty minutes." She smiled at me, not even pretending it wasn't an excuse. "So you'd better get to it, hadn't you? And don't make me bring the bat. Waldo."

The dog instantly jumped off my lap and followed her out of the room without a backward glance. I used the freedom to pour the beer.

Watching Waldo trot off, Abe Frank said, "That's the way Dolores La Marr left after she finished turning me down. Except she kissed me on the cheek first."

"Who was at the party?"

He chewed on the inside of his cheek. "You've seen the arrest list, right?"

"No, but I gather the guys were nobodies."

"Yeah, well, they would be, by the time the cops came in. I know Roselli was there for a while, Eddie Israel, who got killed about a month later, Pigozzi—Bobby Pig—Tony Accardo, maybe Sam. Sam liked Dolly."

"Sam Giancana."

"Yeah, sure. Georgie was there earlier, too. He told me about it. Said it was a really stiff party. Sam was in a bad mood, and everybody was on tiptoe. Couple of the girls, the other girls, not Dolly, they danced some to loosen things up. Georgie said Dolly wanted to leave with him, but one of the guys said she should stay, that they had a special table over at the Rancho for Betty Grable's show. So she stayed."

"Which guy said that?"

"Don't know. Georgie was just talking to me that night, before everything went bad. It didn't mean anything then so I didn't ask."

"But between that time and the time the cops came through the door, all the heavyweights faded and got replaced by nobodies."

"Bookmarks," Abe Frank said. "That's what Sam called them. When the big guys had something else to do, the bookmarks would keep the party going. If they went down to a show the bookmarks would sit in the big guys' chairs until the big guys came back."

"Uh-huh." He was watching me like I was about to jump on him, so I did. "Your photographers were with the cops when they showed up."

He held my eyes, and then he nodded. "I got a lot of regrets in my long, lousy life," he said, "but that's one of the big ones. That I was part of ruining that girl. And now, maybe. . . ."

"Who called you? Who requested the cameras?"

"They didn't call me," he said. "Called the night editor."

"Who? Who called him?"

He licked his lips, and I recognized fear, all these years later. And, I thought, he had no idea how frightened he should be. "Roselli called," he said. "The editor, his name was Bix Wheedon, dead now, said it was Handsome Johnny."

"And who called you in the morning? For the shots in the jail?"

"Police department," he said. "A lieutenant named Spivey. Bent as hell. He's dead now, too."

"Everybody's dead," I said.

Abe Frank looked back at the window, just a sheet of black by now, and heaved a sigh. "That poor, poor girl," he said.

22

In Camera

Senator Wheeler: Welcome back, Miss La Marr.

Miss La Marr: Let's get to it.

Senator Durkee: Just a minute, you—

Senator Wheeler: Mr. Chairman, I believe the witness is mine at the moment.

Senator Kefauver: Wait your turn, Elliot.

Senator Wheeler: As you know, Miss La Marr, this session is being held in camera, meaning—

Miss La Marr: I know what it means.

Senator Wheeler: Meaning that the session is closed to media and all but the committee and their staff.

Miss La Marr: Meaning that you hope some people will think I agreed to come in here and tell you things that would get me killed if they were in the papers. That's what you threatened me with when—

Senator Wheeler: Nobody threatened—

Miss La Marr: When I said I wouldn't testify again. You said you'd subpoena me and hold the session in camera and then I could worry about what my friends thought.

Senator Wheeler: If such a conversation ever took place, I know nothing about it.

Miss La Marr: But you know what? I'm not worried. For honesty and fairness, I'll take a bunch of hoodlums over you guys any day.

Senator Wheeler: I'm sure we're all devastated by your value judgment. But, as you said, let's get to it. How well do you know Irwin Dressler?

Actually, what it said was, "How well do you know ▮▮▮ ▮▮▮▮?" This testimony, like most in-camera testimony, was supposed to have been classified, but Rina had found it and emailed it to me, and whoever allowed it to escape had redacted the names of the living. I only knew it was Dressler they were asking her about because at one point Dolores La Marr referred to him as "Winny" and it had slipped past the censor, who was probably scanning the pages, looking for "Irwin" and "Dressler." I was lying on the bed in my hotel room, up on one elbow, reading through Rina's attachment, mentally filling in Dressler's name wherever it was inked out.

Miss La Marr: I've known him for three or four years.

Senator Wheeler: How well do you know him? Are you friends, or would you call the relationship closer than that?

Miss La Marr: We're friends.

Senator Wheeler: Not a romantic attachment.

Miss La Marr: He's married. As far as I know, he loves his wife.

Senator Wheeler: Then is it a business relationship? Does he take a hand in your career?

Miss La Marr: We're friends. F-R-I-E—

Senator Wheeler: And yet, he was responsible, was he not, for getting you a contract at Universe Pictures?

Miss La Marr: My agent was responsible, not Winny.

Senator Wheeler: And he was responsible, was he not, for getting you a leading roll in the film Hell's Sisters?

Miss La Marr: I was under contract. That's what studios do with people they have under contract. They put them in films, as you say.

Senator Wheeler: We have it on good authority that Mr. Dressler personally persuaded the head of Universe, a Mr. Winterman, to put you under contract and to cast you in that film.

Miss La Marr: Mr. Winterman does what he wants. And what's good authority?

Senator Wheeler: Do you deny, under oath, that Mr. Dressler, Mr. Irwin Dressler, was responsible for these . . . advancements in your career?

Miss La Marr: What a lousy, rotten question. If I say no, which is true, and you've got some cockeyed notion to the contrary, you bring me up on charges. That's what I mean.

For honor, I'll take gangsters any time.

Senator Kefauver: That's the second time you have impugned the honorability of this committee.

Miss La Marr: I'm just getting started.

Senator Kefauver: You might want to re-think that, young lady. Contempt of Congress is not a light charge.

Miss La Marr: Can you bring charges against me for the way I feel, or just for the things I say?

Senator Kefauver: The things you say, obviously.

Miss La Marr: Fine. Then I'll keep my contempt to myself.

My phone rang: Rina.

"Hey, sweetie. How'd you like the house?"

"It was okay. Not as nice as ours. But old Dick really leaned on her, told her the people needed to sell or they were going to lose the place, did this song about how she could steal it. You know, buy it for practically nothing, sell ours, and have a nice new house and a lot of money in the bank."

"What's nothing?"

"Eight hundred fifty thousand."

I said, "That's quite a way from nothing."

"It's not that far under what they were asking, either, which was eight eighty." Los Angeles kids have real estate in their genes. "Anyway, she made an offer, eight thirty-five, and he wrote it up right there, on those people's coffee-table."

"Quite a guy."

"I wanted to cut my wrists."

"But apparently you didn't."

"I was sharpening the knife—Mom lets the knives get really

dull—but about an hour ago, he called to say there was a problem with the title. He said he couldn't—listen to this—he couldn't, *in good conscience*, sell her the house. Can you imagine that? *Dick*? In good conscience?"

"Gosh, that's terrible. How was Kathy about it?"

"Well, you know, she'd kind of gotten herself all revved up. She got past the thing about moving and leaving this place, and she was drawing floor plans everywhere and showing me how much cooler my room there would be and talking about how we didn't really need a pool—"

"Wait," I said. "Eight eighty and no pool?"

"The back yard was a cactus garden. He was going on about how she could qualify for some federal program for saving water. And there were some dinky little solar panels on the roof, and that was a pipeline to the treasury, too. *Money on the table*, he kept saying. So anyway, he'd gotten her all psyched, and when he called to say it was off, she jumped on him a little on the phone. She was chewing on him about how it was his job to make sure the title was good before he got her daughter—that's me—so excited about moving."

"You poor baby."

"So he was going to have dinner with us tonight, but now he's not."

I said, "Awwww."

"Isn't it awful? *Money on the table*."

"Does he really have different-color eyes?"

"Different enough to be a stoplight."

"How's Tyrone?"

"The best," she said.

"Well," I said. "Take care of him."

"He takes care of me," she said, and hung up, having successfully driven a nail of pure guilt straight through my heart.

I lay there for a few minutes, feeling like the guy at the bottom of the avalanche. I was drowning in questions and the cold water of my own shortcomings. The murders of Dolores La Marr, Pinky Pinkerton, and Doug Trent; the attempt on my own life; the apparent nonexistence of the daughter Debbie Halstead asked me to find; Debbie Halstead herself, and whatever the hell she was up to; where Edna had disappeared to; my abandonment, at least for the moment, of Ronnie; Kathy's disastrous taste in men—including, I had to admit, me; my failures as a father; and the possibility of Rina being forced to move out of the house she loved.

Which reminded me.

Just as I started to dial Louie, the phone vibrated, and there he was.

"Like a charm," he said.

"According to Handkerchief?"

"According to the accepted offer, signed by your sleazeball realtor. Ninety thousand above asking price."

"He told Kathy there was a problem with the title."

"Well, there was," Louie said. "He'd sold it to someone else."

I rubbed my eyes. "Okay, good. Did you get the papers back from Handkerchief?"

"Why do you even ask me these things?"

"And you've got the last five hundred for him."

"I give it to him tomorrow, when he calls your buddy Dick and pulls out of the deal."

"And then disappears."

"Handkerchief's good at that."

"Well, I owe you."

Louie said, "Do you ever."

"Who's next?"

"One you never met. Elton Cho, Korean guy. The female half

is his real wife. You didn't even notice that one of the sets of stuff is in an Asian name."

"That's why I have you. Anyway, that's fine, that's fine. Asians inspire confidence. Is he good?"

"Slick as a wet road. Made a fortune buying old buildings in K-town in limited partnership and turning them into churches, tripling the asking price, and selling his part of the partnership to the pastors as the whole thing, without cutting his partners in. Churches are big business in K-town."

"Churches are big business everywhere. Tax-free, too. Is he hungry?"

"Well, sure. That's a limited club, people you can sell a Korean Church to."

"I'll let you know when we need him."

"Kathy ever finds you're behind all this, she'll kill you."

"She'll have to get in line," I said. "Probably behind Debbie. Not the kind of client to ignore."

"And, since you brought her up," Louie said, "I still can't find nothing about Debbie ever having a kid."

"Well," I said, "life is certainly interesting."

Senator Wheeler: And isn't it also true that Mr. Dressler represents the union to which you belong, the Screen Actors Guild?

Miss La Marr: He represents all of them.

Senator Wheeler: He also represents many of the studios, doesn't he?

Miss La Marr: You are so far above my level it's enough to make me laugh. Here's Dolores La Marr's Hollywood, okay? Here's any actress's Hollywood—

Senator Wheeler: Miss La Marr—

Miss La Marr: You try to get an extra part, then you try to get a character with a line to speak, then you try to get a character with a name, then you try—

Senator Wheeler: This is interesting, but—

Miss La Marr: —to get a contract somewhere, and once you've got a contract you try to get a good part without stabbing too many other actresses in the back or having to get into the sack with too many guys in suits. And when you finally get a good part—

Senator Kefauver: Miss La Marr!

Miss La Marr: Then you show up and try to make something work, with a hundred people staring at you and other actresses hoping you fall on your ass, and you go home and cry because you know you can't do it but you can't cry too much because you've got close-ups the next day, and—

Senator Kefauver: Miss La Marr, you will confine yourself to answering the questions we—

Miss La Marr: And you're asking me about who represents who at the top? I don't even see the guys at the top except when I'm trying to stay out of their way on Wednesdays, when they take girls to the Elgin. Or on weekends when they want you to go out to the beach. Like any of them has ever been swimming.

Senator Wheeler: So someone as powerful as Mr. Dressler would be a desirable ally, wouldn't he?

Miss La Marr: We were friends.

Senator Wheeler: You are a member of the Screen Actor's Guild, aren't you?

Miss La Marr: Didn't we just talk about this?

Senator Wheeler: As a member of a union, what is your understanding of what a union does?

Miss La Marr: It soaks you for dues.

Senator Wheeler: Please, Miss La Marr.

Miss La Marr: It's supposed to get you paid better, keep people from cheating you. My father was in the union, in Scranton.

Senator Wheeler: And how would your father have felt if he learned his union's lawyer also represented the mine owner?

Miss La Marr: It would have bugged him. You know, upset him.

Senator Wheeler: Do you know the term conflict of interest?

Miss La Marr: Sure, what do you think, I'm dumb?

Senator Wheeler: I think you're a very intelligent young woman. I think you know exactly how much of a boost it can give a young woman's career to have a—what shall I call it—an advocate like Irwin Dressler in her corner.

Miss La Marr: You got a point there somewhere?

Senator Wheeler: I also think you know how much might be done by a body such as this one, with the influence we wield, to repair the damage that's been done to your career.

Miss La Marr: You don't say. You mean, a bunch of Congressmen are going to say it wasn't really me in those pictures?

Senator Wheeler: There are many ways people like the members of this committee could help you to get past the repercussions of your evening in Las Vegas. Of course, the best way for you to demonstrate that what happened there was all a misunderstanding would be for you to cooperate with this committee. Actions speak more loudly than words.

Miss La Marr: Yeah? Then what am I saying now?

(Miss La Marr walks out of the committee room.)

Girl had guts.

I looked at my watch. It was still early enough that I had two choices about whom to call. I didn't think that either of them would lie to me, but I decided to call the one whom I *knew* wouldn't.

Rina said, "This better be good."

"Why?"

"Mom and him are having a real flamer on the phone."

"Mom and *he*," I said, and then I said, "you mean an argument?"

"*Oh*, yeah. He told her the truth."

"Always a decision that should be given some thought where a woman is concerned. What's the truth?"

"Well, she kind of chewed him into a corner about the title mistake, and he told her that actually he'd had a much better offer, and he was legally required to report it to the seller."

"If you hear a choking sound on my end, it'll be laughter."

"So she said, why didn't he give her a chance to match it, and he apparently said because it was way more than the house would be worth, and she said, well how did he ever think he could represent both of them anyway and wasn't that conflict of interest and he said that he could save her money by kicking back part of his double commission to her, and she said, and I quote, 'There is no fucking way in God's world that's honest, Richard,' and then you called."

"Synchronicity," I said. "The concept of conflict of interest has come up a lot in the last ten minutes. Listen, I need you to check something for me. You said Dolly's mother married some assistant director or something and he got big during a union power squabble and something something."

"Yeah?"

"Well, try to find out more. Find out about the union fight. Who were the two sides? How did it get resolved? Anything you can get. I think maybe the most important thing is who were the two sides, who were the leaders of the two sides."

"Unions. A little boring. The grimy proletariat."

"Might be a murder story."

"You mean the guy Dolly's mother married was involved?"

"And maybe a lot of other people, too."

There was a silence, and I figured I'd impressed her, so I let it stretch out, but then she said, "*Boy* is she ripping him a new one."

23

Miss La Marr Was Far Too Elegant to Dance

The bed was fine, but I wasn't. It took me hours to get to sleep, and then I kept waking up, and the eightieth or ninetieth time I opened my eyes, the sky through the window was that horrifying steel gray that tells you the night is over and the sun will be running things again almost immediately.

So I called down for coffee and took a quick shower before it arrived, and I was sitting there, damp-haired, when there was a knock at the door. I opened it to Tuffy.

"Mr. Frank is swell," Tuffy said. "I got relieved by another guy at three A.M. and got some sleep. Nobody even drove past the place."

"Good." I stepped aside to let him in. "Have you had coffee?"

"Don't drink it. My nervous system is too delicate."

"Juice? Anything? I've got a guy on the way up."

"Nope. Just wanted you to know that Abe Frank is okay and that the man who's been sitting in front of what's-her-name, Ella Cowan, says he hasn't seen nothing either. At least, nothing that got his attention."

"What does that mean?" The door, which I'd left ajar, opened, and a young man, East Indian or Pakistani from the look of him, came in with a big tray. He put it down and removed the linen covering it to show me a vacuum-pump of coffee, a cup and saucer, and two pieces of toast, cut the frilly way, which is to say on the diagonal. He hovered there, waiting for approval. I gave it to him in the form of a few ones, and he left.

"Means she lives in a condo development," Tuffy said. He surveyed the contents of the tray without interest. "White bread," he said. "Refined flour will kill you. Anyways, you gotta get through the gate, which he didn't, and on the other side there's like a dozen big units. Oasis Tower, something like that. So he sat there all night and no one went through the gate until about twenty minutes ago, and that was a limo that a guy came out of and got into and then it left again. She's in Unit Seven, and as near as he can figure, nothing is happening in Unit Seven."

"Good. How's Irwin?"

"Popping out of his skin. Wants to kill everybody. I haven't seen him like this in years, since before he took everything legal."

I picked up the toast and looked at the individually wrapped squares of melting butter that had been plopped on top of it. "Tell me," I said between my teeth, "what's so contagious about the hotel idiocy that says you send the toast up, getting cold, with two foil-wrapped bits of butter, getting warm, so that by the time you get it, you've got butter that runs all over the place when you open the foil and four pieces of dry, cold toast? Why do you suppose every goddamned hotel in the world does it?"

"Jeez," Tuffy said. "And I thought *I* had a bad night's sleep."

After Tuffy left and I flushed the toast down the toilet, I still had a couple of hours before I could even think about heading over to Oasis Towers; Ella Cowan had made it very clear that she didn't see anyone earlier than eleven and that I'd be pushing it even then.

I blew a few hours going over things, making notes on my

laptop and checking the notes I'd already made. Abe Frank had been right when he said everybody was dead; more right, anyway, than he would have been if he'd made the statement a couple of days earlier, before Murder Night. The editor who took the call for the photographer was dead, the cop who'd made the morning call for the second photographer was dead. Raft was dead, Giancana, Roselli, Eddie Israel, Bugsy—the list went on and on.

And it prompted me to recheck the names La Marr had given me when I talked to her. I hadn't talked to Melly Crain, although apparently she was past being helpful, if Dressler was to be trusted. Oriole Finlayson, the woman who wrote *Hell's Sisters*, was still among us; she'd had a nice little second career in the 1970s and '80s writing a series of mysteries narrated by the detective's cat, one of which had been turned into an animated film. So make a mark next to her name: someone to go see, if nothing broke loose first.

I had the distinct feeling that something was going to break loose.

The woman who'd worked in publicity for Bugsy Siegel, Delilah Polland, had failed to answer a number of calls. I had an address, so I figured I'd drive by on the way to see Ella Cowan and just take a look. That left Olivia Dupont from La Marr's original list.

Okay, so what *about* Olivia Dupont?

Google took me to a fan site, "Livvy Lives On," a pixellated shrine to one of Hollywood's Almosts. Except, as it turned out, she wasn't quite as much an Almost as I'd thought. She'd gone on working on the downslope of the industry. She'd played the female lead in a couple of the atomic giant bug movies of the 1950s and done a turn as a female biologist in two quickies about a putatively horrifying guy in a lizard suit who emerged from a

Louisiana Bayou to wreak havoc among people in obscure southern ZIP codes. Movies that cost less in their entirety than what they pay today for ten minutes of the average television series, movies where the entire shoot might be twelve days on uncooperative locations, and the important thing was to hire people who always knew their lines and could handle practically anything in one, or at most, two, takes. No matter what they'd said about Livvy, no one had said that she couldn't get the job done.

And then, in the early seventies, a late-life break: She'd found her way into the Great Shrine of Camp in a series called *Reata*. For three years she'd played a bullwhip-toting rancher named Henrietta "Hank" Hawkins, the sole mistress of a vast spread "in the great Pecos country," as the website put it—a cigar-smoking, bullwhip-toting matron whom some gay people had gleefully embraced as "the butchest character ever in prime time." Apparently, Livvy had been a grand marshal of the West Hollywood Halloween parade in 1979, riding in a Cadillac surrounded by guys in leather dresses, carrying bullwhips.

I was laughing when I got to the picture of her in costume, one foot up on a stump, leaning forward with an expression that probably scared the hell out of cattle, with her arms crossed over her thigh and the whip, curled in a circle, dangling from one hand. I took a closer look at her face and stopped laughing. Livvy's face, twenty-five years after *Hell's Sisters*, answered any number of questions.

The house where Delilah Polland was supposed to live was resonantly empty. I knocked on the door a couple of times and peered through the front window, looking at furniture with dust covers on it. When I felt eyes on me, I straightened and turned. On the sidewalk, straddling a bicycle with black fringe coming out of the handlebars, was a red-headed cowboy of perhaps eight or nine with an expression that said he'd already heard it, no matter what I was going to say.

"She's not there," he said.

"So I see."

He weighed my response, turning his handlebars back and forth. "She fell down."

I waited, but that seemed to be the bulletin in full. I said, "Is she all right?"

He said, "I don't know."

I said, "Well, what about your—" just as a woman called out, "Danny! Danny, come away from there."

Danny threw me an accusing squint and put his feet on the pedals, and I turned to see the woman next door standing in her doorway and giving me a highly critical eye. "I'm looking for Miss Polland," I called out. "Your son says she took a fall, is that right?"

"Who are you?"

"Sorry." I moved less than halfway to her, remaining on the sidewalk rather than setting foot over the magic line at the edge of her lawn. "I'm Edward MacLeish. I spoke with Miss Polland a year or so ago about talking to me for a documentary I'm making on Bugsy Seigel. For PBS?"

The mention of PBS relaxed her a bit. It always does. I use it all the time. Nothing can go wrong, or even get very exciting, with a guy from PBS.

She came down the three steps that led to her door, a woman in her trim mid-thirties with carrot-orange hair. "She took a bad fall, went right down those front steps. Broke both hips. It was terrible, 'cause nobody was around. She was out there, in front of her door, flat on her back on the walkway, for an hour or more before anybody came by."

"That's awful," I said. "How is she now?"

She screwed up her mouth, pulling it to the left, a semaphore of doubt. "She was pretty shaken, mentally. It kind of brought it all home to her. That she was old, I mean, that—you know—she's eventually going to die. Knocked the cocky right out of her."

"The cocky?"

"Cockiness. I don't mean that in a bad way. She was just so full of energy, and she'd worked with all those gangsters and murderers, and she was still here. But after the fall, even after they rebuilt her hips, she wasn't the same. So now she's living with her daughter. In West Virginia."

"Sorry to hear it."

"I've got a phone number. Hang on a second."

She turned and ran up the three steps, letting the screen door bang behind her. Danny looked at me without much enthusiasm.

"So," I said to the kid. "You watch a lot of PBS?"

Ella Cowan, the former showgirl who'd been at the fateful party, had cornered the market in glass grapes, silk flowers, marble-top tables, and those black-and-white silhouette cutouts of girls wearing billowing, wasp-waisted nineteenth-century dresses. There must have been sixty of them on the long wall in her living room.

"Sure, I remember," she said in a smoker's baritone, using a big malachite cigarette lighter to set fire to one of those skinny women's cigarettes I'd thought had disappeared a decade ago. The package announced that this particular Virginia Slim was mentholated, which was almost enough to close my throat completely. "It was a crappy night."

"Probably not as crappy for you as for Dolly."

"Oh, Dolly, Dolly, Dolly. Spare me." Cowan lived in twilight, if the drawn drapes were any indication, and she had the general air of something that would turn to wisps of burning paper if sunlight should strike it. She was still slender, still elegantly proportioned at more than six feet tall, but her face had the peculiar look of fictional youth achieved by those who spend much of their time on the operating tables of cosmetic surgeons: unlined, colorless, immobile, occasionally—as in the too-full lips—improbable. She looked like she'd been preserved cryonically in 1952 and had thawed halfway, and her personality was chilly enough to bear that out.

"Most people seem to have liked her," I said. I was sitting across a marble-top coffee table ten feet long, a veritable vineyard of dark purple glass grapes with green plastic leaves. Cowan had apparently grown used to talking to people who were shorter than she was, and even sitting she tilted her head back so she could sight down her nose at me. She held her cigarette dead-center in her mouth, the plumped lips pursed around it, so she may also have been trying to keep smoke out of her eyes. The total package—hair drawn back so tightly it looked like it hurt, tilted-back head, cool eyes, the mouth pulled tight around the cigarette like a rejected kiss—it all had something of the forties vamp about it, the woman in a B-movie whom even a ten-year-old would never mistake for the heroine.

"She was only nice to the men," she said. "And she wasn't even *giving* them any. She treated the girls like we were extras on a movie set. I'll tell you what she was, although I haven't heard the term in years: she was a cock-teaser. She was all about how wonderful she was, pushing the other girls aside and shaking her little can at the men. No, I didn't like her."

"And yet here you are, talking to me about her."

A long pull on the cigarette, then she took it out of her mouth, leaned her head all the way back, and blew the smoke straight up in the air. "I don't have many visitors." She waved the smoke away and said, "And Irwin Dressler, *himself*, called me up and told me to."

I said, "Must have been persuasive."

"It was flattering, I suppose. I've been off the radar since JFK was president. And even then I wasn't exactly at the level where I chatted with Irwin Dressler every day, which I'll bet is no surprise to you. I only ever saw him maybe four times, and I don't think he noticed me. Had no eyes for girls at all, that one."

"He was married," I said.

"They all were. But I'll tell you, when he called me yesterday I damn near saluted. He was the only person Bugsy ever told me he was afraid of. And that was Bugsy's problem, wasn't it? If he'd had the sense to be afraid of people he probably would have died of old age. Dressler scared me, sure, but to tell you the truth, honey, what's he going to do to me? At my age I don't care whether I've got another five years or five days." The coal on the Virginia Slims glowed again, and she said, flapping her hand at the smoke, "Long as it doesn't hurt."

I said, "That's what's left, huh?"

She said, "This doesn't interest you. You're not old enough yet. What does interest you?"

"The night of the party. Who invited you?"

She was shaking her head before I finished the question. "It wasn't what you'd call an invitation. Tony Accardo picked me out of a line of living statues—that was the act, we were living statues because that way nobody could say we were dancing naked—and sent somebody backstage for me."

"That night?"

"Yeah, sure, but the first time was about two, three months earlier."

"So you're backstage, putting on makeup—

"Having it put on. It was everywhere, right? White greasepaint.

I'm supposed to be marble." She rubbed the cigarette's coal against the side of a big cobalt-blue glass ashtray, just scraping off the ash. "So one of the boys comes in, wants to know can I go. Tony was always a gentleman like that. Not 'Tony wants you,' but 'Tony wants to know can you go?' So I said sure, and what time and like that, and we set it up."

"For the Flamingo," I said.

"One of Bugsy's high-roller suites. Bugsy was dead, then, but they were still Bugsy's suites. When people read about it back then, they probably imagined some kind of hotel room. But Bugsy's suites were palaces. Four, five rooms. Big as this place."

"What was the agenda? I mean, did whoever Accardo sent to invite you say anything about what the evening would be like?"

"Just a party. Drink with four or five of the guys for a few hours, then go down and catch Betty Grable's last show. Maybe go home with Tony later. Like a million parties. Those guys liked girls. Liked to be around them. Liked us to make them feel big. They were macho, remember macho? We were the people they could show off in front of, and we could go *Ooooooo, what a big guy you are,* and they'd know we weren't saving up bits and pieces of the things they told us so we could rat it out to Sam or Mostelli and get them whacked so we could take over their job. Those guys spent a lot of time looking at each other when they didn't think the other one would catch them at it."

"What time did you get up to the suite?"

Her eyes went up to the ceiling for a second and came back down. "Maybe nine."

"Didn't you have a show at ten or so?"

"Ten and midnight. We had floaters, four girls who could stand in if one of us got picked out for the night. Not too hard. All they had to do was stand in the right place and not scratch their nose."

"So you went up to the suite. Who was there?"

She said, "You know, this was just one night out of a lot of nights, and it was a long time ago."

"Try," I said. "I know you can do it."

She stubbed out the cigarette. "No sweetener?"

"Sure," I said. "Two thousand bucks." I pulled some of Dolores La Marr's remaining hundreds out of my pocket and counted out twenty of them.

"The girls," she said. She picked up the big ashtray and put it on top of the money. "What's-her-name, the one who said she was an actress—"

"Kelly Brannigan."

"Yeah. Her. And herself, of course, the darling Miss La Marr. And George Raft, he was there, nosing around La Marr; and Tony the Ant, that's Mostelli; Handsome Johnny; Tony Accardo—my date, so to speak; Bobby Pig, that's Roberto Pigozzi; and Sam Giancana. Couple other guys rotated in and out. Stompanato, he was just a kid then, and one other. . . . "

"Eddie Israel?"

"Yeah, Eddie. Nice guy, Eddie. Caught one in the head not too long after."

"What did you do? At the party?"

"Well, it was a *party*, Jack. Remember parties? We drank some good stuff, we smoked cigarettes—hold on a minute." She tapped the Virginia Slims pack in an expert fashion, and a cigarette obligingly stuck its head up. She put it in her mouth, dead center again, and I hefted the malachite lighter for her. She inhaled and then pulled it out and regarded the glowing tip critically, as though she suspected me of doing it wrong. "And we danced a little," she said when she'd approved of my work. "Sam had brought three jigs up from the lounge—"

"Jigs?"

She sighed. "Black guys. A trio, you know? Piano, bass, drums. Pretty good. See, that's what I mean, this wasn't just a hotel room. Can you imagine a trio, piano and everything, playing in a hotel room?"

She expected an answer, so I said, "No."

"We were dancing, me and Brannigan. You know, dancing like girls who were interested in each other. Just kidding around. The guys liked that. Miss La Marr was far too elegant to dance."

"Someone said Giancana was in a bad mood."

"He was always in a bad mood. But, yeah, he was pretty pissy. Some of the guys—not Tony, not Mostelli, but some of the other ones—were up on tiptoe. Raft was kind of working on him, telling him jokes and stories about Hollywood. Not making much headway. Sam could be a charmer, but when he wasn't, you wanted to look out."

I said, "And then the bookmarks started coming in. What, like ten thirty, eleven?"

"The—oh, yeah, the bookmarks. Stompanato was one of them. Damn, he was a good-looking kid. Three others, in and out. The big guys would melt away and the bookmarks would come in, then the big guys would come back and the bookmarks would disappear, except that as it got later the bookmarks outnumbered the big guys."

"Who was the last big guy to leave?"

The look she gave me over the cigarette was profoundly unfriendly. "Why does that matter?"

"You know why it matters. Last one out, he's the one who gave the cops the high sign."

She sat back on the couch. Then she turned her head and looked at the drapes over the big glass door at the end of the room. She still had a classically beautiful profile. "I don't remember."

"You went to jail that night. You remember."

"Jail," she said. "Couple of hours, laughing with the cops."

"Tell you what," I said. "I'll tell you who it was, and if I'm right, you nod."

Her lower lip came out and retreated again, and she shrugged. I said a name, the only one I thought was possible. The only one without an expiration date, far as I could tell.

She nodded.

24
Heckle and Jeckle

Since I had hours before my plane and I was in Vegas anyway, I swung past the address of one of the women whose names Debbie Halstead had given me and knocked on the door. The harassed-looking woman who answered was probably Debbie's age, maybe thirty-seven or thirty-eight, and the baby squalling in her arms was, she said, ten months old. The house was little and dingy and kind of sad, with that prematurely abandoned look a place acquires when the people who live there don't like it; and the woman, whose name was Petey Ryan—short for Petunia, can you imagine being named Petunia?—was a remarkably unskillful liar. She said the things she'd been told to say and got caught up in *ums* and *uhs* when I asked her a question that took her off the script. What she had to say was, yes, Debbie was an old friend, and yes, Debbie had a daughter. The daughter's name? Uhhh, Tiffany, and her father had taken, uhhh, Tiffany with him when he left Debbie and had *poisoned her mind* against her mother ever since, and wasn't that terrible?

I agreed it was terrible and asked when she had last seen Crystal. When she was ten months old, Petey said, without correcting the name. And when had she seen Debbie last? Eight, nine years ago. And how many years had it been since Debbie's husband sneaked off with the kid?

"Oh, boy," Petey said. She kept her eyes on me but started making little numbers on the tabletop with the tip of her index finger, and I got up and thanked her for her time, and as she followed me to the door, she said, "Wait, I haven't told you all of it."

"It's okay," I called back over my shoulder. "I can fill it in."

I got an earlier plane and thought all the way back to LA, even turning down the generous offer of a bag of peanuts and some water. Debbie's mysterious daughter, Crystal or Tiffany, was as fictitious as Ella Cowan's youthful face, so what had Debbie wanted with me in the first place? Something to stew about.

In the Vegas airport, I'd used my iPhone to download an email from Rina, answering a few questions I'd asked her the night before, and then I'd used the incredibly awkward browser for a little follow-up. The two senators, Durkee and Wheeler, who'd led the questioning of Dolores La Marr, had come from Illinois and California, respectively, which made sense. Dressler's gang was based in Chicago, and Los Angeles was where the movie industry and its unions were. Just to tie the knot a bit more tightly, Senator Wheeler, the Californian, had spent fourteen months in some soft-hands Federal prison for campaign fund irregularities, which consisted of whopping under-the-table donations from a couple of Hollywood unions. Rina also sent me some background on the little kerfuffle among several of the unions in 1952 that had resulted in Dressler's law firm being fired as their counsel of record and another firm being appointed to replace him, although a little less than three years later, Dressler was back in charge. Just your basic back-and-forth.

As Rina said, unions were dull.

Until you think about how much money flows through them.

About how much money is in their pension and health funds. Then unions become very interesting.

I thought I more or less knew what had happened to Dolores La Marr all those years ago, and why. I also more or less knew why she, Pinky Pinkerton and Doug Trent had been killed, and why. I knew, I was *almost* certain, what had happened to Edna. And poor Pyongyang had just gotten in the way.

If I was right about Dolores La Marr, she'd been even sadder than I'd believed. She'd had to live not only with obscurity and solitude and the loss of her beauty and the perpetual taunt of what might have been, but also with the weight of her betrayal. The regret for the person who, in the end, she hadn't been. For all I knew, I thought as I got off the plane in LA, toting my one carry-on, she might have welcomed the end, even through the terror of the moment.

The pity I felt for her had an almost physical weight to it, and it distracted me, interfered with my radar in the LAX parking structure. I'd popped the trunk to toss my carry-on into it before I heard the scuff of a shoe on the concrete behind me.

He was three feet away, all jitters and all nose, a beak that dominated a narrow, olive-skinned face, and he couldn't have weighed more than 140 pounds even though he was as tall as I was. The dark blue shirt bloused out all around him, coming almost to a point where it was tucked into a waist maybe twenty-six inches around. The other thing I noticed about the shirt was that the right sleeve was rolled up, all the way above the elbow, to keep it out of the way of the knife.

He made a rough little sound in his throat, a kind of chortle, probably in appreciation of our relative positions. There he was with a heavy, bone-handled hunting knife in his right hand, its cutting edge honed to a fine and shining line of silver, and his body poised to bring it around in a downward diagonal arc, edge out, that would flay me from throat to navel. And there I was, the doofus of the century, flat-footed, one hand holding up the trunk's lid and the other toting a soft, useless little cloth suitcase.

The noise he made brought the smell of his breath to me, a heavy, queasy mix of rotted meat and speed, and it got to me in a way nothing else had, and I whipped the hand—my left—with the bag in it toward him, and as he gracefully stepped away from it, I brought it back again and lifted it high, as though to try to hit him over the head with it, presenting the picture of failure, my chest and stomach open to him. As he stepped in, I brought my right hand straight up, holding the thin little knife from the trunk lining, and he swung his knife-arm down and onto its upraised point.

My knife slipped between his radius and ulna and jammed, trapped between the bones, and I yanked it toward me, keeping it upright. It hauled him forward, all awkward, angular motion, sharp knees and elbows in all directions, screaming in some language I didn't speak, and as he banged into the back of my car I dropped the suitcase and brought the trunk down with my left hand, cracking his head so hard the trunk bounced back up out of my hand. But by then his knees weren't working, and he went down, clipping the bottom of his chin on my bumper and then again when he hit the concrete. When I rolled him over to yank my knife free, he was bleeding freely from the mouth, so he'd done some serious damage to his tongue.

I kicked his head, hearing a snap that said nothing good about the state of his neck, and then backed away, fighting for breath and scanning the structure for witnesses.

And there he was again, standing five feet away from me, knife in hand, sleeve rolled up, as though nothing had happened to him. It took me a second to process it, but when I looked down, the first one was right where I'd left him and obviously not going anywhere. I thought, *Heckle and Jeckle?* and turned back to the standing one. His eyes were pinwheels of speed and rage and maybe grief, and the scream he emitted was high enough to break me out in goose bumps all over, and I knew I wasn't going to get lucky with the knife again, so I reached into the recesses of the trunk and brought out the Glock I'd taken out of storage before going to Vegas and shot him with it.

The impact knocked him back a few feet, into another parked car. The car began to emit a *whoop-whoop-whoop* alarm and then an authoritative electronic voice said, "Stand away from the vehicle," and both of us looked around, startled, and the *whoop-whoop* started up again and then the electronic voice, and as I sighted the Glock at him, he turned and ran, bending over with both hands pressed to his right side.

The one on the concrete, the dead one, was pitifully light, but even 140 pounds of dead weight is still dead weight, and it took me maybe half a sweaty, cursing minute to hoist him into the trunk and get his arms and legs folded tightly up, like a swatted spider, and even so when I slammed the trunk down, it bounced back up and I had to take out the suitcase before I could get the trunk's lock to engage. I drove out of the structure slowly and deliberately, forcing myself to breathe deeply and evenly, searching everywhere for the second twin or a witness to what had happened, trying to look like someone who'd come off a boring flight, barely awake, nobody worth remembering, and thinking I was succeeding until, when I tried to pay the guy at the exit gate, I dropped change all over the street.

"Twins," I said to Dressler. It was almost an hour later, and I still hadn't caught my breath.

"I've heard of them," he said, rocking back and forth on the couch a little. "Syrian or something. Supposed to be completely nuts." He was looking tired and even a little thinner but a lot more like himself than the last time I'd seen him. And there was that pent-up energy rocking him back and forth and the *something* in his eyes, a little spark like the one in a magician's eyes just before he makes the rabbit pop out of the hat.

But I had my own rabbit, and getting to it was probably going to be difficult. I put my laptop on the table, watching my hands tremble, and Dressler said to the room, "He's going to check his email?"

The front door opened, and Tuffy, who'd beaten me back from Vegas, came back in. He'd already assured me that both Ella Cowan and Abe Frank were still under watch and that nothing had gone wrong. "Got him," Tuffy said. He tossed me my keys, and I caught them. "He's a skinny one."

"Crack," I said. I could hear my voice shaking. "The diet *du jour*."

"I'll get rid of him a little later."

"Just out of curiosity," I said, "how do you do that? Not that I—"

"You're right," Dressler said. "You don't."

I went back to the laptop. "That's what I was saying."

"So that's good, Tuffy," Dressler said. "You take care of that later. Ask Babe to make something for us to eat. You hungry, Junior?"

"I didn't eat the peanuts," I said. I was trapped in Windows Eternity, waiting for my laptop to load, with my knee bobbing up and down two times per second, and I wasn't paying much attention. When I heard the silence, I looked up to find him regarding me as though I'd just spoken the language of flowers or something. "On the plane," I clarified. "I didn't eat the peanuts on the plane."

"So," he said with what was supposed to be a patient nod, "you're hungry."

"I am?"

"You heard him, Tuffy. Just something easy, sandwiches or something."

I said, "Sandwiches would be—"

"When he finishes with his email, he'll eat a little," Dressler said.

"It's not my email," I said. "I want to show you something." I yawned, the nervous kind of yawn. "Sorry. Bad night, bad flight, no peanuts. Killed a man. Takes it out of you."

He didn't even blink. "This is the second body I'm getting rid of for you."

It seemed important to set him straight. "But the first one I killed."

"You never killed anybody before?" His head was cocked slightly to the right, and I had no idea whether he knew the truth, so I didn't take a chance.

"Once."

"Did *that* take it out of you?"

I gave it a minute's consideration, trying to cut through the fog of the present and find my way back to it. "Not right away. He was a pretty loathsome guy. Later, though, it got to me later."

"I'd think it would," he said. "You'll feel better after a sandwich."

His equanimity pissed me off. "Is that what *you* do?" I said. "Eat a sandwich?"

"Me?" He sounded more surprised than I'd ever heard him. "I never killed anybody."

"You? You never. . . ."

"Of course not. I'm offended you would think that. Do I look like somebody who kills people?"

"Well, do *I*?"

"Maybe," he said. "Lot of nice-looking guys kill people. Take Tuffy. Don't you think Tuffy's a nice-looking guy?" Tuffy smiled at me.

"Jesus, I don't know. I suppose. Compared to a lot of guys, yeah, I suppose Tuffy's a nice-looking guy."

"And what do I look like?"

"You look like a man with bad taste in pants."

"They're golf slacks. Golf, you should play golf. Calm you down, lower your blood pressure."

"You don't play golf."

"Not willingly, no. I belong to the clubs because that's where a lot of the deals get made and the money changes hands, but golf is a game for the prematurely dead."

"But you're telling me to play—"

He raised both hands and patted the air at me. "Oh, calm down. I'm just changing the subject, that's all. You were all upset. You needed a boring minute or two."

My phone rang.

"Check your email," Dressler said. "Talk on the phone. I got nowhere to go."

"This'll just take a second." I got up and walked over to the shelf with the carved jade on it. "Hi, sweetie."

Dressler said, "Sweetie, he says."

"It's my daughter."

"So talk to her," Dressler said. "The sandwiches, Tuffy?"

"Mom and Dick made up, sort of. He's got another one for her to look at."

"Not a guy to give up."

"You know what he reminds me of? Do you remember Annabelle?"

"He reminds you of Annabelle?" Annabelle had been Rina's

best friend for a couple of years, the relationship now mysteriously severed.

"Not Annabelle. Pippy. Annabelle's Airedale."

"Annabelle's Airedale."

"No matter how many times you said no, no matter how many times you pushed him away, Pippy would try to hump your leg. There was only one thing he wanted to do in the whole world, and he wanted to do it all the time. Dick's like that."

"Metaphorically, of course."

"It's actually a simile," she said.

"Everybody's explaining things to me lately. Listen, she wants you to go with her, right?"

"Sure. She's pretending it matters what I think."

"Well, unless it's just terrible, love it."

"Sorry?"

"Love it. Get excited about it. Get her to make an offer."

"But you. . . ." I could almost hear it dawn on her. "You're going to *do* something about this, aren't you?"

"That's my damn house," I said. "I mean it's her damn house and your damn house, but she's not going to sell it to make a few bucks for the boyfriend of the week."

"That's not exactly fair."

"Okay," I said, "which issue do you want to address?"

Dressler said, "You talk like that to your daughter?"

"My daughter can take it."

"How old?" Dressler said.

Rina said, "Who's there? Who are you talking to?"

I said to Dressler, "Thirteen," and to Rina, "Irwin Dressler."

"Omigod," Rina said. "Can I meet him sometime?"

"I don't know." To Dressler, I said. "She wants to meet you."

"Me?" Dressler said. "An *alter kocker* like me?"

I said, "He says sure."

"Omigod," she said again. "He's like history in person. Like a Rose Parade float. Did you screw up the first house?"

I said, "I cannot tell a lie."

Dressler said, "Useful to know."

"I've got to go," I said to Rina. "Just be enthusiastic, okay?"

"This isn't about the house for you, is it?" she said slowly. "This is about Dick."

"Fifty-fifty."

"Well, it's okay with me on both counts. Bye."

I put the phone in my pocket. "I pretty much don't tell lies," I said to Dressler.

Dressler nodded slowly. "Sounds like you got something to tell me that I don't want to hear."

"Afraid so."

"What'll it hurt if it waits half an hour? I'm feeling pretty good right now and I'd like to keep it that way."

"Nothing will change in half an hour."

"You'll be not so crazy," Dressler said. "So we'll have a little nosh first." He smiled at me. It was almost friendly. "After all," he said, "you didn't eat the peanuts."

"Within fifteen minutes of our first conversation," I said, "while I was on my way to see Dolores La Marr, I said something to my daughter that was right on the money."

"Easy to say," Dressler said, "since none of us was there to hear you." He was holding down the entire couch, emitting a prickly aura that kept it empty. We'd eaten sandwiches and drunk wine. Tuffy had sprawled his impressive bulk on the carpet about three feet from me, and Babe was sitting on the step up to the dining room.

"Yeah, but I wasn't really so smart, because I promptly forgot about it. But while I was thinking about it, I asked Rina to track down La Marr's testimony in front of the Kefauver Committee. Just in case ruining her wasn't really the point."

"Which means what?" Tuffy asked, and then looked at Dressler as though asking retroactive permission to speak. Dressler was looking at me.

"Rina got it immediately," I said. "She said something like, 'You mean she might not have been just a victim. She might have been a weapon.'"

"This girl, your daughter," Dressler said, "she's how old?"

"Thirteen," I said again.

"Devious mind," he said approvingly. "Although I can't see how Dolly would have been a weapon. Against whom?"

"I'll get there. So at first, when I talked to the people La Marr had known back then, I was looking for people who knew that she had these—friendships—with gangsters. Who knew enough about it—you know, where she'd be, when she'd be there—enough that they could have dimed her out that night. And what I found out was that it was a dead end. Everybody knew, even if they didn't have all the details. Doug Trent said it was no secret."

Dressler said, "But I—"

"*You* were a secret. Probably her only secret. But even so, *somebody* knew about you, or none of this would have happened."

He turned his head toward the dining room, perhaps looking at Babe. "You're saying that—"

"If I don't tell this my way, you're not going to accept it. So let me walk you through it, okay?"

Without turning back to me, he gave me a brusque nod.

"So," I said, "if I couldn't figure out who had the opportunity, the question became, who *profited*? It wasn't like she was all set to play Scarlett in a remake of *Gone With the Wind* and there were four girls lined up behind her, looking for a cliff to push her off. What that meant to me was that it had to be someone in your end of her world, so to speak, someone who had a game in mind. A game with a payoff that would be worth all that trouble."

Now he *was* looking at me, and his eyes were hooded and as still as those of a stuffed animal.

"I decided to look at it from three perspectives at the same time. One was to try to work back from the stories in the paper, try to figure out who planted them, since they were obviously planned in advance. I mean, the newspaper stories were the whole point of the party, what with the big guys gone and just a handful of nonentities in the room by the time the cops and the photographers busted in."

He nodded again, slowly this time.

"Problem is, everybody's dead. The editor who took the call at the newspaper in Vegas that night, the cop who called in the tip for the photographers to come to the jail in the morning. Dead, all of them. So I went at it from the second perspective, her testimony before the committee, to see who they asked her about. You read it. Who did they ask her about?"

"Everybody. Nobody. I mean, they asked her about some of the guys, but it wasn't like they were fishing for information. It was more to incriminate her than anything else. 'Did you know he's a crook?' That sort of stuff."

"That's right," I said. "So I found myself thinking about perspective number three, that old thing about last one out of the room turns off the lights. And I went to work figuring out who the last big guy to leave the party was."

Dressler asked, very softly, "And did you?"

"Yes. But then Rina found something else." This was going to be the hard part. I swiped the touchpad to bring my laptop back to life and turned it toward him. "Did you know that Dolores La Marr went back before the committee? A second time? In a secret session?"

The look he gave me was solid flint. "No. And I don't believe she did."

"Read it," I said. "Look who they're asking her about."

He read it, his lips moving with the words at the beginning. When he got to his own name, he glared around the room as though it angered him that we were there watching, but he kept reading. Then he began to smile, and at the end, he chuckled softly. "She had a pair on her," he said.

"That's what it looks like," I said. "Too bad it's bullshit."

He didn't say anything. Just gazed down at the laptop, putting up a wall between him and whatever I was about to say.

"She probably really said all that stuff, she may even have gotten up and walked out of the room, but I guarantee you that the moment they dismissed the stenographer, she came back in and sat down again."

"Based on what?" The laptop screen went dark but he continued to look at it.

"This shouldn't have been released at all, this bit. That session was held in camera. And even if it had been officially released, it wouldn't have been redacted so sloppily. They never would have let 'Winny' get through."

Dressler said something very softly, with a tiny catch in it, and it took me a second to realize he'd just repeated, "Winny."

"This was leaked to give her an out, in case someone recognized her, back in Washington. In case you heard about it, or someone in Chicago did. They would have found a way to get this to whoever it was."

"Who's *they?*" Dressler asked. "The committee? Why would they do that?"

"It was part of her deal," I said. "She thought they could put things together again for her. You read it right there. They offered to set things straight."

"You don't know what you're talking about," he said. "She'd never have sold me out. Not Dolly." He stopped and listened to himself. "That wasn't who she was."

I didn't reply.

"And if she *did* tell them what—whatever it is you think she told them, why didn't they come after me? Why haven't I ever faced charges?"

"That wasn't what they wanted," I said.

He leaned toward me, his mouth a straight, tight line.

"When you ran the IBEW unions, how much did you personally pocket each year?"

Tuffy said, "IBEW?"

"International Brotherhood of Electrical Workers," I said. "At the time, they controlled most of the behind-the-scenes unions in Hollywood." Dressler was watching me as though he expected me to produce a poisonous snake at any moment. "How much? In a year, how much did you pocket?"

"Two, two and a half mil," he said, and I could see he knew where this was going.

"Let's say two," I said. "If you'd been greedy instead of smart, how much could you have taken?"

"Five."

"And if you'd wanted to dip into the pension fund?"

"Another two."

"So, seven million a year. In 1952. And in 2012 dollars, how much would that be?"

Dressler said, "More than a hundred and forty million. Inflation since that time is a little better than twenty to one."

"In 1952," I said, "you had to let go of those unions. I didn't pay much attention to it when I first noticed it, because you got them back in two, two and a half years, but two and a half years—assuming the person who replaced you was greedy instead of smart—he made almost four hundred million bucks in modern money. I mean the stuff he could have bought with it, back then, would cost almost four hundred million if you bought it now."

Dressler nodded. His eyes were on the dark laptop again.

"This is my guess," I said. "Chicago told you to let go of them for a while."

"That's a good guess." His voice was toneless.

"Here's the rest of the guess. They got a call from Durkee, their own Illinois senator whom they undoubtedly helped to put in office, saying the committee had stuff on you that could be very embarrassing to everyone concerned, and it would be better if you sort of stepped back for a while."

"They didn't tell me the specifics," he said. "They gave me other things to do instead, suggested I'd be too busy to handle everything carefully."

"The California senator, Wheeler, got thrown in the slammer in 1956 for illegal contributions from those unions going back to 1952-53, the years when you weren't in charge. I'd be surprised if Durkee didn't get a pile of cash, too. He was just luckier than Wheeler was."

"So what you're saying. . . ."

"I'm saying that my first guess was right. The whole setup was a plan to turn Dolores La Marr into a weapon that could be used against you. Not to incriminate you, not to imprison you, but to get those unions away from you. For money, plain and simple. Everything that happened to her—the end of her career, the destruction of her life—was just collateral damage. Sort of an accident, like the surgical sponge left in a patient. What they wanted was that money."

"What who wanted?" Dressler seemed almost sleepy.

"One of the guys in Vegas. It was set up in Vegas, between a crook and a couple of bent senators. One other thing. I asked you who knew where she lived, after everything fell apart and she went into hiding at the Wedgwood. Well, her mother did, and the guy she married after *Hell's Sisters* held an office in one of those unions, one of the ones that agitated for a change in management. So whoever set it up probably knew where she lived, too."

"And do you know who it was?" He was reaching into the pocket of his shirt.

"I think so."

He nodded and then cleared his throat. The cords in his neck were almost rigid with tension. "Last time you were here, I told you I had made a mistake, I hadn't made it clear that the malice might still be out there."

"I remember."

He took a slip of paper from the pocket. It had been torn from a small notepad, maybe four inches by five, and folded once the long way. When he opened it, I saw three lines in a small, careful handwriting. "And the reason I made that mistake was because I made an assumption, something I almost never do. But I figured, if there was a guy from back then and I hadn't heard a word about him for fifty, sixty years, he was dead. Even if I didn't know when he'd died, after all this time if he wasn't on anybody's radar, he was dead."

He smoothed the paper on the table with his index finger as though to eliminate the crease. "And I told you, too, that I hadn't kept up with the Internet. So okay, so I still don't know anything about the Internet, but we got guys who do, and one of them, a kid in one of the lawyers' offices in Century City, he came up with something interesting. Here."

He turned the paper around so the writing was right-side up for me, and slid it to me with his fingertips. It was an address in Palm Springs, and beneath that, a name: Robert LeCochon.

I looked up at him at a hard, tight grin I hoped would never be leveled at me, and we said, in unison, "Bobby Pig."

25
The Brand

Tuffy's legs were outlined in fire, a line of hot reddish gold lighted by the rising sun banging off the thicket of pale hair on his calves. He was wearing a blue polo shirt and a pair of beige Bermuda shorts as though he'd been born in them, and he was carrying two large, heavy bags that seemed to weigh nothing at all. Once in a while he'd start to whistle, and Dressler would have to shush him.

At long last Dressler's golf shorts were seeing a golf course. In fact, two pairs of them were, because I was also sheathed in a loud, ugly plaid from the waist down. The waist was so small that the slacks gapped open by about four inches in front, held together by my belt. It felt drafty.

Dressler's grimness lifted slightly every time he looked at my pants.

At eight that evening, Babe had gone to LAX and lifted a set of plates from a car parked in the lot for the international terminal. Then he'd left his car in the structure, stolen a second car, and driven it home to put the plates on it. With any luck, by the time we were finished here, he could get back there and replace both the plates and the car while their owners were still in Puerto Vallarta or Bangkok or wherever.

We'd parked the stolen car with the stolen plates a quarter of a mile from the entry to the golf club around 4:30 A.M. and then found our way onto the course and over a lot of expensive grass in the dark until we got to the fourth tee, where we waited for sunrise. When it began, we were still alone on the course, although from a distance I heard the crack of someone hitting a ball.

"Probably on the first tee," Dressler said. He said to Tuffy, "Driver."

Tuffy said, "Huh?"

"The wood one, gimme the wood one."

Tuffy handed him the club. Dressler stepped up to the ball he'd teed up in the dark, looked down at it for a moment, did a little wiggle with his hips, and knocked it straight down the middle of the fairway.

Tuffy whistled approval and I said, "Very impressive."

"Half the developments in Southern California were negotiated on golf courses," Dressler said. "Every stroke I got closer to par was worth a few million bucks." He slipped the club back into one of the bags Tuffy was toting, and the three of us took off in the direction his ball had gone.

The fourth hole was a long one, with the fairway hooking to the left about 70 percent of the way to the green. If you ignored the bend in the fairway and just kept going straight, you'd be in Robert LeCochon's back yard.

What we hadn't been able to tell from Google Earth and Google Maps was whether the yard was fenced. We hadn't seen anything thick and straight marking the line between the golf course and the yard, but that didn't mean there wasn't something too thin to be visible in the picture.

"Five-iron," Dressler said as we neared the ball.

The sun had risen a few more degrees, a slice of burning

orange on the horizon behind us. As Dressler studied his ball and Tuffy hunted for the five-iron, I went over to Dressler and stood beside him. In my hand was the color printout from Google Earth that told us that the long, low Santa Fe–style house directly in front of us was where Bobby Pig had gone to ground all those years ago, sticking his head out only when Pinky Pinkerton had told Edna to place that call.

"A net," Tuffy said, holding out a club and squinting toward Bobby's house. "Some kind of net."

"Sure," Dressler said. He took the printout, folded it, and put it in his pocket. "To keep his windows from getting broken. He must be pretty confident, not even fenced in like this." He looked down at the club. "That's a seven."

Tuffy said, "So what?"

I said to Dressler, "Are you keeping score or something?"

"Details are important," Dressler muttered, but he took the club, positioned himself above the ball, and whapped it. He watched with surprise as the ball rose and kept going about sixty yards until it was stopped by the net. He said, "Maybe a seven was the right club after all."

I said, "Let's go."

"You didn't have to come, you know," Dressler said, sliding the club into the bag.

"I saw her, remember? I'd be here even if you weren't."

"Calm down," he said. He set off for the net and we followed. "Look at Tuffy. Is he all crazy?"

"I don't know," I said. The top half of the sun, sliding above the treeline behind us, struck a big window in Bobby Pig's house with a blaze of fire, and I shielded my eyes with my hand. "Are you all crazy, Tuffy?"

Tuffy said, "I'm hungry."

"After," Dressler said. "I'll buy us all a big breakfast after.

Once we're clear of Palm Springs. See the tall pine tree to the left?"

I squinted against the glare. "Yes."

"Under there. Nice and shady." He turned and looked behind us. Acres of rolling grass, not a soul in sight. "Good," he said. "This is the tricky part."

Under the pine, which I identified without thinking about it as a Monterrey Cypress, going brown and probably dying in this dry heat, Tuffy examined the net as Dressler unzipped the little shoulder bag I'd been carrying. "It just lifts up over here," Tuffy said.

Dressler said, "Here," handing me a tight, white little ball of wadded-up plastic. "Tuffy, get this on fast. Who knows how long we'll be alone?"

The thin white suits went on right over our clothes and zipped up the front. The only thing that slowed us down was that we had to take our shoes off, put the suits on, and then put the shoes back on before covering them with elastic booties made of the same stuff as the suits. When we were finished, we looked like the guys who handle radioactive materials.

"Put the caps and gloves on," Dressler said as Tuffy lifted the net. "These things were designed for clean rooms, like in computer labs, but they're great for someone who wants to keep his DNA to himself. Science is a wonderful thing."

"What if he's got someone on lookout?" I said.

"Then we kill him or he kills us," Dressler said. "But my guess? My guess is he thinks he's got things salted away. My guess is that he's sleeping like a baby."

The house was a grayish taupe, the approximate color of old, well-dried adobe, essentially a series of rectangles with rounded corners, at the top of a gently rising lawn about fifty feet long. Whoever built the house obviously thought a golf course was a great view, because about half of the side of the house facing us—which I figured was the back, since the street was on the other side—was glass. Big picture windows, either dazzling with the rising sun or framing dark rooms, plus a couple of double-size sliding glass doors, made the reason for the net obvious. Most of the house was breakable.

We were moving silently now, just three moon men climbing the hill. By unspoken agreement, Tuffy and I were in front, where we'd stop or slow any bullets, and Dressler was a couple of feet behind. The slope was minimal, but I could hear him breathing harshly behind me and I remembered, for the first time that morning, how old he was.

Sliding doors are a pain because there's not much anyone can do about a piece of iron or wood laid down on the inside track to stop the sliding half, so I was happy to see, to our left, a standard-size door that, my house radar told me, led to the same kind of utility room I'd passed through to get into Edna's place. I pointed a plastic-gloved hand toward it, and the other two honored my expertise in breaking and entering by following along without any argument.

All those windows were unsettling. It was almost enough to make me doubt the wisdom of the clean-room suits. In our golf slacks, we could at least have poked around for a bit, trying to look like we were searching for a ball that had found its way through the net. Dressed as we were, it would be impossible for anyone who spotted us to mistake us as anything but death on foot.

After living in the city, I found it amazingly quiet out there. One mockingbird, high in the Monterrey Cypress, let loose a trilling salute to the morning as we approached the door, and I saw Tuffy flinch when someone hit a golf ball far away, but other than that, the world was in that silent, gathering-itself-for-the-day mode we miss in the city, buried as it is beneath the clamor of early rush hour. A dry, rustling sound drew my attention, and I turned to see the mockingbird drop down out of the Cypress and then spread its wings and soar up toward another tree, just a generic tree with flat, broad leaves in the neighboring yard.

Tuffy shifted anxiously from foot to foot behind me as I worked on the lock, which was good enough to keep us standing there for two very, very long minutes. They both sighed when I finally managed to turn the knob. No chain, no latch on the inside. Bobby Pig had stopped worrying decades ago.

With the door open about an inch, I pointed at myself and then at the two of them, waving them behind me as I eased the door the rest of the way open. Over my shoulder, I said, just audibly, "Breathe through your mouths. Touch your tongue to the top of your mouth. Stay away from walls and furniture." Then I made the universal raised-finger-to-lips *shhhhhh* sign and went in.

The utility room was half the size of Edna's kitchen, all gleaming brushed stainless steel, front-loading everything: washer, dryer, even a home dry-cleaning unit. Spotless. Along one wall a stainless steel rod had been suspended, and from it, on bright steel clothes hangers, were nine or ten identical pairs of pale blue pajamas. I touched one and felt silk.

Dressler jostled me, trying to get past, and I turned to him and, for the first time, stared him down. With my mouth almost touching his ear, I said, "This is what I do. I'm the expert. You're the amateur."

I turned my back to him again, eased open the door to the kitchen, and went in. I could hear the rustling of their plastic slippers as they followed.

It was an enormous room with a marble-topped island in the center. A restaurant-size range stood against the wall to the left, eight burners. Inset into the wall above it was a bricked rectangle with a black iron door: a pizza oven. The sink and dishwasher were to the right, and straight ahead, beyond them, was a double-wide archway leading into the dining room and, beyond that, the living room. The sun was mostly up behind us now, and the windows in the living room looked out onto the deep bluish shadow cast by the house. A Bentley, dark blue or black, was visible through the giant window in the living room.

To our left, an open doorway led from the kitchen into a hall-way. I took the Google Earth printout from Dressler and undid one of the little convenience zippers in my plastic suit to get my wallet. I slipped out the little pen that came with the wallet and made a quick, speculative sketch: the kitchen in which we stood with the utility room behind it, the two big rooms in front of us, and, to the left, a long corridor running the full length of the house. Off it, further to the left, I sketched in two bedrooms and a bath, and, at a guess, a much larger bedroom with its own bath at the end. I pointed at it, eyebrows elevated.

Dressler looked at it and nodded, and Tuffy, forgetting him-self, grunted and then covered his mouth with his hand as we both stared at him. I tapped the pen against the paper for a sec-ond, thinking. My burglary mentor, Herbie, always said it's the thing you don't expect that'll kill you. I expected whoever was in the house to be in the bedrooms at this hour, so if I were on my own, I'd first make a quick tour of the rooms I thought would be empty, the living room and the dining room, just to eliminate any surprises. Then I'd start listening at bedroom doors.

I headed off toward the archway to the dining room with the two of them a couple of feet behind me.

The dining room was exactly as I'd envisioned it, spacious and floored in the pale wood, probably bamboo, I'd seen from the kitchen. To the far left, beyond the heavy table set for eight, was a doorway into that same corridor. The doorway corresponded with the one I'd sketched conjecturally on my little floor plan. Dressler, behind me, had the floor plan in his hand, and when he saw the open doorway he made a single little click with his tongue, sort of a *tsk*, to indicate either surprise or approval.

The place was remarkably quiet; the sound of our plastic slippers on the floor and the legs of our plastic pants whisking together was practically deafening. On a hunch, I took a good look at the dining-room windows to my right; they were double-paned, almost certainly for insulation against the heat, but double-paned windows are also one of the great silencers, and I relaxed a little. I'd been concerned about the noise of gunfire inside the house alerting the neighbors, but now I removed that from my list of worries.

It was still a pretty long list. For one thing, I had no way of knowing how many people were in the house. And we had exactly one gun among us, the one Tuffy was carrying. Dressler had been insistent that no other firearms would be allowed inside, and at the last moment I'd left the Glock in the trunk of my car. I didn't know what was so magical about the gun Tuffy had, which was a banged-up, ordinary-looking Sig Sauer, but Irwin Dressler didn't get to be Irwin Dressler by allowing himself to be second-guessed.

He was already in motion, heading past me into the living room. All I could do was follow and try to see what had caught his eye.

The room was in full light now, and it made me check my watch: 6:14 A.M. The sun rose earlier here than it did in Los Angeles because of the flat, endless expanse of desert to the east. I should have taken that into consideration. I reached for Dressler's arm to get his attention, but he shrugged me off and kept going.

The far right corner of the living room had been rounded

off and the space filled with a huge fireplace, almost tall enough to walk into. It obviously saw a lot of use; the inside was fire-blackened, and the wall above it was smudged with smoke and soot. But what had drawn Dressler was a scattering of long pieces of rusty-looking iron, three of them, lying on the hearth. They weren't the conventional fireplace tools although they were about the same length, and he had picked one up and was study-ing its end.

He made an abrupt gesture to Tuffy, waving him over. A box of long wooden matches stood to the left of the fireplace, and beside that I saw a lever to turn on the gas in the exhaust-pipe size gas log that ran almost the full width of the opening. Dressler motioned for Tuffy to strike a match, and then he leaned down and turned on the gas.

Tuffy had the match going within a second or two, and the gas caught with a *whoosh* when he tossed it in. I tried to get closer, but Dressler extended the piece of iron between us, point-ing it at me like a sword, and I thought he was threatening me with it until I saw his eyes. The moment I caught his gaze, he dropped it to the end of the piece of iron he was holding, and I looked down at it.

It was a brand. At the end was the silhouette of a plump, happy-looking pig. In a cursive script beneath it, backward, of course, I read Rancho Piggy. From the look of the tip, which was charred and even crusted, it had seen a lot of use.

He gave me the hard, mirthless little grin I'd seen at his house when we identified Bobby Pig, and he put the branding iron down on the hearth with its tip in the fire.

Time was wasting, and this had nothing to do with why I was here. I waved at him to follow, but all he did was turn back to the fireplace and adjust the branding iron to center its tip more precisely in the flame. The flames emerged blue from the gas log but turned a cooler yellow where they flowed around the tip of the iron, like water around a stone in the center of a stream.

I gave up on Dressler and Tuffy, and went back through the dining room and into the kitchen. I stopped and listened again, and then stepped into the corridor.

It had no external walls, and therefore no windows, so it was relatively dim. It suddenly grew a lot dimmer, and I turned quickly to see Tuffy in the door to the kitchen, with Dressler behind him. They stood there, looking, as I was, down the hall.

There were three doors on the left side of the hallway, the first and third closed, and an open door at the far end with the morning light coming through it; the room obviously had either a large window or a glass wall. The open door on the left was between the two closed ones, and when I had moved quietly down the hall to it and peeked around the edge I saw that it was a bathroom. So, my guess was bedroom, bathroom, bedroom.

To my right was a glass-framed tub and shower. Directly ahead were a white marble vanity with a sink at its center and a floor-to-ceiling mirror that reflected me in the doorway, looking a little spooked, staring in with Tuffy just behind me. To the left, near the vanity, was an open door, obviously leading to the bedroom we'd just passed.

Sliding my plastic-shod feet over the marble floor, I went to the bedroom door. There, asleep or unconscious on a narrow single bed, was Heckle, the surviving twin. His skin was a bad gray color and his black hair was damp with sweat. He'd tossed the covers back and bandages sheathed him from shoulder to hip.

Someone pulled me back: Tuffy. Dressler squeezed in front of me, looked at the bed, and said, very softly, "Dolly?"

I whispered, "Certainly." He nodded and looked past me at Tuffy, who wrapped an arm around my neck from behind and dragged me, almost gently, backward out of the bathroom and into the hall. He let go of me, put both hands up, palms facing me in a *stay there* gesture, and went back into the bathroom. Dressler nodded at him and came out to join me. He stood there, looking at the floor, and I heard a soft grunt and something like a stick breaking, and then Tuffy came back out, wiping his hands on the thighs of his shorts. Other than the damp hands, there was no sign that anything at all had happened in the room.

This time, I followed them.

They gathered in front of the second closed door, both looking at me. I shut my eyes, let out all my breath, drew another one, and very slowly turned the knob and pushed the door open about two inches.

A queen-size bed, pale pastels with white posts, neatly made and empty.

I opened the door another foot or so to reveal a feminine room, not frilly or whimsical, but done in soft colors and with more mirrors than most men want in their bedrooms. There was nothing to indicate that the room was occupied—no clothes lying around, no shoes or slippers on the floor. Some women's clothing hung in the open closet to the right, but there was no way to tell how long it had been since anyone had gone through the clothes or had slept in the bed. I could see in the mirror that no one was behind the door.

If I had been alone, I might have picked up something I failed to notice at the time. I was distracted by the two of them peering around me and also by the sharp smell of hot iron from the living room. Whatever excuse I might want to make, the fact is that I closed the door and led them down the hall and into the big, bright bedroom where Bobby Pig lay on his bed, eyes wide, watching us come in.

26
Every Minute You Can Get

He looked terrible.

The bed was king size, but it was still a hospital bed with a high railing running along one side and a cluster of controls on a corded remote just to Bobby Pig's right. He'd raised the head of the bed to about a forty-five degree angle so he could sit up. He was gaunt and wasted, the bones of his skull pushing through the skin and his eyes enormous, glittering like wet stones at the bottom of a hole. The fat that had supported them had been burned away by disease.

A clear plastic oxygen tube ran beneath his nose. His hair was mostly gone, but what he had left was long and combed straight back from a fleeing widow's peak and dyed black in lank strands, pasted to a gleaming scalp. His eyebrows, still thick and bushy, had turned stark white.

"Bobby," Dressler said. "Long time." He followed me into the room, giving most of his attention to the wall of glass at the far end, which faced out onto a white-brick-enclosed courtyard with what looked like metal sculptures scattered around it, each holding a reservoir of reddish fluid. Dressler took it all in, turned back to Pigozzi, and said, "You look like shit."

"I been—" Pigozzi began, and he broke off and swallowed hugely. "I been sick."

"No kidding," Dressler said, looking out the window again. "You gonna die?"

Pigozzi cleared his throat and said, "So they tell me."

"All of this," Dressler said, and suddenly his voice was shaking, "all of this and you were gonna die anyway?"

"You know how it is, Irwin," Pigozzi said. His eyes were burning like those of a man who has lost everything to pain, and he'd never for a moment taken them off of Dressler, even though Tuffy and I were in the room. His voice was a husk. "You want every minute you can get."

"Actually, Bobby," Dressler said, "I *don't* know how it is. I don't know how it is to live like a liar and a thief and a traitor and a sneak. I always tried to do my business, even when it got a little rough around the edges, I always tried to do it honorably. I figured you were the same. I figured everybody was the same."

Pigozzi closed his eyes. I identified the very soft hiss I was hearing as the sound of the oxygen flowing out of the tube beneath his nostrils.

"Nice view," Dressler said. "Good to get all this light like this. I should do this to my bedroom, back at home. You ever been to my house?"

"No." Pigozzi's eyes were still closed.

"These things out here," Dressler said. "You gotta open your eyes, Bobby, so you know what I'm asking you about, okay? These things out here with all the pink stuff in them. What are they?"

"They're hummingbird feeders," Pigozzi said.

Dressler looked at them a moment longer and then said, "Hummingbird feeders."

"I like to watch hummingbirds."

"How about that?" Dressler said. To me, he said, "He likes to watch hummingbirds."

"Lot of people like hummingbirds," I said.

"Yeah? Why is that?"

"They're beautiful," I said. "They're harmless—"

"Tell you the truth, Junior," Dressler said, "I wasn't asking you. I was asking Bobby here."

Behind Dressler, on the other side of the glass wall, a hummingbird dropped down and stopped dead in mid-air, looking in at us. Pigozzi watched it. "What that guy said," Pigozzi said. "I like them."

The hummingbird turned to one of the feeders, inserted its beak with tremendous precision, and hung there weightlessly, feeding.

"And how would you feel, Bobby," Dressler said, "if I sneaked in here some day and cut all your hummingbirds' throats, maybe smashed them flat with a hammer."

I could hear Pigozzi swallow, but he didn't answer.

"I know how you'd feel. You'd be *bereaved*, wouldn't you? Because you're right, they are beautiful, and things that are beautiful should get a pass, don't you think? You were never beautiful, were you, Bobby?"

"Not so's you'd notice," Pigozzi said.

"Me, neither. Wonder what it feels like. I know—*you* know—that not all people who are beautiful are good just because they're beautiful. And even the ones who are good, well, they're not good all the time. Right?"

Pigozzi looked past us at the door.

"He's not coming," Dressler said. "He's dead. Broken neck. Seemed appropriate, since they were twins and that's what happened to his brother." To Tuffy, he said, "Broken neck, right? You broke his neck?"

Pigozzi cleared his throat again and said, "Get to it, you fucker. Just get to it."

"Yeah, okay, right." Dressler sounded like a man who'd forgotten why he'd come. "Tuffy. Go get it."

Tuffy looked puzzled for a moment but then he turned and jogged out of the room. I stood there, listening to the crackle of his slippers on the wooden floor until I couldn't hear them any more. Pigozzi looked at the doorway through which Tuffy had disappeared. Then he reached up and peeled away the oxygen tube.

"So, Bobby," Dressler said. "I'm going to do something for you that you didn't do for her. I'm going to offer you a choice. Not an easy choice, but a choice." He turned as Tuffy came into the room, holding the brand. The tip wasn't glowing, but it was smoking, and I could feel the heat even three feet away. "Whaddya want, Bobby? You want to get shot or you want to get branded?"

Pigozzi tried to talk but went into a spasm of coughing. He was flailing for the oxygen tube when Dressler said, "Me, too. That's what I'd choose, too. Give me that thing, Tuffy." And he took the brand and walked toward Pigozzi, holding the smoking iron in front of him, aimed at the center of the blue silk pajamas covering his chest.

"Come on," Pigozzi said. It would have been a shout if he'd had any voice left. As it was, it sounded like two rocks rubbed together. "You dumb fucker, you pathetic mark. She sold you— she sold you like an old car. A million five, that's what you were to her. Petty fucking change."

Dressler stopped dead where he was. His arm, the arm holding the brand, began to shake, and he let it straighten and hang down until the tip of the brand hissed against the pale wooden floor, sending up a fragrant thread of smoke. "All my life," he said. "All my life I been trying to be something I could live with. And I'm going to give that away for you? A piece of crap like you?" He let the brand fall from his hand and clatter to the floor. "No. You're not important enough."

"Irwin," Pigozzi said, trying to lean forward. "I knew you wouldn't, I knew—Irwin, you won't regret it, I didn't mean what I said about her. I'll—I'll make it up to you, you can have, you can have—"

"This was always one of your problems, Bobby," Dressler said. He sounded sad. "You jump to conclusions." He looked away from the bed. "Tuffy?"

Without hesitation, Tuffy shot Pigozzi through the chest, twice. The sound felt like a punch to both my ears, and outside hummingbirds took flight in all directions.

"Toss the gun on the bed, Tuffy," Dressler said, "and let's get out of here."

The gun bounced once on the mattress and came to rest against Pigozzi's right arm. I said, "Why leave the gun?"

"It was used three weeks ago in a liquor store robbery in South Central," Dressler said. His voice was as thin as the smoke rising from the floor; there was no lower register. "It'll drive the cops crazy." He turned toward the door and froze.

"Is he dead?" It was a woman's voice, and I turned to see Edna. She had a very shiny automatic, probably nickel-plated, in her hand.

"He's dead," Dressler said. He didn't seem very interested in any of it.

Edna had lost the 1940s big-band hairdo, and now her steel-gray hair was chopped about four inches long, a much more stylish cut. Her eyes wandered over the three of us, and when she got to me, she smiled.

I said, "Hi, Livvy."

"Well, well," she said. "A fan."

"Irwin," I said. "Meet the little girl behind most of this. Irwin Dressler, Olivia Dupont."

"Not any more," Livvy said. "Now I'm the grieving widow of Robert LeCochon, and thanks to you, I'm worth about forty million bucks." She glanced back to the bed, which was gradually turning a deep dark red. "He is dead, right?"

"He's dead," Tuffy said. He edged toward the bed.

"Nope," she said. "Just stay there." To Dressler, she said, "He told you, because I heard him, how that little slut sold you out."

"Yes, Miss," Dressler said. He sounded almost courtly. "He did."

"Good. Just want to make sure you know who she really was. It's a bit much to give me all the credit, though. Bobby started this on his own. I just provided creative guidance. Toward the end, he was so terrified of you he almost forgot he was sick. And I look at you and ask myself what he was so scared of. Just another old guy, waiting for the big ending." She waved the barrel of the gun at us, her eyes going back to Bobby Pig for a moment, nothing much revealed in them. "Now, I think the three of you should stand next to each other, facing me, at the end of the bed. Except you, big boy. You face Bobby, since you've just this moment finished shooting him as I rush into the room with a gun in my hand, and when I shoot you in the back, the old fart and Junior here turn to face me, all startled, and I shoot them. Let's see if we can't do this in one take." She raised the gun and sighted down the barrel and said, "Turn around, big boy."

Movement outside drew her attention, and I said, "Hummingbirds," and the glass wall shivered and broke in a million places and cascaded down in a slow-motion waterfall, and one side of Olivia Dupont's face, the side farther from the window, was blown into space, and she went sideways, as though leaping to recover it, and followed the cascade of glass to the floor.

Dressler clutched his chest and let out a groan that sounded like someone prying the lid off a wooden box. As he sank to his knees, one hand grabbing at the blankets and pulling them off of Pigozzi, Debbie Halstead stepped through the wreckage of the window and said to Tuffy, "Pick him up and get him out here, to my car. I'll get him to a hospital."

I was so disoriented by Debbie's appearance and the fact that I wasn't dead that I don't actually remember carrying Dressler to the car, except for one detail:. He was very light, and he seemed to get lighter.

27

The Golden Road

Debbie drove like she shot—efficiently, accurately, and with a minimum of drama. It was almost relaxing.

Even before she'd navigated the car out of Bobby Pig's neighborhood, Tuffy had tucked some nitroglycerine tablets under Dressler's tongue, and within a few minutes he was giving useless orders: *Slow down, there's a stop sign up here, we have to go get the car; hell, no I don't need to go to a hospital. Tuffy will take me to my own doctor.*

Debbie glanced into the rearview mirror and said, "Be quiet," and Dressler shut up, except for the occasional mutinous mumble.

We'd left so quickly, and I'd been so bewildered by Debbie's sudden appearance and Dressler—whom I guess I'd privately considered immortal—going down like that, that I was surprised when we stopped beside our stolen car near the golf club, and Tuffy pulled the golf bags out of Debbie's trunk, along with the little zipped bag I'd been carrying, and threw them into the back of our car. He'd grabbed them out of Bobby Pig's utility room at some point while I was trying to get Dressler comfortable on the backseat of Debbie's SUV.

He helped Dressler into the stolen car, and Debbie said to me, "They're going to stop at the doctor's office. I'll take you home."

I said, "Wherever that is," but stayed in the car. She waited until Tuffy had pulled out, and then put the SUV in gear.

"That car in good shape?" she asked, watching it go.

"I don't know. Tuffy boosted it from LAX. It got us here all right."

"Since you don't seem to know where you live, I'll follow them to the doctor's. Just in case."

And she did, although Tuffy drove like he had a car full of raw eggs, braking at everything he saw and rarely exceeding forty miles an hour, even on the 10 Freeway.

"Who was the one I shot?" she asked.

"An actress. Olivia Dupont."

"Whoa," Debbie said. "She played that bitch with the whip."

"You're not old enough to remember that."

"Cable. Everything's on cable. So the guy on the bed, he was a gangster, right? What was she doing there, a personal appearance?"

"Sort of. She was married to the dead guy in the bed. And she'd been pretending to be someone's secretary. Boss's orders, or maybe her own orders, I don't know."

Debbie said, "Pretending to be? Was there a real secretary?"

"Yeah," I said. "Until two or three days ago. I saw pictures of her in a carton I found in her garage. Little, happy-looking fat lady."

"What happened to her?"

"My guess is, something with a knife. She'll probably turn up in pieces." I sat and thought about what I'd just said, and the sign on Pinky's door popped into my mind's eye. Doug Trent had probably made a courtesy call to Pinky to tell him I was coming, and Pinky had called Pigozzi, as he had probably been told to do if anyone came nosing around about Dolly. The sign was there to hold me off until Livvy could get there from Palm Springs, at least one knife-twin in tow, and sit down in Edna's chair. I was, at least indirectly, responsible for Edna's death.

Debbie shook her head disapprovingly. "Knives are nasty."

She drove in silence for a few minutes, and I wrenched myself away from Edna and said, "She made a pretty good movie, Olivia DuPont, I mean, back in 1950. *Hell's Sisters*."

Debbie said, her attention on the road, "Yeah?"

"Did you ever see it?"

"Nope. I know this sounds funny, but I like TV better than movies."

"Why?"

"Nothing I've seen on film ever fooled me," she said. "When I watch a movie, I see how much money they're spending, and they're still not fooling me. Makes me nervous, all those wasted bucks. I guess I like TV because it's cheap."

"She had a costar in that movie," I said. "Beautiful girl named Dolores La Marr."

"Jesus, Tuffy drives slow." She flicked the brights at him. "Dolores La Marr, huh?" She shrugged. "Nope. Never heard of her."

We were heading toward LA on the 10, the sun a few fingers high in the sky behind us, when I said, "This road? The 10?"

"Yeah?" Debbie said. She pumped the brakes once to warn the guy behind her to back off.

"It replaced the old Route 66," I said. "The dream highway. H.L. Mencken said that the US sloped to the left, and everything that was loose rolled downhill to California. This was the road most of them rolled on."

"I did," she said. She looked over at me. "And not from Vegas."

"I figured."

"He knew—" She lifted her chin to indicate the car Dressler was in. "He knew you wouldn't let me tag around behind you. So he dreamed that story up. If you spotted me, I had a reason for being there."

"Were you around when I went into that office building? Pinky's office building?"

"Saw you come out both times," she said. "When I figured you were going home, the second time, I called you to make sure you were in one piece, despite the way you looked."

I said, "But that means Dressler thought it might get dangerous after all."

"And it did get dangerous," she said. "But who knows what he thought?" She triggered her high-beams a couple of times again to speed Tuffy up. Tuffy responded by hitting the brakes. "He's Irwin Dressler," she said. "He just wanted to make sure every contingency was covered. That's what Irwin Dressler does."

I was halfway asleep when the phone rang. I looked around a bit wildly, saw that we were approaching the grim, warehouse-rich borders of downtown LA, and dug the phone out of my pocket.

"It's over," Rina said. "You should be proud of yourself."

"I'm not," I said. "You have no idea how not proud of myself I am."

"Anyway, it worked. I was all enthusiastic about the house, which was actually pretty nice, and Mom made an offer. Old Dick said it hadn't been on the market very long, so she shouldn't lowball it, but that he'd *hand-walk* it—that's what he said, hand-walk it, as though that makes any sense—through everything. It would go through in no time. Mom was so excited. She'd found a place she liked, and she thought I liked, and she'd have money in the bank. She took me out for dinner, to celebrate." She sighed. "Pizza."

"I'm sorry, sweetie."

"And this morning that sneaky little asshole told her she'd lost the house, somebody outbid her, even though he'd promised he wouldn't show it to anybody else. So she told him she never wanted to see him again, and she meant it."

I said, "Mmm-hmmm."

"And she's been crying ever since. Why does she have to be so *hapless*? Why can't she be more like—more like—"

"Like?"

"Like you. I mean, she should be honest, but not, you know, *clueless*."

"Good people have a problem with people like me and people like Dick, because good people *are* good, and they're truthful, and they think other people are, too. Your mother is a very good person. You should value that. It's one of the things we should both love about her. Listen, just take care of her, okay?"

"Which of you am I like?"

"Rina," I said, "I'm not saying this because I'm your father, but you're not like anybody in the world. You're something completely new."

"Yeah," she said. "Right." And she hung up.

I said, "Yipes," and exhaled so hard it felt like my lungs had turned inside out. Then I put the phone back in my pocket and caught Debbie looking over at me. The moment I looked up, she returned her attention to the road.

She said, "Lucky girl."

ANNA

Part
Five

Part
Five

28

On This Side of the Window

Being dead isn't entirely without advantages.

For one thing, obviously, those of us who are over here have already gotten through the thing living people fear most. It's silly, looking back at it all, how afraid of it we were, when it's really just like going through a window. Without breaking the glass.

All the things that scared me, the things that made me sad, the things that made me climb up on that table, hearing the tragic sound track music in my ears—they were all so silly. Life's greatest joke is that you don't get any real perspective until you're dead.

Life is just there, to be made the best of, until it isn't. And that's all right, too.

Another of the good things about being where I am now, especially for people who were beautiful once, or just healthy and without pain, is that you can decide which person you want to be, out of all the people you've been in your life. You could choose childhood, if you'd like. You don't actually have a body, of course, but it's kind of like it was when you were alive and doing something, when you weren't thinking about being you, but you knew your body was there, behaving itself, and you felt good about how it looked, or worked. So Dolly's young and light and beautiful again, and it thrills her. Although she'll forget about it, over time.

And me? I don't even have an accent.

That nice burglar boy came by after the police were finished with the apartment, and he did the sweetest thing. He stood in the middle of the living room and invited me to go to his place, down on the third floor. He didn't know the rules, he said, but he thought maybe I could leave here and go somewhere else if I was invited. And he was right, I could have. He said he didn't live there all the time, but if I went down there, maybe I wouldn't be so lonely.

But lonely is what I'm not right now. Dolly and I have so much to talk about, now that we're both on this side of the window. I had been alone for so long—Dolly was here, but we could only really see each other's shadows. And she'd been alone, too, and now she isn't. So I said, No, thanks, to the nice burglar boy. We'll stay right here, Dolly and I.

And now new people are moving in, a family with three children. Neither Dolly nor I ever had children, and we're like a couple of maiden aunts. It will be so lively here.

Of course, children are open to things adults miss. Just yesterday the baby—he's about a year old—was in his bassinet while his father was measuring for carpets to cover all that awful black wood, and the baby looked right at Dolly and gave her the biggest smile.

He thought she was *so* pretty.

Author's Note

Writing this book was almost illegally enjoyable. I can only hope it's fun to read, too.

Although Dolores La Marr and most of her Hollywood are fictional, there was a real-life model for Irwin Dressler, the legendary Sidney Korshak. Korshak ran most of Hollywood on behalf of the Chicago mob for decades—studio moguls actually did talk to him daily—and also oversaw the creation of much of modern Los Angeles, including several now-respectable banks that were originally set up to launder money. Dressler's private personality is a product of my imagination, but anyone who's interested in the extent to which the mob—often through Korshak—participated in the shaping of Los Angeles, Las Vegas, and entire state of California might want to read *Supermob* by the investigative reporter (and Pulitzer nominee) Gus Russo. An amazing book.

I used to see Korshak almost daily at his famous table at a Beverly Hills restaurant, where he accepted the obeisances of stars and power-players alike in between calls on his personal telephone, which was swept for bugs and taps several times a day.

Lots of good music went into this book, courtesy of my

exploding iPod. Some of it was from the forties, especially Benny Goodman and the Andrews Sisters, but also Margaret Whiting, Glenn Miller, and Duke Ellington. More contemporary artists who made contributions to my energy fund include The Wombats, the lamented Amy Winehouse, The Raconteurs, Jon Fratelli, Adele, Arctic Monkeys, Rufus Wainwright, Bonnie Raitt, Neil Young, and The Decemberists, among thirty or forty others. Anyone who wants to suggest music to me is invited to do so through the CONTACT TIM button at www.timothyhallinan.com.

My thanks to my demonically energetic editor, Juliet Grames, and all at Soho for plucking Junior out of the ebook ether and slapping him onto the page; to my agent, Bob Mecoy; and to my first listener and most patient audience, my wife, Munyin Choy-Hallinan.

Continue reading for a preview from the next
Junior Bender Mystery

HERBIE'S GAME

PART ONE

"So you see, kid," Herbie said, "we're like Robin Hood. We steal from the rich and we give to the poor."

"How do we give to the poor?" I asked.

"I said we were *like* Robin Hood, not a slavish *imitation* of Robin Hood."

"So we're *sort* of like Robin Hood," I said.

"Yeah," Herbie said. "If you squint."

1

Ur-Hamlet

Eighteen minutes in—just two minutes short of my limit—I was ready to write the place off.

It was a very nice house in a very nice part of the Beverly Hills flats. A very nice car was usually standing in the driveway, a BMW SUV so new the odometer hadn't hit the hundreds yet, and I could smell that canned new-car fragrance through the closed windows. The locks on the house's doors, it seemed to me during my week of taking the occasional careless-looking careful look, would yield to a persuasive argument. No bothersome alarm tip-offs. Inside, I was sure, would be a lot of very nice stuff.

And I was right: there *was* a lot of nice stuff, although most of it was too big to lift. A European sensibility had expressed itself in a lot of stone statuary, some of it very possibly late Roman and some of it, for variety's sake, Khmer, plus a gorgeous polychrome German Madonna in painted linden wood, possibly from the sixteenth century. As tempting as these pieces were, they were all too heavy to hoist, too bulky to carry, and too hard to fence, especially since my premier fence for fine art, Stinky Tetweiler, and I were on the outs.

So I was adjusting to the idea that the evening would be a write-off as I went very carefully through the drawers in the bedroom, putting everything back exactly where I'd found it and counting down the last ninety seconds. And, as is so often the case, the moment when I gave up was also the moment when fate, with its taste for cheap melodrama, uncoiled itself in the darkness, and my knuckles bounced off one of the things that sends a little sugar bullet straight through a burglar's heart: a jewelry box. It was cardboard, not velvet, but it *was* a jewelry box, and it rattled when I picked it up.

Ever since my mentor, Herbie Mott, taught me the rules of burglary, I've practically salivated at the sound of something rattling in a small box.

But . . . the lid was stuck. It felt like it hadn't been popped in years, and the accumulation of humidity and air-born *schmutz* had created a kind of impromptu mucilage. The word *schmutz*, I reflected as I ran a little pen-knife in between the box and the lid, had entered Middle English via Yiddish and German, where it meant, as it means now, *dirt*, specifically, a kind of sticky, yank-your-fingers-back-fast dirt.

The top pulled free from the box with a little sucking noise, like an air-kiss. I shook out one—no, two—objects and aimed my little penlight at them.

And heard the hum of an engine: a car, coming up the driveway.

Hurrying will kill you more often than taking your time will. I looked at the two objects closely, listening for the motor to cut out, listening for the slam of a car door.

One of the pieces I recognized immediately, a glittering little slice of history and bravery—valor, even—in platinum, rubies, sapphires, and diamonds. It looked real, it looked fine, it looked like about $12,000 from a good fence.

The brakes let out an obliging soprano note as the car stopped, and the engine cut out.

The other piece, well . . .

The other piece looked like something that had been made in the dark by someone who was following directions over the radio or some other medium with no REPLAY button. Slap it together from whatever was at hand, don't make a second pass, don't look at it too closely. It bore a sort of *ur*-resemblance to the $12,000 one, in the same way that a supposedly crude revenge play that scholars call the *ur-Hamlet* is thought to be the direct ancestor and inspiration of Shakespeare's greatest hit, but this piece wouldn't have fooled an inanimate object at forty paces.

A car door closed. Then I heard another.

The two pieces were in the same box for a reason. I replaced the lid, slipped the box into my pocket, put the drawer back in its original order, and let myself out the back just as the front door opened.

Wattles once told me he was always happy in the morning because he hadn't hurt anybody yet.

So it's easy to imagine him singing something late-sixties/early-seventies—"Take It Easy," maybe, or "Born Free"—as he clumped out of the elevator in the black-glass, medium-rise office building where he did all the bad things that comprised the business of Wattles, Inc. Easy to imagine him, sport-jacketed and red-faced, following his beach-ball gut down the hall, dragging his left leg behind him like a rejected idea and looking, as he had for twenty years, like he'd be dead in fifteen minutes.

His hair would still be damp. His shave would be aggressively successful. He'd reek of Royall Lyme aftershave, forty bucks a bottle, with the little lead crown on the cap. As he would say, class stuff. Taken together, then: all these characteristics identified Wattles as he undid the cheap locks on the outer door to his office.

Identified him externally, that is. Wattles's interior landscape, a column of dark, buzzing flies looking impatiently for the day's first kill, was tucked safely out of sight.

Tiffany, the new receptionist, was, as always, at her desk, wearing her permanent expression: pretty in kind of a plastic way, happy, perpetually surprised enough at something to be saying, *Oh!* A brunette this week, she was wearing her LaLa the French Maid costume, although Wattles actually preferred Nurse Perky. Still, change was good. He'd had to replace his first receptionist, Dora, when a truly lethal crook named Rabbits Stennet had nearly discovered her secret, which was that she had been modeled on his wife, Bunny, about whom Rabbits went all Othello whenever anyone even looked at her. Rabbits had once backed his car over a parking attendant at Trader Vic's because the man had taken the liberty of turning on Bunny's seat-warmer.

So Dora had been hastily shredded in bulk, all two hundred of her, and replaced by Tiffany: same latex blow-up doll, different nose, different eye color, different wigs.

Wattles had probably squinted at Tiffany as he went to the office's inner door and its array of very *good* locks, because she was sagging a little. He might have heard the soft hiss of a leak, which meant that he would have to find the little battery-powered pump and top her off.

Or maybe just pop the valves and let her deflate, replace her with another one. After all, there were more than three hundred and fifty of her boxed up in the closet, waiting for the mail-order lovers who were the clientele of Wattles's one legitimate business. $89.95 a pop, although Wattles wasn't sure that was the best way to put it.

All the blow-ups leaked sooner or later, thanks to the low manufacturing standards of the Chinese factory where they were produced, which Wattles hadn't complained about because it ensured re-orders. Maybe he'd put a new one at the desk. Nurse Perky again. Or maybe Venice Skater Girl, although that was kind of informal for the office, and the shoes were expensive.

So he was probably singing, full of illegal plans, thinking

about blowing up a new Tiffany, and smelling all limey when he tried to stick a key into the first of his *very* good inner locks and couldn't. It wouldn't go in. He leaned down, grunting a little as the movement squeezed his gut, and saw that the inner tumbler was upside down.

So were the others.

The door had been opened, and whoever had undone those very good locks hadn't even taken the trouble to lock things up again.

He went inside, leaving Tiffany to hiss in desolate solitude, and got the TV remote that opened the panel in the wall opposite his desk, but when he turned to aim it, he put it back down. The panel was open. So was the door of the safe behind it. He didn't even bother to go look.

The one thing that was sure to be missing was *absolutely* going to be the piece of paper that could kill him.

He wheeled his chair over to the window and plopped down, watching the San Fernando Valley work up its daily output of smog. Wattles knew whole battalions of crooks, but he could only think of one person who knew where his office was, could pop those particular locks, and was also enough of a smart-ass to leave them popped.

He could also only think of one person who could help him figure out whether he was right.

Problem was, they were the same person. And this, unfortunately, was where I came into the narrative, because both those people were me.

3
Always Do the Hard Thing First

Trying to ignore all the birds on the wallpaper, I looked at the bird in the brooch with the kind of regret a farmer might feel just before he beheads the chicken his children have named Pookie. It was going to be hard to part with it.

While platinum has been the top of the hill for jewelers for decades, giving the ultra-rich an opportunity to sneer at gold, it's still a relative newcomer to the vault. Unlike gold and silver, which have dangled from wrists and ears since the dawn of the two-syllable word, platinum didn't become available in quantity until the early 1900s. In fact, when the Spanish conquistadors discovered lumps of it in the gold they were ripping from the earth of what is now Colombia, they tried to melt it and failed, and then tossed it away as a nuisance. They called it "platina," meaning "little silver," and one theory was that it might be unripe gold. In the nineteenth century, Lavoisier conquered the metal's high melting point by using oxygen, which, conveniently, he had just discovered. So, by the end of the nineteenth century, there it was: an increasing supply of this beautiful, high-luster metal, brighter than silver and harder than iron, and no one knew what to do with it until Cartier, founded in Paris in 1847, figured out how to use it to support precious stones.

And boy, did they figure it out.

The object in front of me, perhaps an inch and a half in height, blazed with fifty to seventy tiny diamonds, rubies, and sapphires. The stones decorated the platinum body of a bird— the rubies on the breast and the sapphires on the wings, with the diamonds adorning the head. The bird perched behind a graceful, curving grid of platinum in the form of a bird cage.

Which meant that I was experiencing one of those head-on environmental and temporal collisions that frequently remind me that every moment I live contains all the others I've experienced or even read about. I was sitting, surrounded by wallpaper birds, in an obsessively avian room—bird bedspread, bird lighting fixture, bird knickknacks, actual, somewhat depressed-looking birds caged glumly in the corner—in Bitsy's Bird's Nest, the north San Fernando Valley's most _____ motel (I was working on filling in the blank)—and staring at *another* caged bird, this one made of precious stones and platinum on a royal-family-quality brooch crafted in the late 1930s. I was also experiencing a psychosexual collision, since I was smelling nail polish, which I always associated with my mother, from a brush wielded by Ronnie Bigelow, who was emphatically not my mother. Ronnie, her knees tucked to one side, was adding production value to the almost-king-sized, almost-functional Magic Fingers massage bed labeled THE BIRDY RUB, its coverlet decorated in printed parrots the color of healthy lung tissue. Ronnie's eyes took bites out of the brooch as she smoothed a tiny brush over the nail of her right baby finger.

"Why the cage?" she asked.

"It represents the imprisonment of France by Germany," I said. "It's liberation jewelry from World War II. The red, white, and blue bird stands for France, and the cage symbolizes the Nazi occupation. Cartier made these and sold them in Paris under the noses of the Nazis, which was pretty brave, considering the famous Nazi sense of humor." I held it up to the light from the window, and the stones caught fire. "Imagine a willowy French socialite with one of these gleaming on the shoulder of her gown, making small talk as she dances with some Heinrich from the Gestapo. After the war, Cartier changed the design by putting the bird on top of the cage. *Voilà*. Freedom."

"How do you know she was willowy?" Ronnie said. "Socialites eat pretty good, and French socialites probably get their pick of the day's baguettes. She might have been a real beefer." She squinted at the brooch again and then held out a hand, elbow straight, to look at her nails. "I could wear it better than she did." The sight of the hand prompted a frown. "The right hand is the one I always screw up."

The late-morning sunlight was discovering 24-karat gold in Ronnie's hair, which was in the kind of multidimensional tangle predicted by Chaos theory, like a foam of whipped Mobius loops. The brooch would have gone great with it. But—

"If you always screw up the right," I said, "then why start with it?"

"Always do the hard thing first," she said.

"Whatever happened to warming up?"

"So, as I was saying, it would look better on me."

"It won't get a chance to. It's going into Rina's college fund. If I can figure out how to sell it."

"Rina's thirteen."

"And?"

The tip of her tongue clamped between her teeth, she started to paint the thumb of her right hand. "Okay," she said. "Rina's college fund is not negotiable. Why don't you sell it to that awful man with the teensy nose up in the hills?"

The awful man she meant was Stinky Tetweiler, one of LA's

prime fences for connoisseur goods and generally the first place I'd take a piece like this one. But Stinky had tried to have me killed a few weeks earlier, and while I don't generally get personal about business, I wasn't giving him anything as good as this brooch.

"It's too nice for Stinky. Cartier made these things and brave women wore them while the Gestapo basements were squeezing out screams all over Paris."

"What's it worth?"

"Twenty, twenty-five K. At the burglar's rate, I might get twelve." I'd probably get more from Stinky, but the hell with him.

"Was it the only thing you got last night?"

"No," I said. "The other thing is kind of weird."

"Thing, singular? You go to all the trouble to break into that house and you only take two—?"

"What's the first rule of burglary?"

"Don't get caught." She was staring at the partially painted hand as though she was having second thoughts about the color.

"And how do we avoid getting caught?"

"Oh," she said. "Yeah."

"Herbie's Rule Number Three. In and out fast, right? Every minute over twenty or twenty-five that you're in the house—"

"I know, I know. Get out fast. But still, only two—"

"That's why junkies get caught. They take everything. The mark gets home and the whole house is missing and the TV is in the front yard, and he calls the cops and, junkies being junkies, the guy who hit him is probably nodding out at the wheel of his car two houses down."

"Junkies might as well be furniture," she said.

This was new ground. "Do you have personal experience with junkies?"

"No," she said. "I watch the Heroin Channel."

"You haven't mentioned a junkie in the rich and unreliable narrative of your life."

"If my life is a house," she said, "you haven't even gotten to the living room."

"You're just grumpy because you can't remember which town you told me you were born in."

"So, not to change the subject, what's weird about the other thing you took?"

I gave up. Morning chats with an attractive and potentially consenting member of the opposite sex always make me shift focus to one of the lower chakras, and getting Ronnie mad would lessen the chance of that chakra being allowed to go out to play.

"Here," I said. I got up from the chair and went to the bed. "Lift the brush so you won't yell at me when you paint your knuckle." When she did I plopped onto the bed. "Look. This is the Cartier. It's perfect. Immaculate artistry: rubies, diamonds, platinum, the whole shmear. And then there's this."

I held out my other hand. In it was a brooch, of a kind, with an irregular birdcage made of bent wire to house a carved wooden bird, painted red, white, and blue. The whole thing had been glued to a piece of low-budget metal which had, in turn, been glued to a rusty safety pin. The metal of the cage was tarnished and corroded, an uneven spiral that looked like it may have begun life as a watch spring. There was a hair in the glue, and the colors of the paint had faded. Neither the carving nor the painting of the bird was exactly skillful, but it had a certain raw attitude, an improbable vitality.

She touched the tarnished cage and the bars wobbled. A self-respecting parakeet could have busted out in seconds. "Why would you take this?"

"They were together in the box. I thought I'd take them together, try to figure it out."

"I like it better," she said. "Want to give me this one?"

"Would it affect the way we spend the next ninety minutes?"

"Naw. You've been good enough. And, although I'll deny this if you tell anyone I said it, we women experience the occasional meat-dance urge, too, when we're in the company of a competent but not too dominant male who smells good and has nice manners and a knack for abstract thinking. In a pinch, forget the thinking. Let me look at that for a minute while my nails dry." She extended her right hand, the one she'd done first, palm up, and I put the handmade birdcage into it. She brought it up close to her face, looking down at it, and said, "The fancy one is pretty. But this one is beautiful."

"You've got a fine eye."

"I already told you I'd honor your ticket."

"I need to get someone to look at it. Someone who's not Stinky."

"Oh, just take him some flowers."

"He hired a guy to *kill* me."

"Orchids, then."

Somebody knocked on the motel room door. Not aggressive, but confident. I snatched the home-made brooch from her hand and dropped both of them into the jewelry box, which had a label from a chain of budget stores on it, and motioned to Ronnie to do one more button on her blouse, not because she really needed to, but because I wanted to watch. When the show was over, I went to the closet and got my Glock out of the holster that was dangling from the coat hook on the inside of the door. Then, holding the gun in the hand I kept behind the door, I pulled it open and felt my stomach sink.

OTHER TITLES IN THE SOHO CRIME SERIES

Seichō Matsumoto
(Japan)
*Inspector Imanishi
Investigates*

Magdalen Nabb
(Italy)
Death of an Englishman
Death of a Dutchman
Death in Springtime
Death in Autumn
*The Marshal and
the Murderer*
*The Marshal and
the Madwoman*
The Marshal's Own Case
*The Marshal Makes
His Report*
*The Marshal
at the Villa Torrini*
Property of Blood
Some Bitter Taste
The Innocent
Vita Nuova
The Monster of Florence

Fuminori Nakamura
(Japan)
The Thief
Evil and the Mask
Last Winter, We Parted
The Kingdom
The Boy in the Earth

Stuart Neville
(Northern Ireland)
The Ghosts of Belfast
Collusion
Stolen Souls
The Final Silence
Those We Left Behind
So Say the Fallen

(Dublin)
Ratlines

Rebecca Pawel
(1930s Spain)
Death of a Nationalist
Law of Return
The Watcher in the Pine
The Summer Snow

Kwei Quartey
(Ghana)
*Murder at Cape
Three Points*
Gold of Our Fathers
Death by His Grace

Qiu Xiaolong
(China)
Death of a Red Heroine
A Loyal Character Dancer
When Red Is Black

John Straley
(Alaska)
*The Woman Who
Married a Bear*
The Curious Eat Themselves
The Big Both Ways
Cold Storage, Alaska

Akimitsu Takagi
(Japan)
The Tattoo Murder Case
Honeymoon to Nowhere
The Informer

Helene Tursten
(Sweden)
Detective Inspector Huss
The Torso
The Glass Devil
Night Rounds
The Golden Calf
The Fire Dance
The Beige Man
The Treacherous Net
Who Watcheth
Protected by the Shadows

**Janwillem van de
Wetering**
(Holland)
Outsider in Amsterdam
Tumbleweed
The Corpse on the Dike
Death of a Hawker
The Japanese Corpse
The Blond Baboon
The Maine Massacre
The Mind-Murders
The Streetbird
The Rattle-Rat
Hard Rain
Just a Corpse at Twilight
Hollow-Eyed Angel
The Perfidious Parrot
*The Sergeant's Cat:
Collected Stories*

Timothy Williams
(Guadeloupe)
Another Sun
*The Honest Folk
of Guadeloupe*

(Italy)
Converging Parallels
The Puppeteer
Persona Non Grata
Black August
Big Italy
*The Second Day
of the Renaissance*

Jacqueline Winspear
(1920s England)
Maisie Dobbs
Birds of a Feather